D0361649

DIVIDED † PASSIONS

Didsbury Municipal Library
Bag 305
Didsbury, Alberta
TOM OWO

DIVIDED PASSIONS

✝

MICHELLE TISSEYRE

KEY PORTER BOOKS

In memory of my father, Pierre Tisseyre,
Paris, 1909–Montreal, 1995

Copyright © 1999 by Michelle Tisseyre

All rights reserved. No part of this work covered by the copyrights hereon may be reproduced or used in any form or by any means—graphic, electronic or mechanical, including photocopying, recording, taping or information storage and retrieval systems—without the prior written permission of the publisher, or in the case of photocopying or other reprographic copying, a license from the Canadian Copyright Licensing Agency.

Canadian Cataloguing in Publication Data

Tisseyre, Michelle, 1947-
   [La passion de Jeanne. English]
   Divided passions

Translation of: La passion de Jeanne.

ISBN 1-55263-025-0

I. Title. II. Title: La passion de Jeanne. English.

PS8589.I747P3713 1999   C843'.54   C99-930622-7
PQ3919.2.T58P3713 1999

The publisher gratefully acknowledges the support of the Canada Council for the Arts and the Ontario Arts Council for its publishing program.

Canadä

We acknowledge the financial support of the Government of Canada through the Book Publishing Industry Development Program (BPIDP) for our publishing activities.

Key Porter Books Limited
70 The Esplanade
Toronto, Ontario
Canada M5E 1R2
www.keyporter.com

Design: Peter Maher
Electronic formatting: Heidy Lawrance Associates

Printed and bound in Canada

Acknowledgments

I would like to thank my mother, whose childhood memories provided the backdrop for this story, and whose wise advice guided me throughout the writing of it.

I also would like to take the opportunity to extend my thanks to André Maltais, who first suggested that I take the manuscript out of the drawer where it had lain for ten years, and who never stopped urging me on, through weekly luncheons and long walks through the streets of Old Québec, until the job was finished; to Charles Tisseyre, Magda Tadros, Jacques About, Rose de Angelis, Marc and Michelle Ouin, Maurice Dumoncel and Peter Robinson, for their thoughtful reading of the manuscript through its many drafts; to Albina Lantier, for her priceless memories of the political campaigns of her youth and in particular for her company on a memorable trip to Quebec City, notwithstanding her 90 years; to the Ursuline Sisters in Quebec City and in particular their archivist Sister Marie Marchand, for the research she was kind enough to conduct on my behalf; to Ronald Duhamel, M.P. for Saint-Boniface, who took me on a tour of the site of the Carmelite convent where my grandmother was briefly a postulant; to Carole Boily, archivist of the Grey Sisters of Saint-Boniface, who provided me with precious documentation concerning the Saint-Boniface Carmelite convent; to Lucien Chaput, who graciously offered some excellent maps of the town of Saint-Boniface in the period covered

Didsbury Municipal Library

in my story; to Nicole Lafond for her tireless photo-copying; to my son, Merlin Robinson, for his research and suggestions in all matters connected with military history; to my late grand-father John Ahern who left me all those wonderful old books about the Ireland he so loved, and in particular about his hero Michael Collins; to Robert Laffont, for having believed in this book; to Pauline Normand and to Editions Robert Laffont for having given me my chance; to my husband, Peter Robinson, who kept the family ship afloat for the many months during which I literally disappeared into my workroom; to my other living children Liam, Leif, Angus, Brigitte and Francesca, for their patience and understanding; to Madeleine Marmin, my French Literature, Latin and Classical Greek teacher at Collège Marie de France in Montreal, who taught me to love the written word; and above all to my late father who, from the beginning, nurtured in my childish soul the great dream of writing...

For the English version I especially want to thank Anna Porter and everyone at Key Porter Books for giving me the opportunity to fulfill my long-standing dream of publishing in both of the official languages of our country; the late Margaret Laurence whom I got to know while translating *The Diviners* and *A Jest of God* and who, with the unstinting generosity she was famous for, after reading an early draft of the first chapters of this book, urged me to write on; Rudy Wiebe, the translation of whose *Temptations of Big Bear* and *Scorched Wood People* was a huge challenge and a profound learning experience; Ovide Mercredi, who told me the meaning of the word "Manitoba"; John English, for his kind advice and espe-cially for putting me on to the legend of Talbot Papineau; and to my husband, Peter, for his early help in reading and editing the English version.

1

Where

God Speaks

1

Saint-Boniface, December 1915 Night was falling as the train
pulled into the station from the east, under a purple sky.
Here was the last outpost of French Canada west of the
Ottawa River, a place of martyrs, Jeanne's mother said,
where the river once ran red with Catholic blood. Now,
as the special chauffeured automobile sent by the arch-
bishopric turned onto Taché Avenue, the Red River lay
shrouded in snowy winter stillness. Along its broad
expanse in the failing light the street appeared deserted,
desolate. The car came to a stop less than a block from
the Provencher Bridge, at the corner of Masson Street,
where a sixteen-foot plank fence angled away in the
gathering dusk. Behind it, hidden from the street, the
two-story building of weathered wood looked disap-
pointingly small and forlorn. An octagonal tower rose
out of its middle, topped by an open-roofed porch that

looked like a bandshell, and gave it the air of an abandoned seaside residence in the dead of the prairie winter. This squat, truncated tower had once sheltered the large main entrance to the building, which before its present vocation had housed a boys' school and, later, the town hall. Now the grand doorway had been sealed off and a smaller door built to one side, aggravating a sense of vacancy and neglect.

With the temperature dropping and the wind cutting through her, Jeanne scurried up the icy path behind her mother. A sister, short and reassuringly plump, with a bland, ageless face and myopic eyes that squinted through round spectacles, came to the door. Her toothy smile and receding chin, prickly with gray stubble, reminded Jeanne of a dormouse unceremoniously roused from hibernation. "She is the only one who does not live inside the cloister," whispered Mme Langlois to her daughter as they waited in the parlor, an airless, poorly furnished room with creaky floorboards. A chair was placed facing a window in the wall, the other side obscured by a thick metal grille. The sister reappeared, to inform them regretfully that it was impossible to speak with Mother before morning, as evening silence was about to begin. "We do not encourage you to prolong your farewells," she added, with small eyes glinting through thick glasses.

"Remember me in your prayers," her mother said, brushing a perfunctory kiss across Jeanne's forehead. Then, with a look back at her daughter that lingered with something like envy, Mme Langlois was gone, and the darkness had closed around her.

"It's getting late," said the nun. "You'd better get to bed. You'll want to be rested and fresh in the morning. Tomorrow will be a big day for you." She motioned to

Jeanne to follow her up the narrow stairs to a small apartment above the parlor, which was separate from the convent proper.

"Tonight you will occupy the room next to Mme Dragon," she explained, a little out of breath, showing Jeanne to a cell barely wider than the doorway. "She is the mother of our deputy prioress," added the nun, handing Jeanne her habit for the next day. "When her husband died, she left Quebec to be near her daughter. She lives here year-round."

Jeanne was as wretched as an orphan on being introduced to the eccentric, elderly aunt in whose care she has been placed. To her, *convent* was a word that conveyed vastness, the everlastingness of stone, the stately institutions her mother frequented, where she herself had spent so much of her short life. She knelt by the bed and tried to pray, heavy swells of doubt and fear swamping her. Childhood notions of bravery and honor were all she found to cling to now. She summoned up an image fleetingly glimpsed from the window of their compartment, during a station stop in a small Ontario town—a boisterous group of young soldiers, barely older than herself, laughing and cavorting on the platform. Volunteers, all of them, on their way east, bound for France and the front. "You see those young men?" Her mother had eyed her intently. "The power of prayer is directly proportionate to one's sacrifices and privations. These boys are in great need of your prayers. Just think, some day one of them might owe you his life." The Carmelites, Jeanne knew, were possessed of mystic powers. Yet she felt only dread, and the poignancy of kinship. The soldiers were traveling to the east, she to the west. Like hers, theirs was a one-way ticket.

As the train pulled away from the figures on the

platform, snow began to fall. For hundreds of miles it swooped and swirled across the land, daubing itself over frost-blackened fields, snaking its way up windswept hills. Gradually the train left the inhabited world behind, and entered an austere wilderness of dense forest and dark lakes. From her mother had come only withering silence and the endless mouthing of her rosary. Finally they pulled into the station at Saint-Boniface. As Jeanne stepped onto the platform an angry wind leapt at her face, shaking her, scolding her. Later, in the final moment of withheld farewell, her mother's eyes—forever doubting, probing, penetrating the vulnerable core of her inadequacies—peered all the way down to the murky depths of her soul.

Eleven o'clock and still sleep eluded her. She heard movement from the unseen Dragon in the adjoining room. Outside the wind prowled, howled, and rattled the walls.

2

The sister roused her before daylight. Shivering in the subarctic dark she struggled into the heavy, scratchy cloth of the habit she'd been given. Her young body craved only sleep. Warmth. Food. In the drafty hallway the elderly lady speaking with the nun did not live up to her name; Mme Dragon was tiny, frail, and impeccably attired in a long woolen dress and once-fashionable hat, dating from before the outbreak of war. Her round, lidless bird-eyes blinked up in a kindly smile that made Jeanne want to cry.

They proceeded downstairs through the parlor to the chapel, where dawn was beginning to filter through the one tall window. Cracked walls of patched plaster, rough bare floorboards. Creeping dilapidation, and a low ceiling that bore down on the soul. Outside, snow was falling—thick lazy flakes, barely stirred by the sluggish wind, gray against the dull sky. The public section of the chapel was empty, its thirty chairs unoccupied. Through the dense iron grille that sealed off the cloister, shadowy figures were slowly taking shape in the growing light.

An elderly officiant approached the altar. Jeanne stared hard ahead, memory assailing her. The memory of her father's stricken face, fierce wind tousling his white hair, as the sleigh pulled away for the station, of his tall figure, dark against the snow, receding into darkness; of cowering under buffalo furs with the bitter wind flailing her eyes; of apprehension choking her, and swallowing tears that Mother mustn't hear, that blurred her vision, trickled down her face, and seeped between her lips. Now, in the chapel, her chin was trembling, sobs welling deep and rising, garroting, throttling her. She strove to choke back the surge of grief before it burst and with it, the silence of this place; so she gulped it down in great bitter swallows like hated medicine. Up ahead the priest was still whispering mass. Beside her the two old women were bent in prayer. No one had seen. No one had heard. Here in the dingy chapel nothing remained, no hint at all, of the storm that had laid her to waste.

3

By the age of six she was a heart in hiding, her shy façade barely containing her tumultuous nature. Without any warning, emotion would overwhelm her, sweeping away her defenses, spilling out in great gushes that sent her scurrying, red-faced and weeping. Banished to boarding school by a mother whose devotion to

Didsbury Municipal Library

Religion left no room for the distractions of motherhood, Jeanne was subject to erratic infatuations that exposed her needy heart to the careless cruelty of girls. As the dreariness of school life and her efforts at self-camouflage gradually insulated her from her peers, she found lonely solace in the pastel imagery of prayer books, in the legends of the martyrs and saints whose feast days spanned the calendar, in the mystery and pomp of liturgical holy days, in the safety and monotony of the Catholic ritual. Shunned by her schoolmates, she haunted the chapel and the confessional and did her best to curry her mother's distant favor.

For her first communion, Mme Langlois had a dress made for Jeanne—silk-embroidered white organdy, with translucent white chiffon veil to match—which on the day of the ceremony won her the envy of her principal tormentor among the other girls. But it also revealed to her a startling truth about her mother, the elusive idol who seldom left her austere, secluded life in Ottawa, and rarely came to visit her in the convent school in Montreal, whose expectations she could never seem to live up to, whose affection she feared could not be earned.

"You look so lovely," Mme Langlois had whispered after the ceremony, tears spilling down her beautiful face. "Like a saint in Heaven."

On prize-day in the year she turned twelve, the nuns reported to her mother that Jeanne showed great promise of a vocation. That summer, news of her precocious call to the religious life spread like contagion through the coastal village of Carleton in the Gaspé, where the Langlois family had their summer residence. While her father presided on the porch, receiving the endless procession of his constituents, some bearing gifts of cured ham or fresh salmon, others nursing a complaint or bringing a request for assistance, Jeanne followed her mother on her daily calls to the party faithful, who unfailingly marveled at the prodigy. "So she's going into holy orders!" gushed the matrons of the parish. "Which one have you chosen for her?"

"The Carmelites, we hope," her mother would sigh, gazing at her daughter with those doubtful eyes. "But it takes such courage ..."

Every evening, as her husband's local "advisers" began arriving at the door, Mme Langlois fled the fog of tobacco smoke and profanity that, along with the Honorable Charles Langlois's best cognac, invariably accompanied their conferences, and took her daughter off to vespers. After the service, if the sky was fair, they would linger a while on the church steps, chatting with the priest and the other parishioners, who gathered about the young intended bride of Christ like the teachers of the temple around the boy Jesus. Thus was Jeanne caught in a web of her own zealous making. Basking in the unprecedented attention that was lavished on her from all sides, she convinced herself that she was loved at long last, and unwittingly embarked on a course that was to estrange her from her mother for good.

In the months that followed, Jeanne tried her best to believe in her vocation. With the care and ingenuity of a pauper assembling a wedding trousseau, she called upon the entire pantheon of patron saints and heroes of her childhood, from Saint Joan of Arc and Saint Teresa of Avila to Saint Francis of Assisi and Sir Galahad of the Grail. And into the sorry cloth of duty her hopeful heart wove so many threads of honor, valor, and selflessness that the shabbiness of the gown was soon forgotten. Still she had about as clear a notion of what lay in store as a schoolboy can have of the treacherous *fesh-fesh** from looking at a map of the Sahara Desert. She learned only to conceal her raw impulses behind what she called her vocation. Yet there was an ocean of darkness in her soul, a heaving, unfathomable darkness, of which she yet knew nothing at all.

4

After thirty years as prioress of a Carmelite convent, Mother Raphaël de la Providence knew better than to set too much store by first impressions. Nevertheless, by training and long acquaintance with human nature, she was quick to spot physical traits that might thwart a developing vocation. Her own novitiate in Montreal had taught her a healthy respect for the frailties of the human body. There, in a crumbling, unheated building overlooking the St. Lawrence, she had watched helplessly as four of the founding sisters from France sickened and died, overcome by the harshness of the Canadian winter. Then in 1887, as the first Canadian prioress of the new convent on Rue du Carmel, far from the wind and the creeping damp of the river, she had not shrunk from bending the hard Carmelite rule to the realities of an unforgiving climate, allowing for heat in the living quarters, and a minimum of nourishment to sustain health. And yet how many times and with what dismay had she witnessed the defeat of faith through the weakness of incompetent flesh? For the past three years, here in the new home for the order she had helped to establish in Saint-Boniface, conditions had been primitive. The hardships, though only temporary, were an unwelcome

*Fesh-fesh: in the Sahara Desert, a particularly treacherous kind of terrain.

reminder of her own painful beginnings. Postulants came and went, most of them leaving after only a few months.

Mother Raphaël had come to the conclusion that a thickset, stocky build was often the surest guarantee of a lasting vocation. There were of course exceptions, she told herself as she watched the tall, willowy girl enter her small office. A case in point was the deputy prioress: painfully thin, with a bilious disposition, she combated sickliness with a fiery mettle and sheer will that sprang from her boundless faith. Which might explain, thought Mother Raphaël distractedly, the unfortunate habit she had of inflicting on others the ill-humor she mostly felt toward herself ...

"Come in, child," she said to the new postulant. She leaned slightly forward in her heavy brown habit, her stout, compact body pressed against her desk, her large head firmly anchored between thick shoulders. Her black veil framed a plain, wise face, the watchful gray eyes conveying a peaceful strength.

"Come and sit down," she said. "I have just been reviewing my correspondence about you."

Marie Jeanne Églantine Langlois. Born 2 November 1899. Boarded at the Convent of the Sisters of the Adoration of the Precious Blood in Montreal, from September 1905 to July 1915. Only child. Distinguished student. Ardent, pious nature. Has prepared since childhood for her entry into holy orders ...

Be that as it may, thought the nun. The young person standing before her could not in her lifetime have known such conditions as those prevailing in this place. She was tall and slender, delicate-boned and fine-featured, with a head of wavy strawberry-blond hair that ran in rivulets over her shoulders—looking at her, the prioress was tempted to predict she wouldn't last till Christmas. Spring, as she knew too well, was the best time for postulants to begin their initiation to contemplative life, if possible in time for Easter, the great feast that marked the end of Lent and a certain relaxation of the rule after seven long months of fasting. May was the joyful month when first vows were taken, and when a blessed few took the veil for good. During the summer the sisters recovered their strength in the dry prairie heat, fortified by donations of fresh fruit and vegetables from the parishioners, milk and eggs from the Jesuit brothers' farm, and honey, cream, butter, and cheese from the Trappist fathers. In that season a vocation sprouted like seed in fertile soil, and grew and ripened in the summer sun. For those who arrived in winter, after the strict observance of the rule had resumed, the period of initiation often proved too much to bear.

... Daughter of the Honorable Charles Langlois, member of Parliament for Bonaventure, Quebec, who is well known to the citizens of Saint-Boniface as an unstinting defender of the educational rights of French Canadians in the province of Manitoba. A personal friend of the late Monseigneur Langevin ...

Oh, I miss that man, sighed the old nun, to whom the death of the archbishop a few months earlier had dealt a cruel blow.

"You come to us very highly and, might I add, very warmly recommended indeed," she observed, folding her stiff, gnarled fingers over the papers on her desk. "The purpose of the rule under which we live is a simple but demanding one: to open ourselves to the love of God. We believe that giving oneself unconditionally to

Him requires a free and joyous renunciation of all worldly things. *Free* and *joyous*, I stress this because you are so very young ..."

The girl's eyes were pale and luminous, the color of sunshine through water. In their depths the observant nun detected a contracted, quivering emotion which, as she spoke, she was attempting to gauge.

"Our rule is the harness by which our souls are broken to God's will," she resumed, speaking with the gentle inflections of a teacher on the first day of school. "Silence, fasting, penance are only the means by which we strive to know Him. Monseigneur Langevin—God rest his soul," she added wistfully, "—liked to say that we Carmelites serve as lightning rods for the wrath of the Almighty, that with our prayers we protect all those amongst whom we live."

Jeanne shivered under the old woman's penetrating gaze. She felt an impulse stirring deep inside her, the temptation welling up from darkest childhood, the terrible urge to surface, to show herself, to be known. These past months she had been swept along in the seething current. Now, suddenly, a low, sturdy branch was within reach.

"Silence places us squarely in the eye of God," the nun continued. "It frees us from earthly bondage, unfetters the mind, dissipates the fog of everyday existence. Silence hollows, levels, cleanses us. Like the wind sweeping the Great Plain the Indian people here call *Manitouba*, the place where God speaks ..."

"Where God speaks ..." Jeanne repeated.

"Fasting," the prioress resumed, dropping her voice almost to a murmur, "prepares the body to receive the Lord, to be permeated by His love. The body is heavy, the flesh is opaque. The spirit alone is light. Only when we purify the silty waters of the self can the light of love penetrate the soul ..."

Jeanne could only listen, entranced, her unfledged spirit mesmerized by the power of the old nun's words.

5

Alone at the long refectory table, single-mindedly absorbed in the act of eating, basking in the warmth of the stove where a large pot of soup bubbled and simmered, Jeanne devoured her first meal in almost twenty-four hours. As she dared to clean her plate with her last piece of bread, the white-veiled sister who served as cook motioned her to a door on the opposite side of the room. It led to a large unheated hall with tall windows looking out onto the snow-covered yard and the huge fence that blocked any view of the river or the world beyond. The room was so cold that she could see her breath. Pacing back and forth in a futile attempt to keep warm, she wondered whether she had been forgotten. Maybe they would never come for her, and she would freeze to death. By the time the door opened and the prioress finally swept in, followed by the eight other members of the cloister, the brief sensation of warmth that the bread and soup had given her was only a memory.

6

At five o'clock in the morning, in the freezing dark, her feet made contact with the floorboards. The arctic draft coiled around her ankles, slithered under her night-dress, wafted up her naked legs. She struggled into the coarse, heavy robe then sank back onto the hard, narrow pallet. Resisting the urge to lie down, she pulled on wool stockings, wedged her feet into ice-hard shoes, shrugged on her white mantle, the sheer weight of it at last conveying an illusion of warmth. Her head spinning, breath short, teeth miserably chattering, she scurried to the chapel before first light, arriving last again this morning. In the starlight filtering through the tall window, the others were all there, kneeling in the gloom. On toes stiff with cold, she tried to step quietly, but the floorboards creaked with each lurch of her body. As her bruised knees touched the floor she flinched. *Our Father Who art in Heaven*, see me through this one more time. Pain spread upward, sharp as a knife-blade through her bones, pain unrelenting and unendurable. *Please God, help me through this one more day* ... Outside the sky was inky black and she—was inside this dark lair of a body with a beast inside clawing, clawing—*Give us this day our daily ... and forgive us* ... Pain stretching, straining, beyond bearing, beyond numbness, until she could feel neither her legs nor the ground, only hunger, hollowing, gutting her.

At last a shifting in the darkness as bodies settled back on haunches on the floor that was so much harder now than at the beginning. Blood returning to her legs, first the heat, then the dreadful needling, crawling, swarming of ants in dying flesh ...

Eleven-fifteen and mass is over. Time to examine one's conscience, each day more reluctantly than the last—and finally the rationed bliss of steam and aroma and hot soup, spreading all the way down, and the bread that she chewed over and over with eyes downcast, noiselessly so as not to disturb the others. Then, with the beast at bay for the time being, it was back to the chapel for grace again.

Twelve noon. Since Christmas, she dreaded the recreation hall. None of the heat from the rest of the building reached it, and any difference from the temperature outside was surely imaginary. You wore mittens there over your wool gloves. Still, some of the sisters managed to knit. Time for the postulants, and those laid low by illness, to retire upstairs for a brief respite from hunger's dull gnawing. For the past month Jeanne had had company in the other cubicles of the frigid dormitory. Sister Bernadette, whose cough had worsened; Sister Elizabeth, who was too weak to rise. Often she drifted off to sleep, sometimes until the two-o'clock bell startled her awake. But whenever she found the strength, she dragged herself off to the chapel for confession.

Father, I have sinned. The words that bared the soul. *I am not worthy of Thine expectations. Mother was right to doubt my resolve. I thought I was strong, but I am feeble. I thought I was brave, but I am a coward. I resent Mother Raphaël for not looking me in the eye. I detest Sister Cécile for being so cheerful. I am ashamed. I can't pray any more. Father, I have sinned. I doubted myself. I doubted Thee.* She disgorged her failings, the bitterness lingering like bile long after. And the voice answered her from the other side of the grille, a voice like her father's, rich and deep, the voice of a man she wouldn't see again, never, ever again, my God, could this be? Was not silence the sound death makes...?

"The path ahead is long and difficult," said the voice of the priest, who could not see her, whom she had never seen. "It is not unusual to have misgivings, sometimes very painful ones, when you first start out on such a journey. Offer them up to the Creator, ask Him for guidance ..." The voice of forgiveness.

Five o'clock—in the chapel for one more hour, which seemed even longer than in the morning. Darkness had fallen, and the noon meal no longer sustained her. The body weakened further. *Father, why hast Thou forsaken me?*

Six o'clock. A light meal, consisting of one piece of bread (she chewed it slowly, she made it last), a few raisins (she ate them one at a time, sucking her saliva to extract all the sweetness), a glass of hot water (she grasped it between her frozen palms until all the heat had been absorbed, then gulped it down while it was still warm, her stomach churning and heaving with each swallow).

Recess. The depths of misery as the body froze. Sister Bernadette's lips were turning blue. Brittle voices tinkled like glass in the frosty air.

Back to the chapel for evening service. The longest stretch of hours. Silence crowding her without. Emptiness within. By comparison with the recreation hall, it was almost warm, but body heat lost is never recovered.

Eleven at night, and she was back in her cubicle, the weight of the day's failures crushing her. In the beginning she had moved in the silence like a fish released into the sea. Now she muttered to herself almost constantly, sometimes aloud, as soon as she was alone. Silence meanwhile thrived on daylight. Several times a night in the dormitory, the conflicting rhythms of breathing, sighing, coughing, wheezing, snoring, swelled to a deafening roar. Her nerves beset by hunger, exhaustion, unrelenting cold, she pushed icy fingers into her ears. Sometimes she prayed, and the wind answered her, chanting at the windows, shaking the old walls, rattling the building to its very foundations. *Manitou-ba* ...

7

Recess had begun, the bell at last beckoning her to rest. Sunlight was pouring down from the window at the top of the stairs. She climbed them unsteadily, one by one. Though not in the habit of loitering at the window, she often had to stop on the landing to catch her breath. In the cloudless February sky the sun shone brightly. Its radiance, reflected on snow, was blinding. At the far end of the grounds, a figure appeared, black against the gray wood of the fence. A priest, walking fast along the snowy path, picking the hem of his robe up before him. Whereas the priest who said mass was tall and white-haired, the stranger crossing below the window was small and slight, his hair black and bushy, so young she had trouble believing that the voice in the confessional belonged to him. Her heart bolted like a startled colt.

8

"You are suffering."

"Yes, Father ..." From her throat came a kind of croak, barely distinguishable from the creaking of the hard prie-dieu digging into her knees.

"A penitent lives by love and suffering," the voice whispered, so close her head was spinning. "You are courageous and strong, but you must also ask God's help ..."

"Father help me, I beg of you."

She closed her eyes. Here in this space the silence was driven back, defeated by this human voice telling her, Jeanne, that she existed. *You must befriend the silence ... Manitou-ba*, the voice of God. The voice of the unceasing wind, the voice of winter without end. *Father, why hast Thou...?* How many times, her stomach hollow, had she believed she was dying in His embrace? In the darkness the silence howled; the windows shivered, the old plank walls shook and shuddered ... Here she came each day, seeking refuge from the deathly silence and the deadly cold. Here the hurricane no longer roared. Here the silence was stilled, subdued by the voice, gentle as a mother's fingers on a child's fevered brow.

"Was it you I saw, just now, at the window?" He said it so low it was as if they shared the same thoughts. Every day now she dragged herself up to the landing and waited at the window, for the unseemly joy of watching him appear. Today, finally, he had looked up, and she, starting clear away from the window as though ducking a stone, had slumped against the wall in the hallway, her heart in her mouth, her body swimming in a cold sweat.

"Father, help me, please."

The dam inside was about to burst. She could hear the dark rush of water, roaring, thundering.

"You are so young. Life here is—" His voice was sinking through fathoms of water, somewhere in her brain. She hung on to the prie-dieu as it was swept away. Waves of nausea overwhelmed her, for want of warmth, of touch, of sleep.

"Father I can't ..." she shrilled, "I can't ..."

She struggled weakly against the undertow of failure, dragging her under, under. Something hit her, hard, on the cheek.

9

The Archbishop's residence, Saint-Boniface, March 1916

"My Lord, it makes no sense," cried Father Jobin, putting down his fork and looking the archbishop of Saint-Boniface in the eye. "With all due respect, we can't just let her die!"

"François, François," protested Monseigneur Béliveau, settling back in his chair and eyeing his guest warily. This young priest had been close to his illustrious predecessor, the late Monseigneur Arthur Langevin, who had presided over the foundation of the Carmelite cloister. "You know the decision is not mine to make. I cannot order the Mother Superior of the Carmelite convent to send the girl back to Montreal!"

"That isn't what I am asking," insisted the priest. "She is wasting away before our eyes. Besides, I have suspected for some time that she is not here entirely of her own volition."

"How do you know that?"

"I didn't say I knew, only that I suspect. She seems to do herself such violence, to be prey to so much doubt ..."

"Doubt? What kind of doubt?"

"She doubts herself, her courage ..."

"If you'll permit me to venture an opinion, I think perhaps you are much too involved with these good sisters. I know that Arthur himself frequented them, and I know how much he did to facilitate their establishment in Saint-Boniface. But I would not encourage you to interfere too much in their affairs. I am of the opinion that with regard to this, as in all matters of the sister orders, it is wise to keep a healthy distance."

"My Lord, I do not exaggerate when I say that this girl may die if nothing is done. She is not made for the religious life. And let's not forget, she is the daughter of a member of Parliament. Her father has been one of the most vocal defenders of our rights in the House of Commons. We'll need his support this year more than ever. Imagine if she were to leave here feet first!"

The priest's urging had the desired effect. Monseigneur Béliveau shot the younger man an exasperated look, but he could not deny the truth of his words. The Honorable Charles Langlois had made the cause of the French Canadians' right to their own schools in Manitoba his own personal battle. Even as they spoke, a renewed campaign was being launched by the provincial administration to deprive his parishioners of what few guarantees they had left.

"All right, all right, you've convinced me," the prelate grumbled, "but it's not a pleasant prospect."

"If I were you, I would take the initiative of writing to her family to inform them of the state of their daughter's health. By the time the letter reaches them, you will have taken the opportunity to broach the subject with Mother Raphaël de la Providence."

"Those poor sisters." The archbishop sighed. "I always said Saint-Boniface couldn't support a contemplative order like the Carmelites. Arthur knew it, but he so wanted to make them happy ... They've had all sorts of problems just finding enough to eat, especially in winter, because the parishioners they depend on are so poor. The people simply have no surplus to give them, and all the postulants they've welcomed have left, after a few months, usually for health reasons. I really don't see how they can hold out much longer ..."

10

Jeanne surfaced slowly into daylight and the hollow tolling of the convent bell, in time with the sluggish pounding of her heart. All winter long the bell had called out to the parishioners, reminding them of the sisters' dire need, begging for charity to ward off starvation.

She was lying on a narrow cot, in bedclothes clammy with perspiration. She tried to open her eyes, but the light blinded her. She heard a rustling at the door of her room.

"Well, Sister Jeanne." It was the gray sister who had been caring for her since the beginning of her illness. "You're getting better, but you are going to have to start eating, to build up your strength."

Sensing another presence in the room, Jeanne

opened weak, fluttering eyelids. Father Jobin was standing at her bedside, observing her with concern.

"Monseigneur Béliveau has written to your father," he confided, "to inform him of your condition and recommend that he send for you."

Her heart leapt in her chest. She moaned faintly.

"Shh!" hushed the sister softly, pressing a finger to her lips. "Now you must rest. We have tired you enough for one day. Mme Dragon and I are taking turns watching over you. We are right nearby if you need us."

Jeanne closed her eyes. Exhaustion engulfed her.

11

May 1916

Mother never came. In her place, an Angel appeared at the door of the convent.

"I've come for my niece, Mlle Langlois. Would you be so kind as to let her know?"

The Angel wore a long traveling suit, blue as a summer sky, with a little hat and veil to match. Jeanne at first did not recognize her father's younger sister, so seldom had she visited while Jeanne was growing up, and for her part the Angel stifled a cry of dismay at the sight of her niece. Her waxy complexion, hollow cheeks, halting gait and flat dull hair made a striking impression on a person who had known her only as a child at the seaside in summertime.

"Jeanne, it's me, Florence …"

"Florence?" Jeanne's voice was wan. "Mother isn't with you?"

"She had to stay in Ottawa, with your father. She asked me to come in her place."

Jeanne's face registered confusion and disappointment. Something about Florence's explanation didn't fit …

It had been in the dead of winter when she arrived, with the north wind howling in the polar night. Now she was leaving, in the first flush of summer, which, on the great plain that stretches all the way to the Rockies, follows winter without much bothering with spring. As Jeanne and her aunt emerged from the gate onto Taché Street, overlooking the Red River, the suddenness of sunlight overpowered her. She felt the hot breath of the prairies on her skin. Across the street, a tree exploded as a noisy flock of birds suddenly took flight, expanded skyward, wheeled slowly, then dispersed, their sharp, crystal cries tinkling in the pristine air.

Her mother had not come. Already doubt was gathering over the horizon, but the horizon was a long way off. She grasped the Angel's outstretched hand, climbed into the car provided by the archbishop, and glided giddily away to freedom.

2

Sweet

Hermine

Quebec, May 1917 The Rue Sous-le-Fort is one of the oldest streets in Old Quebec, sloping straight up to the Rue Petit-Champlain in the shadow of the Château Frontenac, whose turrets loom above it at the top of the escarpment. It is a narrow corridor dating back two centuries, bordered on either side by grimy stone façades, decrepit with age. On the corner at the top of the street, a young man stood contemplating one of these, looking up at its windows with pale, piercing eyes. He was slight of build, lean and wiry, with fair, freckled skin and an unruly mass of copper-blond hair. His clothes, though clean and well cut, were worn to a shine, an impression only slightly offset by a dapper silk cravat and impeccably polished shoes. Such refinements in a student of limited means usually announce ambition, but in this orphaned son of a former dean of the medical school of the Université Laval, they also revealed a nostalgic bent.

It had been months since Michael O'Neill, who had just arrived by train from Montreal, last visited his hometown, but whenever he returned to Quebec his steps sooner or later led him here, to the haberdasher's shop where his *Canadien* grandparents once worked and lived. Here his mother had been raised and from here she'd departed at the age of thirteen, having obtained the necessary Church dispensation to marry the young man who was to father her eighteen children. It was here, in front of this house at the foot of the stairs to the Upper Town, in the old quarter behind the warehouses that lined the waterfront, that Mick and his brother Arthur, the two youngest, had often loitered as children, as though these old stones still harbored some invisible vestige of the mother they had never known. Now that Arthur, felled at fifteen by typhoid fever, was no more, the house stood as a kind of monument to Mick's own loneliness. An iconoclast by nature, and an anticlericalist since his days at the *séminaire,** he did not come here to pray. Usually, after a moment, he went on his way, filled with a sad, aimless tenderness that blossomed in his heart like sweetbriar on barren ground.

Today, however, he tarried, pacing, checking his watch. He lit a cigarette. Gonzague, you idiot, he muttered, never on time. You'll miss your own damn funeral. Even in boarding school he was always late. Mick chuckled, remembering his friend's schoolboy tricks, like flashing dirty photographs in the john before five or six goggle-eyed toads, who panicked when Arthur, standing sentry outside in the hallway, coughed to signal trouble approaching. Gonzague, you horny fool. At last he

*Séminaire: a private boarding school for boys, run by Catholic priests.

grinned, as his friend appeared at the other end of Petit Champlain. Tall, barrel-chested, his big head jutting between thick shoulders, he sauntered like a pachyderm, taking his time. When he caught sight of Mick his face lit up, but his pace did not quicken for all that.

Stamping his feet Mick held up his watch, dangling it by its chain. The joker just shrugged and laughed at his impatience.

"Hey, big fella! Aren't you stretching it a bit? I was about to leave without you ..."

"Now, don't get excited, you goddamned Irishman!"

"Don't get excited, hell! Have you seen the time?"

2

Turning their collars up against the wind, they hurried up Côte de la Montagne, toward the source of the murmur wafting down from the Upper Town.

"So, how's our man in the big city?" Gonzague teased him, clamping his big bear paw on Mick's shoulder. "At least say it feels good to be home."

Every time they met, Gonzague hoped for the same answer. How could Mick explain that since his father's death, and especially since Arthur's, there was no longer anything here to hold him? That he needed space, as far as the eye could see. That the past was best left behind you, lest it choke you in its bittersweet embrace, especially here in this town where his father had spent his entire life, between his home on Rue Desjardins, behind the Ursuline Convent, and the medical school and the Hôtel-Dieu hospital just up the street. That he would only languish here in the old capital, walled in by the past glory of Quebec, hiding behind its fortifications, nursing its wounded memory of siege and conquest. Gonzague, the rooted provincial, for whom the hub of the universe lay somewhere between the archbishop's palace and the National Assembly, between the Citadelle and the Hôtel de Ville, would probably never understand why Mick's life was now in Montreal, the metropolis to the southwest where the future was being shaped, where the money was being made, in the biggest city in the whole country, spreading its promise at the foot of Mount Royal.

"Sure it feels good. But I'm only visiting. I won't be staying, and you know it!"

"You're crazy, Mick. This town is beautiful. It's so beautiful it's to die for ..."

"The *world* is beautiful." Mick smiled, humoring him. "As for dying, I say we should see as much of the world as we can while there's still time."

Already the square, sloping gently down from the Marché Montcalm, was thick with protesters under a lowering sky. The wind was growing colder as evening approached, yet nothing could chill the ardor of the ever-swelling crowd, shouting their anthem with all their might to keep warm while they awaited the arrival of the anticonscriptionist speakers.

O Canada! Terre de nos aïeux,
Ton front est ceint de fleurons glorieux ...

The sound of thousands of combined voices surged over the ramparts dominating the square, rolled toward the Lower Town and the river beyond and floated off to the distant foothills of the Laurentians, half shrouded in mist.

Sous l'oeil de Dieu, près du fleuve géant,
Le Canadien grandit en espérant ...

Looking down on the throng from the fortifications, groups of young men milled about, shouting and gesticulating. On the other side of the wall, the streets of the Old City had emptied. Farther down, mist was flowing in from the great river. The two students threaded their way along the crest of the wall to a perch at the top of Saint John's Gate.

Ennemi de la tyrannie
Mais plein de loyauté
Il veut garder dans l'harmonie
Sa fière liberté ...

"You should have been in Montreal yesterday. You should have seen it! Fifteen thousand of us at Parc Lafontaine. After the speeches we took to the streets. All day long we marched, until last night when a fight broke out on Sainte-Catherine Street and some windows got smashed at *La Presse* and *La Patrie*."

"What are you going to do if the bill is passed?" Gonzague asked softly, pulling a silver flask out of his jacket pocket, unscrewing the stopper and offering it to his chum.

"I don't know." Mick sighed, lifting the bottle to his mouth.

The whisky went down like fire in their throats. One of these two had chosen McGill, the other had picked Laval. Mick had transplanted himself; he would be a lawyer. Gonzague was rooted here, and planned to be a notary public. No matter. They were friends unto death. And if conscription was passed ... then death it might be indeed, perhaps sooner than either of them knew.

Suddenly a great clamor rose from the teeming square below. The young speechmakers ascended the steps at the front of the Marché, and the crowd roared at the sight of Armand Lavergne, the nationalist firebrand all had been waiting to hear. From the top of the fortifications, in the rain that was starting, the gaggle of young men chanted his name. *La-vergne! La-vergne!* the throng responded in unison. For over an hour the audience shivered under a forest of umbrellas, welcoming each orator in turn with thunderous applause. They railed at the Borden government in Ottawa, which threatened to impose conscription on a country that had already sent three hundred thousand volunteers overseas since the beginning of the war. "Down with conscription!" they shouted, punctuating the speeches with hurrahs and cries of "Down with Borden!" as they huddled patiently under the downpour.

At long last, Lavergne stepped forward to speak, the youthful nemesis (and, rumor had it, illegitimate child) of Sir Wilfrid Laurier, Leader of His Majesty's Loyal Opposition and former prime minister of Canada. The assembly went wild.

As the slight, elegant figure now raised the bullhorn he had brought to make himself heard above the drumroll of rain, the clamor began to subside. At last the young nationalist politician, considered by many to be the most formidable speaker of his generation,* cleared his throat.

"Canadiens!" he shouted, calling for silence, then began: "We are not against conscription for the defense of Canada. It is the duty of a citizen to give his life for his country!"

"That's the truth!" screamed some voices, and the crowd roared again.

Lavergne, barely visible under the big black umbrella

* For Armand Lavergne's speech at the Marché Montcalm, see *Le Devoir*, 28 May 1917.

an aide was holding over him, paused, then called out in a ringing voice, "But I love my people enough to say that we must not give one drop of blood for England!"

"Not one drop! Down with conscription!" they shouted.

"If it's liberty we're fighting for, then let England give liberty to the Irish!"

"Long live Ireland!" yelled Mick, whose father had imbued him with a fierce love for the land of his ancestors.

"Either Canada is a colony, or it is a sovereign nation! I say we are a nation!"

With each new eruption of applause, the opening bars of "O Canada" spread sporadically through the throng.

"The people must be consulted! If the people agree, then the government can have their conscription! But if the people refuse, the country is ours! It does not belong only to Mr. Borden! I have received many letters from citizens in the English-speaking provinces. This many from Toronto!" cried Lavergne, brandishing a thick wad of letters for all to see.

"Hurrah!"

"And these, from as far away as Vancouver! These letters all say that the people in those provinces are opposed to conscription. And they ask the province of Quebec to help them repudiate this government. This government no longer represents us. Its mandate expired two years ago!"

"Down with Borden!" the crowd erupted.

"We demand a referendum!" thundered Lavergne. "So that the government can be given a mandate on this question! And a federal election! So that the people can at last choose a government!"

"An election! We want an election!"

"What we have inherited from our ancestors we will pass on to our descendants! We will ensure that Canadian autonomy is respected! To that end, we shall fight to the last!"

The crowd drowned him in cheers. Now that the rain had finally stopped, the deafening roar rumbled beyond the square, amplified by the fortifications and buildings all around it. The strains of "O Canada" rose up again on the departing tide of people. Shouts of "To *L'Événement*! To the *Chronicle*! Down with conscription!" burst out at the head of the throng, which began to churn and surge forward. On top of Saint John's Gate, buffeted by the wind, the two friends had long since emptied the two flasks of whisky that Gonzague had tucked into his pockets, and now they shivered in their drenched clothes as they watched the crowd, all young men like themselves, wind down the ramparts to join the phalanx heading for the Lower Town.

"Come on, Mick. Let 'em break a few windows if that's what turns their crank. Let's go get warmed up."

3

Laughing and playfully jostling each other, as if by mockery they could dispel the darkness now looming over their lives, the two climbed down from their perch and plunged into the human river flowing from the square into the narrow streets around it. Half carried and half pushed along Rue Saint-Jean, they charged with the others down the Côte du Palais, slipping and sliding on the wet cobblestones. At the bottom of the hill, between the railway station and the docks, they entered an area where cheap rooming houses, dingy hotels, taverns, and warehouses were encrusted along the base of

Cap Diamant like barnacles along the water line on a ship's hull. Here amid the factory smells and the odors of rust, tar, and fried fat bustled a transient netherworld in ceaseless motion: of travelers in transit, sailors on leave, and soldiers bound for the front; of customs agents and railwaymen, traders, land speculators, lumberjacks, and raftsmen on their way north.

After a brief stop in the smoke and noise of the bar of the Saint-Roch Hotel to refill their flasks, the young men set off once again in the damp dark night.

"Tonight, m'boy," Gonzague confided, with a libidinous smirk, "you are going to discover the many faces of pleasure. First-class beauties, boy, nothing but the best, makes me hard just thinking about it—"

"Gonzague, you'll never change," said Mick. "You're worse than a rutting moose, you are."

The fellow had nerve, though, Mick thought. You had to hand it to him. This magistrate's son, who joined the other notables at the basilica for mass every Sunday, sitting piously next to his wealthy mother, who catered to his every whim; this prince of a boy who could afford to impress the most sought-after debutantes from here to Montreal, preferred to wallow in disreputable dives.

"See, what did I tell you, here we are."

For a while now they had been walking along dark, narrow side streets, glistening wet from the rain. Suddenly, between two grimy façades, a carriageway gaped in the shadows like the mouth of a cave. Gonzague ducked into the darkness, with Mick in tow. Their steps echoed smartly beneath the stone vault that led into a tiny courtyard, dimly lit by the upstairs windows, beyond which yawned the gate of the former stable, now empty and abandoned. On the right they spotted a recessed door, with a small window and a lace curtain that stirred as they approached.

"You're expected?"

"*We're* expected, Mick, m'boy ..."

Gonzague's rich baritone purred with excitement and anticipation. The door opened. A woman's face emerged from the gloom.

"The judge's son! Bringing company, are we!"

A female voice, husky and lewd.

"As promised, Eulalie. Boy, have I got a thirst ..."

"I'll take care of that, dearie."

They entered a darkened hallway at the end of which a patch of amber light glowed like a promise. Up close, it was a kind of smoking room, with yellowing walls and aging furniture, a worn carpet, and one window covered with faded lace. Its central feature was a wooden stairway.

"Eulalie Larivière!" Gonzague gathered up the woman's ample waist with one arm and pulled her up against him with gusto. "My pal here is one of the world's finest, 'cept he studies too much. He needs to be shown a thing or three, you get my meaning? Bring him a glass and while you're at it, bring a whole damn bottle for me."

"You want me to call them out on the landing so's your friend can see 'em?"

The lady of the house was a matronly wench with yellow hair, charcoal eyelids, and a fleshy red pout, whose pride in her status as madam to the worthies of the Grande Allée reared up at the slightest praise.

Gonzague turned to his friend. "Want to pick your own, or you prefer the chef's surprise?"

"You know I don't like surprises," muttered Mick, accepting the offered glass.

"Ah, but your chum here ordered something special, just for you," protested the woman, lifting the young man's chin with a folded fan which she held rather comically in her fat little hand, and striking what she fancied was a classy pose. "How old are you, honey?"

The boy's neck stiffened, ever so slightly, like a horse refusing the halter.

"Old enough," he glared.

"One thing's for certain," guffawed the tall Gonzague, giving his pal a slap on the back, "the kid's a virgin."

"What do you know?"

"Don't lie to me, and anyway, if you aren't, pretend you are. They're even nicer to you if they think it's the first time, isn't that so, mother?"

"Isn't a man beautiful at that age! Just look at that face, a real angel. Anyway, dearie, my girls here are clean, and they're young, and as for the customers, we take them by appointment only, understand? All the big shots come to my place, sweetheart, no old whores and no bums allowed."

"Come on, take your share," said Gonzague, handing Mick one of the two bottles of whisky he'd purchased at the Saint-Roch, "we mustn't keep heaven waiting."

4

Upstairs the hallway smelled of floor wax and cheap perfume.

"This one is special," Gonzague whispered to Mick in front of one of the doors. "The prettiest, youngest girl in the house. Guaranteed to make you climb to the ceiling every time ..."

He can say whatever he likes, after all, he's paying, Mick thought to himself, swallowing hard. His heart was pounding. What's the matter with you, boy?—damn! A small, delicate girl in a negligee appeared at the door, thick brown hair cascading over narrow shoulders.

"Hey, it's the lovely Hermine! Look after my chum," Gonzague called out from the next doorway along. He puffed out his chest and swaggered, his arms around two fleshy vestals, one a blond, the other a redhead, with breasts like udders under their flimsy gowns.

"You coming in?" asked the little-girl voice close by. The door closed behind them. They were alone. Heart in his throat, tail between his legs. Get a grip, damn it! In the lamplight, she was pretty and young, very young in fact, and utterly naked under her negligee. A little doll's face, with the eyes of a tired child, and pale, delicate skin beneath the rouge. She took the bottle from his hands with a fetching wriggle of her pert little body, then rubbed up against him enticingly, though her smile contrasted with the mournful gray of her eyes.

"What's your name?" she asked in her soft, reedy voice.

"Michael."

"You are English?"

"Not on your life!" he bridled. "Irish!"

He pulled away, took a few steps around the room in an effort to dispel the discomfort he felt in the presence of this girl, whose eyes behind the make-up were those of a battered child, this stray waterlily washed up in the muck of the harbor. He felt only pity and shame, and would have liked to retreat, but next door already there was revelry and laughter. The room was small, with a brass bed over which loomed a pastel icon of the Sacred Heart of Jesus, and on the dresser, the chest of drawers, the bedside table, a small forest of candles, like the ones lit for prayer in churches. There must have been fifty of them, at least, all round the room.

"Why all the candles? Do you have customers in the archbishop's palace?"

She came closer again, shrugging her negligee off her

frail shoulders, unveiling large breasts, almost too heavy for her fragile frame. She eyed him uncertainly, with a hint of fear at the edge of her eyes.

"Come on, don't be nervous," said the hoarse little voice. "You want me to undress you?"

She sat down on the bed, her small hands settling on his trouser buckle.

"Why don't you light them, just to see?"

"Right now, you mean?"

She got up, turned her back to him, struck a match. Leaning over the dresser, gathering her long hair with one hand behind her neck, she lighted the candles one at a time; the little flames, reflected in the mirror, bathed her soft breasts in a golden glow. She came back toward him, turned off the lamp, and the walls came alive with quivering shadows. She filled the glass he was holding out to her. He emptied it in just a few gulps. She poured him another, then one more. The room shimmered and swam with light and shadow. She loosened his necktie, removed his jacket, unbuckled his belt. He had no more desire for her now than earlier, but next door against the wall the cavalry was charging with everything it had.

Mick let her sit him down, then collapsing crosswise on the bed, shut his eyes. Drank too much too quick, O'Neill, you coward, should get the hell out of here ... Light small fingers, unfastening his trouser buttons, searching him, fondling him, and suddenly the warm wet wonder of her mouth, drawing from a well so deep, at the very root of him, dredging up sharp, fierce pleasure, building, building, swelling, surging to a blazing burst of blinding light ... too soon ... too soon ...

Head so heavy it felt like a stone. Need to sleep but not here. He was empty. Scruples, pride, even pity, gone.

On the ceiling the light from the candles still flickered sadly. The girl was standing by the bed, rinsing her gullet with whisky.

"Tell Gonzague I'll see him at home," he said, straightening his clothes without so much as a sideways glance at her. On the way out he left what little change he had on the dresser. Above it in the mirror he caught a glimpse of himself stealing out, a well-dressed, fair-haired picture of shame.

3

*Birth
of Venus*

1

Carleton, Quebec, July 1917 One would have been hard put to find two more different women than Madeleine Langlois and her sister-in-law, the Angel, also known as Florence. Like her brother Charles, Florence was tall and blue-eyed, but, unlike him, slender and fine-boned, with a vivid complexion and sun-streaked hair that bespoke her love of the outdoors. She was well-read, well-traveled and, like her brother, possessed of a gentle, affectionate nature. A full year had elapsed since the summer she had spent bringing her niece back to the world of the living, a year during which she and Jeanne had become very close. Florence had been widowed early in the war. As the tale was told in the family, she had loved her husband almost to distraction, but she was still so young and pretty that Jeanne, who had barely known her uncle, had trouble seeing her as a widow, or even a woman of her parents' generation. A tad eccentric, oblivious to chatter and gossip, she regularly indulged her love of painting and was often to be seen driving her buggy dressed in an old shirt and a pair of trousers that had belonged to her late husband, hauling her easel and canvas off to some favorite location.

That morning, she and her young charge had risen at the first blush of dawn and set off without delay, so as to arrive at the foot of the mountain before the sun was too high. Having left the horse at a farm where Florence bought her butter, they spent the better part of the day scaling the steep slope of Mount Saint-Joseph, which towered behind the seaside village of Carleton and could be seen from far and wide. The climb was laborious, through dense undergrowth and brushwood, but Florence knew the terrain, the conquest of this peak being a ritual of hers, performed every year in early summer.

"There's another place I like to go," Florence was saying, taking in the breathtaking scenery stretching below them, as far as the eye could see. "In the Laurentians, north of Montreal. I go there in the fall, when the colors are at their peak. Antoine left me a small hunting lodge up in the mountains. You get there on horseback from the valley. I must take you there one of these days ..."

Florence's husband, Antoine Talbot, had been one of the first French Canadians to volunteer for service overseas in 1914. Born to wealth in an upper-class Outremont family, he had risen quickly through the officer ranks, then died a futile death, leading a suicidal charge against the German machine guns at Ypres in the spring of 1915. However, that was not how the government had put it to his young widow.

"I finally learned the truth," Florence had explained to her niece the previous summer, "because not all of his men died with him. Two years ago one of them came to see me in Montreal after he was demobilized. A young second lieutenant, barely more than a boy, it seemed to me. The same shell that killed Antoine blew off both his legs ... He said that just before leading their men over the top, Antoine looked him in the eye and said, 'If you make it out of here alive, find a way to tell my wife my thoughts were of her.' Poor Antoine, he got what he wanted in the end."

Jeanne has listened to Florence's story, lying on the beach, by the remains of their picnic. Lulled by the intermittent roar of the waves, by the hiss of pebbles rolling in surf, practically floating on the warm sand, her whole body absorbing its heat, she was still so weak and exhausted that she had barely registered that last, strange comment. In any case, she recalled, she herself had been nursing a wound of her own that day. She had finally seen her mother again, that very morning, for the very first time since her return from Saint-Boniface. It seemed that Madeleine, hitherto her daughter's zealously protective guardian, had had no part in the decision to send Jeanne to her Aunt Florence's in the Gaspé for the summer. It had been the recommendation of the family doctor, in the absence of her mother, who had been in a closed retreat at the Convent of the Order of the Five Wounds, and seemed in advance to have washed her hands of the whole matter. That morning, as she laid eyes on Jeanne, her mother had said, "What did I tell you, Charlie, you can see for yourself she's not as ill as all that ..."

Those words smote her like the lash of a horsewhip to the face. Worse still, they poisoned what was left of the summer. By fall, when Jeanne was sent off to complete her education at the Sacred Heart Convent school in Montreal, her lifelong hankering after her mother's affection had begun to wither and die. The thought of having to face so much indifference and coldness was as unbearable to her as the glare of even a distant fire to a person who has suffered burns.

"You must miss your husband terribly," she said, picking up on Florence's reference to her husband's bequest.

"I loved him too much," murmured Florence, bitterness stealing over her gaze like a shadow flitting over water. "Antoine loved me in his own way, but he was very unhappy. It's probably for the best ..."

Florence spoke with a serenity that was incomprehensible to her niece, the more so because the events she referred to were still so recent. She had been mad about a man who "loved her in his own way," while at the same time wishing for his own death? How was such a thing possible? The mystery was too great, the reality it concealed too painful. Far in the distance, across the Baie des Chaleurs, the coast of New Brunswick was slowly emerging from the morning mist.

2

Charles Langlois had written to his sister, announcing his arrival. The House of Commons was to remain in session throughout the summer, amid the storm unleashed by the debate over conscription, so that his visit would necessarily be a brief one. Nevertheless, as an election could be called at any time, he would be touring his riding, as he did every summer. He rejoiced at the news that Jeanne had preceded him, and looked forward "to the family being reunited," which Jeanne understood to mean that her mother would also be coming, as was naturally to be expected. How could she have presumed to hope it might be otherwise? Still, she feared the sight of her mother and her inevitable disapproval.

The black cabriolet driven by the Honorable Charles Langlois appeared on the road, hugging the shoreline, then turned up the dirt drive through the field of daisies to Florence's house. Jeanne's father climbed down first. He was a giant of a man, sixteen years older than his wife, with a shock of white hair and a slow, deliberate gait that lent him a kind of lumbering majesty. He was still very handsome, but despite his commanding appearance, noble features and strong, jutting jaw, his was a docile disposition. Coming round to his wife's side, he stopped to pet his horse, smiling sheepishly at his daughter, as he did whenever his wife was about. As though his love for her were a guilty secret, thought Jeanne, who, seeing her mother emerge from the shade of the carriage, felt her heart contract with grief.

Madeleine Langlois was a darkly beautiful woman, whose religious zeal for self-mortification had not altered her youthful appearance. Her brown skin, dark eyes, and jet-black hair hinted at Spanish or, more accurately, Montagnais Indian ancestry. As small and shapely as her daughter was tall and slim, she was hatless as usual, and clad in an unfashionably long-sleeved, high-necked black wool dress, much too warm for the season. Mme Langlois stepped down from the carriage with her head held high. When the two sisters-in-law embraced each other stiffly, eyes averted, cheeks barely touching, they were displaying more than just their disagreement on the subject of Jeanne. For if Charles Langlois had a soft spot for his sister (in fact, it was just about the only aspect of his former life that his marriage had not altered), his wife heartily disliked her sister-in-law, and the feeling was mutual.

"Well then, Charlie," said Florence, calling her brother by his childhood nickname, "what's the news from Ottawa?" Her tone was serious. She understood and shared her brother's political interest, the heavy sense of responsibility, more than his wife ever would.

"Not good, I'm afraid." They followed the others into the house, where an elaborate tea had been prepared. "Since Vimy, voluntary enlistment has not kept up with the casualty rate. Our soldiers over there can't keep up. The government is taking advantage of the situation by wrapping itself in the flag, egged on by all manner of Orangemen from Ontario and elsewhere, who are demanding conscription at any price. Meanwhile Bourassa, Lavergne and the others continue their agitation. That being said," he added, "they are right when they say that a referendum would settle the matter. Indeed, Laurier agrees with them."

"Give women the vote, Charlie, and I guarantee you conscription will never be passed into law," Florence said sarcastically, knowing her brother's conservative views on the issue of female suffrage.

"The government won't hear of a referendum," he continued, sidestepping her challenge. "They are determined to call an election. They plan to run on conscription and patriotism, to maintain themselves in power even at the cost of completely isolating Quebec, which will vote against it, it's inevitable. I fear the consequences of such a divisive election ..."

Like an animal worrying a wound, thus keeping it from healing, Jeanne could not keep from looking at her mother, who was listening to the conversation, her gaze shifting impassively from her husband to her sister-in-law and back again, never once alighting on her daughter. As far as she's concerned, I no longer exist, Jeanne told herself bitterly. Her mother was no longer an impenetrable enigma, but a harsh, finite reality.

3

Each year the coast filled up with vacationers from Montreal, Ottawa, Toronto, and as far as Boston, New York, and Washington. The house to which Mick O'Neill had been invited belonged to some rich Americans who came up for the scenery, the warm sea, and the salmon. It was a large white villa facing the ocean, its shingled walls partly concealed under a cascade of climbing roses, its weathered wooden fence overwhelmed with great masses of flowering sweet-briar, which unlike the sparse clumpy grass of the lawn thrived in the sandy soil. The street in front of the house was already lined with gleaming carriages and flashy new motorcars. A fashionably dressed crowd had invaded the garden, clustering around damask-covered tables laden with pastries and cakes by the silver trayful, and large crystal bowls overflowing with freshly picked berries. Amid the milling guests a few local farm boys hired on as waiters flitted from group to group, hovering shakily before each guest, refilling empty champagne glasses. Mick was offered one as he arrived, then another as he advanced into the press of young women, radiant in their summer dresses, chatting and smiling under their multicolored hats, the sheer variety of which astonished him. Like a dandelion seed sailing in the breeze, he drifted blissfully along in their fragrant midst, emptying his glass each time it was filled, and gradually made his way toward a rose-covered arch at the back of the garden, next to which a small group had gathered.

"Mick! Come, dear boy, let me introduce you!" cried the MP for Bonaventure when he caught sight of him. Magnificent in a white summer suit that matched his snowy hair, the man towered head and shoulders over the group. When they had met through the good offices of an influential lawyer, the senior partner of the firm where Mick would be articling that fall, the august parliamentarian and the aspiring barrister had immediately taken to one another. In the months that followed their paths had crossed often, at political meetings in Montreal and elsewhere in the province, and that summer, with an election in the offing, Charles Langlois had asked Mick to come and give him a hand in his riding. Mick had jumped at the opportunity. His modest income, bequeathed to him by his father to pay for his education, did not provide him with the means to afford a seaside vacation. For almost a month now he had been touring the villages along the coast, meeting the local kingmakers, who received him with all the respect due to a protégé of the man who had represented them in Parliament since 1900.

"Here is a young man who is going to make his mark ..." declared his mentor to the group.

Mick didn't hear the remainder of his introduction. Straight ahead of him, under the arched, rose-covered trellis, framed in splendor and drenched in sunlight, a girl had just sprung from his innermost hopes like a blond Venus rising from the sea. The bewilderment that befell him at that moment probably owed as much to the cloudless blue sky and sapphire sea as it did to a vision of golden hair flowing thickly over beautiful shoulders, of slender limbs glimpsed through the transparency of a summer dress, of luminous eyes, translucent as water, looking through him without seeing. In a flash, however, the apparition had floated off and away in the direction of the house. Mick for a moment followed the girl with his eyes. Then, at the risk of offending the guest of honor, he mumbled an unintelligible apology and departed in pursuit.

4

She had taken refuge inside the house because she could no longer endure all those faces crowding in on her, damp hands pressing her, eyes scrutinizing her. What did they want from her? Wandering through the maze of empty rooms, she met only one servant carrying a heavy tray and asked her the way to the ladies' room. She was shown down a hallway, to a place the size of a closet. Locking herself inside, she leaned her back against the door. Gradually the narrow space, the bare wooden walls, the relative silence quelled her breathlessness. She closed her eyes. *You are suffering* ... the voice of the confessional, whispering in her memory from the depths of a Manitoba winter. Suffering, yes, in her pride and dignity. This unease only fed her exasperation with herself, with everyone. Except the Angel, exempted from spite for kindness over and above the call of duty.

Not wishing to return immediately to the garden, she followed the hallway to a veranda overlooking the woods at the back of the house and startled a young man standing at the window with his back turned. His unruly copper-blond hair was wreathed in cigarette smoke. Before she could retreat, he turned to face her, his whole body exuding tension, like certain overbred horses. He had a narrow, angular face that broadened out at the forehead and temples. His pale, piercing eyes conveyed an intensity, almost a fierceness, that was both mesmerizing and oddly chilling. She made for the screen door and escaped down the wooden steps into the garden.

5

August 1917 To succeed, a young man is prepared to make many a compromise. A wealthy and powerful man takes him under his wing. This man has a cherished daughter, the apple of his eye, who soon evinces a weakness for the ambitious young fellow. To please his mentor and rise a few notches in his estimation, the young man prepares to sacrifice a part of himself, which he may in later years come to regret.

Such, however, was not to be the fate of Mick O'Neill. From the moment he first glimpsed her amid a halo of roses, like a pagan Madonna smiling from a flowered niche, he was violently smitten with Jeanne Langlois. Having followed her into the house without so much as a notion of whom he was pursuing, he appeared before her and froze, spellbound, speechless, like a first-time hunter who suddenly has in his sights the game he has been tracking, but realizes at that moment that he has forgotten to load his rifle, and can only look on, powerlessly, as his prey vanishes into the underbrush.

As for the other young holiday-makers of eligible age, despite all the months of debates and anticonscriptionist demonstrations, the Canadian Parliament had sealed their fate, by passing into law the compulsory military service bill. A kind of frenzy took hold of those young men and women in their headlong rush to outdistance the tidal wave of war that would soon engulf them and tear them away from the life they knew. All through that fateful summer of 1917, the garden parties and receptions that followed one upon the other had a strong political flavoring. Mick made the rounds assiduously, all the while praying for another apparition of the beautiful creature who had ignited his imagination in a far more significant way than had his brief initiation to carnal amusements. But the nymph, who was not sighted often in Carleton, remained invisible, in seclusion, it seemed, at some distance farther up the coast.

One fine August afternoon the little band of young men and the girls around whom they orbited was once again assembled. Mick, fortified by the plethora of political discussions overheard since the beginning of the summer, had become the designated interpreter of the day's increasingly tumultuous news. Here he was, standing under a bower, reading aloud to his new cronies from a newspaper he was holding open in front of him. Only a few days ago in Montreal, a bomb had exploded the home of Lord Atholstan, owner of the *Montreal Star* and a vocal advocate of conscription. The perpetrators were still at large and the police were pursuing their investigation. "Almost time!" one of the fellows announced, glancing at his watch. Whereupon the group, quickly going into action, crossed the lawn and made for the street, pulling into its wake in step with the boys all the girls present.

Suddenly Mick was beside himself with joy. There, not ten feet in front of him, was the very girl he had almost lost all hope of ever setting eyes on again, golden hair blowing across her lovely face, straw hat firmly clamped with one hand to her head, one lovely elbow jutting skyward in an attitude so consummately erotic that he was instantly overwhelmed. She hesitated, like a leaf twirling in the current at water's edge, then, finally allowing herself to be carried along, caught up with the merry crowd as it piled into half a dozen motorcars. Having skillfully maneuvered so as to squeeze next to Mlle Langlois in the back seat of a late-model Studebaker sedan, Mick stretched an arm behind her along the seatback and ventured a bold smile. As the drivers revved their engines and took off, single file, toward the railway station, the feel of female warmth against him threw him into turmoil. He ceased to register the chatter of the other passengers, to feel the jolting of the car on the bumpy road or the hot breath of wind on his cheeks through the open window. His head was swimming in the scent of young girl, in the closeness of golden, gossamer hair, of rose-petal smooth skin. Blood rushed to his face. The thing between his legs was painfully aroused. He looked gingerly down at his wide open jacket baring the crotch of his pants. God don't let her lower her eyes ...

As they arrived at the little station the driver, for a prank, jammed on the brakes and swerved to the right, provoking wild laughter from the girl in the front and pressing Mick's neighbor into him in a way so painfully pleasurable it paralyzed him. Finally the car stopped. The distant whistling of the train could now be heard. He pulled his arm free and got out first. Too giddy to offer Jeanne his hand, he waited for her nonetheless. The shrieking of the locomotive grew louder. The young people poured onto the wooden platform, just in time to cheer the black monster pulling into the station, panting and pawing mightily, spewing great clouds of steam into the air, shaking the small building down to its foundations.

"Do you come every day to wait for the train?" Jeanne asked him, as he strode purposefully up the tracks toward the locomotive.

"Yes, mademoiselle," he answered without slowing his step. "The engine driver brings me the papers from Montreal."

The driver, catching sight of him, poked his head out of the window of the locomotive and dropped a bundle of newspapers, tightly bound with rope. Mick caught the heavy parcel in mid-flight and, drawing a purse from his trouser pocket, threw it up to the driver. The fellow emptied it, counted his money, shouted, "*Correc'!*" above the hissing of the engine, and dropped it back straight into its owner's hands.

"What are you going to do with all these newspapers?" asked Jeanne.

"Sell them."

"Hey, Mick! You got yesterday's *Devoir* in there?" one of the group called out.

"You bet!" Mick sliced through the rope with his pocket knife. "Not to mention *La Patrie, La Presse*, the *Gazette*, and the *Montreal Star*."

He handed the fellow a copy of *Le Devoir*. The others gathered round.

"Hey, look at Bourassa's editorial!" cried the first customer, reading from his open paper. "'*Stériles violences*' ... he said. Bourassa is denouncing the bombers! There's going to be one hell of a trial when they catch them."

"We're in a real mess, all right," grumbled Mick, a cigarette between his teeth, counting his change. Then, speaking quietly to Jeanne without taking his eyes off the coins in the palm of his hand, he added, "I could drive you home, later, if you like ..."

Wherever he went in the vast riding of Bonaventure, the Honorable Charles Langlois's organization provided Mick with a vehicle for his personal use. In Carleton, he even got to use the Langlois horse and buggy when the owners were not in town. His proposition, he knew, was risky. Charles Langlois's daughter, he had learned, was spending the summer with her aunt, who acted as her chaperon. But perhaps, in his capacity as her respected father's assistant...?

6

The cabriolet was speeding along the coast toward the village of Bonaventure. The Langlois's pretty black mare trotted out in front, head up, mane flying in the wind. The sea was deep indigo in the declining light of early evening. In the distance a rag-tag band of squawking seagulls glided and wheeled above the foam-flecked water. It was mid-August. Soon summer would be over. The chill of autumn was already in the air.

"What are you going to do if you are called up?"

Mick turned his head toward the one asking the cruel question. He saw perplexity, even—dare he hope?—concern, in those ineffable eyes.

"I can't believe they are going to enforce that law." He spoke angrily, the excitement he felt at her closeness fueling his indignation. "Or else they'll have to use force, at the risk of blowing up the country. If they're planning an election, it's because they know they would lose a referendum. We're not the only ones opposed to conscription, you know. In the other provinces, there are a lot of people who are against it."

"They say if women were allowed to vote, it would never pass."

"Maybe, but there is no way this Tory government is going to give you the vote, you can be sure of that."

"What are you going to do?"

"I don't know yet," Mick answered morosely. "I'll see when the time comes. I don't see how they could force me to go and fight for the British Crown. Do you know what is going on in Ireland, as we speak? My grandfather crossed the Atlantic to escape hunger and oppression, and would they send me back, to risk my life for bloody England?"

Jeanne's curiosity grew with each word. This rebellious

streak of his intrigued her, perhaps because she herself had for so long harnessed her will to pleasing someone who didn't care. Sometimes the memory of the glory-bound young soldiers she had once glimpsed on the railway platform of a small Ontario town haunted her, and she wondered how many of them were still alive.

"Look, it's so beautiful!" she said, to raise his spirits.

They had reached a place where the road hugged a cliff, at the bottom of which the breakers crashed over the rocks in a roar of surf. Mick reined in the horse, bringing it to a halt. The wind was up. The waves swelled and subsided, like giant breathing. Mick was watching her. He looked bereft. Suddenly his anxious eyes locked onto hers. They seemed to mirror a wild hope, which the road, escaping straight ahead as far as the eye could see, and the windswept ruggedness of this stretch of coast conspired to incite in Jeanne also. On an impulse, whose very boldness excited her more than the act itself, she planted a kiss on the boy's mouth that left them both gasping, as much for composure as for breath. Jeanne didn't like the contrariness she felt stirring within her, the giddy excitement and the dizzy fear, but she couldn't suppress a surge of exasperation at the young man's astonished expression, as he clumsily tried to help himself to more.

"Now I have to go home," she stammered, embarrassed. "Florence will be worried ..."

"I'm leaving for Montreal in a fortnight," he said plaintively. "Do you think I could see you again?"

He was beseeching her with pathetic eyes. Her heart was pounding. What had she done?

"I'll have to ask Florence."

He gave the reins a gentle yank, and they set off again, at a walk.

7

Summer was almost over. Florence had decided, as a kindness to her niece, to give a small reception in honor of the young men who, like Mick O'Neill, were soon to be called up.

The company began arriving at sunset, just as a giant moon was rising from the ocean, almost filling the horizon. Jeanne watched its silvery disk slowly diminish in size as it rose into the night. She was almost resigned to returning to Ottawa with her parents, and Florence promised to invite her often to Montreal. Had it not been for the war, she could have taken that opportunity to see Mick. He had come out to Florence's twice more since that day on the cliffside. He made her aunt laugh with his tales of political shenanigans and derring-do. Her father had said he was a young man with a bright future. "An unbeliever—an atheist," objected her mother, who knew from the priest that he hadn't been seen at church since the day he'd arrived in the area. That was enough to make him attractive to Jeanne, who otherwise welcomed his attentions with mixed emotions. For although his visits flattered her budding feminine pride and reinforced her unwillingness to return to living under her mother's thumb, Mick already thought too much of her for her liking. His devotion to her, a miserable creature who hadn't even merited a mother's love, devalued him in her eyes. For the scar Jeanne was nursing was still too fresh, too painful to touch. In truth, the kiss she had so imprudently given had been no more than a wild rearing up against constraint. But the blaze it had ignited in Mick was wreaking havoc with him. A short time ago he had been his own man, a cocky, ambitious young buck ready to take on all comers on his way up to fame and fortune. Now he was consumed with her alone, with the obsessive need to see her again and again, to make her part of his life once and for all. He would have trekked every day like a pilgrim to offer his devotion, but the riding of Bonaventure was immense and Florence's house, isolated as it was on the coast, away from any village, could not often be inserted into his daily itinerary.

They dined that festive night on lobster boiled in sea water, and champagne. The Honorable Charles Langlois gave the toast, and they drank to victory and the speedy return of the young soldiers-to-be. After dessert (a fabulous Saint-Honoré that was Rose's specialty; Rose was Florence's cook) Jeanne caught sight of Mick quietly slipping out of the dining room. There was something strange about him that piqued her curiosity; he was unlike any boy she had ever met. She rose and followed him out to the veranda, where she found him staring into the darkness.

"Didn't you like Daddy's speech?" she ventured.

"An admirable speech," he replied, turning to face her. "Your father is a wonderful speaker."

Silence fell between them, rooting them both to the spot.

"Your father is a man of peace," he went on. "Like Laurier, which is why I admire him. But peacemakers, in the end, are always repudiated by both sides. They are forever getting caught in the cross-fire."

"Sometimes they win," murmured Jeanne. "If you believe his cause is already lost, why are you here and not in the street with Armand Lavergne?"

Mick gave her a sharp look and blushed as his mind harkened back to his wild night with Gonzague. Blessed darkness masked his embarrassment.

"Because your father is an honorable man, and unlike Bourassa, the ideals he defends are not dictated to him from the mouth of a priest!"

The young man turned once again to face the night, drawing deeply on his cigarette. Jeanne, awkwardly, turned to leave him.

"Wait!" he stammered, suddenly beside her. "Wait," he repeated softly, then fell silent again.

"You're leaving tomorrow ..." she offered, her voice wavering.

He was so close to her now that his whole body quivered with nervousness. He was looking at Jeanne with such intensity that she feared she might blurt out some foolishness. She lowered her eyes.

"I was wondering," he began uneasily, "if I might, if you would object, if I wrote to you from time to time ..."

The words burst from him in volleys, punctuated by deep breaths.

"Yes, I mean, no, of course, I would have no objection ..."

Mick took another deep drag at his cigarette. It was now a smoldering stub that burnt his fingers. Stifling an oath, he flung it over the railing into the darkness. He was burning up all right. He wanted to hold her, to kiss her, so much it was agony, but he made no move to do so. The screen door had just creaked open. They were no longer alone in the darkness. Mme Langlois's silhouette was plainly visible in the light from the doorway. Jeanne and her mother eyed each other warily, then all three retreated to the soft murmurs of the reception room.

4

No

Turning Back

It was the middle of October. The member of Parliament for Bonaventure, his heart heavy with foreboding, had packed his bags and was preparing to submit, for the fifth time in his career, to the judgment of the people. He could only thank God that he had no son. How he felt for those young men, many of them French Canadians, waiting in the trenches for reinforcements. So many were dying over there. Still, this election was going to tear Canada apart. There was going to be more violence, more civil strife.

The maelstrom unleashed by the imposition of conscription had split the country, just as Henri Bourassa and his newspaper, *Le Devoir*, had so often predicted, and as Laurier had always dreaded. In Montreal, at the end of August, rioting crowds had been dispersed by club-wielding policemen on horseback cantering over the cobblestones of the Rue Notre-Dame, and since then the situation in the province had been deteriorating rapidly. Several *assemblées contradictoires** had been canceled because of threatened pandemonium and violence. In the streets of the city, mobs burned government candidates in effigy and everywhere one heard screams of *Traître* and *Vendu.*** All the while, Laurier and his Opposition candidates appealed for calm, promising to hold a referendum if they were returned to power and urging all those who could to volunteer for the defense of Canadian soldiers already in Europe. In the rest of the country the conscriptionist wave swept all before it. In the midst of this tumult, the government, leaving nothing to chance, found it expedient to pass a special Wartime Elections Act giving the vote to mothers, wives, widows, daughters, and sisters of soldiers, while denying it to other women whose loved ones had not yet enlisted. At the same time, Canadian citizens born abroad, speaking the "language of the enemy" and naturalized for less than fifteen years, had their right to vote simply canceled outright. For the Opposition, the dice were loaded, and Charles Langlois knew it.

The day before he left, he called his daughter to his study. The place he chose for this interview was significant, for they both knew that her mother would not venture there, because many of the books it contained were *à l'Index**** and because the smell of tobacco permeated the place. Her father's library was Jeanne's favorite room. Books, magnificently bound in leather, gilt-edged, with exotic titles in several languages, filled

* *Assemblées contradictoires*: public debates among candidates of various parties in an election.
** The Québécois term "vendu" means "sell-out," but is much more injurious in French, having the same connotation as "traitor," and implying that one has sold out to "les Anglais."
*** *à l'Index*: listed in the *Index Librorum Prohibitorum*, i.e. of books prohibited by the Catholic Church.

its bookcases from floor to ceiling. It was a shrine, her father was fond of saying, an Ali Baba's cave filled with wondrous treasures, that one entered on tiptoe.

Outside in the wintry sky the sun was a glowing ember, slowly sinking behind blackened trees soon to be stripped of last leaves by the chilly rains. Her father, standing at the window in the failing light, greeted her warmly.

"Ah, my little Jeanne, I'm glad to see you," he exclaimed, even though he'd just seen her at lunch. "Come in, come in. I have something important to tell you."

He drew a match from the silver case on the mantelpiece and removed the wrought-iron fireguard.

"I haven't yet mentioned this matter to your mother," he began, leaning over to light the twigs and strips of newspaper carefully arranged under the logs in the chimney, "because I wanted to have an opportunity to speak to you first. After all, it's you it concerns, and I want to know your feelings on the matter before going any further."

He drew himself upright and stood with his hands in his pockets, a little stooped, gazing at the flames that were darting out from under the logs. The fire crackled faintly as it licked at the fragrant wood. He took a deep breath and turned to face his daughter.

"I have just today received a letter from our young friend Mick O'Neill. I take it he's been writing to you regularly—for some time?"

Jeanne nodded in silence, wondering where her father's questions could be leading. Mick had indeed been writing to her, often and at great length. In his letters he rarely spoke of her or of himself; he described his new life as a lawyer-in-training with the prestigious Montreal firm of Lynch O'Connell Doyle, amid the chaotic events shaking the city. Was she wrong to receive his letters? Would her father reproach her?

Jeanne was almost certain that her mother opened her mail before giving it to her.

"Here, perhaps you'd better read it yourself," said her father, his voice thick with an emotion she could not identify.

Jeanne took the letter. She read the beginning over several times, trying to make sense of the words scrawled there in a hand she recognized.

... I fully realize that this may come as a surprise to you, and naturally expect you to question the haste with which I appear to be acting. However, my feelings for Jeanne are such ...

She gave her father a startled, questioning look.

... that I would be deeply saddened to be leaving the country without taking away with me some hope that she might await my return. I venture to hope that your opinion of me has not changed, that you still believe in my prospects for the future, and that consequently you may see in me a suitable husband for your daughter ...

Jeanne was thunderstruck. She had not expected this. Mick's proposal aroused turbulent emotions. She was flattered, of course, but that was not all she felt: an instinct deep inside her balked and stiffened at the prospect like a yearling at the bit. Her thoughts raced, trying to gauge the implications of accepting or refusing. On the one hand she could see the possibility, barely conceivable and perhaps unattainable because of the war, of removing herself from her mother's dominion. The lure of freedom beckoned from that imagined future. The price was tying her destiny to that of this young man whom she hardly knew. But if she refused, there could be only more of the dismal, solitary life she had always known. Finally her father's calm, affectionate voice rose above the clamor of her thoughts.

"He's just been called up. He's to join his unit at Valcartier next month," he was saying. "Of course it's a big decision, one you mustn't make lightly. I don't want you to feel pressured."

She said nothing. She did not feel capable of discussing such intimate matters with her father, kind though he was. Her thoughts turned to the only person in whom she could really confide. She must speak to Florence.

"He's rather shy, I know. Raised without a mother, without much contact with his sisters. That being said," her father added with the shadow of a smile, "every man needs a woman's civilizing influence, and I suspect that given the right woman to draw him out, he will make someone an excellent husband. Quite apart from that, as you know, he has a brilliant career ahead of him. Life at the side of such a young man would never be dull ..."

As she watched him stoke the fire with the poker, Jeanne couldn't help wondering what "civilizing influence" her own mother could possibly have had on this gentlest of men.

"Then of course there is the matter of his mobilization. I would like to be able to promise you that we will win the election and that the legislation allowing for conscription, once we put it to a referendum, will be repealed. But I think it my duty to tell you the truth as I see it. Quebec will vote for Laurier, and the majority in the rest of the country will vote for the government. It is a battle Quebec can only lose. In practice, that almost certainly means Mick will be called up ... I'll tell your mother about his marriage proposal. I've no doubt," he sighed, as though to himself, "she will have her own views on the subject ..."

Jeanne could see the line clearly drawn between them: on one side, her father, using all his diplomatic skills to champion his young protégé; on the other, her mother, railing against Mick's anti-religious views, which he did nothing to conceal.

But the anticipated confrontation did not take place. "Let her be married," Madeleine decreed, with the soft-spoken peremptoriness her husband knew was final, "as soon as possible, before she has the opportunity to sin." To her daughter she later added, cryptically: "Be very careful. You may come to regret not having given yourself to Our Lord."

2

"So your mind's made up, is it?" muttered Mick. He threw a handful of twigs onto the fire that was crackling, spewing swirls of sparks in the crisp autumn air. He and Gonzague were preparing to return to Quebec City at the end of a successful hunting trip in the valley of the Jacques-Cartier River. They had killed a deer the day before, and today had loaded it into the Ford borrowed from Gonzague's mother for the occasion. Mick had been moved when they had found the doe lying where she had fallen on a blood-stained carpet of autumn leaves, as graceful in death as she had been in life. Even after two days in the peace and silence of the bush, he felt as agitated as the day he had left Montreal.

"There's no use talking about it," Gonzague was saying, with a graver expression than Mick had seen on him in all the years of their friendship. "There's a war on over there. And it's time we got it over with."

The two chums were sitting on a tree trunk that must have fallen in a recent storm. Yellow leaves still clung to its branches.

"Gonzague Prud'homme," murmured Mick incredulously, "I would never have believed you of all people would enlist."

"First of all, I don't really think I have a choice, and anyway, ever since my cousin Georges was killed, the atmosphere at home has become unbearable. But I'll tell you, Georges didn't die for France or for England. When you die in a Canadian uniform, boy, there aren't many can still argue that your country is just a colony of Great Britain. As for Canadian sovereignty, we've got it now. We took it, old friend, at Vimy. We won that one. Not the French, not the English. We did it, Mick, never forget that."

"It's hard to believe that in a matter of days you'll be at Valcartier, even if it is just a few miles from here. I respect you, Gonzague, you know that. Dammit, I'll even go so far as to say I admire you. But my mind's made up as well."

"What are you going to do?"

"I'll do what I have to ... As long as the Canadian army remains under British command, you won't find me in it."

"You crazy Irishman—misplaced honor is all well and good, but are you sure your Jeanne Langlois doesn't have something to do with it?"

"She sure as hell will have something to do with it if ever she'll have me. Do you think I'm going to go and get myself killed or, worse, maimed for life if I have so much as a chance she'll say yes?"

"You've got it bad, haven't you? What if she says no?"

"She won't."

"But how are you going to manage to get yourself exempted?"

"Well, there you are, Gonzague, that's where you can help me."

"Sure I'm willing to help, but I don't see how ..."

Mick got to his feet and went to get his hunting rifle, a Winchester model 94 that had belonged to his father. He sauntered back toward Gonzague, but this time he sat down again at some distance from his friend. Then he pulled his canteen out of his jacket, having previously filled it with whisky, uncorked it and guzzled half its contents in one gulp.

"The hell are you doing?" Gonzague exclaimed in alarm.

"Gonzague, you remember, we always said, friends for life unto death, right?"

"Yeah, but *Christ!*"

"You gotta help me!"

"Yes, but what? What do you want me to do?"

Mick laid the gun across his knees, cracked it open, pushed the cartridge into the magazine.

"Now, don't move, Gonzague old friend, don't move a hair. But after, that's when I'm gonna need your help ..."

Mick swallowed what was left of the whisky. Then he cocked the Winchester, laid it gingerly on the ground before him, and with his left hand grasped it by the tip of the barrel, with his middle finger over the mouth of it.

"Mick! Are you crazy! Mick, goddammit—"

Carefully he lifted the rifle butt with his right hand, and then he slammed it down.

3

Ottawa, November 1917

The following week Jeanne Langlois was called to the telephone to speak to her father, who was calling from New Carlyle.

"Jeanne, how are you?" crackled the distant but familiar voice.

"I'm fine, Daddy, what about you? How's the election?"

"Oh, mine's not going too badly," he said, in the plucky tone that only election campaigns seemed to arouse in him. "Unfortunately, Henri Bourassa* has just given us the kiss of death by coming out in support of Laurier. The press in the rest of the country has gone on the rampage. To them, Lavergne's and Bourassa's brand of anti-imperialism is anathema. They are not ready yet for Canadian nationalism. But we'll take Quebec, there's no doubt about that. How is your mother?"

"She left yesterday for her annual retreat with the Sisters of the Precious Blood," answered Jeanne, who knew her father too well not to suspect that he was calling precisely because he knew that her mother was absent.

"Listen, Jeanne, I'm calling you because I've had some bad news concerning young Mick O'Neill."

Jeanne's blood ran cold.

"I've just received a telegram. He's in hospital. It seems he was involved in a hunting accident."

"An accident? I thought he was helping you with your campaign."

"He's been offered a position in the firm he's articling with. That's why he stayed in Montreal. It seems he has been badly wounded. I've written you a letter and when you receive it, I want you to call me so we can talk about it. Take care of yourself."

4

Mick spent three weeks in the Hôtel-Dieu hospital, where his father had practiced the surgical arts for so

* Henri Bourassa: member of Parliament and founder-editor of *Le Devoir*: arguably French Canada's most influential daily newspaper of the day.

many years. The wound he had inflicted on himself was considerable. The bullet had blown off the knuckle along with his finger, and the pain was excruciating; he had lost a great deal of blood, but the worst had been averted thanks to his friend's presence of mind. Gonzague had tied a tourniquet, doused the wound with alcohol, and applied a clean compress made from the oversupply of clean underwear his mother had forced him to pack. He had also gotten him to the hospital, driving all the way in from Sainte-Catherine-de-la-Jacques-Cartier to Quebec City in record time. The nuns, several of whom had known Mick's father well, in the days when he was chief surgeon at the hospital, showered him with attention. Once he was strong enough for conversation, they delighted in recounting the exploits of Dr. O'Neill, who had been the first disciple of Pasteur at the faculty of medicine, and the first surgeon at the hospital to introduce asepsis in the operating theater.

When Gonzague came to visit it was in the uniform of a second lieutenant in the Royal Vingt-Deuxième Régiment. His mother had had his brass tunic buttons gilded, and his officer's boots and Sam Browne belt specially made to measure by her saddler. He was about to sail for Halifax.

"You crazy fool," the big guy murmured when he saw Mick, lying so pale in his hospital bed. "And all for a bit of skirt!" he quipped, with a smile that didn't quite mask his emotion.

"I want to thank you for what you did ..."

"Hey! For life, unto death, right?"

"Yeah, except that now you're shipping out just when I wanted you to be my best man!"

"Hell, she say yes?"

"Not yet, but she will, don't you worry."

"Mick, before I go, there's something I have to ask ..."

Gonzague's expression darkened.

"It's my mother," he said, lowering his voice and gazing deeply into his friend's eyes. "She can't take it. Me being her only son and all. Éloïse is a wonderful daughter to her, but for Mom it's not the same ..."

"Ask me anything, Gonzague, you know you can count on me."

"Look after her, will you? Call her from time to time whenever you're in town for a court case, drop in for a visit, it'll do her good."

"You sure she won't resent—"

"You're like a second son to her, trust me."

"Understood. You know my word is worth more than my signature ..."

5

Ottawa, January 1, 1918 Night was falling on the frozen canal. She was skating, her hands tucked into the beautiful ermine muff Florence had given her that very morning. Her aunt's feet were too cold, she said, and she had gone to sit in the red-painted sleigh, wrapped in a shaggy buffalo rug, her breath rising in little clouds as the horses stood patiently under their blankets, shaking their heads from time to time and snorting loudly in the cold. Jeanne's skates sped over the smooth hard ice, turning and whirling with abandon. Her father had won his election, along with the sixty-two other Liberal MPs in the province of Quebec, including their leader, Sir Wilfrid Laurier. In the other provinces the Liberals, the party that had proposed putting conscription to a referendum, had been annihilated. A few days before Christmas, Mick, back on his feet and officially exempted from military service, had come to Ottawa to see her and had formally asked her to become his wife. He would soon, he said, be in a position to join the prestigious firm of Lynch O'Connell Doyle in Montreal as a junior associate. His future was assured. As a token of his affection, he had given her an aquamarine, mounted on a gold ring, "to match the color of your eyes," he'd said, an extravagance that must have cost him whatever savings he had.

The wheels of her life were turning again, she was being pointed in a direction not entirely of her choosing, launched on a course not quite of her making, but one that led outward and away, and from which there would be no turning back. She skated furiously on in the deepening gloom, drunk with the speed and the cold, intoxicated with the effort she demanded of her muscles. The hiss of her skate blades echoed between the high banks of the canal, in time with her breathing and the pounding of her heart. Farther, faster, as she mulled her decision, ignoring for a few moments longer Florence's hand waving from the beckoning warmth of the sleigh.

5

Adieu

Botticelli

With April 1918 came a cold, windy spring. Winter
dragged on. The malignancy of war spread to every corner of daily life, beginning with the long lists of the dead
in the morning paper. The country had not recovered
from the December election. Compulsory enlistment
had failed in every province. Of the hundred thousand
men called up since the law had been passed, three-
quarters had requested exemption. Not a single convoy
had left Halifax for the battlefields of Europe, where the
slaughter continued unabated, and the need for reinforcements was ever more cruelly felt.

In Quebec, the methods of recruitment were becoming more brutal. On the evening of Maundy Thursday a
riot broke out in Quebec City after some spotters,* on
the lookout for young men of draft age, arrested a man
who at first failed to produce his exemption papers. For

* Spotters: government agents whose task it was to "spot" draft
evaders.

several days pandemonium reigned. Spotters were beaten by rioters. The eight hundred soldiers of the Quebec City garrison were not enough to control the crowd of several thousand people who set fire to the police station and ransacked a federal recruitment office.

In the end, a battalion of soldiers was sent up from Toronto as reinforcements. Not one among them could speak or understand French. Sharpshooters fired on them from the rooftops, wounding four. The troops opened fire, killing five rioters and setting off an uproar in the province. Meanwhile in London the British government declared its intention of imposing conscription on Ireland. The perceived iniquity of that measure stemmed in part from the fact that it sought to force the Irish to defend, on behalf of others, a principle—self-government—that had long been denied them at home. The day conscription for Ireland was passed into law, all the Irish nationalist MPs left the House of Commons and returned to Dublin to sit as Dáil Éireann, the self-proclaimed Irish National Assembly. Meanwhile, in France, word was beginning to seep out of widespread mutiny in the French army the previous year, of entire units rebelling against their commanding officers, of hundreds of desperate soldiers, driven to desert by the horror and futility of the carnage, recaptured and summarily executed by firing squad. Everywhere the plague of war was spreading, pitting friend against friend, brother against brother, sowing internal havoc and division within the nations themselves.

Jeanne and Mick were married without fanfare on a dark rainy day in Montreal. The ceremony was held in the morning (in time for the newlyweds to catch the noon train to New York) in the grandiose setting of Notre-Dame Cathedral. It was a sign of the times that only the immediate family and most intimate friends had been invited. It would not have been seemly to make too spectacular a display of this wedding, when so many young women were mourning a fiancé or a husband, and so many families a son, brother, or father. Moving slowly up the aisle on her father's arm, Jeanne was stepping onto a straight and narrow path that led she knew not where, except to the young stranger in a morning coat whose pale eyes stared nervously in her direction. His accident had changed him. His wound still bothered him, and the pain, even though he did not complain, made him silent and remote—at least that was Florence's interpretation of his sometimes touchy behavior during the rehearsals. As Jeanne approached the altar his face was inscrutable, his eyes as intensely watchful as the first time she'd seen him. They turned to face His Lordship Archbishop Bruchési, whom Charles Langlois had asked to celebrate the wedding mass.

In his sermon the prelate spoke at length about divine love, self-abnegation, and self-sacrifice. His voice echoing beneath the blue-and-gold vault of the cathedral, he enjoined the bride to follow the example of the Virgin Mary, "who offered her body to God that the Savior, Who redeems all the sins of mankind, might be born." He exhorted her husband to do his Christian duty, comparing him to the tiller "who sows the seeds from which will spring the harvest of the future, the next generation of sons and daughters of our Holy Mother the Church." He spoke of life's travails "that are so much more easily borne together. Remember, lastly, every day of your lives, the words of Our Lord Jesus Christ and that essential rule of conduct which He bequeathed us and which we must hold to now more than ever in these dark times: Love one another, as I have loved you. In suffering and in joy. In suffering especially, for in joy it is easy ..." Love. Pain. The two notes of the chant learned among the Carmelites. To suffer. To love. Her soul rebeled against such finality.

2

After the ceremony the wedding party repaired under the pouring rain to the Ritz, where a modest reception had been planned, to give the newlyweds time to change into their travel clothes and the guests a chance to drink to their health before going to see them off at Windsor Station. Jeanne went up in the elevator as soon as she arrived. The anteroom of the bridal suite was filled with flowers, a small extravagance by which her father had wished to atone for the informality and restraint of the ceremony and reception. In the bedroom a mountain of elaborately wrapped gifts was on display. A complete change of clothes, chosen by Florence, was laid out on the bed. Jeanne had spent the last hectic fortnight at Florence's home in Outremont, on the flank of Mount Royal, where she lived alone with her chambermaid and her cook. Florence had involved herself far more in the whole business of the wedding than her own mother. The trousseau, even the wedding dress had been chosen by and with Florence, and everything handmade by her own dressmaker from the latest Paris designs. Amid all the fittings, rehearsals, teas, and heart-to-hearts, Jeanne had recaptured some of the carefree camaraderie of their last summer holidays together. She had left her regretfully, as she had just left her father at the foot of the altar. She was no longer Langlois, she grieved as she began to undress. Her name no longer belonged to her, and neither did the new one she now wore.

Suddenly, someone was knocking, making her almost jump out of her skin. Pulling her heavy white satin wedding gown back up around herself, she sidled up to the door.

"Darling!" It was Florence's voice. "Do you need any help?"

Jeanne let her in.

"But you're crying! Let's see those tears, you poor thing!"

Florence tossed her pretty beaded purse on the bed and wrapped her arms around her niece.

"There, let it out," she crooned, stroking Jeanne's head softly. "Getting cold feet, are we? You're not the first. Go ahead and cry. It's like rain after the thunder, it will do you good."

Gradually her sobbing subsided. She raised her head and smiled uncertainly through her tears.

"Come, let me help you into your clothes. Here, look in the mirror. You see, even in tears you're still the most beautiful bride I've ever seen. Now cheer up. In a few hours you'll be in New York. You're starting a new life, Mme O'Neill. And you have a brand new husband who only wants to make you happy, I'm sure."

Wet snow was falling on Sherbrooke Street when the wedding party emerged from the Ritz to board the waiting carriages for Windsor Station. As their landau pulled away, clattering over the cobblestones, Jeanne caught sight of her father just as a strong gust knocked off his top hat and tousled his white hair. She felt a pang of tenderness for the big, vulnerable man, who stood half a head taller than the knot of people huddled behind him, grimacing in their spring overcoats at the rawness of the weather. On the platform he wept when he kissed Jeanne goodbye. Her mother, who had attended the marriage ceremony but not the reception, was at his side. "I will pray for you," she said with a knowing look. Jeanne's eyes sought out Florence's in the little crowd. The two women exchanged fervent farewells. At that moment the photographer snapped the picture of the newlyweds departing. It would show a young woman, elegant in a small-waisted suit, her chignon tucked under a broad-brimmed hat, her expression delicately blurred by the little veil, next to the enigmatic young man in top hat and morning coat to whom she had bound her fate.

3

Jeanne thought of her mother now as snow flailed the dark landscape rushing past the window. Mick had disappeared almost as soon as the train pulled out of the station. He seemed restless, had removed his top hat, unbuttoned his morning coat and his detachable collar. Jeanne had smiled, noticing for the first time that he had not taken the time to change before boarding the train. He had lit a cigarette and, inhaling mightily, had excused himself, pleading a monstrous thirst.

Jeanne felt more relief than pique at his apparent lack of appetite for her company. She was secretly grateful for the few minutes alone in the privacy of their stateroom, time enough to regain her composure and collect her thoughts after the excitement of the morning. Outside the snow was falling obliquely, in soft fat flakes driven by the wind. Jeanne gave herself up to the rocking motion of the train. New York would be but a pause between the past and the future, a future in which Florence would figure prominently. She closed her eyes, and gradually sank into a deep torpor.

Some time later she was roused by the door of the

compartment crashing open. Mick stood for a moment with his arms resting on the doorjambs, his weight shifting from side to side with each movement of the carriage. He looked disheveled and his eyes glittered oddly. The train lurched into a bend. He stumbled inside, kicking the door shut behind him, and tottered precariously forward. The train straightened and he lost his footing. Suddenly he tumbled at Jeanne's feet. She bent over him, sprawling there, and held out her hand to help him. Mick's blond head lolled from side to side. He looked up at her, slack-jawed, eyes shiny with mirth. "Let down your hair ..." he slurred, like a man waking from deep sleep, "... so beautiful when you let it down ..." Jeanne, obliging, leaned over him. Her hair fell in curtains around her face. As the train rounded another sharp bend, he suddenly grabbed her outstretched hand, pulling her down, knocking the wind right out of her, not seeming himself to feel the blow. His arms locked around her, squeezing tightly. She gasped for air but he breathed harder and his hands were moving, traveling down the slope of her back, and lower still, groping, grasping, then pushing up, slipping up under ...

"Mick! Stop! Let me go!"

She struggled, trying to pry herself free, but he only pressed her more tightly. "Jeanne," he breathed, an urgent, plaintive whisper, "Jeanne!" She fought him but he was stronger, much stronger than he looked. He was beyond listening, beyond hearing, keenly absorbed in the writhing and wrestling of their two bodies, and through it all, breathing her name over and over. Now he was on her, crushing her, grinding her. The floorboards were rattling, shaking, deafening her. Now his mouth was all over hers. She reared up, trying to push away from the smell, the sour whisky taste.

"Jeanne," he groaned into her ear, "so beautiful, Jeanne," over the chaotic jolting of the train. His hands shoved up under her skirt, tearing at her flimsy silk bloomers. He squirmed and twisted against her, then all at once plunged, forced, wounded her with his hard flesh. He was moaning, grunting, gasping, surging, working himself to frantic agony and then, at the height of it, collapsed, groaning. In the shameful rawness a spreading wetness, as she tried with all her might to shift him, to roll the dead weight of him onto the floor. She sat up gingerly, her whole body shaking, aching. Hot tears welled up, constricting her throat so she could barely draw breath. She pulled herself back up to the seat, and stared at the figure sprawled at her feet, at the ugly finger of shriveled flesh lolling out of the unbuttoned trousers. She huddled against the window of the quaking train. *You may yet regret not having given yourself to Our Lord.* A white-hot coal of loathing ignited in her stomach, heaving to her throat as she rushed to the tiny water-closet and retched and sobbed and retched again. The train plunged on.

4

The canyons of New York that spring were teeming with men in uniform. The vast city hummed with exuberant optimism and the pride of a nation still unsullied by the carnage in Europe. In the lobby of the Waldorf-Astoria, where he was waiting for his wife, Mick O'Neill was pacing expectantly. She was late, but his impatience to see her was tainted with apprehension and shame. Ever since waking up on the floor of the train, his head pounding, his mouth dry and sour, his clothes in disarray, he had been searching for a way to erase the blot he had made on the cover page of their marital copybook.

What unbearable thirst had possessed him? Where had it come from? Exhaustion? Insomnia? Or the need to dampen the urge she aroused? Ever since that first glimpse of her, on the porch in Carleton that summer afternoon, he had been desperate to have her. Now, he had behaved like an animal, a wild, filthy brute ...

Glancing at his watch, he flinched with self-loathing. That morning, he had risen at six, taken his usual cold shower, a habit acquired in boarding school, and dressed in the bathroom as she slept. Lighting his first cigarette of the day, he scribbled a short note, asking to meet for lunch, then went down to breakfast, leaving a curl of smoke in the room behind him. Having spent the morning with an Irish-American journalist with Sinn Fein contacts in Ireland, he had stopped at Van Cleef and Arpel's on the way back to the hotel and spent a small fortune on an exquisite gem of a watch for his new wife—the tiny gold watchface encased in petal-shaped diamonds, in the shape of a daisy—with the hope that she might forgive him.

5.

Even though she was late for lunch, Jeanne crossed the hotel lobby at an unhurried pace. As she walked toward Mick, his eyes registered not a flicker of recognition until she was directly in front of him.

"Jeanne?" he said finally. "What have you done to yourself?"

The expression that spread over his face when he recognized her was beyond the merely comical.

"You don't like it?"

"Why did you do that? What possessed you?"

"Do I need your permission?"

He looked stricken, uncomprehending.

"You had such beautiful long hair. You know how I ..."

"I thought we were going to have lunch," she said coolly. "I don't know about you, but I'm famished ..."

His eyes hardened perceptibly, and he seized her arm. "You did it for revenge, is that it?"

"Let me go," she whispered, trying to free herself, "people are watching!"

"Very well!" he glared, releasing her. "You'll have to excuse me if I don't join you. I have other, more pressing matters to attend to."

He strode quickly away, his hand in his coat pocket, still clutching the small velvet case containing his purchased apology. Jeanne was left alone to ponder her meager victory. There was no sweetness in it, only the sickly taste of fear. She was beginning to see how hopeless it all was. All she had done was change her jailer. But this time she had bolted the shackles on herself. For all time, forever. A life sentence, from which death alone could release her. She blamed her father, her mother— even Florence. Why had she not warned her? She railed against fate for dealing her such a bad hand. Suddenly very tired, she went up to the room and fell into bed. She slept without dreaming until dinner.

6

Three

Fates

"Jeanne, darling, do tell me what happened? Surely it can't just be that childish business about your hair?"

Jeanne shuddered, hugging herself. They were sitting under the awning on the terrace behind Florence's house in Outremont. The last two weeks had been exceptionally hot. The peonies along the flower beds were already bowing under the weight of their white and purple blooms. A warm breeze stirred the long, hanging strands of a weeping willow at the bottom of the garden. Florence sat in a blush-colored silk kimono, opposite her niece. The glass-topped wrought-iron table was strewn with the remains of their lunch.

"It suits you, I must say. Mind you, it does rather make you look like a boy. A very pretty boy! But I can understand him being a little taken aback. Why didn't you tell him?"

Jeanne looked up at the green canopy billowing in the breeze.

"He wants us to leave for Carleton at the end of the month. We'll spend two weeks with my parents. Apparently he and Daddy have some business to discuss. It's going to be perfectly dreadful. After that he has to come back here but I wouldn't mind staying on, at least for a little while ..."

The two men did indeed have a great deal to talk about. Since the debacle of the December election, which Bourassa, the arch-foe of conscription, had described as a great victory for the French Canadians, Quebec, its isolation from the rest of the country now complete, had been left without representation in the government. In April there had even been calls in Parliament for the imposition of martial law in Quebec, for the internment of Bourassa (he was, after all, the grandson of Louis-Joseph Papineau, the leader of the bloody 1837 Rebellion), and the suppression of his newspaper, *Le Devoir*. In Quebec, however, where Papineau was a hero, and the pious Bourassa close to a saint, the sound and fury in the House of Commons only threw more oil on an already well-stoked fire.

"Then you'll have to come and spend August with me."

Jeanne grinned gratefully at her aunt.

"In the meantime, you'll have plenty to occupy you."

2

Indeed, Mick had bought a house on University Street, into which the young couple had just moved. It was a handsome limestone townhouse, covered in ivy, with a flat roof. The rooms were airy and well-lit, with tall windows and high ceilings. The living room had a large fireplace and looked out onto the campus of McGill University, on the other side of the street. It housed

Mick's innumerable books, some inherited from his father who, though a surgeon and professor of medicine, had also been known as a keen man of letters. There were volumes on anatomy piled alongside the complete works of Shakespeare and Victor Hugo, tomes of Gaelic poetry, and legal treatises in three languages, all waiting to be stored on the bookshelves Mick had had built into the walls. In a corner of the room the Victrola, a wedding gift from Florence, raised its petunia-shaped promise of fun. Much remained to be done to make the house fit to receive anyone, but Jeanne had little heart for the task. She was tired and listless and often fell asleep in the middle of the afternoon. She sank into something resembling nostalgia, although she had no past that she wished to return to, and wept bitterly over her fate.

Meanwhile, Mick filled his days with unremitting work, and spent several evenings a week at the Reform Club, a favorite meeting ground for prominent Liberals. On those nights he came home late after a lengthy dinner, well doused with wine and a virile abundance of liqueurs. Depending on the degree of his inebriation, he would clamber upstairs and fall into bed fully clothed, or stand swaying in the middle of the room, smoking one last cigarette and mumbling to himself, a preamble that Jeanne dreaded. For after flicking his cigarette stub into the bedroom fireplace and stepping unsteadily out of his trousers, he staggered over to her bed in his shirt-tails, and clambered in. She learned to expedite her loathsome marital duty by submitting without protest, for when alcohol had him, any resistance served only to excite him.

These infringements on her young female dignity were to Jeanne a source of daily anxiety. No one had ever spoken of these things to her, and she could not bring herself to speak of them either. There was only one place to discharge this burden, one place of refuge silent enough to hear the unspeakable. She chose a church far from her home. But the priest, anonymous and unseen, offered no comfort.

"Your husband is only doing his Christian duty, my child," came the whispered verdict through the metal grille. "You must do yours, in accordance with the holy sacrament of marriage. You give too much heed to the voice of pride, which is by no means a venial sin. Still, God loves you as He loves all His children. You must ask His forgiveness. For your penance you will say ..."

At that point Jeanne committed the unpardonable sin—she bolted out of the confessional without waiting for her sentence. She fled, with a heart full of rage and insuperable fear of divine retribution.

As the days wore on she grew thinner, the color drained from her cheeks. Soon she stopped eating altogether. Florence expressed alarm at her deteriorating health. One day when they were having lunch, Jeanne fainted as she was getting up from the table after failing to eat a single bite. Florence sent for the doctor, who after a brief examination said, "It seems congratulations are in order, Mrs. O'Neill. Your symptoms are quite normal for your condition. Mme Talbot tells me that you are leaving for the seaside in a few days. The fresh air will do you a world of good. There's nothing for it now but the waiting. I'd say you're expecting early in the New Year."

Jeanne was appalled by the diagnosis. Had she no control over her life? Things just kept happening to her, out of ignorance, ineptitude, incompetence. But Florence was moved to tears by the news.

"I wish I could have been so blessed," she said, hugging her niece. "Just think of it! To bear a life, separate from you, and yet of your own self ... To be able to love that way, without restraint, forever ..."

To love without restraint, forever. Holy orders and marriage. The injunction was the same. The course she was on was an inexorable one.

3

"I am expecting a child."

Jeanne's words shattered the silence of the dining room. Mick looked up sharply from his plate, some kind of emotion blurring his features. For once his feelings escaped him uncensored by his pride, an event so rare that Jeanne failed to understand what she was seeing. She had no notion of his feelings for her, and had come to believe that he had married her only to advance his ambitions.

"Have you seen a doctor?" he finally managed.

"This afternoon. I fainted."

"You weren't hurt, I hope?"

"No. Florence called the doctor."

"Ah, dear Florence," he said with a hint of sarcasm. "How is she?"

"She invited me to come and spend a few weeks with her after you leave to come back here."

"I have nothing against that. You'll certainly be better off there than in town this summer."

For the duration of her pregnancy, Mick, drunk or sober, abstained from his nocturnal visitations. He took to inquiring after his wife's health and even bought her flowers on occasion. The general tone of their relations gradually improved. When they parted at the end of July, Jeanne insisted on seeing him to the station.

The two-week stay at her parents' had been trying. Her mother, observing some dissension between them beneath all the civility, had taken to waiting on Mick's every need. She barely spoke to Jeanne, however. She displayed no compassion for her daughter's weariness and bouts of nausea. "It's too late to complain," she seemed to say, "you chose to sin, now pay." Jeanne, who in girlhood had been both fascinated and piously repelled by the mortal "sin of the flesh," now could not comprehend why such a grotesque act, routinely performed in broad daylight by dogs, carried such a fearful burden of mystery, terror, and guilt.

4

Gaspé, August 1918 Summer was slowly slipping away. At sunset Florence took to making a fire to ward off the evening chill.

"You're very silent tonight," she observed, eyeing her niece. She dropped another log onto the hearth. "Did your mother's visit upset you?"

Madeleine Langlois had come to lunch. Her visit had been brief.

"To her I don't exist any more, since I left Saint-Boniface."

"I'm going to tell you something," Florence hesitated, as though about to contravene a long-standing resolution, "about your mother. Did she ever tell you how they met?"

Jeanne thought a moment, then shrugged bemusedly.

"When your father met your mother," Florence began, striving for tact and nuance, "he was thirty-two. He was from a good family, well educated, and quite well traveled. He was very good-looking, and of course rich, our father having made his fortune in real estate. As for Madeleine, she was sixteen. Her father, a butcher, worked in an abattoir. She was uneducated, penniless, and already working in a factory to help feed her large family. But she was pretty, intelligent, and extremely determined. Your father, like a lot of other bachelors his age, liked to have a drink with his pals. They would go into the East End in their cars and try to pick up some girls as they came out of the factories. They took them dancing, in return, I imagine, for certain kinds of favors. That was how Charlie met your mother, only he fell head over heels for her. Madeleine was anything but a harebrained *midinette.** She made sure Charlie would end up marrying her."

"You mean ..."

Florence stopped, looked somewhat anxiously at her niece, made up her mind and pressed on.

"He was just crazy about her," she exclaimed. "I was only thirteen at the time but I remember what a fuss their marriage caused in the family. My mother never really got over it. That is the reason you've always been told both your maternal grandparents were dead. When you were growing up, your mother kept them away. She was ashamed of the fact that her father had had to sign his name with an X on your parents' marriage certificate. She had great ambitions for your father in those days. It's ironic, but if she hadn't pushed him so hard in the back all the time, he might never have considered a career in politics in the first place."

"Come to think of it, I never really knew my other grandparents either ..." Jeanne said, her heart sinking under the weight of these revelations.

"There is also a reason why you never knew them. My parents were convinced that your mother had tricked

* *Midinette*: 1920s–50s term designating a young shopgirl, dressmaker's apprentice, factory girl, etc. The real meaning is "easy pick-up."

Charlie into marriage. They were completely mistaken of course. Charlie on his wedding day was happier than I've ever seen him. But Madeleine felt humiliated by our family's haughty attitude. Very quickly, she refused to have anything to do with any of us. At first my parents dismissed this as vulgar posturing, but once Charlie was elected and moved to Ottawa, and he and Madeleine began socializing with the Lauriers and their circle in the national capital, I think they regretted not making her feel more welcome."

"And the quarrel lasted until their death?"

"Oh, yes. Your mother is a vindictive woman. Deep down, however, she must have remembered all the sermons she'd heard as a child about eternal damnation for carnal sin. As she saw it, you, poor little Jeanne, were that sin personified and incarnate, the flagrant evidence of her guilt. For years I've watched her launder her conscience at your expense. And when Father Plantin came into her life, she abdicated her role as a wife and mother with such complete ostentation that she managed to shock everyone all over again."

Jeanne shuddered at the thought of her mother's confessor, a sinister hooded Capuchin monk whose dictates regulated every detail of her mother's life.

"What was she like before she met him?"

"Well, she was pretty, and saucy, and coquettish, and French, and an overnight sensation in the stuffy, conformist little world of Ottawa. From the day she set foot in the national capital in 1900, when your father was first elected to the House of Commons, she dazzled everyone, the men with her beauty, the women with her dresses imported at great expense from Paris. She had a pleasant singing voice, and soon became a fixture at Lady Laurier's musical gatherings on Sunday afternoons.

Ottawa matrons viewed her with envy, and there were Anglo-Saxon mutterings about her being half-Indian, and about Charles having married beneath his station."

"I can't imagine her as a socialite, let alone a fashion plate!"

"That she certainly was, until the arrival at her church of a new confessor, under whose influence she changed quite radically. There is no doubt that he convinced her that the only way to redeem her sin before God was a life of abstinence and privation. Practically overnight, she became obsessed with religion. Sadly, her transformation irreparably damaged your father's career. When you turned sixteen, the age at which she'd met Charlie, she panicked. Your entry into holy orders was her way of ensuring her own redemption. She visualized herself as the mother of a saint, I'm sure. I have to say that when I heard what she was planning, I was furious with Charlie for allowing it and I told him as much. You were so young! When the archbishop wrote to him about your illness and asked him to come for you, he called me. He couldn't leave Ottawa because of the debate on conscription, and your mother refused to accept that you had to be rescued. So I went. And my God, the state you were in!"

Jeanne listened in stunned silence. She couldn't help admiring her mother for refusing to submit to an obscure fate. She had seized life by the throat and imposed her will, on the man she had chosen, and on her world.

Florence stood up from the couch and went over to the Victrola. She selected a disc and dropped it carefully onto the velvet-covered turntable. The opening measures of a tango filled the room. Florence held out her hand, and Jeanne rose to the challenge. She loved these sessions, even if she had had a clumsy start. She liked the sensation of Florence guiding her, the grace and assurance with which she moved.

"Antoine was a wonderful dancer," her aunt sighed, winding her arm around Jeanne's waist. "God, how I loved that man. I couldn't eat, I couldn't sleep. I loved him so much. I would have done anything to please him, anything he asked. We were engaged for two years and it nearly drove me crazy. I lived only to see him, to be with him."

"You're still very sad ..."

"Oh, well ..." Florence said wistfully. "If he had come back, I would probably have requested an annulment."

"An annulment?"

"Things started to go wrong on the night of our wedding. You should have seen me." Florence smiled bitterly. "All aquiver with love and anticipation ... He sat down on the bed, fully dressed. He looked exhausted, white as a sheet, and so unhappy. He made me sit on his knee. He apologized. He said I had to give him time. After a few days, he decided it was better to sleep in separate rooms. He never even told me why. I tried to put on a brave face, but I was devastated. When he enlisted, I couldn't help thinking it was the only honorable way out for him ..."

The music had ended and the needle, having reached the end of the groove, was scratching and bumping against the label.

"You could marry again, Florence, you are young enough."

"At the rate they're slaughtering the men," Florence said doubtfully, "who knows how many will return. Those who do will certainly have a wealth of nubile young girls to choose from. For every able-bodied man, there will be ten eager souls, much younger and more appetizing than a thirty-one-year-old widow like me. You should consider yourself lucky, darling, to have a husband who is not in danger of dying somewhere far away, and who is willing and able to give you children. You may not love him now, but you'll come to value him more when you see the generation of spinsters this war is going to leave in its wake."

That night in her bed Jeanne lay listening to the steady roar of waves breaking on the sand. When she held her breath and sucked in her stomach, she could feel a small, hard bulge low down in her belly, which hadn't been there the week before.

5

Florence and Jeanne were sitting on a rock, looking out at the crashing surf. The wind was sweeping out to sea, bowing the tall grasses all around them toward the choppy water. The morning air had a cutting edge to it, a reminder of how early winter came to that part of the country. They got up, pulling their shawls tighter against the force of the wind, and retreated homeward in search of warmth.

"Quick! The woodstove, tea and toast!" cried Florence, mincing her steps with cold.

They left the wind howling on the doorstep. In the sudden silence of the house, they heard a muffled sound of distress from somewhere in the back, in the direction of the kitchen. They followed it cautiously, and found Rose, crumpled on a chair, crying into her apron.

"My goodness, Rose," said Florence solicitously, "what's happened?"

Rose was Florence's cook and housekeeper. A sturdy, ruddy, gray-haired woman, the mother of ten grown children, she had for many summers supplemented her family's income by working for Florence's husband's family.

"It's Gabrielle, Madame ..." she wailed, in another paroxysm of grief.

"My God, what's happened? She's not ..."

"Dead? No, Madame. But she might ... as well! Better ... to die ... of shame...!"

Gabrielle was Rose's youngest daughter. The previous fall she had gone to work as a servant for a wealthy doctor in Quebec City. Since then Rose and her family were subjected every Sunday to the admonitions of the parish priest. Every sermon began and ended the same way: praise for the salubriousness of life on the land and the moral fortitude to be derived from family life, hard work, and the Catholic faith, followed by dire warnings of the danger that lurked behind the allure of the city, where hopes were dashed on the cobblestones of poverty, and the soul consumed in the fires of the flesh.

"Where is she?"

"Here, in Carleton," answered the sobbing woman in her lilting Gaspé accent. "She had to leave her job. She was let go. She's pregnant!" She hid her face in her apron again.

"Who is the father?"

"The eldest son of Dr. Gratton, Madame. He's the father!"

"Heavens, how old is he?"

"Eighteen, Madame. He's studying at the university. When his father found out, he threw Gabrielle out on the street. He didn't care how she would get home. And him a doctor, Madame! If my Gabrielle wasn't so careful and hadn't put a few pennies aside to come back, God knows what would have happened to her. I wouldn't have believed that such heartless people could exist!"

"And where is she at this moment?"

"At home, for now. Her father would kill her if he knew. I told him her employers went on a trip and sent her home for a holiday. She's lucky she's a big girl and it doesn't show yet. But in a little it'll be as plain as the nose on her face. Her heart is broken, Madame. Her life is finished, and she's not sixteen yet!"

"My poor Gabrielle," said Florence when the girl appeared the following afternoon. She had matured since the previous summer. Her healthy young body was fuller, softer. Her dark complexion and thick black hair had acquired a new luster that only enhanced the china blue of her eyes. It was easy to see how such a rustic beauty would arouse the appetite of a red-blooded young male. She showed none of her mother's desperation, only an eerie calm. Her downcast eyes seemed empty even of shame—the shame that was written so plainly on Rose's face. Jeanne, seeing Rose holding her daughter's hand, felt a pang of envy.

"I asked your mother to bring you here," said Florence, motioning the women to the sitting room, "because I have a proposal to make to you."

Gabrielle looked up at her with eyes devoid of any feeling. Florence offered to take Gabrielle back to Montreal with her.

"We can say my chambermaid has been taken ill and had to leave, and that I have asked Gabrielle to come and work for me. When the baby is born, I'll arrange to find a home for the child. No one here need ever know. In time you will be able to put this behind you, and Gabrielle will still be quite young enough to start a new life. When is the baby due?"

"Around Christmas, Madame," answered Rose, clutching her daughter's hand more tightly.

Florence rose to her feet, smiled reassuringly, and

motioned to Jeanne to follow her out of the room. She fetched a shawl and her old straw hat.

"Poor thing, she's terribly young to bear a child out of wedlock," she sighed once they were outside. "What a dreadful ordeal. Can you imagine, having to give up a child you've just borne! Meanwhile, the heartless boy who did this to her will pursue his studies unmolested by anyone. Then he'll go on to a career, marriage, and a nice, tidy, respectable life. That said, there is something you could do to help."

"Ask me anything you want!"

"She is expecting her child a little sooner than you, which means she will probably be just about recovered by the time of your confinement. You could take her in as nursemaid to the baby for the first few months. Gabrielle is a good girl. We can't let her life come to an end when it's hardly begun ..."

7

Into the Shadows

"Don't you read the papers?" Mick cried. He seemed agitated, almost angry, as he greeted the three women on their arrival at Windsor Station. As they stepped off the train, he rushed up to grab their suitcases, and herded them toward the exit, away from the waiting porters.

"I don't mean to startle you, ladies," he puffed, leading his charges out to his car, a newly acquired McLaughlin-Buick canvas-top convertible, which his wife hadn't yet seen. "But here we are in the middle of an epidemic."

Indeed, although an Allied victory in Europe seemed imminent, a new specter now loomed on the horizon. Influenza had broken out in the trenches, then come ashore in New York in May. By August it had reached Quebec and it was now spreading across the province at a terrifying rate. As the disease was extraordinarily virulent and often deadly, the population was being urged to avoid public places, and as far as possible to stay home.

Mick opened the car door for his wife and saw Florence and Gabrielle to a cab. He had changed over the summer. He sported an elegant tweed suit and a reddish mustache. Even the way he walked seemed more purposeful and assured. Clearly, business was good, and joining the firm had made him more self-confident. The last few months had changed Jeanne too, Mick observed as he got behind the wheel of the new car, which he had meant as a surprise for his young wife. There was a new radiance to her complexion, a new s_ness to her still adolescent form. As always, she aroused him, but her pregnancy banned him from her bed. As they drove wordlessly through the dusky streets, Jeanne, as usual without a compass when it came to reading her husband's moods, took offense at his silence. The old malaise settled between them before they had even reached home. She resented him, and held him responsible for her misfortune. Her body was swelling like a ripening fruit. It no longer belonged to her. All her energies were commandeered, mobilized around the growing, moving core that seemed to take up more space inside her with each passing week, hampering her sleep and her digestion. Under these discomforts there lurked a fear, fed by allusions gleaned at random—her husband's mother had *died in childbirth*; he was the seventeenth of eighteen children, twelve of whom had been *stillborn*; Gabrielle's eldest sister had *died of the fever*, leaving three orphans. *Children thou shalt bring in sorrow forth ...* The punishment inflicted on Eve. *You will regret not having given yourself to Our Lord ...* She stole a glance at the man now driving her destiny. Even in profile his was no ordinary face, with its high forehead, aquiline nose, and pale, piercing eyes, but she felt nothing for him now but rancor.

Montreal was a ghost town. The Health Board had shut down schools, theaters, movie houses, and concert halls. Even the churches had closed their doors. No soldiers were to be seen on the streets. All leaves had been canceled, all military personnel confined to barracks. The city's eight hospitals were understaffed, as patients flooded in and doctors and nurses were themselves decimated by the epidemic. In outlying areas, the shortage of doctors was so severe that fifth-year medical students were being sent out to the countryside. Over a thousand new cases, and more than one hundred and fifty deaths, were recorded daily. The streets were empty as only emergency vehicles—ambulances and doctors' cars had overall priority—cars requisitioned to transport the sick, and hearses to carry the dead were free to move about the city.

The car Florence was driving was clearly identified by a white streamer marked Volunteer Aid in bold lettering. Florence, like many women of her class, had answered the call for volunteers, to care for the sick in the poorer neighborhoods. This morning she was hastening to the aid of a war veteran's family, whose anxious neighbors had reported them ill. Driving east along Sherbrooke Street, she passed a tram going in the other direction. It was one of those converted by municipal order to transport the dead to the cemetery. Her blood ran cold as it trundled eerily by. She turned into the Rue Panet. The population seemed to be following the Health Board's instructions to the letter, for not even a child could be seen on the deserted street.

She got out of her car, picked up the blankets and supplies from the back, and climbed a rickety set of stairs to a second-floor flat. No one answered her

knock. Quietly pushing open the door, she let herself into a dark hallway. The floors were bare. The air inside was almost as cold as the street. Soon she heard what seemed like a faint stirring somewhere at the back. It was a feeble sound that got more disturbing as she drew closer—the sound of a child gasping for breath. In a room at the end of the hallway, next to a kitchen where the stove had been out for hours if not days, she found an entire huddled family. In the bed amid the dirty blankets, a lifeless woman lay cradling a tiny gray corpse. Two small boys were curled up against her, too sick to move and barely breathing. Beside them a little girl, pale as death, slept fitfully in the arms of her father, who merely stared at Florence with sunken eyes. One of the little boys began to cough, his limbs twitching and jerking pathetically. Florence hurried to his side. He was struggling for breath, his small rib cage contracting over and over, too weak even to raise his eyelids. Gently Florence felt his forehead. It was damp, and as cold as the air around them. She unfolded the blankets she had brought and spread them over the children, then rushed off to light the stove and put some water on to boil. When she returned a few minutes later, no one stirred. Father and daughter were asleep. Next to them, the sad little cough had permanently ceased.

3

On the last day of October 1918, a Thursday, Jeanne, driven to distraction by loneliness and boredom, picked up the telephone and ordered a hackney cab. Since her return from the seaside a month before she had been languishing at home, at Mick's insistence. In the meantime, a cold gray autumn had settled on the city. The rains had come and stripped the trees, baring them black against the bleak sky.

The carriage drove up Park Avenue, along the eastern flank of Mount Royal, and turned into the affluent streets of Outremont. It pulled up outside Florence's house just as she was returning from her morning ride. Florence's horse boarded at the Shakespeare Road Stables, on the side of the mountain that sloped down toward Côte des Neiges. She was still in her riding clothes.

"Jeanne!" she cried from the top of the steps. "You should have called before coming here!"

"But you weren't at home ..."

"It doesn't matter," she scolded, affection fueling her alarm. She signaled Jeanne not to come any closer. "Esther would have warned you not to come. There is sickness in the house. Esther's husband has fallen ill, and now Gabrielle. The doctor is very concerned about her. Oh, it's my fault," she hastily added, seeing Jeanne's dismay. "I should have called you, but I didn't want to alarm you. You must go home at once and not come out again. You're already exposed enough with Mick going out to work every day! I promise I'll come and see you as soon as the doctor assures me that it is safe to do so. I would never forgive myself if you fell ill!"

4

Florence telephoned two days later. Her voice seemed hoarse and halting. Gabrielle had just lost her baby, she said. Yes, Gabrielle was out of danger. No, she herself was not ill. Just tired after staying up for two nights caring for the poor girl. Jeanne would always remember that thin, reedy voice. A week later, on Armistice Day, while the rest of the world rejoiced, the Angel died of pneumonia.

A part of her niece died with her. At Florence's insistence, Jeanne had not been informed of the danger she was in.

Her daily telephone calls had been received with no more than guarded formality—"She's better today, Madame, but not well enough to come to the phone"—from Esther, the chambermaid, who had been sworn by her mistress not to reveal the gravity of her condition. However that day it was not Esther who had answered the phone, but her husband, a gruff, taciturn sort, himself barely recovered from his bout with the virus, who bluntly informed her that "Madame died during the night," omitting even to ask who was calling.

The news fell on Jeanne like a truncheon. The brutality of it stunned her. Despair overwhelmed her. But her grief turned to anger when, on the orders of her doctor, she was forbidden even to attend the funeral.

Florence at least was given a proper burial, with her family and friends in attendance. So many that autumn had lost loved ones to the epidemic, only to have their dead piled aboard a tram car, hauled directly to the cemetery, and buried in a bare box (there was a shortage of coffins, for which no casings were allowed, as these required bigger holes to be dug and that took too long) without even a brief ceremonial oration from their parish priest. To them Florence's modest funeral would have seemed a most solemn affair. "The Honorable Charles Langlois, Member of Parliament for Bonaventure, member of the King's Privy Council, and brother of the deceased, was in attendance along with other members of the Langlois family, including his son-in-law M. M. D. O'Neill. Mayor Médéric Martin was also present, as were ..." read the obituary in *La Presse*.

The day after the funeral, Jeanne brought her own wreath to the grave of her beloved aunt. There was no tombstone as yet. No grass covered the mound of frozen earth. It was strewn with wilted flowers. As Mick waited on the path for her to finish her devotions, snow began to fall. Horror welled up inside her as she stared at the barren ground. Beneath it, unspeakable things were beginning to happen. They were happening to Florence. Sweet, lovely, youthful Florence. She would have welcomed a sudden faintness or nausea to relieve her of the horror, but life, cunning and triumphant, had never throbbed more vigorously in her veins. Was surviving the worst of misfortunes? She felt more orphaned now than if she had lost both Father and Mother. She raged against the pain. She railed at a God who had punished Gabrielle (or so the girl believed) for her sin with the loss of her child. She rebelled against a faith that forced itself on the minds of its adherents with horrifying threats of divine retribution. What justice could there be in the death of your baby, Gabrielle, she thought, or in the thousands of other immolations throughout the country? What crime were they atoning for, those millions of young men murdered before they could live, those widows and mothers bludgeoned with grief, those young spinsters condemned their whole lives to mourn some man they might have loved and had never met? What if the heavenly Judge was not a judge but a Butcher, of babies whose mothers succumbed to the sweet lure of love, of widows whose nieces refused his calling, of those rare soldiers who had somehow escaped slaughter, and of their wives, and the children they had barely known? For no apparent reason the Butcher had spared Jeanne and the baby she was carrying. Justice was blind. The Judge was demented. Florence's friendship had lasted in her life about as long as a rainshower in the desert.

5

For Mick O'Neill too, the year 1918 ended on a tragic note. Three weeks after the armistice was signed, Gonzague's mother received a letter from the Government of Canada. *Missing in action*, the worst sentence of all for a mother, who until her dying day will never cease to hope, to believe, that some day, by some miracle, a mistake, a misunderstanding, a clerical error come to light, her son will come back. Some time later she received his Military Cross, posthumously awarded. Promoted to the rank of captain, with an entire company of fully one hundred men under his command, Gonzague had distinguished himself with acts of bravery during the battle of Arras. He had vanished in the murder and mayhem of the first of November, ten days before the last shot was fired.

6

In her will Florence left her only niece her jewelry, her books, and a hunting lodge in the Laurentian mountains. The two houses she had inherited from her husband were to revert to the latter's family. The remainder of her assets she willed to her brother Charles, to dispose of as he wished. Among these was discovered a striking and unusual portrait of Florence that none of her family had ever seen. It was a large canvas, life-sized. The artist had portrayed her bare-shouldered in a dark velvet evening gown, under a brooding night sky. The silvery tinge of her skin, reflecting a stormy moon, and the large opal eyes conveyed a sadness, a loneliness, that Jeanne had never seen in her aunt. The painter had chosen a dark palette, as a composer might a minor key, to create an atmosphere of drama and mystery. Jeanne was fascinated with the painting and wondered why, in all the times she had visited her aunt's home, Florence had never shown it to her. Perhaps she didn't like the reflection it gave of herself, and yet it depicted her as even more beautiful than she was. Perhaps it was the facet of her personality it revealed that Florence had wanted to relegate to the closet where it was found. Jeanne's father did not care for the portrait and had needed no coaxing to part with it in favor of his daughter. Mick, on the other hand, was immediately taken with it. It was now prominently displayed in the living room in University Street, above the baby grand piano.

8

Epiphany

Montreal, January 6, 1919 The pains began early in the evening of Epiphany. It had been snowing heavily all day. University Street was buried under a thick blanket of loosely packed flakes that glinted in the light from the streetlamp outside the living-room window. Gabrielle, who was slowly recovering from her misfortunes of the fall, and whom her new mistress had delighted at Christmas with a brand new pair of skates, was busy helping Georgette, the new cook, prepare the *galette des rois.* In it she had just concealed, instead of the custom-ary dried pea, the precious louis d'or that had belonged to the first Langlois to arrive in New France in 1653, the discovery of which in one's slice of *galette* designated one King or Queen for the evening. The Honorable Charles Langlois and his wife were expected for dinner, along with a lawyer friend of Monsieur from Quebec City, a young bachelor who had no family in Montreal.

Jeanne by now was very big and found navigating her

way around the house, up and down stairs and around the furniture, increasingly difficult. Her back troubled her and she was subject to excruciating cramps in her legs at night. She slept poorly, her body constantly shifting and rearranging itself around its bulging middle. The baby was very active and seemed to Jeanne almost frighteningly strong. A terrible fear haunted her, for in spite of all her efforts she still could not imagine how it was all going to end, or by what divine intervention the unseen being that spent so much of its time thrashing about inside her was going to appear. In the mirror each morning she stole a glimpse at her navel, now stretched beyond recognition, pondering its purpose with foreboding. But her questions found no answer. There was a timid knock on the bedroom door.

"I have brought Madame her tea," said Gabrielle, entering the room where Jeanne had been resting before the arrival of the guests. "It is almost five o'clock. Does Madame wish me to prepare her dress?"

Gabrielle put the tray carefully down on the bed. Her brief apprenticeship in Quebec City had taught her the use of the third person singular when addressing her employers and turned her into a polished *domestique*, a station in life which her mother, Rose, viewed as a step up in the world. Rose herself, on the other hand, had never aspired to the life of a servant. In Florence's lifetime, she did not *serve*, but rather *worked for* her mistress, being at heart that most ancient of egalitarians, a Christian in the purest sense. For if her religion taught her to accept without question the limitations of her own status along with the authority of her social superiors, it did so by preaching the paradox that all were equal before God, and that none was better than his neighbor in the eyes of Jesus. Thus Rose's total lack of subservience toward Florence, stemming from a Christian awareness of her own worth, had been a true measure of the respect which she bore her.

Jeanne sat up in bed and took a sip of tea. Then, moving with great caution, she lowered her feet to the floor, into the slippers that Gabrielle had placed there for her. Taking the latter's outstretched hand she slowly pulled herself upright and took a few steps toward the wardrobe. Suddenly there was a hot gush between her legs, and looking down, she found herself standing in a puddle of warm water, and shivering violently. Terrified at the thought of prompting another such effusion, "The doctor!" she whimpered to Gabrielle, who looked on aghast, rooted to the spot. Finally, Jeanne's legs gave way beneath her.

When she came to, she was lying on her side across the bed. Her wet nightdress clung to her skin, and she shivered under the mohair throw with which Gabrielle, presumably, had covered her legs. She pulled her knees up a little and lay curled up, shaking with cold and fear. In her huge belly the baby's kicking only focused her dread. After what seemed like a very long time, Gabrielle knocked on the door again, but this time she let herself in without waiting for an answer.

"The doctor is on his way, Madame. He says to rest in bed until he arrives."

"The guests, Gabrielle. Has my husband been told?"

"As soon as he arrives, Madame. Georgette and I will look after everything. Madame must rest," added Gabrielle, producing a basin, some towels, and a clean nightdress.

Soon the pains came, the dreaded pains she'd heard whispers about. They came at intervals and mounted in intensity. At each onset her panic grew, the vice of it tightening inexorably, pain surging through her before subsiding, leaving her cowed and broken at its ebb, even as the next one began building. Finally the doctor bustled in, waited for the lull, and examined her abdomen. Jeanne's eyes widened, as though to decipher some sign in the doctor's face that would help her understand what was happening. The pain was a wall between herself and the world beyond her body.

"The great day has arrived, it seems," the doctor said. "How frequent are the pains? Every ten minutes? Five minutes? My, but we're in a hurry! All the better, it will be over that much sooner. I'll be downstairs when you need me. In the meantime, everyone is drinking your health. A little courage, now. Gabrielle here will call me when it begins, won't you, Gabrielle?"

When it begins? The doctor's words still rang in her ears when the next wave came crashing over her, breaking her will, smashing her consciousness, dragging her ever closer to the terrifying edge. There was no longer any respite between assaults, and the wounded animal cries she could no longer contain. Through the cruel fog she sensed a commotion in the room, a coming and going and murmur of voices. Suddenly the panic and humiliation of a male hand parting her thighs, driving its way up inside. Through it all, the pain gathered, building, swelling, towering dreadfully, terrifyingly. *One last little effort!* Then a rending, overwhelming agony, and sudden release, deliverance.

Then she sank into blessed darkness. Somewhere a male voice was saying, "You have a daughter!" She opened her eyes and then the miracle—slippery wet, naked (somehow the thought had never occurred to her)—in the doctor's hands, shiny black hair stuck to the tiny skull, red little face, and that small lusty voice.

Tears were streaming down Gabrielle's face as she bent over her and placed the baby in her arms. The child had stopped crying. The small wrinkled face was turned up at her mother and her dark eyes blinked in the light from the lamp. Moments later Jeanne, having drifted so close to the chasm between life and death, sank at last into blessed sleep.

2

When Gabrielle left the room, cradling the baby in her arms, Mick was waiting, stock-still, in the shadows at the top of the stairs. The house at last was quiet, his in-laws, the doctor, and his guest having taken their leave. He watched Gabrielle go by and then made for the bedroom door. With his hand on the knob he hesitated, then changed his mind and followed Gabrielle down the hall to the nursery.

"How is she?" he asked stiffly.

"Oh, Monsieur, come and see. She is so beautiful!"

"I mean my wife. How is she?"

"Madame is fine, just fine, Monsieur," answered Gabrielle reassuringly. "She's very tired, naturally, she just needs sleep."

Cautiously he approached the cradle where Gabrielle had just laid the child. "It's a terrible ordeal for a woman," his father-in-law had confided earlier, hearing his daughter's cries, one floor above. "After Jeanne was born I swore to Madeleine that she would never again be subjected to such a harrowing experience. I kept my word." Perhaps this was the key to the submissiveness with which this man, whom his son-in-law admired, allowed himself to be led around by the nose by his madwoman of a wife. Mick had told himself that he would never allow such a calamity to befall him yet inwardly he squirmed with remorse at his wife's solitary suffering. And then he saw the infant, a human being such as he had never before laid eyes on, an apparition so moving that, for a moment, confirmed atheist though he was, he felt himself in the presence of something divine. For here was a creature so perfect, so alive even in the stillness of sleep, so entirely other; a fullfledged life mysteriously sprung from the darkness of his desire and the secret depths of its mother's body, a being of such unimaginable helplessness and frailty that he could not fail to be touched profoundly. Gabrielle thought she saw tears gleaming in his eyes.

3

March 1919 Since the birth of his daughter Mick O'Neill had spent very few of his evenings at home. Again tonight, he was late coming in. To tell the truth, he was spending as little time as possible in his own house, where he sometimes felt as though he had inadvertently wandered into a hospital or, heaven forbid, a convent. The servants spoke in hushed voices. The stillness was broken only by the swish of a starched white uniform, and a quiet bustle of trays, basins, and laundry up and down stairs. Gabrielle was in complete charge of the child, whom he passed in the hallway, either crying or sleeping depending on whether she was being taken in to her mother to be fed or off to her bed after nursing. A feminine stuffiness permeated the house, concealing one knew not what prudish indecencies. At first he had attempted a clumsy *rapprochement* with his wife. He had brought flowers, and lingered at her bedside, trying to sound reassuring.

"It seems everything went well, then?" he had begun, tentatively, with obvious embarrassment. "The doctor said it wasn't too painful?"

"He said that?" Jeanne had replied rather sharply. "That's just like a man, isn't it."

"Have you decided what you want to call her?" he mumbled, a little alarmed at her pallor and extreme weariness.

"Catherine," she answered.

The decision, it seemed, was final, the result of a selection process that did not include him. From then on, he found ways of occupying nearly all of his time elsewhere.

Under the auspices of his employers—who were Irish Catholics like himself, but born in Montreal, where the Irish were English-speaking—his career was flourishing. He was often invited to dine at the home of important clients. He was now a regular at the Reform Club, as it was useful for him to be seen there in the company of some of the most influential Liberals in the province. Louis-Alexandre Taschereau, minister of labor and public works in the provincial cabinet, took an interest in him. Taschereau, the scion of a prominent Quebec City family who had known Mick's father well, was said to be an intimate of the premier, Lomer Gouin, who according to the newspapers was thinking of retiring.

The cause of Ireland occupied a great deal of his time. In December, for the first time in their history, the Irish had voted massively for the secessionist party Sinn Fein. Eamon de Valera, who had been elected president *in absentia* of the new National Assembly in Dublin while still a political prisoner in England, had escaped from prison. Public opinion in the United States, where Americans of Irish descent were now twenty-five-million strong, had pressured the House of Representatives to approve a resolution enjoining the Paris Peace Conference to look favorably upon the right of the Irish people to self-determination. But in Paris President Wilson remained noncommittal, and the incidence of violent clashes with the police in Ireland continued to increase. The Irish diaspora in North America, to the rebels an inexhaustible source of money and, much more covertly, of arms, was mobilizing.

This year, Mick had participated even more enthusiastically than usual in the Saint Patrick's Day fund-raising effort. Sinn Fein flags had been given pride of place in the traditional parade, and during the banquet at the Windsor Hotel that evening, de Valera's Saint Patrick's Day message to the Irish people had been read aloud: the Irish language was dying, he warned, the younger generation barely spoke it any more. Without its language, Ireland would cease to exist. It was incumbent on this generation to save it, or it would be lost forever. The only means to achieve that salvation was for Ireland to free herself from the yoke of England, for over the centuries, the English had tried by every available means to stifle Gaelic, going as far as to outlaw the teaching of it for more than one hundred years of her history.

Returning home that night, feeling sentimental after an evening of many toasts and rousing speeches, Mick was thinking of his father, who had spoken fluent Gaelic. He pictured him marching with the other dignitaries at the head of the Saint Patrick's Day parade in old Quebec City, still snowbound in mid-March. He could still see him, dressed in his Sunday best, crimson-faced under a volley of snowballs aimed directly at his top hat which his prankster sons had launched from the cover of a nearby snowbank. Then he was remembering a scene from a few years later, when he was seventeen, tramping through the mud and shivering with grief behind his father's casket. He had walked at the head of a huge procession swelled by family, friends, colleagues, students, and patients of the deceased, and a throng of onlookers, whom Dr. O'Neill had, in the course of his long life, delivered into the world or helped in some way, and who that day seemed to number half of the population of the city of Quebec. They had accompanied him to Saint Patrick's Cemetery, and all along their route the bells of Saint Patrick's Church, of the Notre-Dame-de-Québec basilica, of the Anglican church, and of all the neighboring parish churches echoed in the spring air as they went. For Mick, that day, they had tolled to an empty sky.

Mick's memories of childhood, half-forgotten and yet so near, had been stirred that very morning, although he hadn't realized it at the time. Except on his wedding day, he had not set foot in a church since his father's funeral, but he had felt compelled to join the throng that poured into Saint-Jean-Baptiste Church to attend the thirty-day memorial service for Sir Wilfrid Laurier, who had died the previous month. For weeks, in towns and villages across the province, people had gathered in their churches to pray and reminisce. *Peace, tolerance, respect* had been the message recalled and repeated in homilies from every pulpit. Language, religion, and responsible government. Even Laurier's old foe, Bourassa, in the pages of *Le Devoir* had grieved along with the rest.

4

The following day, for the first time since Catherine's birth, Jeanne decided at the last minute to accept a dinner invitation. Miss Edwina Marshall, an important new client of Mick's, was a wealthy, elderly spinster whose brother had fought the Boers. She lived in a palatial red lava-stone house on Drummond Street in the elegant heart of English Montreal. It was a bitter March evening, and as Mick always worked quite late, Miss Marshall had sent her chauffeur and luxuriously appointed Pierce-Arrow, the seats of which were covered in mink, to fetch Jeanne. The door was opened to her by the butler, a distinguished-looking man with slicked-back hair, a high forehead, and a florid complexion; his fleshy pout and dour monocle expressed a haughty sensuality that to Jeanne seemed strangely at odds with his modest social station. He relieved her of her coat, handing it to a maid in a starched black-and-white uniform who hovered behind him in the vast hall.

"If Madame would like to follow me," he said with the kind of French accent that Jeanne until then had heard only at the French embassy. She was shown through a cozy den, where a fire roared in the marble hearth, to the spacious conservatory that served as a winter garden.

"Mrs. Michael O'Neill," the butler announced, this time in heavily accented English, from which, curiously, the French inflections were now absent.

Jeanne's entrance did not go unnoticed. In her high-waisted, black sequined dress that camouflaged her recent pregnancy and emphasized her slender arms, her bobbed hair held in place by a fringed, black headband, she turned every head in the room. She was immediately approached by a tall, severe-looking woman, of imperial demeanor.

"Mrs. O'Neill," said the unsmiling woman, with a British accent. "Miss Marshall is anxious to meet you. Do come this way."

Just then Jeanne caught sight of Mick motioning to her from behind a high-backed cane armchair. In it sat a tiny, frail, elderly woman with a cloud of white hair.

"Oh, Michael," exclaimed Miss Marshall in a quavering voice that matched her bird-like appearance. "What a pretty girl! My dear," she chirruped, extending a bony hand whose cool dry touch reminded Jeanne of a budgie's claw, "you are even lovelier than I'd been led to expect. Thank you, Hutchison," she added, dismissing the woman, who, Jeanne now saw, was her lady-in-waiting. Then she turned to Mick. "Be a kind fellow and introduce your darling wife to the other guests for me?"

The couple made their way toward a small group to whom the butler was serving sherry, looking down from his considerable height with what could only be described as benign condescension. All eyes turned as Mick and Jeanne approached. A semblance of complicity passed between them, perhaps due to the fact that, apart from the butler, they were the only ones here who spoke French. Flawlessly bilingual since childhood, they both had such an ability to blend into whatever company they happened to be with that people to whom they did not divulge it never suspected they were of "the other race." All of the guests that night were English-speaking. Several were members of the old English establishment of Montreal, their pedigree attested to by the transcendent plainness of their clothes, as if they wished to distinguish themselves from the lavishly dressed and bejeweled "new money" that smelled of contracts obtained from friends in the federal cabinet. Far too often during the war, government money had ended up on the front lines as shells that failed to explode, guns that misfired, tainted rations, and broken, leaky boots that rotted feet. But the war was over now, and profit, no matter how ill-gotten, has no odor, except perhaps the heady scent of power.

Dinner was served, and as the guests made their way

to the dining room, Jeanne for the second time that night noticed how female eyes sought out and lingered on Mick. The annoyance it gave her surprised and irritated her. When everyone was seated, the chair to Jeanne's right remained unoccupied.

"I'm expecting my nephew," the hostess explained. With a hint of pride, she added, "He should be here any moment now. The poor boy has just resumed his internship at the Royal Vic. Even when he has an evening off, he often has to cancel engagements at the last minute ..."

"I noticed yesterday in the *Star* that Rachmaninoff is going to be at His Majesty's on Sunday," someone said. "I was in New York last February when he came, and I'm not going to miss him this time!"

"Poor Rachmaninoff," sighed Miss Marshall, who seemed even tinier perched at the head of the table. "His country is going through a dreadful time."

"The Bolsheviki are gaining ground all over, even here," interjected a banker from St. James Street. "In the paper this morning there was an article on the riots in the textile workers' strike in Massachusetts. The police finally dispersed the demonstrators, but red flags were spotted in the crowd. The threat is real."

"But that's small stuff," rumbled a beefy-looking gentleman. "Look at Germany—it's in a state of anarchy. Communist agitation is everywhere."

"Tell me, Michael," twittered Miss Marshall with an innocence Mick knew to be feigned, "aren't those people going hungry?"

"Indeed, ma'am. They are without bread, without work, and without anyone to lead them. The Allied blockade is largely responsible for the agitation."

"But, my dear fellow," the banker broke in, "that is the price of defeat! The purpose of the peace conference is to ensure that the German aggression of 1914 can never be repeated. The Hun are a warlike people who must be brought to heel once and for all. The future of peace in Europe and the world depends on it."

"It is always dangerous to starve an entire people," Mick replied evenly. "However, one humiliates a nation at even greater risk."

The intentness with which he stared at the banker did not escape Miss Marshall's attention.

"How lucky we are to live sheltered from so much misfortune!" exclaimed the lady of the house, a little breathlessly. "Look at my poor butler," she continued in a hushed voice, "I am almost ashamed to have hired him. Just imagine, a prince of the Romanov household, raised at the court of the Tsar! The revolution has ruined him. He arrived here without a penny to his name."

"But happy to be alive, I'll be bound," thundered a male guest, diamond cufflinks glinting as he cut his roast beef.

Directly across the table from Jeanne, a tall, elegant woman suddenly looked stricken. Around her, discreetly knowing looks were exchanged. An uncomfortable silence rippled up to the head of the table.

"Today must have been especially hard for you both," Miss Marshall commiserated, speaking to the banker and the woman, who was evidently his wife. For the last two days, returning Canadian troops had been parading to cheering crowds through the streets of Montreal. The Fifth Canadian Mounted Rifles had arrived the previous evening, and the Ninth Field Ambulance that very morning.

"Our Malcolm was with the Patricias," said the man, his voice faltering, eyeing his wife with obvious concern.

"The hardest part of all," said the woman, whose

trembling voice Jeanne was hearing for the first time, "wasn't so much to see those boys returning." She stopped, and the strain showed in her face. "The hardest," she repeated, and you could hear the bitterness now, "was to see all those French Canadians yesterday, thousands of them, worshiping at the altar of Laurier! He was the one, while our boys lay wounded and dying, he was the one inciting the people to betray and abandon them!"

"Slackers," someone growled, "cowards."

"While our children were being butchered."

Jeanne watched her husband throughout this exchange, wondering what he was thinking. Her natural sympathy for the bereaved mother had quickly turned to indignation at the scathing tone with which she spoke of Laurier, whose death had plunged the Langlois family into mourning.

"Laurier be damned," grunted the man with the diamond cufflinks. "At least he won't be ramming his cursed French schools down our throats in Ontario. That man has done more to divide and destroy this country than Bourassa and Lavergne and their whole gang of subversives."

"That's why I keep saying," interjected the banker, "that in these situations it pays to be firm. For example, we could have solved the problem right after the Plains of Abraham. Britain is as much to blame for the mess as the Lauriers of this world. Britain allowed the French to retain their religion, their places of worship, their clergy, their schools, their language, their government, their separate legal system. That is how they prospered and multiplied to the point where they can now threaten the very fabric of the nation!"

Jeanne looked wonderingly down the table at Mick.

He was expressionless, sitting stock-still and looking calmly down at his hands, his maimed left bearing eloquent silent witness to his true feelings on the matter. At that moment the glass door of the dining room opened and a tall young man in military uniform entered.

"Darling! At last!" exclaimed Miss Marshall with heartfelt relief. "You poor boy, come and have something to eat. Dear friends, for those of you who don't already know him, this is my nephew, Dr. Louis Marshall."

The young man caught his aunt's hand in mid-wave and, bending over to kiss her, murmured an apology for his lateness that seemed to enchant her.

"But you're still in uniform! You haven't even had time to go home to change." She indicated the seat next to Jeanne, who was still flushed with suppressed anger.

Her nephew sat down, smiling affably at his neighbors as he did so. In the wavering candlelight his dark eyes sparkled with intelligence. A servant brought him soup.

"You see," sighed the lady of the house, "we're already serving dessert, but no matter. You are a splendid fellow to have managed to free yourself. Louis served in France," she explained to her guests, "with the Ninth Field Ambulance, when he was still a medical student at McGill. He was part of the faculty welcoming committee greeting his old unit at Bonaventure Station this morning. That is why he is still in uniform ..."

The late arrival of the newcomer mercifully changed the topic of conversation, and the dinner went on without incident. However, as soon as the guests rose from the dinner table, Jeanne signaled to her husband and claiming fatigue on this, her first postnatal outing, took her leave of the hostess. Outside the damp cold froze her bones.

"How could you sit there listening to those people

without saying something?" she demanded as Mick silently busied himself with the starter crank.

"A waste of time," he grumbled, shrugging his shoulders. The motor coughed two or three times then started up loudly. "Those people will never change their opinion."

"But they think—"

"They don't think. They need to blame someone for the death of their son."

"But you heard what they said—"

"They were just repeating what their parents taught them. We've got more than our share of people like that on our side as well."

"There was a time when you would have answered them," Jeanne muttered, shocked at what she took to be indifference on his part. She realized that she had rather liked the hotheadedness he had displayed when she first met him. Now all he thinks about is humoring his clients, she thought to herself.

"There was a time when I was as stupid as them," he said.

Since his best friend had left for the front and disappeared forever in a blaze of glory, he no longer seemed able to care much about the question. If Gonzague had lived, had returned safe and sound—if even now he might return, things could perhaps be different. But alas, there was no longer any hope of that.

PART TWO

1

Andante Cantabile

Senator Bernard's country home on the lakeshore was visible from the road behind its wrought-iron gates. A short gravel drive led up to it, between banks of red and white roses that nodded and bowed in the breeze like a floral honor guard. The house was built of stone, and the back of it opened onto a spacious terrace, where groups of guests were already sipping drinks. Wide stone steps led down to a beautifully tended lawn sweeping out toward the lake, where a dock and several boats bobbed behind a screen of mauve and white phlox. Halfway between the house and the shore rose a single giant oak. Under the shelter of its vast reach a string quartet was playing chamber music, eyes anchored to their music stands, their movements measured and precise, amid the leisurely milling guests.

Mick had made no bones about the fact that this party was the agreeable pretext for a political meeting. Similar gatherings, large and small, were being held all over the country in the wake of Sir Wilfrid Laurier's death, and in anticipation of a national leadership convention in August, the first in the party's history.

"We are finally going to heal the wounds of conscription," the senator, a portly man with woolly white hair, was saying. "The time for rumors is past. We now have the means to unite the party, by demonstrating once and for all that the Liberal defeat of 1917 was the result of a gigantic swindle."

"Are you saying we can actually prove there was election fraud?" interrupted Mick with a hungry glint in his eye.

"We will provide case after documented case of wholesale manipulation by the Borden government of the overseas soldiers' vote: cabled instructions from members of the Union cabinet, relayed through the office of the High Commissioner in London, allowing for recruitment of British soldiers, American citizens, even British employees in Canadian hospitals in England, to vote in a Canadian election! But there's more: British citizens were given Canadian forces uniforms along with lists of names, and directions to all the polling stations in London."

"Any other evidence?"

"My dear fellow, we have evidence galore! Soldiers' letters from home, withheld by the censor if they were found to contain encouragements to vote against the government. Bogus cables, purportedly from relatives in Canada, sent to soldiers by government order and charged to government accounts, advising them not to oppose government candidates in the coming election.

We are even in a position to reveal the existence of a committee of senior army officers, with an office in Piccadilly, whose mission it was to root out soldiers with outspoken Liberal sympathies so that they could be sent to the front without delay. Even the wounded in the hospitals were warned that a vote for Laurier would buy them an early one-way ticket back to the front! Revelations without precedent, my friend, which are going to make our convention very, very interesting indeed!"

"Well, Mick!" interrupted a red-haired young woman, who had just joined them.

"Éloïse!" cried Mick, with a rare show of emotion. "How the devil are you? How is your mother?"

She wasn't pretty, Jeanne observed, but her pleasant face and intelligent eyes lent her an unmistakable charm. Her cream-colored dress and the green bandeau she wore in her bobbed bright hair brought out the milky whiteness of her complexion and of her plump, shapely arms. She kissed the senator and introduced herself to Jeanne with a handshake that was as firm as any man's.

"Éloïse Prud'homme," she said, with an engaging smile. "We met at your wedding." Jeanne barely had time to apologize for not recognizing her. "My goodness! You're not expected to notice things like that on your wedding day."

"How would you know?" Mick teased her.

"Oh, you!" she huffed, with mock indignation.

"I have a feeling I'm going to have my ears pulled again, Senator, don't you?"

"Éloïse is incorrigible, but we always forgive her. Mick, what do you say we go and fill the glasses of these charming ladies?"

"They want to shake us off," said Éloïse, watching the two men stroll off. "Fine. Let's take a walk. That'll teach them."

Jeanne willingly followed her out to the lawn. She liked Éloïse's vivaciousness, and the familiarity with which she treated Mick intrigued her.

"Have you known Mick long?"

"Heavens, yes!" she exclaimed. "A long time. I knew him when he was still in short pants. You would not believe the pranks he and his brother Arthur got up to, and the thrashings Mick got. He always took all the blame on himself to protect his little brother. I used to be friendly with his sister."

"You're from Quebec City?"

"Yes ma'am! His sister Marguerite and I went to the Ursulines* together. My brother Gonzague and Mick were inseparable. Their house was on Rue Desjardins, and ours was on Rue Couillard."

She was twenty-four, five years older than Jeanne, still single ("No Abélard in sight, I must have been born in the wrong century") and she had one all-consuming interest: politics, to which she devoted all of her time. Her father, Judge Évariste Prud'homme, had died suddenly shortly after the armistice, upon learning that his only son Gonzague, in whom he had placed all his hopes, had been reported missing, presumed dead, on the battlefield just a few days before the end of the war. Her mother, who had lived for her only son, entered the Ursuline convent, leaving her daughter a considerable fortune. That was when Éloïse had decided to leave Quebec City to make her life in Montreal. Her life in society had never been easy: her first ever *at home* at the Château Frontenac had been sabotaged by Cardinal Bégin, when he had declared

* *Ursulines*: the Ursuline Convent School in Quebec City.

dancing to be a mortal sin, thus prompting her father to cancel the whole event. And now, unlike most young women in her position, who would have divided their time between the social circuit and charitable work, she haunted the back-rooms, the smoke-filled redoubts of the party of her father, who had died a *rouge** as he had been born. She could smoke cigars with the best of them, but for now she was content to light up a cigarette, at the end of her long ivory cigarette-holder.

"Now there's a man who would do just fine as a stand-in for Abélard. Unfortunately, and quite understandably, he's looking at you, not at me."

Turning her head slightly to follow Éloïse's gaze, Jeanne looked up toward the terrace and felt the man's gaze on her almost before she saw him.

"Who is he?" she asked, turning her back to the house and savoring the sudden complicity. "Should I know him?"

"You do so at your peril," whispered Éloïse knowingly, as they strolled toward the lake.

"My goodness, is he so bad?"

"No, no." Éloïse laughed delightedly. "I'm teasing you. He's a Russian, if you please, an aristocrat, no less."

"There are a lot of them around these days," Jeanne remarked, remembering Miss Marshall's butler a few months earlier, and trying to give herself a worldly air.

"Yes, they come here for the climate, because it reminds them of home, and because they know the language. Most of them speak French better than you or I."

"He's beautiful ... What's his name?"

"Vladimir Sergeievitch Shpazhinsky," Éloïse intoned with exaggerated difficulty. "Those Russians have such impossible names."

* *Rouge*: Liberal.

"What is he doing here? Is he a Liberal?"

"Don't look so incredulous, maybe he is!"

Jeanne marveled at her new friend's high spirits.

"He has many friends. Women adore him. He's invited everywhere. I've heard he's a very good painter, but he doesn't exhibit his work. He has to earn a living, his family lost everything. If what they say is true, his father was an equerry to the Tsar."

"You know him?"

"I have never had the honor of being introduced." She said it with a hint of self-deprecating irony in her voice which, Jeanne was beginning to suspect, was meant to conceal a sensitive nature.

"Well, you two, I had a time finding you!" said Mick just behind them. "Come on, Éloïse, I've saved you a seat at our table."

Not only were they the only two people left on the lawn, but in the course of their chat they had wandered down to the edge of the lake, where their light-colored dresses blended in with the phlox along the shore.

2

Lunch began with champagne and ended with ripe strawberries, smothered in rich cream and sweetened with maple syrup. Jeanne's tablemates lingered on to argue the relative merits of Fielding and Mackenzie King as leader of the party.

"As for me," Éloïse declared, with the added fervor wine imparts, "I will never get over the loss of Talbot Papineau. He was *predestined* for the office of prime minister. Imagine for a moment, if he hadn't died at Passchendaele! The grandson of Louis-Joseph Papineau, hero of the 1837 Rebellion! Handsome, dashing, brave, passionate, a war hero, bilingual, and what a speaker!"

As the debate grew more intense, Jeanne, light-headed with wine, dessert, and the bracing country air, rose from the table and strolled out toward the spreading branches of the massive oak tree. Under its broad reach, the chamber ensemble had resumed playing. A cool breeze was blowing from the lake. Leaning back against the trunk of the great tree, she let her eyes wander out over the pastel cloud of phlox to the sparkling water beyond, her senses seduced by the melancholy music that was dissipating like a flowery scent in the open air.

"Ah—the *andante cantabile* that made Tolstoy weep ..." sighed a voice that seemed to come from the very trunk of the tree. "You like Tchaikovsky, mademoiselle?"

He came round to face her, leaning at arm's length against the tree. Jeanne tried to remember what Éloïse had told her about him—she had mentioned horses—his father an equerry to the Tsar. His eyes were laughing, teasing, but gently, not enough to wound.

"I startled you," he apologized, his hand resting almost too close to the place where her bare shoulder met the rough bark. His gray eyes sought hers boldly. He seemed to reach into her, like a man helping himself to a sweet without waiting for it to be offered. Then, taking her hand and lifting it slowly to his lips: "I should introduce myself, mademoiselle," he said. "Vladimir Shpazhinsky."

Jeanne felt the softness of his mouth on her skin. She tried to lift her eyes to glance at him again.

"*Madame ...*" she managed to correct him.

"What, already?" He held her gaze for a moment longer, then gave a little shove and stood clear of the tree. "What a shame ... You are blushing?" he said, with a hungry smile. This man is at least thirty-five years old,

Jeanne thought to herself, and he's making fun of my age and my shyness. But her heart was racing with unaccustomed excitement.

"So tell me," he said, "who is the lucky fellow?"

"I am," came Mick's voice from a few feet away. He was standing there, eyes flashing, his whole body exuding tension, his face an unreadable mask.

"Mr. O'Neill," exclaimed the Russian with consummate assurance, "what a pleasure to see you! You are indeed a fortunate man."

"You've met?" asked Jeanne, with a coolness that, a moment before, she would have thought herself incapable of. Mick shook hands with the stranger.

"Last winter, at your aunt's funeral," he answered, without looking at her.

"You knew my Aunt Florence, Monsieur?"

"She was my pupil," the man replied quietly, looking away toward the open water.

"It's time to leave, Jeanne, it's getting late." Mick took her unceremoniously by the elbow and marched her off toward the house as one does a child one is going to punish. Mick's arrival on the scene had had the effect of a glass of cold water flung in her face. Mortified at having let herself be humiliated but too proud to show it, she waited until they were close to the house to tear free of his grasp. She climbed the steps to the terrace two at a time, almost knocking down Éloïse, who was coming down to join them. Jeanne spluttered an apology.

"He's always had a temper," whispered Éloïse, who must have witnessed the scene from afar. "Don't hold it against him ..." She spoke with a blissful, slightly glazed smile that further annoyed Jeanne, who was utterly sober now.

The O'Neills said their goodbyes and drove home in

silence, the air between them thick with resentment. As Mick sat grimly at the wheel, eyes front, Jeanne's thoughts wandered back to the party, trying to remember the stranger's face. She realized she had noticed almost nothing about him. She became irritated with herself, fearing she had looked foolish in the eyes of such a worldly, experienced man, by blushing like a schoolgirl under the effect, she told herself, of too much wine.

When they arrived back at University Street, their five-month-old daughter's wails could be heard even before they crossed the threshold. Jeanne, whose milk had suddenly begun to flow, ran upstairs to the nursery, where she found Gabrielle pacing the floor with the screaming infant in her arms.

"Gabrielle, for heaven's sake," cried Jeanne, unbuttoning her dress, the front of which was already soaked with milk, "you should have given her a bottle, you know I told you—"

"She didn't want it, Madame, I tried everything."

"Give her to me," Jeanne said, gesturing impatiently as she slipped into her bathrobe. The baby began sucking greedily as soon as her mother's nipple brushed her lips. Gradually the tension left Jeanne's body. She surrendered herself to the physical comfort of nursing, to the sweet smell of baby and milk, to the quiet reverence of their communion. Gabrielle produced a brush and, standing behind Jeanne, began brushing her hair with slow strokes, the fingers of her free hand resting lightly on her head, gently massaging her scalp, as she sometimes did, without being asked, since the baby had been born. Jeanne, feeling the womanly warmth of her against her back, became deliciously drowsy. The baby had fallen asleep. Gabrielle gathered her up in her arms and took her off to the nursery.

In her room, lying on her bed, Jeanne's thoughts drifted back to the lawn at Senator Bernard's; to Éloïse, with the two little dimples that her good nature seemed to have etched in her cheeks, marveling once again at her extraordinary verbal agility, and the tenderness sheltering under her bravado; and finally to the Russian, whose company had so disturbed her that she couldn't remember how tall he was, or the color of his eyes, or whether he had stood three feet or three inches away from her. As her thoughts drifted into dreams she dozed off, and found on awakening that dusk was falling.

3

Jeanne awoke the next morning from a dreamless sleep into a crushing sense of dread. For a moment before she opened her eyes she thought she was back in Saint-Boniface, the rosebud of her youth pinched off before it could bloom, her future forgone before it had begun. Her body ached as if she had been chafing in the horsehair shirt prescribed for self-mortification, her jaw was tender from, she thought, gnashing her teeth with hunger in her sleep ... Someone was knocking very gently on the door. She opened her eyes, and remembering what had happened, felt an irrational longing for the barren safety of her convent bed. Then the fullness in her breasts reasserted the reality of Catherine, and so much that was now good in her life. She remembered getting up from the floor and locking the door, quite unnecessarily as Mick had made no attempt to return. The door was still locked, and she now recognized Gabrielle's timidly insistent little rap.

"I'm sorry for waking you up, Madame, but the little one was crying ..."

The baby had found her thumb and was sucking it

furiously. Two tiny pearls of moisture sat on her round little cheeks. Jeanne took her daughter into her arms.

"Would Madame like her breakfast now?" Gabrielle hesitated, without looking at her.

"What's wrong, Gabrielle?" asked Jeanne carefully. "You don't seem your normal self this morning."

"Oh, Madame," answered the girl, tears leaping into her eyes, "last night ... I couldn't help hearing ..."

Jeanne cringed at the allusion. Mick had appeared at her door quite late, his shirt unbuttoned at the neck. The lapels of his white dinner jacket were smeared with cigarette ash, his face gleaming with perspiration. She guessed at once that he must have been drinking steadily since their return. Indeed he had. As soon as they had arrived home, he'd gone straight to the sitting room and opened a bottle of whisky. He'd sat there brooding in his chair until the gathering gloom had made him want to get up to turn on the lights. After several attempts at getting to his feet, he'd staggered across the room, feeling for the light switch in the semi-darkness. It was the noise he'd made bumping into the cabinet of the Victrola that Gabrielle had first heard. Going up the stairs he'd stumbled repeatedly, swearing each time in a black rage. Then she had heard some terrible shouting in Madame's bedroom, followed by the door slamming and Monsieur muttering to himself in the hall on his way to the study.

Jeanne had never seen him quite so drunk before. Usually, depending on the amount he had imbibed, alcohol had one of two effects on him: in the early stages it relaxed him, made him more talkative, amusing, entertaining. For this reason at social gatherings his talents as a raconteur were much in demand. In the all-male context of the Reform Club however, he drank faster and more, and this produced the other state, which Jeanne before Catherine's birth had come to dread. But last night was different. He was far beyond any bodily cravings. Almost incoherent with anger, he'd sprung at her like a puma, threatening and shoving until she fell, hard, onto the floor. In falling she had struck her jaw and he had stood over her, raging at her for a while longer. Finally he'd gone, slamming the door so hard it should have leapt off its hinges.

Georgette, the cook, entered with the breakfast tray, the newspaper, and the first mail of the day, which Jeanne opened as she finished feeding the baby.

"*Madame,*" said the short note written in an unknown hand. "*It will be a pleasure to put Mme Florence Talbot's horses at your disposal. Please telephone me at your convenience at the Shakespeare Road Stables.*"

"*With best regards,*
"*V. S. Shpazhinsky.*"

4

Once she had made up her mind to see the man who had apparently been Florence's riding instructor, Jeanne found herself procrastinating, partly out of shyness and inexperience, and partly out of fear of opening a Pandora's box of emotions, hitherto bolted shut by an instinct for self-preservation that Mick's recent vindictiveness had merely reinforced. Finally, two days before she was to leave for Carleton for the holidays, her indecision exacerbated beyond bearing by the prospect of spending the entire summer without having seen him again, she picked up the telephone to call him, half hoping she had left it too late. The phone rang and rang, each ring jangling her nerves like a surge of current. Four. Five. She was about to put down the receiver when a voice came on at the other end.

"Shakespeare Road, Shpazhinsky," said the voice in English. "Hello," he repeated, "Shpazhinsky speaking."

"Mr. Shpazhinsky," she said finally. "Jeanne O'Neill here."

"Mme O'Neill!" The voice was delighted, solicitous. "I had almost given up hearing from you. How are you?"

She recognized the slight Russian inflection in his otherwise impeccable French.

"I'm afraid I'm not giving you very much notice. We leave for the Gaspé the day after tomorrow ..."

"No, no. It will be a great pleasure, certainly. Please. Feel free."

Abruptly she relaxed. He made it all sound so simple and straightforward, and in fact, before her pregnancy, Florence had sometimes spoken of taking her riding on the mountain. The apprehension and excitement of a few moments ago now seemed childish. On the telephone he sounded quite ordinary—courteous, pleasant, but quite ordinary really.

And yet that afternoon when he came out of his small office adjoining the main stable building to greet her, the effect he had on her was anything but ordinary. In his rolled-up shirtsleeves and riding breeches, his hair tousled as if he'd been sleeping, he seemed younger than she remembered. Shpazhinsky's gaze was so direct he seemed to be reading her thoughts. She became so engrossed in trying to suppress the havoc this caused inside her that she didn't understand what he was saying. Already he was heading back toward the stable and she followed, aware of the gravel crunching under their boots, now that she no longer had to channel all her attention into avoiding his eyes.

"The gray is the gentle one," he was saying. "Florence liked him best."

The fact that he called Florence by her first name intrigued her, even worried her a little. Had they been friends? Why then had Florence never mentioned him to her? Remembering her inability to recall anything about him after that first time at the senator's, and taking advantage of the fact he was walking ahead of her, Jeanne observed him intently. He was not as tall as she had imagined. Not much more than me, in fact, she mused, realizing that the impression he had left her with was one of height.

"I am glad you came," he said without turning around. "I was beginning to think I wouldn't see you again."

"I didn't know whether I should answer or not," she blurted, before she realized the interpretation that could be made of her words.

He pushed open the door of the stable, the top half of which had been left open because of the heat.

"Then you are as honest as you are pretty," he said, his eyes connecting with hers in the same way they had under the huge oak, that day. He was almost too close to her. He smelled of horse, and of leather, and ...

He disappeared into the tack room, then reappeared with an English saddle over his arm and a bridle slung over his shoulder; he let himself into one of the stalls. In the semi-darkness Jeanne gradually made out the shape of a magnificent dapple-gray with a black mane and tail. Shpazhinsky was speaking softly to the animal and stroking its great neck.

"So you were Florence's riding master?" Jeanne asked rather pointlessly, just for something to say. The man's proximity in the dark, silent stable was unsettling.

"I had this privilege," he replied, eyeing her steadily, over the quiet creaking and clinking of saddle and stirrups as he tightened the horse's girth.

"The last time I saw her she was coming from here, and ..."

"She was dressed just like you," he answered, pointing to the riding habit which Florence had had made for her as part of her trousseau, in the happier times of their tea-parties over dress patterns just before the wedding.

"Yes, we had the same one, we were the same size, although I have never had the opportunity to wear it."

"I knew who you were the first time I saw you," he said, removing the halter and expertly slipping the bridle over the animal's head. "The resemblance is striking."

She remembered the way his eyes had held her, that day up on the terrace, and the question leapt into her mind: "Did you love her?" But she was not bold enough to ask it. He was not looking at her that way now.

The horse was now saddled. Shpazhinsky backed him out of his stall. "His name is Pushkin," he said. And he led him out into the daylight, his hoofs clattering on the cement floor of the stable. He picked up a low wooden stool and placing it at the side of the horse, under the stirrup, he held out his hand to her. Jeanne took it, stepped onto the stool, put her foot in the stirrup and, as she drew herself uncertainly up onto the horse, Shpazhinsky seized her by the waist and lifted her effortlessly onto the saddle.

"Don't be so nervous," he laughed, "you make the horse nervous too."

"I'm sorry," she said, red-faced, "I haven't ridden a horse since I was twelve ..."

"Then pretend you are twelve! With practice you can make perfect again, you will see."

He disappeared again into the darkness of the stable and emerged leading a beautiful chestnut mare with legs so long and delicate that they seemed in danger of snapping at the slightest stumble.

"This is Lara," he said, mounting. "She is very nervous. Unfortunately she was mishandled the first two or three years of her life. Florence gave her to me to train because she didn't like riding her."

Shpazhinsky set out first, leading the way down the short gravel drive, past the ring and the jumps. As they reached the field at the back of the stables, he quickened his pace to a trot. Jeanne felt a surge of exhilaration as her horse caught up with his and the hot breath of June blew her damp hair, now unfashionably long, away from her face and neck.

"You know, when I left Russia I never thought it would be for good. I am very lucky to find a place where I can feel at home. This is such a big country. In Europe I always felt the horizon so near, almost closing in, every square meter of it either inhabited or cultivated, everywhere you see the hand of man. Here, in winter, walking in the woods, I can almost imagine I am at my mother's in the country and that one of my little brothers is going to appear on the path in his little sled."

Jeanne listened with envy, aware of the impenetrable loneliness of memory, of the inadequacy of words to convey the fullness of a past intimately lived, but she admired the French he spoke—rich, concise, and grammatically pure.

"When I was a boy," he continued, "I would spend days drawing in the woods. In the evenings I would try to produce a decent watercolor out of the sketches I had made."

"Yes, Éloïse said you were a painter."

"Oh, not any more," he said, pulling ahead of her on the narrow path and ducking into the wood.

"Do you still have family in Russia, Mr. Shpazhinsky?" she asked, cursing the bashfulness that seemed to empty her head whenever she opened her mouth.

"Vladimir! Please. Don't be so formal," he cried, then in answer to her question, "My father died when I was small. Perhaps it was just as well for him."

"You mean because of the Revolution?"

"Actually, no. My father was the son of a landowner who had been governor of a province where there were many Poles. After the Polish revolt in 1830 was brutally crushed by the authorities, my grandfather resigned his post in disgust and retired to one of his estates in Ukraine. The repression of the Poles continued to haunt him so much that to soothe his own conscience eventually he freed all his serfs, including his servants, keeping only those who wished to stay on as paid employees. I hope I am not boring you with this genealogy?" he said, turning toward her with an apologetic smile that enchanted her.

"Having lost most of his manpower, my grandfather had to sell almost all of his lands, and my father and his brothers had to make a living for themselves. My father went into the army, where he became an officer, and at twenty-four he was made an equerry to Alexander II, the Tsar who gave the serfs their freedom. His duties took him to St. Petersburg, where he met my mother, married her, and lived long enough to give her four sons. It was his marriage that sooner or later would have been his undoing, if he had lived."

Jeanne, giddy with his confidences, listened in a state of rapture. As the path got progressively steeper she could feel Pushkin lunging at the hill with his shoulders, working his powerful neck up and down like a lever against the pull of gravity.

"My mother, whom he worshiped," he continued, "was a catastrophe for his career, because she was a passionate opponent of the autocracy. She would never even have considered an equerry to the Tsar as a suitor were it not for the fact that he came from a family that had committed an unpardonable sin against its own class. To her, bored and rebellious daughter of a senior civil servant in the Ministry of the Interior, my father combined the natural attractions of his character and looks, to say nothing of his birth and upbringing, with the irresistible allure of a man who was viewed with suspicion in St. Petersburg society, whose frivolity and obsequiousness to the court she despised. My mother's father had powerful friends in the police, and as long as he was alive he shielded her and my father from harm. She was beautiful, bright, educated. She spoke four languages and liked to surround herself with artists of all kinds. Her salon was frequented by the most progressive intellectuals in St. Petersburg, and therefore closely watched by the police. In summer she would entertain all these people at the family estate in Ukraine, which my father had inherited. Here, this will interest you," he said authoritatively, as though he had known her for a long time, and Jeanne suddenly wondered whether Florence had sometimes spoken to him of her.

"She was friendly with the Davidovs," he resumed, "who also had estates in the area, and sometimes visited them at their home in Kamenka. One day, on one of these visits, our calèche passed a bearded, white-haired man walking alone, very fast, on the side of the road, and I remember my mother reverently pointing him out to me as we drove by. It was Piotr Ilyitch Tchaikovsky, whose genius the great luminaries in the capital still refused to acknowledge."

As they rode on, the ground leveled off and the trail skirted a small clearing.

"But my mother also knew many politically dangerous people, and after the assassination of Tsar Alexander II, life in the capital became impossible. The secret police and their informers were everywhere, arrests and executions multiplied. By then my father had died of cholera, at thirty-four, four years younger than I am now, think of it ... My mother retired to the country and never lived in St. Petersburg again. But to answer your question, no. My mother is dead, my three little brothers were killed in the war, and my country is drowning in blood."

Without warning he gave his horse a nudge and Jeanne followed, overawed by his sudden burst of bitterness. Soon the path widened into a broad dirt track between the trees.

"But I don't understand," she said when she caught up with him, intimidated by his silence yet eager for him to continue. "If you were brought up as an opponent of the regime, why did you leave?"

"I was so young then," he answered, looking straight ahead of him. When he wandered off thus, following the meandering thread of his memories deep into the maze of his past, he seemed almost oblivious of her presence, leaving her free to watch him as he spoke. Turned from her, his face in profile was more generous than his full face, less dominated by his melancholy eyes and small, moody mouth. "It was 1905. I was in the capital studying fine arts. I was bored and frustrated, stifled by the atmosphere of repression, the hostility to new ideas, the police surveillance. It was a time when students could be arrested on the street just for walking in a group. The future looked bleak. We were losing the war with Japan, a war everyone thought we could so easily win. And then, on a cold Sunday in January, a peaceful demonstration by hundreds of thousands of unarmed workers was savagely broken up. Hundreds of men, women, and children were shot down in the streets in cold blood. In response, hundreds of thousands of workers all over Russia went on strike. Many universities simply closed down, because the students and their teachers were all in the streets. In April, after the annihilation of the Russian fleet by the Japanese in Tsushima Strait, rioting broke out everywhere. In June there was a major insurrection in Odessa, on the Black Sea, almost a civil war between striking workers and students and revolutionaries on one side, and the army and police on the other. More than two thousand died before it was over. Meanwhile, political assassinations multiplied.

"That summer my mother, who, being a keen student of history, was only too familiar with the chaos and barbarism unleashed by the French Revolution, became convinced that bloody revolution was at hand and that decent, compassionate, thinking people like herself and her friends were about to be swept up in a tidal wave of vengefulness and hatred, to make way for God only knew what. In August she packed our bags and took us all to Paris, where I enrolled at the École des Beaux-Arts and my brothers were placed in a good school.

"In October the whole of Russia went on strike. In many parts of the Empire, the peasants went on a violent rampage. Finally the Tsar gave way and granted the people some of the freedoms you Canadians take for granted, but more importantly, he gave Russia an elected consultative assembly, the Duma, something liberals like my mother had pushed for, for years. At first my mother was exultant. Her first impulse was to return to Russia at once, but news from home soon convinced her to stay on in Paris until things settled down. For two weeks in December, violent insurrection gripped the city of Moscow. The revolt was ominous because the Muscovite upper class was sympathetic to the revolutionaries, even to the extent of financing them, and the troops of the Moscow garrison were rumored to be demoralized and perhaps even capable of joining the rebels. Eventually the revolt was crushed, but not before a thousand died, many more were executed, and whole areas of the city were left ravaged by artillery fire. In Paris we received constant reports of savage repression throughout the country, executions, hangings in the thousands. Pacification measures continued well into 1906.

"Finally, at the end of April, after we had been in Paris for eight months, the Duma was inaugurated. My mother, throwing caution to the wind, again packed up her belongings, her servants, and my two youngest brothers and went home, to witness what she thought was the dawning of a new age."

"You didn't follow?"

"My brother Maxim and I stayed behind. He had examinations to write and had decided to spend the summer with friends in the Midi before returning home in autumn. As for me, I had no desire to leave Paris. It seemed to me that an entire lifetime would not be enough to see all there was to see, to learn all that I wanted to learn. I spent four years there in a kind of trance, drinking too much and painting too little. I became acquainted with a coterie of artists who were much more iconoclastic and adventurous than I, and whose exploits of experimentation intimidated and exasperated me. They seemed obsessed with the *form* of things. To me, to be an artist is a little like being an astronomer. You try to steal glimpses of the Infinite and then strive to convey the wonder of it with the feeble human means at your disposal. It seemed to me that these young geniuses had become so absorbed in the mathematics of their interpretation that they had lost all ability to *communicate* what they actually saw."

He stressed the word, turning to look at Jeanne, as if he wanted to be sure she understood.

"Perhaps I was simply jealous. If God were just, I would have been born a musician. Music has such immediacy, it can produce emotion out of nothing. By filling the head, and overwhelming the heart. Completely artificially it can make you feel joy or sorrow, longing, triumph, defeat. Not vicariously like books, or even poetry. By commandeering directly, without intermediary, the most intimate of the senses, the most secret access route to the deepest part of the soul. Take Tchaikovsky," he went on, with the enthusiasm of a true teacher. "No one has more potently expressed the torment of love, the violence contained in the act of living. There are people who don't like his music, who find it *overdone*. But life is overdone, exaggerated, excessive—life is nothing but extremes of joy and suffering, beauty and ugliness! An artist is not simply an illusionist but an oracle, a medium. Through him some part of reality is revealed. An artist who expresses only his individual reality in terms that others can't understand is an egotist whose works are destined for oblivion. He who lives only for himself does not survive his own death. Of course there are certain affinities that attract us to a particular painter, or writer, or composer more than to some other. When this empathy exists, communion can take place. Otherwise it is like trying to find one's way in a country without knowing the language. Definitely, the language that Tchaikovsky spoke was Russian ..."

He was hard to follow, through the twists and turns and sudden shortcuts of his thinking, but no one, not even Florence, had ever spoken to Jeanne this way. She hung on his every word, and the more she drank them, the thirstier she became.

"You love your country very much, don't you, Monsieur—?" Shpazhinsky shot her a questioning look. "—I mean, Vladimir."

"The Russia I love is dying," he replied morosely. "Perhaps it is already dead."

"One night last winter," Jeanne said, attempting to steer him away from the shoals that she had unsuspectingly caused to appear before him, "I went to dinner at the home of a wealthy client of my husband's. Her butler caught my attention."

Shpazhinsky raised an eyebrow.

"Oh, don't tease!" she said with a pinched expression that prompted a burst of laughter from the Russian. "He seemed completely out of place somehow, he was too distinguished-looking, too ... *aristocratic*. The lady of the house later told us that he was a prince, a Romanov, who had been forced to leave everything behind and, having arrived here penniless, had been obliged to become a butler to earn a living. Do you know who I mean?"

"You must be referring to Dimitrov, the old scoundrel. An officer in the first White Volunteer army. He is a reactionary monarchist anachronism. Between his kind and the Bolsheviki, Russia will slowly bleed to death. The tsarists want time to stand still, while the Bolsheviki would pull history up by the roots if they could. Neither is remotely interested in what Russian people want, and yet both claim to speak for Russia. Only the people can speak for Russia, and their voice has never been heard ... You see," he added wryly, "I have talked myself in a big circle."

They had indeed gone all the way round the mountain, and were now at the other end of the field they had crossed when they were just setting out on their ride. Jeanne's heart sank a little at the prospect of her tête-à-tête with Shpazhinsky coming to an end.

Back in the stableyard, he helped her down off her horse.

"You see," he said, eyes twinkling, "it wasn't so hard. You look as though you've been riding all your life."

"Thank you, I enjoyed it very much, Vladimir Sergeievitch," she said, turning crimson as she uttered the patronymic.

"You see, it is not so hard to say," he said, watching her intently. "You must come back again, when you return from your holiday."

"I would like to," she stammered, losing what was left of her composure.

"Don't worry," he said, "next time will be easier."

He watched her back the huge McLaughlin-Buick haltingly around. Mick, like most lawyers and men of business who lived in the heart of the city, preferred to take the streetcar to work, and Jeanne had only just learned to drive. Finally the car lunged forward and drove off amid a loud crackling of gravel.

2

Portraits

of the Artist

1

June 1919 De Valera was in New York. Word had come more than a fortnight earlier that the Irish MP and president of Sinn Fein, of the Irish Volunteers and of Dáil Éireann, the Irish National Assembly, had been smuggled out of Ireland. He was in America to mobilize support and money for the independence movement, and ultimately to secure recognition for Irish independence.

For Michael O'Neill the news came not a day too soon. His life had been purgatory ever since the morning, two weeks ago, when he'd awakened fully clothed on the couch in the study, his head aching and his mind a clouded morass of guilt involving his wife the night before. What he did remember was the cozy little scene he'd come upon in the senator's garden—her flushed cheeks and rapt expression as she listened to the Russian, the fear and surprise in her eyes when he'd made his presence known, and the burning fury that had plagued him all afternoon. But of his actions the night before, no clear recollection remained. Still, the terrified look in young Gabrielle's eyes as he met her on the stairs had made him think better of breakfast, and he'd left that morning without a word to anyone.

Since then, Jeanne had become more estranged from him than ever. She seemed to withdraw deep inside herself, and there was a vigilant guardedness about her that he had not noticed before. His pride was sorely tested by all this, and as he loaded the suitcases onto the Ocean Limited, he couldn't help feeling glad of the respite her leaving would afford him. Time, he told himself, would put things into perspective; what loomed so large now, exaggerated by a mutual silence that fed on resentment and the constant irritant of daily contact, would soon appear as trivial as it truly was. A separation now would help her forget, which for all practical purposes was as good as forgive. Having decided to go to New York to meet with de Valera's people, he was putting Jeanne and the baby on the train to Carleton, where they were to spend the rest of the summer.

As he stood on the platform, steeped in the gold light of sunset, Gabrielle appeared at the window of the sleeping car holding Catherine in her arms. The child wriggled with delight at the sight of her father. Mick grinned back, chuckling to himself.

"Bye, Kit!" he waved, calling her by the Gaelic nickname he'd long substituted for the first name chosen by his wife.

The whistle blew, and as the engine started up ponderously, Jeanne herself came to the window. The two of them, waving at one another from the safety of impending distance, smiled: he to reassure himself that there was indeed no cause for worry, and she the better to shield from him the true state of her mind.

For two days since her visit to Shakespeare Road she had been immersed in delicious turmoil, her mind feasting on the words and images that had been thrown her way like bones to a hungry dog. Her imagination had fastened on a constantly shifting picture, painstakingly pieced together from the succession of glimpses she had stolen of Shpazhinsky's face. His words she endlessly reviewed as a miser counts his gold, tirelessly repeating them to herself like a child learning declensions, until she remembered each inflection by heart. When the thrill it gave her began to wear off, she would retrieve yet another image from the treasure-trove in her mind. She was obsessed by the memory of his eyes searching her, flushing her like a startled bird, of his quick strong hands on her waist. There was such pleasure in these recollections that she tried to refrain from indulging in them too much, lest they lose their freshness and intensity.

As the train pulled away she peered gratefully on Mick's swiftly receding form. She looked forward to the weeks alone, particularly as the entire month of July was to be spent in Florence's house, well out of Carleton and her mother's meddlesome reach. Florence had specified in her will that she wished the house to be put at the disposal of her niece for one month every summer, and Jeanne was thankful for the opportunity to remove herself from the society of family and acquaintances for a few weeks before moving on to her father's house in August. A short while later, as the train crossed Victoria Bridge and the Saint Lawrence River on its way out of the city, the wealthy homes on the western flank of Mount Royal were set ablaze by the setting sun, as the city huddled in the shadows at its feet. Jeanne gazed back at the mountain with a twinge of excitement.

Somewhere beneath the foliage, in the darkening woods, lay the hidden path that had sheltered their ride.

2

The next morning Jeanne awoke early, just as Catherine was beginning to squirm in her small wicker traveling cot. She picked up the baby and, drawing the thick green curtain more securely across her sleeping berth, began nursing her while everyone in the Pullman car still slept. At Matapédia they switched trains. They were now on the Gaspé railway line, once promised and then delivered by her father, as his campaign workers never tired of reminding the Bonaventure electorate each time he took to the hustings. As the train wended its way down the valley toward the coast, Gabrielle suddenly leapt to her feet.

"Madame! The sea! Can you smell it? Oh, may I open the window a little wider?"

As she did so, Jeanne felt it too, the sudden pungency of salt in the air. Her eyes filled with tears as a wave of emotion engulfed her. For what the sea wind had so unexpectedly stirred, along with the forgotten smells of her eighteenth summer, was the memory of hope. After the long numbness since her aunt's death, her heart was springing to life in a bitter gust of grief. Just then Catherine, who was in Gabrielle's arms at the open window with the wind ruffling her downy hair, wrinkled her nose and uttered a series of sneezes, punctuating each one with an impish grin in her mother's direction. *What the Lord taketh away with one hand, He giveth with the other.* Even after so many months since leaving the convent, she could still hear Father Jobin's rich, deep voice in the confessional and feel the power of his compassion, which had somehow seen her through the black months in Saint-Boniface. The love of her child was so trusting, so unconditional, it lifted her out of the distress that a moment ago had overwhelmed her. Soon they caught their first glimpse of the ocean glittering under the summer sun. Florence was gone, never to return, but some part of her lived on in Catherine, in the resemblance all three of them shared. She took the baby into her arms and held her closely, kissing and caressing her, for the remainder of the journey.

At the Carleton station they were met by Gabrielle's brother Théo, a brawny lad in his twenties. The two had been close as children and their reunion was a noisy, tearful one. After Théo had loaded their bags onto the driver's seat of the calèche he'd acquired second-hand, in hopes of profiting from the tourist trade, they set off for Florence's house, which was about halfway between the villages of Carleton and Bonaventure along the coast.

As they turned into the long drive that led up to the house, Jeanne and Gabrielle recognized a white figure standing on the porch, waving a handkerchief for all she was worth. Rose had not seen her daughter since the previous September, when she had left under Florence's protection to have her child—the child that no one here must ever know existed. Many things had happened since then, and Rose had suffered through long silences, interrupted by cataclysmic bursts of bad news coming from Montreal. First Florence's death, announced in church by the priest, and then Gabrielle's letter containing the veiled but unmistakable references to "Lisette, the poor girl I told you about" who had lost her baby to the epidemic. She hadn't even had the consolation of comforting her daughter, and her sorrow had been all the lonelier to bear as there was no one in whom she could confide, not even (in this instance, least of all) the parish priest. Since Christmas the news had been mostly good, however, and she was deeply grateful to Jeanne for rescuing Gabrielle from the hopeless situation in which Florence's death would otherwise most certainly have left her. For eight months she had pined and fretted in secret, but now she allowed the strenuously maintained edifice of her composure to crumble in a moment at the sight of her youngest daughter stepping down from Théo's carriage with a baby in her arms.

<h2 style="text-align:center">3</h2>

The sound of the sea was like breathing, deep and regular. The waves broke in long sighs on the coarse sand, which was strewn with fine pebbles where the sunlight caught and glinted. The beach was soggy this morning, its surface pockmarked, riddled with tiny craters left by the night's rain, soon to be wiped clean by the wind. The rhythm of the sea had gradually permeated Jeanne's consciousness, smoothing it like sand, leveling and cleansing her perspective until the people and events in her life seemed as peaceably remote as the dark blue horizon. Her days had settled into an unhurried routine of long walks along the shore in the mornings on fine days, or gathering flowers in the field behind the house if the beach was too blustery, and quiet hours in the afternoons while the baby napped and Gabrielle helped Rose in the kitchen—a regimen very like that under which Florence had liked to live. Twice a week Théo came round to take his mother and sister to town to buy groceries, and Jeanne had Catherine and the house to herself for the day. As Jeanne sat rocking the baby to sleep, to the quiet flapping of the blind in the afternoon breeze, she gazed at the child's plump little face, the delicately veined, almost diaphanous eyelids, the long dark lashes resting on her cheeks, the skin so fine-textured no pores could be detected, as smooth as the petals on a rose. She had never before had the opportunity to study anyone else's face so closely; nor had she wanted to. Now, besides Catherine, there was Shpazhinsky. She remembered the urge she had felt to stare at him as though to fill herself with the sight of him, until his features were indelibly imprinted on her senses. After the weeks spent here, even the images of him that she cherished most faithfully had faded, and the euphoria they produced had worn off. The hunger inside her was dulled, and her heart, finally, had found some kind of peace.

Jeanne tucked the baby snugly into her cot and went down to the sitting room. It looked out onto the sea. Florence's absence was palpable, in this room as it was in all the others. Everything in the house was still exactly as they had left it in September, but without her, the sheen of familiarity with which the past had hitherto endowed it had been stripped away. Despite the comfort of this place, where she had once been happy, Jeanne knew that she would find no respite from the loneliness that hollowed out her days. She wandered through the house, searching for a trace of Florence's passage, her fingertips absently skimming over inanimate objects where her aunt's fingers might once have lingered. Jeanne had always loved the sunny space of the tiny, cluttered room that Florence called her studio; now it was a chapel, filled with relics of her beloved friend. The dozens of unframed canvases leaning against the wall all testified to Florence's love of the Gaspé landscape. From here the two of them had often set out, drawn by a certain quality of light or by the drama of a windy day, in those last two summers of Florence's life. Her aunt had studied art for two years before her marriage and her paintings had a naïve elegance, a clarity of color that admirably conveyed the beauty of this place. The room was filled with her possessions, from the small bookcase crammed with books of art criticism, poetry, and travel, atop which squatted an earthenware pot bristling with paint brushes, to the paint-spattered wooden tray littered with half-used paint tubes. Here was her easel, and flung carelessly over it, as if its owner had been called away momentarily, the paint-speckled old smock she had worked in.

In a corner of the room stood the Canadian pine wardrobe, painted a cornflower blue, where Florence kept her art supplies. Jeanne opened it. It was well stocked with canvas and various types of paper, boxes containing pastel and charcoal crayons, watercolors, inks, chamois skins, more pots for mixing colors, and at the very back a large brown portfolio that Jeanne had not seen before. It was pigskin, reinforced at the corners, and tied together with silk cord on three sides. The inside of the cover bore an inscription in half-faded ink, which at first glance seemed curiously illegible until she realized that it was written in Cyrillic script. It didn't take her long to decipher the name of the portfolio's original owner. Jeanne ran her hand over the soft, worn leather of the cover. The paper on the inside of the binding was yellowed with age. She wondered whether it dated back to his student days in St. Petersburg. She felt a kind of reverence before this stray evidence of his past, this lost companion of his younger self. There was something oddly moving about this forgotten repository of his early strivings languishing at the back of a cupboard in a remote corner of the Gaspé coast. The mere fact that

Florence had had it in her possession spoke volumes about her friendship with the man to whom it had belonged. She must have been far more to Shpazhinsky than a mere social acquaintance for him to have made her a gift of so personal a nature.

As soon as she began leafing through the contents of the portfolio, Jeanne realized that the watercolors, charcoals, and inks it had been used to store were not by Florence at all—although she was the subject of every drawing it contained. There was even a series of sketches for the mysterious portrait that now hung in the living room on University Street. But the stunning thing was that nearly all of them were nudes, and they struck Jeanne as the most daring and the most sensual depictions of a woman's body that she had ever seen. It was as though the tender boldness with which she had felt herself almost physically caressed when she first caught Shpazhinsky's eye, that afternoon at the senator's, had somehow materialized in his art. Unlike the somber nocturne of the portrait, the woman he celebrated in his drawings had all the warmth, gaiety, and softness of the Florence Jeanne had known, and which she now recognized as the attributes of a woman loved. With what serene self-confidence she had inhabited her body, now abandoned to the profanations of the grave. As she pored over the drawings of Florence lying or reclining in sleepy abandon amid the languorous disarray of an unmade bed, Jeanne was caught up in a swirling rush of admiration, envy, jealousy, longing, self-pity, shame, and despair.

Florence, Florence, she mourned, there is no one else. Since her arrival here she had achieved a fragile peace, mainly through the comforting reminders of Florence that surrounded her. Now that peace had been shattered. She was suffocating with need, she was haunted by questions. Were you lovers? she wondered, ashamed as though she had been peeping through the keyhole or eavesdropping at their bedroom door. Was it possible to be so radiantly oneself before a man? Why could she see no immodesty, only vulnerability, in Shpazhinsky's portrayal of her? Seeing Florence through her lover's eyes, Jeanne admired and loved her all the more. She had loved, she had been loved, as she had deserved to be. But then why, if she had herself experienced joy, had she not tried to dissuade her niece from marrying someone she did not love? Jeanne could never bring herself to believe that Florence had not had her best interests at heart. But what had her aunt been thinking of? Having loved and been loved, or so it seemed, did she not wish the same happiness for Jeanne? For the first time since Florence's death, Jeanne felt abandoned. What closely guarded secret could possibly explain this painful enigma and restore peace in her heart? Did *he* know? Would he tell her? All those afternoons she had spent with Florence, all those confidences, and yet there had never been the slightest mention of him. Why? Did she not think Jeanne worthy of her trust?

There was nothing left to say. She felt sapped, hollow. Still there was the question of what to do with the portfolio. Instinctively she knew that she could not leave it here to be discovered, one fine day, by some God-fearing relative of Florence's late husband. Her aunt had taken such pains to keep her relationship with Shpazhinsky— whatever it was—secret when she was alive, that the secret must be kept still. There was nothing for it but to take the lot back to Montreal and return it to its original owner without further ado. There was no need for Mick or anyone else to know the intimate details of Florence's love life. The main difficulty lay in the size of the portfolio; it could not be easily concealed and was bound to stand out amid her other baggage—unless perhaps she were to flaunt it and, if asked, to say that Florence had given it to her, years ago, but kept it at her seaside home in anticipation of their future painting excursions together. Just to be on the safe side, she inserted several watercolors of her own, along with a good padding of full-sized blanks, at the front and back of the portfolio, and put it safely away in the cupboard in Florence's bedroom, where she now slept.

4

New York, July 1919 The door of the tenement opened slightly, and a pair of wary eyes sized up the visitor.

"Yes?"

"Michael O'Neill, from the Montreal section."

The lock-chain fell and the door swung open.

"Come in, come in, we were expecting you. My name's Sean Lynch," said the man, who spoke with a New York accent.

Mick entered a large room; at the back, two long tables had been placed end to end. A huge green-white-and-orange Sinn Fein flag adorned the far wall.

"Mr. de Valera's assistant is leaving for Dublin this afternoon. He should be here any minute."

Almost at once there was a knock on the door. Lynch went and opened it, and made the introductions.

"Liam O'Neill, this is Michael O'Neill, from the Montreal section."

"O'Neill, say?" said the fellow, shaking Mick's hand. He was young, in his early twenties, tall and powerfully built, with a strong handshake. "Do you know where your people came from originally?" he asked.

"From Cork," answered Mick. "My grandfather came from there."

"Well, think of that—that's where I'm from," said the young Sinn Feiner in a lilting Irish brogue that enchanted his Canadian namesake. "When did your grandfather arrive in Canada?"

"He left Ireland in 1832, during one of the lesser famines."

"You don't say. My own grandfather made the trip that year, but he didn't stay. He'd got on a boat with his brother, but the two had a falling out during the voyage. When they got to the other side, they split up, and my father went home to Ireland a few months later—"

"My grandfather," interrupted Mick, "crossed the Atlantic under identical circumstances! In the family we've always wondered what happened to the other branch."

"What was your grandfather's name?"

"Brendan," said Mick, his eyes widening incredulously. "Brendan O'Neill ... And yours?"

"Seamus!" grinned the Irishman. "Brendan was his brother's name. They were barely more than boys when they parted ways."

"Did you know him? Did he ever tell you what they quarreled about?"

"I only know that when he returned to Cork, he married the very girl his brother had left behind. He died, however, long before I was born, in the rising of 1867."

As they spoke the two men had moved toward the tables at the back of the room.

"Let me honor his memory—with this," Mick said, setting down the briefcase that had not left his side since his departure from Montreal the previous night, and sliding it toward his newly discovered cousin. "It gives me great pride," he continued, in a formal tone that reflected the solemnity of the occasion, "to hand over to you, on behalf of the Irish community of Montreal and Quebec City, an initial contribution to the Irish Republican loan, of $20,000."

Liam O'Neill opened the briefcase and whistled approvingly as he examined its contents.

"The Minister of Finance, Michael Collins, will be very appreciative," he said with quiet sincerity. "This is a magnificent contribution. Ireland is forever beholden to you for this."

"I know how much is needed." Mick nodded gravely. "What is the latest news from over there?"

"The war is intensifying. Ireland is full of enemy troops. There have been arrests and reprisals. The British Crown has nothing to offer the Irish people but armed occupation. In fact, the British troops are inflaming public opinion to such a degree that Sinn Fein has never enjoyed so much support. Even the Catholic Hierarchy declared last month that the only way to resolve the conflict was to put an end to the armed domination of Ireland, and they demanded that the Irish people be allowed to choose for themselves the government under whose authority they wish to live. Think of it. In 1916 there was almost no one willing to take our side, whereas now ..."

5

Bonaventure, August 1919 Every summer, the house was full of nuns. This year Madeleine Langlois had enticed four of them away from their Ottawa convent to act as her spiritual ladies-in-waiting for the summer. Early each morning they could be heard rustling off to mass in their long habits, and their company so entertained Madeleine that she would let the rest of the house sleep in until her return from church. Besides the sisters,

Jeanne, little Catherine, and Gabrielle, there was another new addition to the household that summer. Her name was Claire, and although fully fourteen years of age, she looked barely more than ten. She was pale, thin, and prematurely stooped, and her sallow little face was heavily scarred, as were her arms and legs. As a small child she had been regularly beaten by her drunken father, and later, after he had finally deserted the family, little Claire was taken to the Ottawa cloister of the Sisters of the Five Wounds, the religious order to which Madame Langlois had ties through the good offices of Father Plantin. There the child was left, abandoned on the front steps, and there she had been found, waiting listlessly in a little heap in the corner of the portal. She was then all of eight years old. At length it had been suggested to Madeleine Langlois that she could perform a resoundingly good deed by adopting the waif, which she promptly did, with the eagerness of a politician planting an IOU—this one, presumably, to be collected from the Almighty at a later date. This probably explained her treatment of the girl, who from the moment she entered the household was never allowed to forget, indeed was constantly reminded of, her debt to society and, in particular, to her adoptive mother.

Claire had been raised on a steady diet of hard work and prayer, but her status in the household was much lower than that of the humblest servant girl, who at least drew wages for her pains. Nevertheless, the sight of the poor foundling forever scrubbing, polishing, washing, folding, starching, ironing, mending, helping with menial chores in the kitchen, and generally providing Madeleine with her God-given pound of flesh, never failed to afford her benefactress the satisfying feeling that she had been truly generous, and never elicited from the visiting sisters anything but displaced admiration. "The little one is earning her place in Heaven," they would murmur to each other as they bustled by. Often they would be on their way out to the beach, where they could be spotted a short time later, veils billowing in the wind, skirts ineffectually hitched as high above their black-shod ankles as they dared, as wave upon wave soaked the heavy cloth up to their knees, giggling giddily like middle-aged schoolgirls as they boarded a small fishing boat for an afternoon's outing. Theirs was a gentle, innocuous presence, and Charles Langlois did not take exception to the annual conversion of his house into a quasi-nunnery. They kept Madeleine busy, happy, and thus thankfully out of his hair—most of the time.

"With all due respect, sir," Mick was saying, in an unusually brusque manner, "I trust it won't be necessary for me to go into the reasons why I won't attend ..."

He offered his father-in-law a cigarette and gave him a fierce look. The two men as they talked were standing on the veranda, looking out at the sea.

"Yes, I understand, Mick," Charles Langlois answered patiently, "but if you'll permit me, I would advise you not to make a show of it. I'm sure you'll agree that such opinions could be detrimental to your career. Find a credible excuse to stay away and then stick to it. It won't be simple, you know. The entire city will be turning out for the event. No-shows will be noticed."

"Charlie! I can smell tobacco smoke in here!" shrilled a female voice from the interior of the house.

"Come, let's go sit under the pergola. There's a nice breeze blowing."

Mick had always admired his father-in-law's quiet dignity. Even in the face of constant criticism, he remained as unruffled as his white summer suits, which were always crisp and neat even on the muggiest days. He moved unhurriedly, with giant majesty, as though going out of doors had been his intention all along. They sauntered toward the small arbor, which was covered in white climbing roses. The white-haired older man sat down in his wicker rocking chair facing the ocean, and motioned to his son-in-law to take a seat.

"God only knows," Mick said, in an angry tone, "why French Montreal should turn out in droves to see the Prince of Wales—a conquered people kissing the boots of the conqueror's descendants!"

"You know as well as I do," replied the member for Bonaventure with his usual equanimity, "that the Crown is our best protection against racists and bigots. It is the guarantor of our religious and linguistic rights, our bulwark against Americans and Orangemen alike. The people know that, and they will make sure that the future king is heartily reminded of his duties and responsibilities toward them."

"All the same, sir," Mick spoke with barely contained sarcasm, "I've just returned from New York where I met with people who've had firsthand experience of the British Crown's magnanimity. Why, hasn't it just recently shown its generosity by outlawing the Irish National Assembly, duly elected by the Irish people!"

"You're entitled to your opinion, and I respect your convictions, Mick, you know that. But take my advice and keep them to yourself. Public sentiment at the moment is running very high in favor of this visit and of this Prince. French Canadians may have refused conscription, but the war is over, it's been won, and many of them willingly laid down their lives for a cause that history will record as just. Our country is still in its infancy. It will need bright, passionate men like you to lead it to full nationhood. Men of vision and above all compassion, strong and farsighted enough to lift our peoples out of the quagmire of the past, to enable them to transcend the limitations imposed on them by tradition and the accidents of history. It matters little, in the end, whether you are there or not, on September 2. That stopover was more or less an afterthought, stemming from a spontaneous request from His Royal Highness himself. He seems to have more political acumen, for all his youth and inexperience, than our own protocol people, since he deemed it unwise to bypass Montreal on his way out west, even though he is scheduled to return for a longer visit later. Nevertheless there will be functions, on the occasion of that second visit, which you as my son-in-law, and Jeanne as my daughter, will be expected to attend. What you don't want is for some obscure Orangeman in Ontario, ten years from now, to cast doubt on your patriotism or your perceived loyalty to the Crown on the basis of some trifling oversight of a decade before. In politics, as you know, it's best to leave nothing to chance."

Mick drew mightily on his cigarette and answered, less belligerently this time, "I'm grateful for the advice, sir. I assure you I don't take it lightly. I shall certainly look forward to reading your speeches in the papers."

"One day, my boy, it could be you making speeches to welcome a future king to our city. In the meantime you should never allow yourself to lose sight of your broader goals. What about Jeanne—is she planning to go?" added Charles Langlois, motioning far down the seaweed-strewn beach toward the parasol under which his daughter sat reading.

"She's free to do as she chooses. I imagine she will. She's not necessarily bound by everything I think and do," Mick added stiffly.

"Just as well, perhaps. Good. Well, if she does go, she'll certainly *be seen to go*. Look at her. Who could fail to notice her?"

Mick nodded in agreement, but the thought was painful to him, like his old wound when it rained.

3

The Sin of Music

Dawn broke gray and misty that second of September as the population of Montreal prepared to welcome the Prince of Wales on his unofficial stopover before continuing his journey west. There was plenty of residual enthusiasm for one of the figureheads of the victory that many Canadians had fought so hard to secure. The jubilation of that triumph still hung in the air as, all over the city, along the forty-mile route that the Prince was to follow, homes proudly displayed the Union Jack, along with the other Allied flags. Long before nine o'clock, huge crowds gathered around Windsor Station. As the visit was an unofficial one, there was no band, but the bells of nearby Saint George's Church pealed out patriotic airs. At ten o'clock precisely the royal train, with its huge engine bearing the royal coat of arms and the two royal standards at the front, drew into the station. The gates were opened and the mayor, accompanied by civic, military, Church, and other dignitaries, was ushered down the platform. The Prince, looking slim and boyish in a gray morning sack suit and matching gray fedora, appeared at the door of his private coach and, seeing them approach, promptly stepped down to meet them.

2

The stableyard seemed deserted. Jeanne got out of her car, picked up the portfolio, hesitated, then laid it back on the seat again and shut the car door. A sleepy stillness, humming with the chant of insects, hung over the low buildings in the heat of late summer. The door of the small office was open. There was no one inside. As she walked past the tack room she could hear the snuffling of horses in the stalls nearby. Coming out of bright sunlight into the cool of the stable, momentarily disoriented in the sudden darkness, she began cautiously making her way down the line of boxes where great dark horse shapes quietly loomed. She heard whispering in one of the end stalls, punctuated by the rasping of a currycomb against a horse's hide. Her whole body shivered with tension. The Russian had loomed so large in her mind for so long that she felt a kind of physical terror at the imminent prospect of his presence. All summer long in her mind she had rehearsed this moment. Now that it was finally upon her, she realized too late that the situation, unlike the controlled conditions of one's imagination, was volatile and utterly unpredictable.

She started at the sight of him and shrank back slightly. He had his back turned and with long, easy strokes was rubbing down the chestnut mare Lara, patting her neck and muttering to her in a low, soothing croon. The mare's box was thick with dusty sunlight coming in at a small square window. The rich, pungent odor of horse and fresh straw, of oats, leather, and manure seemed to go to her head. She watched in silence as he ran his hands over the horse's back and rump. The mare's muscles rippled to his touch.

"Do you always groom them yourself?" she blurted, in a panic lest he suddenly catch her gaping at him. Shpazhinsky turned his head and gave her a questioning look, which soon dissolved in amusement when he saw how deeply she was blushing.

"Only Lara," he answered good-naturedly. "It calms her nerves before going out."

"I'm sorry, I'm a little early, I ..."

"No, no. Come." he said. He smiled, but his eyes, as large as a child's in proportion to the rest of his face, looked out from such a melancholy depth that she was not able to sustain his gaze for long. "You can keep me company while I saddle her. Did you have a good holiday?"

"Not very exciting, but restful, I suppose. And yourself?"

"I read your father's speech this morning in *La Presse*."

"He didn't get to give it, you know. There wasn't time. The Prince's motorcade took so long, through all the crowds, that there was only time for the mayor's welcoming address."

"Still, it was a good speech. You must be very proud."

"Yes, he was one of the dignitaries invited to the luncheon on Mount Royal in honor of the Prince. I went to Windsor Station in the morning, just for the fun of it. Daddy was on the platform with the mayor and the others, to meet the train."

"And did you meet His Royal Highness?"

"Oh, no! I wasn't part of the delegation, I was in the street with everybody else! You wouldn't have believed the crowds, and the shouting, and shoving, just to catch a tiny glimpse of the Prince getting into his Rolls-Royce. Especially when just about everyone there voted against conscription. From everything I've heard and read, he was met with the same delirium everywhere he went."

"People need gods," Shpazhinsky said, easing the bit into the mare's delicate mouth. "Even the Bolsheviki understand this very well. They got rid of the Tsar, that fallible little god of flesh and blood, only to replace him with History—a far more ruthless and inexorable deity, but neatly predictable, or so they claim—in whose name tyranny once again is alive and well in Russia ..."

He frowned and, stroking the animal's velvet muzzle, seemed temporarily to lose interest in the conversation. Then, leaving the mare in the box, he crossed the aisle to where Pushkin, saddled and bridled, stood waiting. He tightened the saddle a notch, and adjusted the stirrups. By the time he came out again, leading the tall gray horse by the reins, the silence of the stable was almost oppressive. In a moment however he was helping Jeanne into the saddle. He smiled up at her, his eyes conveying their unsettling blend of candor, knowledge, and unselfconscious power.

They set out, and all at once the many pleasures of a beautiful summer's day—the sun pummeling her back, the hypnotic shrilling of crickets, the twitter of birds in the foliage at the edge of the wood, the shiver of aspens, leaves shimmering in the hot breeze—crowded in on her senses. And when, reaching the open field, they broke into effortless canter, the exhilaration of moving through space at speed set her rioting pulse pounding in time to the horse's hoofbeats, hammering the ground with her joy.

"I spent July in Florence's house," Jeanne ventured,

pulling up behind him on the narrow path into the wood.

"Oh?" he said, barely turning his head. Jeanne sensed that he would skirt the subject of Florence if at all possible.

"The weather was exceptional," she pressed on bravely. "I found a copy of *The Idiot* and finished it in three days. It was the first time I'd read any Dostoyevsky."

"Ah, Prince Myshkin and Rogozhin!" he declaimed sarcastically. "The saint and the brute, the two extremes vying for the Russian soul. Nowhere else in the world is such passionate idealism found side by side with monstrous barbarity."

They rode on in single file along the shady path. Shpazhinsky seemed moody and irritable for some reason, and Jeanne hung back, silently waiting for the moment to pass.

"You knew my aunt well, didn't you, Vladimir Sergeievitch?" she finally asked, point-blank, as they reached the edge of a small clearing.

"You could say that," he answered, gazing at her steadily. Jeanne's cheeks were flushing hotter as her resolve began to wane. Aware now of the enormity of the indiscretion she would be committing when she returned the portfolio, she lowered her head, her hands tightly gripping the reins. Then suddenly she seemed to cross the point of no return in her own mind.

"I still miss her so much," she said, raising her eyes to meet his.

"She was very fond of you," he answered guardedly, as though speaking from some entrenched outpost of remembrance. But he was already nudging his horse forward again. They reached the dirt track that led back around the mountain. The path widened and the tangle of tree branches opened out onto blue sky over their heads. Jeanne felt the pall of self-absorption that had momentarily threatened to stifle her dissipate in the glorious September sunshine.

"Did you know," Shpazhinsky said, "that the composer Tchaikovsky most admired was Mozart?"

"But their music is so different ... Tchaikovsky's is so ..."

"Emotional? Tchaikovsky was a man who suffered, and he poured out his suffering in his music. Music to him was a way to purge himself of his pain, a powerful remedy, like Greek tragedy, catharsis. Mozart's music is like a vision of platonic perfection. Tchaikovsky too was in love with Beauty, but he was not on intimate terms with her, like Mozart. Tchaikovsky was tormented, bullied by his ideal. Sometimes he was moved to destroy his own work. When Mozart composed, it was like taking dictation, he never changed a single note ... Here, when we get back," he added, nodding toward the cluster of buildings squatting at the lower edge of the field now just ahead, "I have something to show you that will interest you."

Jeanne started inwardly at the thought of the portfolio, wondering again whether she would dare give it to him, along with the secrets it contained, her knowledge of which its return would inevitably disclose.

Back in the stableyard they dismounted and allowed the horses to drink from the big wooden trough on the ground by the stable door. Shpazhinsky disappeared briefly into his office. Outside Jeanne stood waiting, oozing sweat, dust clinging to her skin, the sun beating down on her head in the hot, dry breeze. Soon he reappeared, holding what looked like a large book.

"Here," he said, handing it to her. "I am lending it to you. It was a present, very precious. I know you will enjoy it."

It was an album of gramophone records entitled: *Great Masterpieces—A Selection from Tchaikovsky's Late Symphonies.*

"How kind, Vladimir Sergeievitch. How can I thank you?" she stammered. She looked up into his eyes and was drawn with such force that for a moment she almost lost her footing. Then, gathering all the courage she could muster, she somehow pressed on: "Vladimir Sergeievitch, I too have something to give to you ... In the car ... I'm not sure if I should have, but I found it in Florence's studio this summer and ... I thought you would want to have it back."

He acknowledged the information with complete inscrutability. His gaze appeared to recede into itself, yet there was nothing veiled or dissimulating about his look. It was as if between them he had raised a barrier of glass. He seemed to be able to conceal himself while remaining utterly exposed. The top of the car was folded down. Jeanne had only to reach in, to lift it out of the front seat. Her mouth was dry, her stomach clenched. She wished the ground beneath her would open and swallow her up. But Shpazhinsky had already seen the portfolio. With a perfunctory "May I?" he plucked it out of the car and was beginning to untie it.

"They are very beautiful," Jeanne found herself murmuring as she watched him examine the portfolio's contents. He looked up sharply, as if he had momentarily forgotten her presence.

"You really think so?" he asked, catching her lightly by the chin.

"Yes," she answered helplessly. He released her and gave her a friendly little pat on the cheek. "I also have," she forced herself to go on, "the portrait you painted of her.

She left it to my father but he gave it to me. I had no idea—it wasn't signed—if you want it back I will gladly ..."

"You don't like it?" He smiled, crossing his arms and keeping his eyes firmly fixed on hers.

"Oh, but I do," she protested, looking down at her feet. "I've always found it so mysterious, so unlike the Florence I knew, and at the same time so believable ..."

"I'm glad you see that," he said, with obvious amusement but not condescendingly. "It was for a joke. She wanted a portrait of herself as 'femme fatale,' so you see, perhaps I succeeded in granting her wish. But you keep it," he added encouragingly. "If you like it, I'm happy."

He seemed neither disturbed, annoyed, resentful, nor even embarrassed, all of which she had dreaded each time she had imagined his reaction. She felt a tremendous relief at having been "forgiven" for trespassing into his past. She had somehow survived the ordeal of confession. She thanked him. He held out his hand in parting and she took it. But he took his time releasing hers.

"It was kind of you to go to the trouble," he said finally, motioning toward the portfolio. He opened the car door and Jeanne climbed in.

"Come back soon!" he said.

3

Watching her drive slowly away, Shpazhinsky's face resumed the melancholy expression that was its natural cast. The girl stirred his manhood, along with his grief. Since Florence's death he had been celibate, for the first time since his student days. She even stirred long-buried memories of Nadia, a fierce beauty who had viewed love as a reactionary bourgeois pastime and devoted herself to making revolution instead. They had both been picked up by agents of the Okhrana,*

* *Okhrana*: Tsarist secret police, forerunner of Soviet KGB.

but his grandfather's string-pulling at the Ministry of the Interior had obtained clemency for only him. Jeanne was as beautiful, without the fierceness. She was an innocent brimming with passion, a ripe fruit asking to be picked. He knew only too well he had but to reach, and catch her deliciously as she fell. She was so young, poised on the brink of womanhood. Certainly the jealous little man who was her husband was not equal to such a bride. He knew the type—ambitious, hard-bitten, fundamentally mystified by women, but not interested enough in them to bother to understand the one he had chosen. He was suspicious enough, though—Shpazhinsky had seen that much—and he would not be one to stand idly by if sheer gravity were to impel his prized possession into the arms of another man. This was not blasé, cynical St. Petersburg, where infidelity was tactfully ignored by the injured party for the sake of appearances or personal advancement. This society was altogether different. Its people were ruled by priests and the fear of sin, none more dreadful than the sin of pleasure. The tender coupling of man and woman was here reduced to a grim duty, sanctioned only by holy matrimony, for the sole purpose of reproduction. Adultery here entailed immediate and permanent ostracism. Even Florence, a widow with no children, had fretted lest their being seen together give rise to suspicion. Away from the horses they had met only irregularly, always at night, at his apartment in an anonymous part of the city. The portfolio held vivid memories of one such occasion, when the bitter cold had kept them in for several days and they had whiled away the time between lovemaking, she as his model, and he casting his nets of lines, striving to capture her elusive grace. His body had longed for Florence then, for the delicate ridge of her collarbone against his cheek, for her slender limbs enfolding him, for the smell and yielding softness of female flesh ... And now, here was this fawn-like creature whom Florence had loved and protected, this child who so resembled her. He could see himself losing his head over such a girl. In a way it was a sensation he craved, out of loneliness, as one might crave vodka. Twenty years ago he would have indulged himself without a moment's hesitation. But things were different now. The rules here were so punitive. Nothing but a great deal of harm could come of it. He sighed deeply, and pushed the thought to the very back of his mind.

4

Jeanne's thoughts were as wayward as wild horses. The palms of her hands slid on the leather steering wheel. Sweat trickled between her shoulder blades. The road ahead of her barely registered on her consciousness. She started out of her skin each time a bump brought her back to reality and the very real business of driving. Without realizing it she was experiencing the birth of an emotion for which she had no frame of reference other than the wickedness darkly warned against in childhood. It was a feeling she had harbored so secretly that she had never even thought of giving it a name, much less pondered its implications.

Shpazhinsky was now enthroned like a saint in the chapel of her imagination. The gramophone records he had lent her were his sacred relics, a talisman with which to conjure his presence. Joy overwhelmed her: he existed, he was alive, God was kind. Providence had put him on her path, had made him known to her. How else could she account for such a clear conscience, and the gratitude with which her heart was bursting? She realized that until now she had never believed very strongly in anything. Her belief in the sanctity of what she was experiencing was as complete, and as guiltless, as the heretic's conviction. The very notion of heresy was attractive to her, because of the solidarity she now felt with all those whom society had cast out. Shpazhinsky the exile was one of those, and the thought of being, however tenuously, connected to him by some common bond thrilled her. Time itself lost all reality. Part of her wanted to linger in the moment just past, straining to prolong its spell, while the rest of her was spurred relentlessly onward by curiosity and the alarmingly powerful desire to see him again.

5

She had to wait before she could make use of the talisman. When she arrived home it was already late. She rushed to change out of her riding clothes and wash the horse smell out of her skin and hair—for once she was thankful for Mick's incessant smoking. The house was silent. Gabrielle was not yet back from her afternoon walk with the baby, and Georgette would soon be starting to prepare dinner.

As Jeanne stepped into the deep, claw-footed bath, she remembered all the miserable baths she had taken as a child, and later as a young girl, forbidden to remove her long nightdress lest she catch a glimpse of her bare self, constrained to the awkwardness of washing herself under the yards of heavy cloth, then having to endure the cold, wet feel of it clinging to her skin, while she struggled to dry herself and pulled on her underclothes. She recalled the first time she had dared disrobe and enter the water naked, and how anxious it had made her. It had taken her weeks just to feel at ease in the water, to stop preposterously fearing someone would catch her even with the door locked. Even now, she still suppressed an urge to reach for her bathrobe whenever she heard someone passing in the hall. But not today. Never before had her nakedness felt so right, so pleasurable. The water enfolded her like an embrace; if she closed her eyes she no longer clearly knew where her body ended and the water began. Her sense of her own vibrant existence was so intense that it seemed death itself could only be some supreme form of being, boundless and transparent. She was determined to remain suspended in warmth until the last possible moment, nursing her newborn happiness, treasuring the beautiful Russian diminutive she had found inscribed in familiar handwriting on the cover of the gramophone album: *To Volodya, lovingly, F.* It sounded like a river, or a song. A secret name with which to baptize her obsession, an incantation to exorcise her loneliness.

6

The talisman that Shpazhinsky had entrusted to her was fearsome in its power. It drew her helplessly down to unimagined depths, into dark magical woods filled with foreboding. It delivered her defenseless into the tyranny of absence, and the torment of hope suddenly taking flight and rising high above, a soaring vision of impossible happiness, only to be brutally felled by murderous Fate. Each time the recorded music ended, Jeanne would awake from her trance, moved to intense pity for the composer whose tortured heart poured itself out in his music. She remembered Shpazhinsky's words—*nowhere has the torment of love been more potently described.* The magic it worked was intoxicating. After the first few bars, the tinny sound of the Victrola was forgotten, overwhelmed by the music that seemed to well up from the depths of her own mind, so penetratingly familiar were the emotions it conveyed. A powerful talisman, requiring her merely to close her eyes to summon the beautiful face of Shpazhinsky. It commanded self-surrender, as complete as that which had been asked of her in Saint-Boniface, but which her soul, try as she might, had then steadfastly refused. The music transported her to another world, where the heart soared and the senses exulted, a world far from prying, reproachful eyes, where she could indulge herself without restraint or shame. Music opened the locks that let her nature flood out. In that other world divine judgment was not to be feared, for music, as the ancients knew, was the voice of Creation itself. *Manitouba* ... The voice of God.

Someone coughed discreetly and Jeanne looked up in surprise from her daydream. Gabrielle was standing in the hallway at the door of the living room, holding little Catherine in her arms. The baby's cheeks were rosy with sleep, her eyelids heavy, her big blue eyes serious, as a baby's eyes on awakening always are. Jeanne got up and kissed her tenderly.

"I'll take her for her walk today," she told Gabrielle, taking the baby into her arms, "you can take the afternoon off if you like."

She went back to the Victrola and, with one hand, carefully removed the thick black disc from the velvet-covered turntable and slid it into its pocket in the album. Then, taking it and the baby upstairs to her room, she tucked it away in a drawer of her commode under a pile of nightdresses, and went out.

7

Jeanne resisted for as long as she could before surrendering to the keenness of her need. As the days passed, the music that she listened to over and over each afternoon took possession of her soul. Soon she lived only for those moments when the music held her in its spell, and she could indulge her imagination in ways that would have shocked her innocence a short time ago. As with any addictive drug, however, the sensual and emotional excitement that it produced soon gave way to loneliness and longing. She thanked heaven that in giving her this potent poison, Shpazhinsky had also provided her with an antidote: by entrusting her with a cherished possession, which she was obliged to return to him, he gave her the perfect excuse for seeking his company, and reassured her that he would be waiting. This time, there would be no summer-long delay to give her fascination time to wear off. Instead, Shpazhinsky had found a skillful way of forcing the budding flower of her desire, so that when Jeanne was once again before him, the toxin that had been introduced through her senses had invaded her whole self. Though her decorous nature made her struggle to conceal the nakedness of her heart, she was still so guileless that no one could have failed to notice how vulnerable she was.

8

Jeanne's addiction was progressing so rapidly that by October, her interest in riding had intensified to a thrice-weekly habit. One day at the height of the autumn, she found Shpazhinsky in the stableyard, huddled over a clumsy black object with an accordion-shaped snout. He looked up and smiled triumphantly, but said nothing as she approached.

"Jeanne," he said finally. Her heart stopped. He hadn't called her "Mme O'Neill" for weeks now, but neither had he called her anything else. It was as though he had unexpectedly taken a step toward her and was suddenly close enough to touch.

"I have a big favor to ask of you," he went on, smiling, still fiddling with the camera, and keeping his eyes on what he was doing. "I have had this since my Paris days. I haven't used it for a long time but I want to get back to photography."

His tinkering produced a series of clicks that seemed to satisfy him. Finally he looked up and smiled at her mischievously.

"Would you let me do a few portraits, sometime when you come to ride?"

"Of me, you mean?" asked Jeanne incredulously. Over time, Shpazhinsky had acquired in her eyes the stature of an oracle, mysterious and all-knowing, whose every manifestation of interest moved her to paroxysms of gratitude. She had forgotten that it was he that had first invited her here, and who each time never failed to renew the invitation (there had never been any mention of *lessons* between them), and she wanted to kiss his hands. Hers was the love of a starveling for the stranger who takes you into his house and invites you to his table to share his meal. Shyness combined with her pride to afflict her with such a terror of exposing her true nature that she feared sometimes he might take her for a simpleton. Shpazhinsky, however, who handled her like a nervous colt, was not fooled.

"I am not asking permission to take pictures of scenery," he chided, teasing her. "Don't pout—someday you will know what makes you so interesting and it will ruin you! Come," he said, waving her toward the waiting horses.

It was a breathtaking day. The variegated color of the maples was at its zenith and the palest yellow among them seemed to drip sunlight into radiant pools of gold. The air was warm, but with an edge to it that poignantly heralded the long dark months to come. It was a day for making the most of the present, for stealing the last glorious moments of the season before its priceless tapestry was blown to shreds by the north wind. Shpazhinsky took four photographs that day, and from the unhesitating way in which he chose the site, pose, and angle of each shot, it was obvious that he had composed every detail in his mind well before. At first Jeanne was intimidated by the camera's probing eye, but soon she learned to trust the homely instrument, and to look upon it as a depository for her innermost thoughts, to be decoded by Shpazhinsky later in the privacy of his darkroom, once she was no longer there to feel exposed. He had opened a window into her soul, and each time he peered in, the look she returned to him boldly invited him inside.

9

Winter was now but a turn in the wind away, and the cold gray days came soon enough. One afternoon, with snowflakes dancing through the air in advance of a bitter nor'wester, Shpazhinsky came out to meet her holding a magnificent lynx cap which he unceremoniously fitted on her head, ruffling it the way one does a child's hair.

"It was a gift from my mother when I left home," he explained, "to protect me from the St. Petersburg cold. I am lending it to you for the picture. There. You look like a tsarina."

Jeanne eyed him warily. He had once described the Empress of Russia to her in most unflattering terms, ascribing to her and her confidant, the infamous Rasputin, a large portion of the blame for precipitating the Revolution. Had it been allowed, he argued, to come about democratically, there might have been a very different historical outcome.

"Don't worry, that is a compliment," he chuckled.

Jeanne mounted her horse as Shpazhinsky, glancing past her, held the reins. His eyes narrowed suddenly as he caught sight of a black automobile parked on Shakespeare Road, a hundred and fifty yards away. Its appearance coincided with Jeanne's presence for the third time this week.

"Is anything wrong, Vladimir Sergeievitch?" she asked, noticing the change in his expression.

"Wrong?" he repeated absently. "Not much light today," he complained, scanning the low sky. "Maybe we can make a dark, dramatic picture. But we must hurry, the day is getting short."

On this urgent note they set out through the withered field, toward the barren hillside where the stark spines of trees stood out, brittle against the faded carpet of leaves. As they entered the wood, the sound of the horses' hooves resonated in the hollow silence, and that roused in Jeanne an instinctive reverence, such as she had once felt in the cavernous naves of churches. The trees seemed to pray to the muted sky, as stone pillars were meant to pray to the painted heavens of cathedrals, although stone pillars never seemed, somehow, to really leave the ground. Churches squatted, trees soared. As they neared the lookout, which Shpazhinsky usually skirted to avoid the sightseers who milled there whatever the weather, suddenly the whole mountain exploded with the sound of cannons.

"Punctuality is the courtesy of kings," he said, glancing at his watch.

The twenty-one-gun salute! Of course! The royal train was due in Windsor Station at two-thirty, but while the rest of the population crowded along the city streets in anticipation of the Prince's motorcade, and her own father was on hand to welcome the Prince back to Montreal, Jeanne had forgotten what day it was. To her that morning, it had simply been a Monday, and Monday was one of the days she lived for.

"Is your father in town?" Shpazhinsky called out, up ahead of her on the path.

"Yes!" she answered. "He's spending the week here. He'll be taking me to the ball on Thursday ..."

She fell silent. Shpazhinsky had slowed the pace of his horse in order to wait for her. Their eyes met and Jeanne looked uncomfortably away, for her innocuous remark hid the unseemly hope that, knowing where she would be that night unaccompanied by her husband, he might somehow contrive to be there himself. Shpazhinsky made no answer and rode on for a time in silence, scanning the surrounding woods for a suitable setting for the picture he envisaged.

"Over there," he called out, twisting back in the saddle and gesturing to the right. He trotted off and dismounted before she had caught up with him.

As she slid off her horse he caught her, his hands capturing her to help her down. She felt the pressure of his thumbs just below her ribs, stifling her breath. For a moment his eyes locked onto hers, destroying her will, scooping her out like flesh from an oyster, deliciously numbing her muscles. At last he released her with a comic growl of hunger, as a man forced to deny himself a sweet, in deference to a fractious liver, devours it with his eyes. Then he turned away, and the withdrawal of his touch left a burning emptiness in its place.

Shpazhinsky stalked off up the bank and she followed, their feet swishing through the damp autumn leaves, breaking the silence like paddles rippling the still waters of a lake. He motioned her toward a clump of birch trees near the top, white bark peeling off the trunks in flesh-colored ringlets. Jeanne placed herself in front of the trees and turned to face him. Jumping down from a rock a little farther up the slope, he took a few steps toward her, and, reaching out at arm's length, tilted the angle of the fur cap slightly on her head. Then, placing both hands on her shoulders, he smiled and settled her back against the smooth white bark.

"Now," he chanted softly, holding her by the chin. "Look ... at ... me."

He strode back up the hill and adjusted the camera.

"Eyes, Jeanne, eyes!" he admonished, clicking the shutter.

Shpazhinsky had already trained her to stay perfectly still after he had taken the first exposure, so that he could move in and take the same pose again at close range. Frozen as if by a spell, she watched him come nearer, all her senses on the alert, her heart thundering in her chest, like a doe caught out in the open, its every muscle primed for flight. But it was not with fear that her blood was pounding.

"Look ... at ... me. Good."

He looked up, releasing her from the pose. The chill in the air froze his breath. It flushed his cheeks and rimmed his nostrils and turned the blue of his eyes to water. He was very near now, though Jeanne had not moved, so near that with only a step he could stretch out his hand and touch her. She felt his fingertips brush her cheek.

Suddenly there were voices, ringing out from somewhere under the trees, growing louder as they came nearer. Shpazhinsky turned his head in the direction of the noise and doubled back wordlessly down the bank to where he had left the horses. It was not unusual to meet other riders or people out strolling in these woods. Some, Shpazhinsky even knew to say hello to. But something in his demeanor today unsettled her. The cold pecked relentlessly at her face. Apprehension needled the palms of her hands. By the time he returned she was shivering uncontrollably.

"It's nothing," he said, gesturing as he jogged up toward her. "Just some riders, one I know. They're gone now."

He took her almost roughly by the hand, and began pulling her along in the direction he had just come from.

She complied, a little breathlessly. "What is it?" She was not certain whether to laugh or be alarmed at the sudden change in his behavior.

Shpazhinsky ignored her and forged on, with a look of grim determination that was just exaggerated enough to keep her wavering between laughter and dismay. When they reached the horses, he took her forcibly by the waist, heaved her up into the saddle, and stalked off toward Lara, who had begun rolling her eyes and twitching in the raw air.

"Are you angry, Vladimir Sergeievitch?" she asked lamely.

"We can talk later. First you must see with your own eyes," he called back to her as he took off down the path at a fast trot. Jeanne followed docilely, bewildered by his abrupt change of mood, clinging forlornly to the hope that all would soon be explained and that she would somehow find herself back in his good graces.

Once out in the open he took a slight lead and arrived back in the stableyard at a walk, a little ahead of her, which gave him time to dismount, not in the middle of the yard as was his habit, but right up by the stable door, which could not be seen from the road. Jeanne, as expected, followed suit.

"Don't be alarmed," he said, taking Pushkin by the bridle and looking up at her with a seriousness that withered her heart and alarmed her very much indeed. "I didn't tell you before because you might have looked. Someone is following you."

"Those riders?" she exclaimed after a stunned silence.

"No. You must be very careful when you leave, not to look. On the road, a little up from here, is a car. The same car as last time you came here, and the time before also. Parked in the same place. This is not a coincidence."

"Are you sure, Vladimir Sergeievitch?"

A wave of unease swept down her spine. The cold made her eyes smart.

"I would not be telling you this otherwise. I have more experience than you when it comes to being followed," he said, in dead earnest.

It was all too much like a trap springing shut. She felt as lost as one can be on an open plain at the onset of a blizzard.

"You must not stay any longer. It will look bad for you," he cautioned, his voice softening.

"But Vladimir Sergeievitch, what is going to happen? What should I do?"

She made no attempt to contain her distress and, for once, didn't care who knew it.

"Let me help you. Come on Wednesday," he said, lowering her and for the first time holding her in his arms. "Do as you do normally," he went on. "We'll ride as usual and can talk then. Until then, act as if nothing happened."

He released her, gently lifting the lynx cap off her head and smoothing her hair back into place. Then, taking her firmly by the shoulders, he swung her around, aimed her in the direction of her car, and pushed her gently forward.

"Now, go," he said in a voice that did not invite a backward glance.

On her way out, Jeanne noted with distress the presence of the car Shpazhinsky had described. Still deeply shaken by the tenderness he'd shown just moments before, she grappled with the intensity of it, striving to maintain an even keel. Careful not to deviate from her usual route home, she drove unhurriedly though her nerves screamed for speed, her foot cramped over the accelerator pedal, her hands gripping the steering wheel, as frightened as an inexperienced cabin boy alone at the helm in a gale.

10

Till Wednesday then. Jeanne huddled inside that promise like a bird fluffing out its feathers against a chill wind, but she was waylaid en route to her heart's destination by a mishap so trivial that the scale of its insignificance was matched only by the magnitude of its consequences. Because she did not see Shpazhinsky on Tuesdays, these were long, empty days, airless hollow spaces, waystations, nothing more, between the days that mattered, stones in the current for crossing to the other side of a life bisected by absence. In the afternoon the dressmaker arrived for the final fitting of the gown she was to wear to the ball in honor of the Prince of Wales. Small adjustments were needed, and another fitting was now to take place on Wednesday. But the hard-pressed seamstress, who was already working around the clock for several other clients with the same deadline and could not be pinned down to anything more definite than "afternoon," had unwittingly condemned the young woman she was working so hard to please to twenty-four hours of harrowing uncertainty. Because Wednesday was a day when Shpazhinsky was unavailable before three, Jeanne, hoping against hope, put off canceling their meeting until the last possible moment. Just to complicate matters, her parents that night were expected to dinner, when she longed more than ever to be left in peace, to nurse her anxieties at leisure. However her father's schedule since his arrival from Ottawa left him just one evening free of official duties and functions, none of which Mick would be attending. Dinner on Wednesday was the only opportunity the two men would have to see each other.

As soon as he had stepped off the train on Sunday night, the MP for the riding of Bonaventure had gone straight to a last-minute briefing with the mayor and the executive council, of which he, in addition to his duties as a parliamentarian, was a member. The first half of Monday had been taken up with preparing for the royal visit, which had gotten under way on the dot of 2:30 p.m. The royal train had pulled into Windsor Station right on schedule, heralded by a victory peal from the bells of Saint George's Church across the street. Emerging from his private car at the rear of the train, His Royal Highness, dressed in the uniform of the Welsh Fusiliers, had stepped, nay, bounded onto the platform as the military band played the first six bars of "God Save the King" and the guns on the lookout on Mount Royal boomed out the royal salute. As Mayor Martin, robed in ermine and wearing the ponderous insignia of his office, came forward to greet him, the Prince strode jauntily toward him, smiling broadly and extending his left hand (his right was almost crippled from handshakes sustained by the thousands in the course of his tour of the West). He fairly beamed, with the same boyish enthusiasm that had seduced Montrealers during his brief stopover in September. Here was a prince, thought Charles Langlois as the young man shook his hand and expressed his delight at seeing him again, here was a prince who worked hard at his job and did more to promote good-will toward the Crown than all of the King's ambas-sadors combined.

"You can imagine," Jeanne's father was saying, describ-ing his impressions of the royal visitor to his daughter and son-in-law two days later, "how tired he must be at the end of that grueling two-month tour ..."

They were sitting in the O'Neills' living room, the men enjoying an apéritif. Jeanne was happy to see her father, but her mother's aloofness exasperated her. She wondered why she'd even bothered to leave Ottawa, as she stayed resolutely away from all public functions and spent her time in seclusion, praying and reciting rosaries. Mick's presence, however, was more unsettling, for the latent hostility she had long felt toward him was now leavened with fear. Even though she had learned from childhood to endure the most absurd constraints, the nerve-shattering wait all that afternoon for the seamstress, who had finally appeared just as she picked up the telephone to call the Shakespeare Road Stables, had finally gotten the better of her self-control. Inwardly she screamed in the straitjacket of polite com-posure, heart beating, breath heaving against the tide of hysteria relentlessly rising within her.

"But you can take it from me," her father was saying, "and I've spent the better part of the last two days in the company of His Royal Highness, no matter how dull, how tedious the task, he is invariably gracious, and seems genuinely delighted to be here. He has a rare gift for enjoying himself and the people just love him. The soldiers in particular have a soft spot for him. He fought in France, of course, like them, but also, whenever he sees men in uniform he stops to talk to them. On Monday before leaving the station, even though there was a huge crowd clamoring for him just outside, he took time out to chat with some of the First Canadian Grenadier Guards that were acting as his guard of honor." Mick shifted uncomfortably in his seat.

"Oh come, Mick, you have to admit the Prince is immensely popular. Hundreds of thousands lined the streets to see his motorcade, and the enthusiasm of the crowds was extraordinary. A group of Laval University students down from Quebec City ran alongside his car almost the whole way. When we got to City Hall, they started up 'O Canada' and 'God Save the King' and soon had the whole crowd singing under the mayor's windows, and that went on the whole time we were inside. Then when the Prince reappeared, the cheers and the applause were tremendous."

"Forgive me," said Mick with contained sarcasm, "if I find the whole thing rather mortifying."

"Oh hush," Jeanne snapped, prompting a sharp look from her husband. "Let Papa tell us what happened."

"Well," her father sighed, trying his best to ignore the tension, "later His Royal Highness was at it again. There was a civic reception at City Hall. After a brief rest at his hotel and dinner, ten thousand citizens lined up to be presented to him. The police had a job keeping the crowd moving, four abreast, in an orderly fashion. As for the Prince, he stood the whole time, smiling graciously and saluting the people as they went by. Tired as he may have been, he—"

"He never once sat in the chair!" his wife interrupted

indignantly. "Why on earth you bothered to have it brought here all the way from Ottawa, just to have that boy make a fool of you again, I'll never know."

Charles Langlois glanced warily at the diminutive figure scolding him from across the room. She was incensed at him for lending the replica of the Speaker's Chair, which Lady Laurier had had made for him after the defeat of 1911, when his stint as Speaker of the House of Commons had been ended.

"That really is of very little importance, my dear," he soothed, with characteristic self-effacement.

"It was just the same the last time he was here," she clucked on, her face darkening by the second, "when they dropped your speech from the luncheon on Mount Royal."

"But, Madeleine," her husband cajoled, "you know very well that was because they were far behind schedule. The Prince, you'll remember, had a train to catch."

"Be that as it may, Charles. The French-language papers all reported your speech, and in most cases reprinted it exactly as though you had delivered it. The *Gazette* was the only one that didn't even quote from it, barely mentioned your presence, you, a member of Parliament and of the King's Privy Council, a former Speaker of the House and a prominent citizen of this town!"

"But, Mother," Jeanne interjected, exasperated. "Daddy's speech yesterday at Place Viger was reported in the *Gazette* this morning. They even called it 'a graceful speech.'"

"A most gracious speech, sir," added Mick, after a deliberate silence. "But I wonder if naïve isn't the right word to describe His Royal Highness's address in response to your very apposite remarks."

"My dear fellow," Charles Langlois replied, gratefully

picking up the glove that his son-in-law had thrown down, "surely you must agree that his speech was bold, even inspiring, in the way it tackled the fundamental question of Anglo-French coexistence in this country, and yet, just as remarkably in someone so young, tactful in the extreme."

His son-in-law's eyes narrowed, his gaze hardened.

"Inspiring, tactful, certainly. But with all due respect," Mick continued, with a restraint that reminded Jeanne of a predator about to pounce, "extraordinarily naïve when he dares to extol the wisdom of what he calls *the policy of racial unity in Canada*, based on, of all things, the British model of freedom of speech, freedom of language, and mutual respect! One is left to wonder whether His Royal Highness thinks us all cretins or whether he is himself terminally simple, to congratulate us for achieving the same heights of political harmony as that attained in his homeland. Perhaps he has forgotten that his own government is at this very moment engaged in a bloody campaign to crush democracy in Ireland! Exhibit A: the suppression, only weeks ago, of the democratically elected parliament of Ireland, which is now an illegal body in the country whose people it represents. Exhibit B: the state of siege which the Irish people must daily endure, their land ruled and occupied by hated foreign troops. A modest oversight, but there's more. Has the Prince of Wales recently been taken on a tour of the clouds that he should come back to this city and talk to us about freedom of speech, freedom of language, mutual respect? Does he not know, or does he think we are unaware of the fact, that the latest judgment of the Privy Council in London on the Ontario schools question, a matter that we all know to be particularly close to *your* heart, sir, that very judgment upholds and enforces a policy whose sole purpose is to assimilate us by prohibiting the teaching of our language to our own people outside this province, in spite of our constitutionally protected rights?"

Mick had not raised his voice, but the intensity of his indignation seethed in his inflection and his particular emphasis on certain words, in his eyes, and in his whole countenance.

"I take it you don't agree with the more didactic approach taken by *Le Devoir*, which chooses to take His Royal Highness's words as a cautionary statement of what *ought* to be?" his father-in-law replied, warming to the debate.

"It has to be said, sir, that in the climate of immoderate adulation which not only the Prince, but by association the King and Great Britain herself are presently enjoying, our bitter struggle against conscription and boundless oceans of blood notwithstanding, *Le Devoir* in its editorial went as far as it dared in exposing the Prince's almost laughable obtuseness on the subject. What can he have seen of the country from the succession of private wagons and private hotel suites and carefully orchestrated official receptions—"

"Oh come now, Mick," Charles Langlois finally interrupted him, his face coloring slightly against his snowy hair, "you can't seriously believe that tens of thousands of people can be 'orchestrated,' as you say? Can you be suggesting that the huge crowds that have turned out all over Montreal, day after day, wherever he's appeared, were made up of nothing but hand-picked, loyal *Anglais*? Of course we have problems in this country, grave problems, that I grant you," he conceded, "problems that are inextricably woven into our history, grievances whose redress will require a tenacious political will. I for one have certainly never been in favor of sweeping them under the rug. My position on the matter is in Hansard for all to see, and in all my years of grappling with it I have never compromised. But I believe it is our duty to shape the future, rather than allow ourselves to be shaped by the past. It's not enough to rail against injustice. It only exacerbates the very divisions we should be trying to heal. Build this country, improve it, that is where you should be investing your passion ..."

Just then Gabrielle appeared in the doorway of the living room in her starched uniform, holding little Catherine in her white nightdress, with rosy cheeks shiny from her bath. At the sight of her the four seated adults let out a chorus of *ahhhs*, and Jeanne thanked heaven for the diversion, knowing how belligerent Mick became when he drank. But as she was not usually privy to their discussions, she couldn't suspect that the two men took as much pleasure in their verbal jousts as others might in a game of tennis, and that except in the presence of ladies, most notably his wife, her father too enjoyed a good stiff chaser with his rhetoric. Mick, however, was still relatively sober, and in any case, when his daughter appeared the rest of the world ceased to exist. Drawing deeply on his cigarette, and peering through a veil of smoke, he watched attentively as the smiling infant, now a blossoming nine months old, was passed from knee to knee.

When Madeleine's turn came to hold her grandchild a strange thing happened. A change came over her, a change that Jeanne, in her distracted state, had not seen before. It was as thorough a transformation as when a momentary break in the clouds floods the landscape with sunlight. Her mother's eyes danced and the smile spreading over her face provided a glimpse of the dark beauty that had enthralled the hapless young journalist Jeanne's father had once been. The baby responded instantly, snuggling up close to her grandmother and cooing contentedly.

Jeanne's thoughts drifted away like leaves in the current, and almost immediately plunged into an abyss of want. Her sense of deprivation at having been kept from seeing Vladimir that day was acute. A traveler in the desert who finally arrives at an oasis only to find the well dry could not have been more distressed. The next oasis was Friday, two days' march away and to her, that night, it might as well have been at the ends of the earth.

4

A

Royal Ball

1

Vladimir Sergeievitch Shpazhinsky, Esq.
is cordially invited to attend
the Citizens' Ball
to be held in honor of
His Royal Highness
The Prince of Wales
on Thursday the thirtieth day of October
nineteen hundred and nineteen
at nine o'clock
at the Windsor Hotel

R.S.V.P.   Black Tie

Vladimir stared hard at the gold-embossed card that had
for weeks been lying amid the clutter of photographs,
cufflinks, shoehorns, and ashtrays on the desk top that
doubled as his dresser. The mere thought of seeing the
girl made his manhood stiffen and throb like a schoolboy's. Second adolescence, he shrugged. He reached for

his vodka glass and drained it all at once. As far back as he could remember, there had always been women in his life, to love or simply lie with, to comfort and be comforted by. Finding an outlet for his libido had never been a problem, and was not even now, he told himself, looking askance at the fine strands of white lacing his ash-blond hair, like the first yellow leaves on a maple in early autumn. No, his quandary was that his desire, like a stray dog that had found its master, could no longer be satisfied with any other.

Yesterday afternoon and the unaccustomed misery of waiting and waiting for her to appear had made it all perfectly clear. He wanted her, longed for her. He was infatuated, with no reasonable hope of satisfaction. Still, there was something oddly pleasurable about this intensity of feeling, even if it was mostly painful—perhaps because he had too often experienced the chronic depression of the uprooted person, and too long survived in an emotional desert, but most of all because he knew that Jeanne was his for the taking. She responded as vibrantly to him as the strings of a piano when its keys are barely touched. But it wasn't just wanting, it wasn't that simple. If it had been, he probably would have helped himself to her by now. Nor was it just residual loyalty to Florence that held him back. There was something about her, something untouched, like new snow, that made you reluctant to mar its smoothness and yet invited you to leave your imprint in it; something deep and impressionable that, were you to possess her, would make her wholly yours. She made him realize that what he sought was more than just a balm for his loneliness: it was to surrender his will, as though to blessed sleep. A kind of peace in which to lose himself completely. But he was falling in love with a child, and his longings had an urgency and violence that he hadn't experienced in twenty years. For all the tenderness, affection, and pleasure Florence and he had shared, he had not lost his head then the way he was losing it now. And there was no denying that, for all the relative freedom he now had, priests and their watchdogs were as prevalent and powerful here as the secret police and its spies had been back home in Russia. The black car that was following her meant that there would be nowhere to hide—that no matter what lengths they might go to, they could not shield their relationship from view. Assuming they could have kept any secrecy from being eroded and jeopardized by the evolving urgency of their mutual need, a day would inevitably come when her husband would be in possession of incontrovertible proof. Then not only would any liaison come to an abrupt end, but Jeanne would be cast out of her society. She would cease to be viewed as anything but an adulteress, an unfit mother, a disgrace to herself, her husband, her parents, and her friends. He hadn't even the luxury of pretending that she might resist him. He knew that he had only to touch her ...

He tore off the black necktie he had been struggling with and tossed it aside on the bed. He poured himself another glassful from the half-empty bottle. On the desk he picked up the faded photograph of his mother and his three brothers in its antique silver frame. *Volodya*, they had called him, and he could still hear their voices ringing out as they ran down the front steps toward him, each time he came home from St. Petersburg on holiday. He looked at each cherished face, now wiped from the plane of existence save for vestigial images such as this. His own beautiful mother, not six years dead, who had lost each of her sons in turn and seen the country she so fiercely loved devastated by war, and then convulsed in revolution. Brave, bold Maxim, last seen in Paris, where he had spent that too brief springtime of his life before returning home to Russia; Maxim who, following in their father's footsteps, and to his mother's unremitting sorrow, had invested his precious youth in a career in the military, only to be cut down early in the war, along with his entire generation of junior army officers, by the scythe of German military technology. And the two little ones, Pasha and Aliosha, who had refused to take advantage of the exemption from military service to which their rank entitled them; who had thrown their lives into gaping death and been consumed like blades of grass before a raging brush fire ... *Volodya*, they had called him, and nothing encapsulated the loneliness of his long, unpremeditated exile more than the name by which no one ever called him any more. Florence in a tender moment had once asked him the Russian diminutive of his name, and had sometimes used it in her letters to him, but it had never come naturally to her lips. *Volodya*. The name he'd left behind along with everything else ... Ghosts! His life left nothing but ghosts in its wake.

He looked around him at the walls, which, as in the rest of the apartment, were almost completely papered over with drawings and photographs. The most recent ones, all of Jeanne, had gradually taken over the space once occupied by a rogues' gallery of friends, former loves, and acquaintances. He stared at his pitifully unmade bed. There was at least one way in which all this might have some usefulness. Pain, after all, is good for the Russian soul! he declaimed angrily to himself. He lit a cigarette, unbuttoned the detachable collar of his dress shirt, and, grabbing the bottle by the throat, flopped morosely onto his creaky bed. He raised it to his lips and swallowed, hard, like a man administering anesthetic to himself before digging a bullet out of his flesh.

2

As Jeanne and her father alighted from their limousine in front of the Windsor Hotel, a great boom was heard on the flank of Mount Royal. A cry went up from the crowd of onlookers that had gathered to await the arrival of the heir to the British throne. The entire sky burst into incandescent bloom, lighting up the night with a gigantic effigy of His Royal Highness the Prince of Wales, set between a fleur-de-lys and a maple leaf like an enormous jewel between two lesser gems. It slowly opened out like some otherworldly flower, then faded and drifted earthward in a lazy shower of sparks. No sooner had this first configuration subsided than a second explosion was emblazoned on the night sky, this time with the coat of arms of the Prince of Wales, bearing the words *Ich dien*, the ancient motto of the Black Prince, in letters of fire, beneath banderoles blazing with the twin inscriptions *Bienvenue* and *Welcome*.

Looking up, Jeanne kindled the thought, warming her desolate heart by its tiny flame, that wherever he was in the city tonight, Vladimir would have heard the deafening staccato of fireworks and perhaps at this very moment was gazing skyward. He had become her principal frame of reference. Her need to see him was so pressing that it sought him everywhere. Everything around her, directly or indirectly, spoke to her only of him. Her very heartbeat was like some primal symptom of what ailed her. His absence obsessed her so that she sometimes felt as if she were outside herself. She spent a lot of time trying to imagine what the world looked like through his eyes, so that she sometimes fancied that she had become him. And yet she had not even lived. How could she know, let alone presume to guess how such a person as he might see the world? And although her thoughts of him strayed well beyond the bounds of what was called morality, they were only thoughts, she told herself, as harmless by comparison with the actions they evoked as were these fireworks with the bombs that had fallen nightly in the trenches during the Great War: although they lit up her soul, they broke no ground in the daily living of her life.

"What a marvelous display," her father was saying as they went in, "a masterpiece. I must congratulate the Hand Company people in Ontario. They've really outdone themselves!"

As they left the excitement of the street behind and entered the hushed, richly carpeted lobby of the hotel, a feeling of futility descended on her. Even though she knew that there were thousands of young women in the city tonight who would have given their eye-teeth to be where she was, she in turn would have paid any price to be allowed to vanish in the night and go to Vladimir, wherever he was. Indeed, had the opportunity arisen, Jeanne realized that she would not even have known where to find him. She did not figure in his plans. There was no room for her in his life. Unlike Florence ... the memory of the nudes he had painted, of the intimacy they revealed, smote her like poison in the heart.

As they reached the entrance to the Windsor room, the footman bellowed out their names. A new alertness quickened her pulse and brought all her senses sharply into focus. Somewhere in this ballroom, perhaps, Vladimir might be waiting. Somewhere in that anonymous throng of men and women ... But in the darker recesses of her mind anxiety lurked. All of Montreal high society was here tonight. Its most glamorous women, its most beautiful debutantes, dressed in their most dazzling finery, were assembled for the occasion. Jeanne scanned the crowd over and over again, picking out the prettiest, most elegant women and sorting through their male entourage, but to no avail. She couldn't help feeling a twinge of envy whenever she sighted a particularly attractive female—and there were many there, young debutantes in model gowns of every hue and texture: silk, satin, velvet, taffeta, chiffon, charmeuse, lace, or tulle, in pale pink, coral, shrimp, salmon, old rose, flesh, turquoise, Nile green, robin's egg, heliotrope; trimmed with sequins, beads, or Paris flowers, ornamented with garlands of roses or orchid corsages, even the occasional train and tiara, and the inevitable ostrich fan, in colors chosen to match or contrast with their gowns. Indeed, she couldn't help imagining that Vladimir, if he were here tonight, would not be indifferent to so much elegance and beauty.

As she made her way docilely on her father's arm, smiling distractedly as he greeted and introduced her to friends and acquaintances, the orchestra at the far end of the hall struck up a tune. Couples that had been idling before the stage during the break quickly reformed and resumed dancing, while newer arrivals joined them on the floor.

"Let's go and have a look at some of the other rooms," she asked her father almost pleadingly, for she now dreaded the very sight that she had been longing for moments ago. For the merest glimpse of Vladimir with his arm around the waist of some beautiful stranger would have been more than her frayed nerves could bear.

"But, Jeanne dear, don't you feel like dancing?" her father asked in surprise.

"Oh, Daddy, you know I don't know how to dance. I'd only embarrass you …" she said lamely. She was only half lying. Florence had taught her the tango, nothing else.

"Nonsense, my dear! I had better teach you quickly, before the Prince arrives. What if he asks you to dance? You'd have to say yes, you know." He smiled, taking her by the hand. It had been years since she'd held on to his hand, but it still seemed as huge as when she was a child. "Come on," he added, leading her onto the dance floor, "let me show you."

They were well into their third number when a hand landed lightly on Jeanne's shoulder. Her heart leapt in her chest.

"Hello, you two!"

Éloïse's singsong voice burst upon her consciousness. "My goodness, Jeanne, you look like you've just seen a ghost!"

"I'm sorry," Jeanne stammered, "you startled me!"

"My dear Éloïse, how elegant you look!" said Charles Langlois as she kissed his cheek.

She wore a long silk sheath of emerald green, with a matching satin bandeau, and a white feather aigrette in her red hair. Quite unwittingly, she had just sent Jeanne into another fit of nerves. She had not expected to run into Éloïse (had it really been so long since they had spoken to each other?) and yet here she was. Vladimir too could turn up at any moment! Once again her eyes began sifting restlessly through the crowd.

"… Hey!" repeated Éloïse, and Jeanne realized that her friend was speaking to her, and that she hadn't understood a word she'd said. "You are on another planet tonight!"

It was nearly eleven o'clock when the three orchestras fell silent, signaling the imminent arrival of the guest of honor. In the Rose Room and the Ladies' Ordinary, the crowd deserted the dance floor and streamed toward the main ballroom. The hall itself had been elaborately decorated, the color note being the British red, white, and blue. Flags of the Allies hung from the ceiling, while between the tall windows were draped panels of red, white, and blue bunting, with Montreal's civic crest bearing the quintessentially Canadian motto *Concordia salus*—salvation through concord. Above the stage at the back of the room, where the orchestra was again preparing to play, shone the Prince's crest in electric lights, with the royal arms over it and the legend *God Bless Him* in gold letters on a mauve background. As the guests gathered expectantly into two lines on either side of the main doorway, conversations resumed in a discreet murmur. News rippled through the crowd that HRH, having just arrived from another ball organized by the Grand Army of Canada, Vimy Post Number 4, at the 65th Armory, had been spirited upstairs to his rooms by the reception committee.

"I was invited to the military ball on Tuesday night," Éloïse whispered to Jeanne. "You should have seen him make his grand entrance under the fanfare of trumpets in his gorgeous uniform, between two rows of officers in full regalia. What a sight for sore eyes!"

At last the skirl of Scottish pipes down the hallway put an end to the small talk. As the orchestra launched into a fervent rendition of "God Save the King," the Prince made his entry, flanked by Mayor Médéric Martin and followed by the reception committee and members of his own suite. Jeanne watched him progress up the ballroom between the two lines of applauding guests. She was struck by his extreme youth and the surprising ingenuousness of his smile. He was very slim, his narrow frame, thin face, and pale complexion—though his cheeks were slightly flushed—lending him an air of frailty not normally associated with royalty. At the same time, he seemed entirely at ease in the role that fate had assigned him. His performance was as flawless, as seemingly effortless as that of a trapeze artist at the circus. He was as natural as it was possible to be, even though his naturalness, her father had explained, was the product of lifelong discipline and training. Like any other blue blood in the midst of commoners, he seemed to stand alone, but unlike most, whose distance from the masses was further emphasized by aloofness bred over centuries of hereditary rule, a kind of stoically accepted loneliness was what set him apart. Yet, according to everyone who'd met him, the Prince displayed the same ebullient zest for enjoying himself as any other young man in the aftermath of the war. It was easy to understand why the press, in its trite way, constantly referred to him as Prince Charming. As he reached the end of the double receiving line, the heir to the throne chose as his first partner a young woman gowned in pink satin holding a pink feather fan, who was said to have been in love with Talbot Papineau, the prime minister who never was, and whose death at Passchendaele in 1917 had broken so many hearts.

3

The house was quiet. The two servants had gone to bed and Kit had been sound asleep for hours. Jeanne and her father were still at the ball. Mick O'Neill sat in his armchair, a crystal decanter at his elbow. A cruel beast was gnawing at his heart. So far, the evidence was circumstantial, but incriminating nonetheless. Why else would she contrive to meet three times a week, come sun or rain or hail, with a man? A little convent girl like her was easy prey for such a man as that, with his bloody accent and his big calf-eyes, not to mention his reputation. Wasn't he getting a bit long in the tooth to go after game that young? What was he, anyway, if not a walking anachronism? The world he came from had ceased to exist. What could he possibly have to offer her? All he had was a past. No future, nothing ahead of him but melancholy old age. And yet the first time he saw them together at the senator's he knew; he'd smelled it, the way a dog smells danger. With time, however, that memory faded and there hadn't been any reason to pursue the matter further. Not, that is, until a few weeks ago, when he came home for lunch unexpectedly, with flowers for his wife, as he often had since the birth of their child—only to be told that Madame was out for the afternoon, and then, in reply to his questions, that yes, Madame often went out in the afternoons, every Monday, Wednesday, and Friday, in fact. Where did she go? he asked—and what husband wouldn't want to know where his wife disappeared to on such a regular basis. Madame didn't say. But she was dressed for *riding?* The revelation hit him like a fist to the face. For days he'd waited, hoping the lady herself would come forward, or at least make some passing reference to this consuming interest of hers. But her unbroken silence on the matter had told him more than he cared to know. The decision to have her followed was a radical one, but his wife was still so young, so innocent: he'd done it as much to protect her as anything else.

He scowled, the whisky reigniting his anger as it went down. The girl was a fool, an impulsive little birdbrain who made no effort to gauge the repercussions her behavior was likely to have for her own and her family's good name, for her husband's career, for their little Kitty's future. A wave of resentment engulfed him then, irrepressibly, like nausea but more odious, clouding his mind and blurring his vision. Suddenly his perception changed. Recalling that the Russian was a friend of Florence's, a person for whom he'd had such respect, and summoning his own wholly favorable impression of the man until Jeanne came on the scene, he now saw his wife as little better than a she-dog, sniffing and panting after the male, importuning him with her visits, making a damned fool of herself, and, by association, of her husband for not doing a better job of reining her in. To think she dared to bar him from his own bedroom! A second later a sneering vision appeared to him through the alcoholic fog in his brain, of the two of them locked in frenzied coupling. Another emotion tightened its noose around his throat. Hatred swept over him, wresting from him what few shreds of self-respect he had left. The decanter on the small ornamental stand beside him stood empty, having disgorged its evil genie. A strange calm descended on him then, as though a heavy burden had been lifted from his shoulders. A kind of numbness stilled his heart. He closed his eyes, and, to all appearances, slept.

4

On the stroke of midnight, supper was served. After the Prince had retired to the Oak Room to sup in private with a small privileged group, the other guests repaired to the Rose Room, the Green Room, and Peacock Alley for a buffet, delivered to the tables by the male guests, whose inexperience in the role of waiter was in a few instances compounded by a measure of inebriation, with disastrous if comic results. Jeanne went through the motions like a sleepwalker. The scene before her was almost one-dimensional in its irrelevance. Sounds reached her as if through fathoms of water. Vladimir would not be coming. The deprivation she felt was unendurable.

After supper the dancing resumed and the young Prince was again the focus of attention as he whirled his partners through fox-trot and one-step, to songs like "Johnny's in Town" and "Smiles," said to be his personal favorites. Although at first he singled out only ladies with whom he was already acquainted, the Prince now began requesting introductions to others, whose dancing or appearance had caught his eye. Thus it was that Jeanne suddenly found herself face to face with the young man, as he greeted her father in the warm personal manner that so endeared him to all who met him.

"M. Langlois, what a great pleasure to see you here, sir," he said, as usual extending his left hand. He spoke in a languid, slightly nasal drawl. "I was wondering if you would do me the kindness of introducing me to your lovely young companion here," he added, with a mildly ecstatic smile for Jeanne. "I'd be thrilled if you'd honor me with this dance, *mademoiselle*," he continued, after her father had quite distinctly presented her as *Mrs.* Michael O'Neill. "I'm mad about dancing, you know."

His Royal Highness's speech was almost imperceptibly slurred, his eyes unusually bright, but his dancing was as surefooted and graceful as any she'd been treated to all evening. He seemed almost weightless in his movements, and was as easy to follow as his mood was infectious. He seemed completely absorbed in the rhythm of the music, moving with a nonchalant grace, underlaid by the subtle tension that results from pleasurable concentration.

"This is the most fun I've had in my life," he went on in the rather stilted monotone of the English upper class. "I'm really dreading going back. *M'maaah* is such a dreadful bore."

Jeanne said nothing. Instinctively she grasped that her dancing partner, having consumed a liberating amount of booze throughout the evening, was merely thinking aloud, and that his thoughts were meant to skip like stones over water before sinking from sight. It would have been a considerable faux pas for her to have commented in any way. She noticed that when he wasn't smiling, his thin face, mournful eyes, and sad little mouth gave him an almost pathetic air. Unlike Shpazhinsky, whose magnetism suggested and stemmed from an intense and fascinating inner life, there was a wistful, unfledged, and ultimately shallow quality about the Prince that made her pity him, but without arousing her curiosity or eliciting from her the kind of empathy that might have made her want to know him better. This emotionless pity spared her the agony of tongue-tied, over-awed self-consciousness which that night bedeviled many an eager debutante.

The dance ended, the Prince thanked her, she curtsied again, as she had on being introduced, and watched him move on, his gait smooth, almost gliding, toward Madeleine Taschereau, lovely in a simple white chiffon frock embroidered in pink and green, whom he had twice danced with before supper. As the Prince came up to her, however, one of his aides was seen to slip a hand under his elbow and speak discreetly in his ear. The Prince replied by petulantly stamping his foot and snapping his finger, exclaiming "Oh rot!" quite audibly before excusing himself and following the aide, who clearly had already selected someone else for His Royal Highness to dance with. Suddenly, for no apparent reason, Jeanne felt herself choke with sobs.

"I'm so tired, Daddy, please take me home!" she said, turning to her father, and focusing intently on the far wall behind him to avoid looking into his face.

"What, so soon? But it's only one o'clock—are you sure you want to leave?"

Her father's genuine concern brought Jeanne to her senses. Why alarm him with incongruous behavior? Who in their right mind would want to leave now, moments after dancing with a future king? What better way to arouse suspicion? Jeanne took a deep breath, and finally gave her father a dry-eyed smile.

"There," she said. "I feel better now. I thought I was going to faint. It's so stuffy in here."

"Are you sure? We can go right away if you don't feel well," said her father solicitously, the look of puzzlement gradually ebbing from his eyes.

"No, let's stay. I feel much better."

5

The lights were still on in the house on University Street when Jeanne and her father returned around three o'clock that morning. The crinkle of dry leaves on the windblown pavement was the only sound in the chill night as Charles Langlois walked his daughter, shivering in her black satin wrap, to her front door. Declining her invitation to come in for a nightcap because of the lateness of the hour, he kissed Jeanne goodnight, and she watched him, by the light of the streetlamp, get back into his car and drive off into the darkness. Jeanne closed the front door, and seeing the lights on in the living room, was about to turn them off when she nearly started out of her skin. Mick was sitting stock-still in his armchair by the dead fire. He was wide awake and very pale.

"Goodness, Mick," she stammered, her heart pounding with dread, "you're still up! It's after three in the morning ..."

Mick's eyes narrowed. He leaned forward, lowering his head like an animal smelling fear.

"I don't need you to tell me what time it is," he glowered.

"I'm going to go to bed, I'm dead tired," she ventured, as airily as she dared, instinctively backing out of the room.

"Madame is tired, is she?"

As she reached the foot of the stairs, he lunged out of his seat, seeming to cross the room in a single bound, and caught her by the wrist. Jeanne let out a sharp cry.

"In whose arms did we amuse ourselves tonight, I wonder?" he growled, tightening his grip. "Or had we perhaps arranged a secret rendezvous, thinking no one was watching?"

"You've gone mad!" Jeanne struggled to free herself. Her anger at being unjustly accused, added to the knowledge that she would have given almost anything to have done precisely what she was being accused of, exacerbated the pain he was inflicting on her. "You know I was with Daddy all night. For God's sake, stop it, you're hurting me!" she cried, trying in vain to twist herself free.

"Think I believe you, you lying—"

"Mick! Stop it! You're drunk—"

"Shut your mouth!" he roared. "You dare to speak to me! You dare to look at me!"

He pushed her roughly up the stairs, forcing her to

scramble up ahead of him in a futile attempt at escape. From then on he was silent as he inflicted his pent-up rage, undiluted by thought or voice, on her body. He pushed her into the bedroom and shoved her onto the bed. No more reproaches, no more reprimands, only his hands mauling her, and the frightening strength that alcohol gave him. He took a long time to go off, priming himself frenziedly, pounding himself into her until she was raw, and then the brief seizure, the tremor deep inside his body, and he was done. He withdrew himself, rose to his feet, and left the room without so much as a backward glance, not bothering to shut the door behind him, which for some reason unnerved and humiliated her even more than if he had slammed it with all his might. She managed to get up and close it quietly, her hands shaking so badly that for a panic-stricken moment she thought the lock would not catch.

6

Mick awoke as usual on the dot of seven, his head throbbing as if from a blow. For a few seconds before his eyes registered the grayness of a cold November dawn he was still in his dream, on an empty rain-soaked street in pitch darkness, with his little brother Arthur calling to him somewhere in the night. But his brother's voice wasn't that of the seventeen-year-old he had been the year typhoid had claimed him. It was a voice from his boyhood, a call he'd heard so many times—once one Easter, when the five-year-old Arthur had sunk up to his knees in the soggy clay of an empty lot near their father's house and stuck fast, and so often as they were growing up, when some practical joke they'd played had back-fired and the irate victim had come chasing after them, Arthur as usual lagging behind him ...

Gradually the pounding in his head took over his consciousness. Sitting up slowly, he looked at his watch. The memory of the previous night, with its apex of savage pleasure, stuck in his brain like a shard of glass. He squirmed with shame at the thought of it, but his remorse subsided as the flames of jealousy began licking at his soul. His fists tightened and the pain in his head turned ugly. He reached for his cigarettes, and stood up gingerly. His aching mind craved clarity. He lit up a smoke, wondering whether to follow his impulse, which was to skip the coffee that his dehydrated body was demanding, and slip out of the house into the bracing autumn air. He hated these "mornings after" with their attendant stirrings of self-loathing. As always, his instinct was to turn the page and leave behind what could not be undone. There would always be time to bring things around when everything he was striving to build for himself began to benefit her in more tangible ways—and her pathetic infatuation had finally run its course. The private detective had been instructed to be discreet, but obvious. By now her friend could have no doubt in his mind as to the viability of their little idyll.

5
Life
Sentence

1

For Jeanne, Monday came almost as a surprise. Dazed and so brittle she feared breaking down at the sight of her husband, she had wasted the weekend avoiding him. She needn't have bothered, for Mick, grim and silent behind his newspaper, or else closeted in his study with his legal briefs, had stayed well out of her way. On Saturday afternoon she had bundled Kitty up in her pram and taken her for a walk through the grounds of McGill University. The six days since she had last seen Vladimir—since he had taken her in his arms, and she had realized that her life was about to change in some cataclysmic way—had sapped her resolve and eroded her will.

Today, she did not go out in her riding clothes as she normally did. Instead, she folded her tweed habit into one large hatbox, and her leather riding boots in another, both of which she carried out to her car just before lunch. She drove down to Morgan's, followed at a distance by the stranger Mick paid for the purpose, parked on Union, and marched into the department store carrying her two parcels. She made her way to the ladies' room at the opposite end of the store and changed into her riding habit in one of the stalls. There, she struggled into her fall coat, much more tight-fitting over her riding jacket than she'd anticipated. She then headed for the Sainte-Catherine Street exit of the department store in a sort of panic. She was still so shaken by the events of the night of the ball that the humor of this brazen schoolgirl prank escaped her completely. Her heart beating with raw anticipation and an impatience that was joyless, she felt none of the excitement she was used to experiencing just before seeing Vladimir. She hailed a taxicab and gave the driver the Shakespeare Road address.

The ride seemed interminable, through unruly horse and motor traffic. She couldn't remember when she had gone so long without seeing him, speaking to him, being near him. Now that the moment was imminent, time was winding down, the car losing speed; her very breathing had slowed to the point of ceasing altogether. At last the low buildings housing the horses came into view, and the taxi puttered up the gently sloping road to her destination. Jeanne paid the fare hurriedly, her mind racing now, flying ahead to where he would be waiting, to where she would finally find and overtake herself once more.

The faded blue sky was littered with scudding gray clouds. The cold wind whistled and moaned outside the dark stable. Inside, the air was warm and heavy with animal smells. When she reached the last two stalls, she found Lara's empty, and Pushkin standing quietly under his blanket, munching on his oats as if she weren't expected at all. She found the tack room deserted also, and the door of the small office, which was usually left open, had been locked. She glanced bemusedly at her watch: 12:45. Why would he have left without her, knowing that she was rarely able to get here before twelve-thirty, sometimes later? It made no sense. She walked around to the side of the big barn, where he usually kept his car. No sign of it either. Then, as she rounded the corner of the building, she heard noises coming from the other side of the barn, where the hay and other supplies for the horses were kept, and she saw a man in overalls forking horse dung and dirty straw from a wheelbarrow up onto a mountain of manure. The man looked up and touched the peak of his cap in greeting. Jeanne felt sure that she had never seen him before.

"Excuse me," she began uncertainly, "is Mr. Shpazhinsky here today?"

"No, Madame," the man answered laconically. "He's gone."

"Gone?" The word stuck in her throat like a fishbone. She struggled to retain her composure. "When do you expect him?"

"Oh, I don't, Madame. I told you, he's gone," came the reply.

"Can I reach him here tomorrow, do you think?"

"No, Madame, he's—wait a minute," he interrupted himself. "You must be Mrs.—" He hesitated, searching his memory.

"O'Neill, yes, I have an appointment every Monday ..."

"He said to saddle up for one o'clock. Guess it must be about that time, then," he drawled, pulling his watch out of the pocket of his overalls. He stuck his pitchfork in the ground next to the manure heap. His thick hands were red with cold. "Won't be long," he said.

"You did say he won't be coming," Jeanne reiterated, feeling increasingly unnerved.

"He called all his clients over the weekend," the man replied over his shoulder, walking off toward the stable. "Guess he didn't reach you, because he left a letter here in case you came by. It's in the office," he added, disappearing into the building.

Jeanne became even more agitated, knowing the office was locked.

"Excuse me," she called after him, but the man ignored her, or else didn't hear.

Jeanne had no desire to go riding alone. She was anxious to get back, fearing that her watchdog might become curious and look for her here. But the man was back in no time flat, holding Pushkin at the ready. Jeanne feared antagonizing the fellow by appearing to change her mind at the last minute. She stepped onto the stool and pulled herself up into the saddle.

"Would you be kind enough to get Mr. Shpazhinsky's letter for me?" she added, with a forced smile, cursing the man's unconcern.

"Just a minute then," he answered gruffly, taking a tobacco pouch and a pipe out of his pocket and beginning to stuff tobacco into it as he went. She watched him saunter over to the office door, put his pipe in his mouth and, holding it between his teeth, fumble around his pocket for the key. Finally he was walking back toward her, not a whit faster than before, and she had to stop herself from reaching out and snatching the letter from him.

Jeanne thanked the man, counted mentally to ten, gathering the reins and fussing with her gloves so as not to appear too eager to hasten off, and then nudged Pushkin into a walk. She followed their usual route, straight across the field into a biting wind, then up the leaf-strewn sheltered little path. From the silent woods, the birds had long departed, and the muffled sound of Pushkin's hooves matched the beating of her heart. She ambled on to the clearing where they always halted. Pushkin's ears twitched to the creaking of the swaying treetops high above them. She felt the bracing cold of the air on her face as she opened the envelope, and as she recognized the vigorous, impatient handwriting she could almost pretend that the tears that leapt into her eyes were as much due to the weather as to the emotion that gripped her.

2

For Vladimir Sergeievitch Shpazhinsky the last few days had passed altogether differently. Friday morning, his mind made up, he had paid a visit to his employer, Lady Ashbourne, an old friend dating back to his early days in Montreal, before the war. He reminded her of a discussion they had had the previous summer; she had suggested that she might have more agreeable employment for him. At the time he had had no desire to leave Shakespeare Road, but now he needed to know, as soon as possible, whether the offer was still good.

Lady Ashbourne, the wife of a wealthy trader who had been knighted by the King, listened sympathetically to his curious request. Though she didn't tell him so, a rumor had already reached her concerning Shpazhinsky and a young woman whom he saw often, on his own time, whenever she came to ride the horses. Even without this knowledge, she might, knowing him as she did, have guessed that his succinctly invoked "pressing personal reasons" had a feminine component. Nevertheless she was struck by the alteration in her friend's demeanor. He looked harried, his hollow cheeks and sunken eyes betraying more than physical fatigue. Under the circumstances, she was happy to confirm that his acceptance of her offer was not too late. She wished him well, encouraged him warmly to keep in touch, and asked no questions.

All weekend as he made his preparations, packing up his few belongings and the voluminous result of all the years spent trying to give visible form to the images in his mind, he was plagued by an urge to telephone her, arrange a meeting, and tell her himself what he was doing and why; but try as he might, he could not deceive himself. This line of thought was about one thing, and one thing only—seeing her again—and he knew that if he did, wild horses would never be able to drag him away. He would create the very situation he wanted at all costs to avoid. So far he had done her no harm. He knew she wouldn't understand, that she would suffer in her nineteen-year-old way—perhaps she would hate him, and soon forget him. As for him, the years of accumulated loneliness made this denial unendurable. Had he to leave his life behind again? Was he to be condemned eternally to this internal exile with no pardon possible? Was he atoning for the lives of his brothers, and the murdered millions of his countrymen? Or merely propitiating his own conscience, and the imperative voice of responsibility that is inseparable from love? Whatever the motivation that compelled it, he had written her a letter instead. Once, twice, three times, trying to expurgate from each successive draft the accursed sentimentalism that gushed from his pen and trivialized his intention by playing on the very emotions it purported to renounce. Finally the weight on his heart had lifted a little, but immediately another mirage shimmered before him—to take it to her, himself, on Monday morning, after her husband had left for work ... and then the silly futility of the scheme had dissipated the illusion. Even if the fellow wasn't there, he would find out sooner or later. The purpose of his leaving was to spare her. Anything else he did would betray that purpose. She would be presumed guilty without further proof required.

Late that night he had driven by her house. All the windows were dark except one, on the ground floor. His thoughts had flown to her then, like birds escaping from a cage. Then he drove on alone into the night, as though plunging slowly into cold dark water.

Now that he had put himself physically on the train, he recalled the warm sunlight of a June day, when he'd startled her under the tree at the senator's. He remembered the luminous purity, the vulnerability, of her aquamarine eyes. He had done her no harm ...

The train rushed south.

3

Jeanne,

Shortly I will be getting on a train to Kentucky, where I have accepted a position training horses. Please don't hate me for leaving. There was no other way. I do not hold your happiness in my hands, only your misfortune, which is also my own. I am leaving you Pushkin. He is as much yours as he is mine. You have brought me much joy.

V

Cruel comfort, exquisite sorrow, the poison of farewell laced with the opiate of love at last spoken, this was the bittersweet potion he forced her to drink. The terseness of his words drove the finality of his leaving into her heart. Now that he had removed himself from her life for good, her own shackles cut more deeply. The very devotion she felt for him became another link in the chain that bound her. All her hopes were now stripped from her, in a single gust like leaves from a tree, leaving only the bare dead wood of memory. She turned Pushkin's head around and rode back to the stable.

Jeanne thanked the stableman, taking pains not to allow the bleakness and hopelessness she felt to color her voice and expression. Picking up her cumbersome hatboxes, she walked unsteadily to the end of the tram line at the top of the road, where the streetcars doubled back toward Côte des Neiges. Mercifully, the tramcar was nearly empty at that time of day. On Sherbrooke Street she found a taxi to take her back to Morgan's. She changed back into her street clothes and returned to her car, wondering bitterly how long it would be before Mick heard the news and called off his bloodhound, who, unbelievably, was still sitting in his car farther up the street, reading the newspaper. Now that Mick no longer had the power to prevent her from seeing Vladimir, she no longer feared him. Her pride and upbringing kept her from expressing the hatred she now lucidly felt, but it festered, unmollified by gestures of contrition (no doubt prompted by the routing of his rival) such as the Hudson's Bay seal coat he had made for her at Holt Renfrew, Montreal's most exclusive furriers, to celebrate her twentieth birthday.

4

The dark days shortened. Jeanne grew despondent. Unexpectedly she lost her breast milk. Her weaning of little Catherine further deprived her of comfort. For a while she continued to ride, more out of loyalty to

Pushkin, who enabled her to console herself by feeling sorry for him, than out of any desire to spare her husband the confirmation of his suspicions. If anything, she would have liked to inflict some of her suffering on him. Winter closed in. She became listless, craving only sleep. It took Gabrielle to suggest that her illness might have a straightforward explanation. To this Jeanne reacted with revulsion, though she was soon forced to acknowledge the obvious. The thought of having to undergo so many months of physical wretchedness, with an orgy of anguish and suffering at the end, horrified her. She loathed the act that had caused this. During all the weeks she had mourned Vladimir's departing, nothing would have brought her more solace than to have been carrying *his* child. But she was being punished for her adulterous longings. It didn't matter that her deeds had remained beyond reproach. Either way the sentence was the same, to cower, to suffer and repent! As it always had been, and no doubt ever more would be.

The more her pregnancy progressed, the more she was haunted by insane loathing of the life she carried. When she finally felt the first flutter of movement deep within, this unnatural repudiation of her own flesh frightened and horrified her. As much as she dreaded the crucible of childbirth, she had emerged from it a mother, the mother of Catherine. She loved her little daughter as fiercely as any she-wolf her cub. She struggled endlessly with the fear. Anger and remorse tore at her sanity. She came to see herself as a monster, unworthy of living. Perhaps death would be merciful and end her suffering.

The prospect of fatherhood flattered her husband. He interpreted his wife's pregnancy as a sign of pardon, an undeserved gift, for which he showed gratitude and contrition. His pride had been placated by the defeat of his rival. Now that he had been freed from jealousy's grip, he took his wife's uncommunicativeness in stride. Time, he told himself, time heals all things. Professionally his reputation was spreading. As a litigator, he was well served by his prodigious memory. His encyclopedic knowledge of the law, his meticulous recall of legal precedent, not to mention the biting wit that judges found so entertaining, would one day make him practically unbeatable in court. He had just won a difficult case and, at twenty-four, been offered a full partnership in the firm. His success was assured. Soon his beautiful young wife would reward him with another child, perhaps even a son. He could afford to be magnanimous. Judging by its beginning, 1920 was going to be a very good year.

5

March that year went out like a lion, with one of those memorable blizzards against which subsequent ones are measured for years to come. The wind had piled the snow so high against the house that at seven in the morning, when Gabrielle took Catherine downstairs to breakfast, it covered the windows facing onto University Street. When she opened the front door to bring in the morning paper, she found herself before a wall of snow which, judging from the way it shut out the growing daylight, looked to be very wide as well as deep. It took Mick an hour to shovel through it and open a passage out to the street. As the streetcars had stopped running, he strapped on his skis and set off under a clear blue sky. He slogged his way to the office on Place d'Armes, through deserted streets of pristine whiteness. The snow sparkled and glittered in the brightness, muffling all sound, hushing the city to arctic silence. The storm had toppled telephone poles in several places along the way. On the main thoroughfares, Sherbrooke, Sainte-Catherine, and Dorchester, snow-removal crews were hard at work, their task rendered more strenuous by the mild weather. The heavy snow stuck to their shovels, while teams of plow horses wearing nose-bags and blinkers pulled the municipal works department sleds, their wood-slatted containers hauling veritable mountains of snow.

By evening the trams were running again, albeit slowly, through streets lined with twelve-foot snowbanks. Inside the streetcar, passengers sat and stood in damp coats, wet snow clinging to their overshoes, steam rising from the heated wicker benches. The air, hot and humid, smelled of wet wool. When Mick arrived home Gabrielle met him at the door, red-eyed and visibly agitated.

"Something the matter, Gabrielle?" he asked, stamping his feet to loosen the snow from his overshoes.

"Madame has not been well all day," blurted the girl, taking his coat, "she's not very well at all."

"Is she ill? What's wrong with her?" Mick interrupted. "For God's sake, don't beat around the bush!"

"She's been bleeding, Monsieur," Gabrielle answered, her eyes wide with embarrassment and fear.

"Bleeding? You mean ..."

"Yes, Monsieur," she repeated, biting her lower lip and holding back tears.

"Did you call the doctor?"

"I've tried several times, Monsieur, but he's not in."

"Not in? Did you leave a message?"

Mick didn't wait for the reply.

"Where is she?" he called, bounding up the stairs.

"In her bed, Monsieur," Gabrielle answered, behind him.

He burst into the room, and found Jeanne lying on her side, her face turned toward the wall. She lay perfectly still, giving no indication that she had heard him come in. He approached the bed and bent over her, waiting for a sign. Her eyes were open, staring hard at the wall, straight ahead. She did not turn or look up at him.

"Jeanne," he whispered anxiously, "are you all right?"

She turned her head slightly, then began to moan softly. Her gaze was tense and accusing. Her pallid face glistened with perspiration.

"I'm calling the doctor," Mick muttered, rushing out of the room.

As the phone rang at the other end, he was relieved that neither his nor his doctor's line had been put out of operation by the storm. However, the doctor, he was told, had not yet come in. His wife explained that the state of the roads had made him late in his house calls. As the weather had made it much harder for patients, especially children, to get in to see him, he had more people to look in on than on a normal day. In the calm, courteous voice of one used to speaking to distraught patients and relatives, she assured him that he was expected at any moment, and that she would personally make sure he returned Mick's call as soon as he arrived. In the meantime, was there anything she might be able to help him with?

"This is Michael O'Neill," he barked into the telephone. "My wife is expecting a baby and she is very ill!"

"If you'd like to give me an idea of her symptoms, I'll certainly pass them on, and I'll see that he calls you the minute he comes in," the woman repeated in a soothing voice.

"Damn it all, I'm not going to wait while she bleeds

to death! Tell him I'm taking her to the Royal Vic and to meet me there as soon as possible!"

"But he may not want you to move her ..."

There was not a second more to lose. He rushed out of the house to the car. He took a long time starting it, but the cold air did him good. His nerve was returning. He left the car running, hoping to warm it up a little, and dashed back to the house. He ran out again carrying the buffalo furs he'd called out to Gabrielle to fetch from the cedar cupboard in the cellar, spread them on the front seat, and charged back inside, climbing the stairs two at a time. Gabrielle was having trouble wrapping Jeanne's coat around her.

"She mustn't sit up, Monsieur. She's got to keep her feet up so it won't get worse."

As he lifted his wife off the bed, he saw the blood-soaked towels among the bed sheets where she had lain.

"Gabrielle!" he called from the top of the stairs. "Go and spread the covers on the back seat for her! If I put her in the front, she'll have to sit up," he added breathlessly as the girl ran past him.

Mick was not a big man and Jeanne, slender and fine-boned though she was, was by no means a small woman. He carried her carefully out to the car, watching his step as best he could in the dim light of the streetlamp. The temperature had dropped since nightfall, and the snow that had melted during the day was hardening treacherously underfoot. He laid his wife gingerly on the back seat and covered her with the furs he took from Gabrielle, who stood shivering in her shoes on the icy path he'd hacked out of the snowbank that morning. Jeanne's eyes were closed now, her eyebrows knitted in pain. She was shivering so violently that her teeth chattered, but still she said nothing.

"Now go inside and call the hospital. Tell them to have a stretcher ready for her!" Mick shouted, jogging around to the driver's side, his words going up in puffs in the frosty air.

Mick pulled away from the curb, gathering as much speed as he could for the climb up University Street. At the top of their hill hulked the turrets of the Royal Victoria Hospital. Halfway up, the car began losing momentum. The wheels skidded and spun over the frozen slush. As he pumped the accelerator, the strain of containing his anxiety, of keeping the pressure of his foot on the pedal light and steady, caused a sweat to break out all over his body. Finally the snow-chains on his tires crunched into the ice and the car jerked forward. His foot played the pedal like some musical instrument as he listened intently, trying to divine from the varying pitch of the wheels' whine whether to press for speed or let up, to allow the chains to bite. Slowly he inched the McLaughlin-Buick up the incline, until finally they were over the top. After they crossed Pine Avenue, the rest of the way up to the Women's Pavilion, although steeper still than the hill he had just negotiated, presented no further difficulty, for it had been heavily sanded throughout the day in order to keep the way open to ambulances. As soon as they pulled up in front of the entrance, two orderlies jogged out, carrying a stretcher. The nurse met them in the lobby.

"We've been expecting you, Mrs. O'Neill," she told Jeanne reassuringly. "Dr. Stanley has just called in to say he's on his way. The doctor on duty will take charge until he gets here."

She turned to Mick as they were wheeling Jeanne away.

"If you'd like to go up to the waiting room," she told him, "the doctor will join you as soon as possible."

Mick did as he was told. He had an instinctive fear and mistrust of hospitals; in particular he hated the helplessness of being in that alien environment, where one was forced to hand over responsibility for one's fate to strangers. The fact that his own father had been a doctor didn't help: for all his knowledge and brilliance, he had been powerless to save Mick's mother when one of his colleagues had, in accordance with the ordinance of the Catholic Church, let her die in the process of saving their eighteenth child. That child had been Arthur, and now he too was dead. And no doctor had been able to do a thing to prevent that either.

The waiting room was empty, no doubt due to the storm. Mick sat tensely on the edge of his chair, watching as the clock parsimoniously measured out the seconds and minutes, listening to it tick on and on, trying to conquer the fear that was coiling up inside him like a spring, building, building. The door swung open. A doctor he didn't know, who seemed barely older than himself, entered the room.

"Mr. O'Neill?"

Mick nodded, rising to his feet.

"I'm Dr.—"

"Save the mother!" he cried, losing control. "Do whatever you have to but for God's sake, save her!"

Only then did Mick realize that he was holding on to the doctor by the lapels of his white coat. The latter was much taller than he, and more powerfully built.

"There's no question of that," answered the resident reassuringly. He made no move to extricate himself, thus allowing Mick to recover his composure with the minimum loss of face. "I'm afraid the fetus is nowhere near term, and can't possibly survive. Your wife has lost quite a lot of blood. Dr. Stanley has decided to anesthetize her. If you want to wait, he'll be out to talk to you when it's over."

Mick sat down again, dazed at his own outburst. He wanted to ask whether she was in real danger, but he said nothing. Besides, how would they know whether she was going to pull through? Once the doctor had left the room, however, he gradually regained his composure. Perhaps if they didn't have to concentrate on saving the baby ... But every time he closed his eyes, the memory of blood on the sheets jolted him like an accusation.

6

"We're going to give you a little ether, Mrs. O'Neill. When you come to, this will all be behind you," Dr. Stanley had said. The two men in white coats stood over her: the older man, whose familiar face and pleasant, fatherly manner were reassuring, and his taller, younger colleague, who, though he made no attempt to placate her fears with bedside-manner optimism, still, somehow, invited trust. The nurse placed the gauze-covered mask over Jeanne's nose and mouth. She struggled briefly, suddenly roused from exhaustion and hemorrhage-induced lethargy by the instinctive need to breathe, but the nurse holding her head whispered softly from somewhere just behind her, *Just breathe in now, dear, just breathe in*, as the gas entered her lungs, and she was delicately separated from herself, peeled away like a tracing from her soul underneath.

"Mrs. O'Neill. Mrs. O'Neill." Someone was calling, distantly. "Wake up, Mrs. O'Neill."

Jeanne opened her eyes. A woman's face entered her field of vision. A homely, caring face. *It's all over now, dear.*

You're going to be fine ... But she hadn't the strength to hold on to the apparition, and drifted off again.

Later she awoke to the pinkish glow of a snowy dawn. Outside the high window of the hospital room, still immersed in gloom, she could make out the dark outline of trees against the sloping whiteness of Mount Royal. She was alone. Something was missing. The pain was gone. *It's all over.* The baby. She'd poisoned it with her anger, banished it from her future. She realized too late how much the child had already laid claim to its mother, how deeply their kinship had taken root. The unnatural aversion that had infected her feelings for the baby had been bled from her, leaving only tears and merciless, useless memory.

She heard the door open. Someone was coming in quietly. The room was still in semi-darkness despite the growing daylight. When he reached her bedside she recognized the doctor who had seen her on her arrival at the hospital. He stood on the side of her bed opposite the window, so that she could see his face clearly. He was tall, dark, with thick curly hair, like a portrait of Saint John the Baptist. He looked tired.

"How are you feeling?" he asked. His voice was deep, soothing—a voice startlingly like one she remembered from her distant past.

"Was it ... a boy?" she asked in a pathetic whisper. "Please ... tell me ..."

The young man's gaze was direct. "Yes, it was," he answered, as gently as he could.

Jeanne closed her eyes and tried to choke down the sobs that were heaving up inside her.

"It happens," the doctor said softly. "Don't fight it. It'll do you good to cry."

But still there was no release from the grip tightening round her throat. Her face contorted in a painful grimace. She hid behind her hands.

"Dr. Stanley spoke to your husband last night," the doctor continued. "He wants to keep you under observation for a few days. You've lost some blood and we want to make sure you don't lose any more. The duty nurse will give you ergot to help things along."

The doctor's little speech had given Jeanne the leeway she needed. She collected herself sufficiently to look up briefly.

"Thank you," she managed, "for telling me ..."

Then the last of her defenses collapsed, swept away by the wave of grief surging through her, bursting through the tangled anger and resentment, fear and remorse that had held her back for so long—one at last with her pain.

6

The Pride
of Pardee

1

Quebec City, 6 June 1920 In the Rue du Parloir the wind
was shoving Mick along like a recalcitrant child. As he
neared the stone portal of the Ursuline convent, he was
overcome by a feeling of unease, whose origins he was
instinctively, characteristically, loath to question. And
yet it wasn't only Gonzague's parting words to him three
years before—*Look after her ... whenever you're in town for a
court case, drop in for a visit, it'll do her good*—that resonated
in his memory this morning. The sight of these old walls
brought back memories of his childhood in the house
on Rue Desjardins, right behind the convent—of the
days when he scaled the convent wall on Rue Sainte-
Ursule to steal plums from the nuns' orchard. Once he
had jumped down and landed in the middle of recess,
like a fox among chickens, sending little convent girls
squawking in all directions. This three-hundred-year-
old institution had nurtured those of his sisters who
had not died before his birth, and whom he had barely

known as he was growing up. But his sisters were not the only ones with whom he neglected to keep in touch; he reproached himself, filled with remorse toward the woman he was coming to visit for the first time in months. He could never be certain his visits really alleviated her grief ...

He pushed the heavy door open, entered the main hall, stepped up to the *tour** and rang the doorbell. On the other side of the round, brass grille, a shadow stirred.

"With whom do you wish to speak?"

"With Mme Prud'homme, please," murmured Mick uncomfortably.

Following the unseen sister's instructions, he crossed the hall to the door of the nuns' parlor and entered. His unease increased once he was inside the small bright room. Its walls were bare save for a painting representing La Bienheureuse Mère Marie de l'Incarnation.** The partition separating it from the cloister featured three arched windows, each opening filled in with a double grille, through which one could converse with a member of the cloister. After a time that seemed longer to Mick than it actually was, a door opened and a black-robed, white-veiled figure appeared dimly before him through the metal screen.

"You are sweet to have come, Mick," said the voice, gentle and familiar, on the other side.

"Mme Prud'homme ..."

---

* *Tour*: in a monastery, reception area consisting of a rotating armoire for passing letters, parcels etc. from outside into the cloister. In the Ursulines' convent in Quebec City, there is also a heavily screened window through which a visitor could make inquiries.
** La Bienheureuse Mère Marie de l'Incarnation: founder of the Ursuline convent (1639).

Mick's voice faltered. He felt an orphan's distress at her bereavement.

"Éloïse tells me your wife has recently had to bear a great hardship," came the voice. "Tell me, how is she?"

"She is beginning to feel a little better, thank you ..."

"And your daughter, how is she faring?"

The surge of emotion he felt for this mother who had watched him grow up was no match for the finality of the barrier between them. His was a primal, physical need to see, to recognize in her face, in the features she had handed down to her late son, the irrefutable, in-the-flesh confirmation of his own past. Instead, her disembodied voice unnerved him.

"She is doing wonderfully, thank you. And you? Your health is good, I trust?"

"Yes, dear Mick, you are kind. Are you going to attend the Corpus Christi celebrations at the basilica? Saint Patrick's parish is to join up with Notre-Dame for the mass and procession, this year. All the Quebec City Irish will be there."

"I'm just on my way there, as a matter of fact," he only half lied.

"I want to thank you for looking after Éloïse the way you do. I know Gonzague will be grateful to you for watching over her on his behalf."

"You know Éloïse is like a sister to me."

Mick, whose militant rationalism was usually unrelenting, was now thoroughly ill at ease. He had known Gonzague's mother in her glory, dignified, tall, commanding, regal in fact, reigning over her entire household like a queen. Married late in life, a first-time mother at the age of forty, her only weakness had been her son. She was as besotted with him as an old man with a dancing girl, forever showering him with gifts and indulging his heart's every whim. Before her quiet refusal to believe in his death, Mick was utterly defenseless.

2

The Ursuline chapel was slowly filling up. Before the glittering gold of the main altar, Mick hurried through a semblance of a genuflection. Noiselessly he sidled up to the figure kneeling before the burial plaque marking the grave of General Montcalm, whose soldiers had once carried his bleeding body here through the tumult of defeat. The man he was meeting was a soldier of a different kind, in a volunteer army that had been fighting the English for seven hundred years. His struggle was for Ireland, whose victory the trumpeting angel atop the pulpit carved by Levasseur seemed already to be heralding.

Mick knelt next to the young man, who seemed deep in prayer. A few moments later, the fellow signed himself, acknowledging Mick with a subtle nod. The two men rose, signed themselves before the altar, and proceeded together down the center aisle, between walls bearing treasures rescued from pillage in the French Revolution, like the *Jésus Chez Simon le Pharisien* that hung above the entrance, the two halves of which—one discovered in the north, the other in the south of France—had been reunited by chance in Quebec City, sometime in the year 1820.

3

"All set then?" inquired the Irishman, almost shouting above the wind in the Rue Buade.

Since their first meeting in New York the year before, Liam O'Neill had been in sporadic written contact with his Canadian cousin. He had arrived in New

York a week ago, and met with de Valera at his head-quarters in the Waldorf-Astoria, on behalf of Michael Collins, commander-in-chief of the IRA, whose personal envoy he was. De Valera had left New York on a tour of the American West, and Liam had come north to complete a transaction that Mick had been planning for months; he was to return at once to the Emerald Isle with the product of their labors.

"I'll say we're set!" bellowed Mick, hanging on to his cap. "Everything'll be over and done with by ten o'clock tonight."

"Praise God," said the Irishman, shrugging his head into his shoulders to shield himself from the wind. "Churchill's been boasting again about the forty tanks and twenty-eight airplanes he's sent to do us in. The British railway workers' union has just let us down, even if the workers over in England are still refusin' to load munitions for the government. We can count on nobody but ourselves alone now!"

"But you seem to be doing well! Sinn Fein's just won the elections in two of the northern counties. That's unheard of!"

"Meantime they're still sendin' us their tanks, and their warships, and their armies. 'Tis far from won yet, Mick!"

"In any case, every Irish man, woman, and child in Quebec City will be turning out this morning. It's your lucky day!"

Since his father's death Mick had always been scathingly sarcastic about anything remotely connected with religion. But he felt no qualms about attending mass today. He knew his visitor to be a fervent Catholic: the first question he'd asked on the telephone from New York was about the times at which it was possible to attend mass. Even Collins, the most wanted man in Ireland, never missed mass and went to confession every chance he got, so Liam assured him. If the British only knew that! But the beloved hero of the Irish people was safe and sound in their midst ...

4

After high mass at the Notre-Dame-de-Québec basilica, the procession gradually assembled on the square in front of City Hall. Four hundred orphans of the Soeurs de la Charité, followed by hundreds of children (boys first, then the girls) from the various communities in the parish, led the march. They entered the Rue Buade, along the church wall, then turned in front of the arch-bishop's palace, under the benevolent stare of Monseigneur de Laval, eyeing them from the top of his monument. As they poured into the Côte de la Montagne the fierce wind swooped down on them, ruffling their hair, roughing up their banners, as it plunged toward the Rue des Remparts and the wide river below. Behind the children came the cadets of Saint Patrick, followed by the cadets of the Académie Commerciale, and the students of the Séminaire de Québec, each group led by its very own brass band. Next came a flock of choirboys in red robes and white surplices, strewing flowers that swirled and scattered in the wind. Behind them marched a hundred priests from the seminary, and a large contingent of clergymen of all orders. Finally, preceded by a colorful detachment of the Pope's own Zouaves in blue-and-red uniforms, gaiters, and képis, came the billowing canopy, and under it Monseigneur Marois, the *vicaire-général*, in his gold moiré chasuble, holding aloft the Holy Sacrament in its magnificent gold monstrance, flanked by a deacon and subdeacon, their skirts flying. Monseigneur's white cope flapped like great wings and the wind threatened to lift the canopy right out of its bearers' grasp.

Behind them was arrayed a phalanx of local worthies: Lieutenant-Governor Sir Charles Fitzpatrick, the Honorable Louis-Alexandre Taschereau, solicitor-general for the province, the chief justice of the Superior Court, Sir François Lemieux, senators, ministers, members of Parliament and of the National Assembly, along with the judges and members of the liberal professions of the city of Quebec. The howling wind bullied and worried them, knocking off hats, pummeling standards, even breaking a few banners. All along the steeply winding slope that descended toward the Lower Town the population knelt in prayer under the raging gusts. At the bottom of the hill a wooden *arche de triomphe*, constructed specially for the occasion, spanned the road, its decorative foliage and flowers tearing and scattering in the wind. The procession filed under it in full sail, then turning into Rue Notre-Dame, trudged on toward the Place Royale.

The canopy came to a stop before the steps of the church of Notre Dame des Victoires, where a richly ornate altar had been prepared. On the square, among the crowd of faithful, could be heard the flapping of standards and banners. Every window of the buildings lining the square had been festooned for the occasion with flags and bunting and garlands of flowers that quaked and trembled under the lash of the wind. Monseigneur ascended the steps, pressing his biretta to his skull with one hand, his cope ballooning behind him. Then, holding aloft the monstrance, as the crowd fell to its knees he turned to face the square.

5

The procession had moved on, through the Rues Sous-le-Fort, Saint-Pierre, Saint-Antoine, Sault-au-Matelot, small side streets that offered the hope of respite from the angry wind. Doggedly it ascended the Côte de la Montagne, harried by furies swooping down from the top of Cap Diamant, threatening rain at any moment. Inside the little church of Notre Dame des Victoires, Mick and Liam sought refuge from the weather. Over their heads a model of Samuel de Champlain's ship, the *Don de Dieu*, hung by a sturdy thread. She might have been the ship of Destiny itself, for all that she seemed to be held aloft by nothing save the grace of God. The main altar of white and gold was carved in the shape of a fortified castle, representing Quebec, the only walled city in the New World. Above it a radiant Virgin Mary, to whom Frontenac believed he owed his victory over the English, looked serenely down. It was to pray to her that the Irishman had asked to come here ...

6

The fierce nor'wester that had blown all day had driven away the clouds and dried the rain. The waters of the Saint Lawrence were finally calm. On the other side of the river the distant lights of Lévis glimmered faintly. In the port of Quebec an American merchant ship called the *Pride of Pardee* hulked blackly against the stars. It was only a short walk from the customs office with its columned façade, vaguely suggestive of Dublin, to the ship. In her hull lay two cratefuls of Vickers .303 machine guns, imported from Britain by the Canadian army in the spring of 1918 to train conscripts before shipping them off to Europe, and stockpiled since then in a munitions depot at the Valcartier military base.

Purchased on the cheap by an accredited scrap-metal merchant of Mick's acquaintance, the Vickers machine guns, unlike their American-made counterparts, had the advantage of being of the same caliber as the British ammunition captured by the IRA in Ireland. The guns would cross the Atlantic concealed in the *Pride of Pardee*'s legitimate cargo of scrap machine-grade steel, bound for the Belfast shipyards.

"All the paperwork is in order," Mick concluded, handing Liam a wad of documents. "The lads in the customs office saw to that."

"A superb job, Mick. Commander Collins thanks you all. Our victory will be your victory. It's only a matter o' time, now."

At the foot of the gangway, the two men exchanged an emotional embrace. Then the Irishman went up alone into the darkened ship, yet another friend gone, perhaps never to be seen again. Mick strode quickly away, and drawing from his pocket the treasured silver flask Gonzague had given him, drained it in long, greedy gulps. An unquenchable thirst afflicted him ... Still, you've done well today, he told himself. A regular triumph. You deserve a toast, no doubt about that. And yet something inside was not quite right, hadn't been since this morning. "Jeanne," he muttered, as if to an invisible listener. His Jeanne. Damned Jeanne, always at the back of his thoughts, like background noise you didn't hear until all other sounds had subsided. She was his private, ancient wound, the hurt he did not admit to, like a disease, secret and shameful. It had been months since she'd let him near her. Since her return from the hospital he hadn't dared even contemplate it. He never had known how to handle her. Slowly but surely, she was driving him crazy ...

"There are ten ways to skin a cat, long as you're nice and you show some *amour* ..." Gonzague's familiar teasing voice came to him, welling up from the deepest recesses of his memory.

"Damn fool, Gonzague," he mumbled, sentimental as always when the booze was on him.

"Aw, come on boy," the voice within continued, "might as well get it where you can. Short and sweet is best, I say. Better than nothing, which is what you've got anyway. Face it, Mick, you foolish boy, in the dark they're all alike ..."

He wandered for a while through grimy back streets, the spectral voice inside his head seemingly guiding his steps. Emboldened by whisky, he soon found himself before a carriage entrance, the site of a youthful debauch he had almost forgotten. The lair of Medusa, Eulalie Larivière! "This one, Gonzague, you rake," he told himself, "will be for you." He turned into the murky passage, his head spinning with queasiness, like a soul contemplating the void. In the gloom Eulalie's door loomed, waiting to swallow him. How could it have only been three years since he'd last stood here?

"You need an appointment!" hissed an indignant voice through the partly open door.

"I am a friend of Gonzague Prud'homme ..."

"Who? Oh, my God!" The voice suddenly relented. "Come in, come in ..."

PART † THREE

1

Resurrection

1

Ottawa, Easter 1924 Kitty awoke, drawn from sleep by her grandmother's whispered entreaties. At first there was only unfamiliar darkness, but then she remembered. Mimi and Grandpapa's house, the long train ride yesterday, and the nice redcap who looked after her. Mummy was on the platform blowing kisses through the window of the train ... She rubbed her eyes in surprise. It seemed only moments before that she had been lying wide awake, unable to get to sleep, even after Mimi had peeked in on her way to bed.

"Is it still nighttime?"

"The sun won't be up for a while yet. Come, we mustn't waste a moment," her grandmother added dramatically. "I'm going to turn on the light, are you ready? Close your eyes ..."

The light from the bedside lamp was so bright, even

through closed eyelids, that the little one hid her face in her hands.

"Your eyes are still asleep, aren't they, my little angel?" murmured Madeleine Langlois tenderly, running her fingers through her granddaughter's fine blond hair. "Look, your clothes are all ready, just as we left them last night."

Kitty remembered. Blinking hard, willing herself awake, she jumped eagerly out of bed. All her impatience and excitement of last night had returned. She pulled on her bloomers and her long gray stockings under her nightshirt, and stepped into the thick gray pleated skirt that scratched (Mimi said it was a good way to show Jesus how much she loved Him, and such a small discomfort compared to the sacrifice He made to save us all from everlasting Hell). "Imagine," she had said the night before last, which was the day Jesus died, "imagine the sorrow of His poor Mother, standing so pitifully at the foot of the Cross where her only Son, whose birth had been promised her by an Angel sent by God, hangs lifeless from nails driven through His hands and feet. Oh, imagine her pain, her grief! Do you think that Jesus would have inflicted such cruelty on His Mother, do you think that He—the Flesh of her flesh!— could have brought such horror down upon her if not for the sake of us, poor sinners, here on Earth?" And in her heart Kitty felt a surge of love and pity for the poor Virgin Mary, and a great awe.

Mimi was doing up the buttons of her granddaughter's blouse. She herself was dressed all in black and wore a black woolen kerchief on her head, as befitted the task they were about to perform. She helped Kitty into her Red River coat and pulled up the hood, so wide it almost hid her face. She tied her red wool sash for her, and put on her mittens.

"It's almost five o'clock. Time to go," she whispered conspiratorially, leading the way noiselessly down the stairs. They set off, Mimi penitently gloveless in the predawn cold, holding Kitty's little mittened hand. Silently they walked the several blocks to church, their heads bowed, Mimi's in prayer, Kitty's in reverent anticipation. They were, Mimi said, the "Women Apostles," to whom Jesus chose to first reveal that He had risen from the dead, and who believed before any of the "real" apostles. "Jesus chose them because their faith was so strong," Mimi said. "Stronger than Peter's, who denied Him three times before the rooster crowed, stronger than Thomas's, who doubted even when he saw Him with his own eyes."

Going to church this Easter morning, they were retracing the steps of these Holy Women to the Sepulchre, where Jesus's body had been entombed. Pontius Pilate had it sealed and watched over by sentries, to ensure that none of His disciples could come under cover of darkness to remove His body and claim to the others that He had fulfilled His prophecy. As they turned a street corner they caught sight of the church. Mimi slowed her step. "Look there!" she breathed, fixing her gaze on the dark portal at the top of a flight of stone steps. "The Sepulchre!"

Kitty held her breath. She looked up in awe at her grandmother's beautiful face, tear-streaked and red-nosed with the cold, then at the somber door. She did not dare speak. She shivered a little in the bitter wind. Suddenly a sharp crack burst the silence, as the metal bolt on the inside was pulled back. Slowly the heavy door creaked open.

"And behold," her grandmother fervently intoned, "there was a great earthquake: for the Angel of the Lord descended from Heaven, and came and rolled back the stone from the door, and sat upon it. His countenance was like lightning and his raiment as white as snow. And the Angel said unto the women, Fear not: for I know that you seek Jesus, who was crucified. He is not here: for He is risen, as He foretold. Come, see the place where the Lord lay."

They started up the stone steps, at the top of which the softly flickering glow of candles seeped out from the dark church through the door that had opened as if by a miracle.

2

Ottawa, June 1924 Mimi had had the dress specially made by the nuns while Kitty was away. It was by far the most beautiful article of clothing the child had ever been given to wear: white organdy, with an ankle-length flounced skirt and a veil to be worn with a crown of fresh flowers, which had just been delivered from the florist's shop. There was also a pair of white lace gloves, an ivory-beaded rosary, and a small gilt-edged missal bound in white leather, in a carved ivory case with a little handle of white silk cord. And white silk stockings, and white leather shoes.

"It looks like a wedding dress!" Kitty exclaimed with delight.

"That's because it is a wedding dress," Mimi replied, beaming. "Today you'll be married to Jesus, and there will never be a more important day in your life. And for you," she went on, taking Kitty's hand, "it will be even more special than for other little girls. Most of them have to wait until they are seven before they are considered grown up enough to be married to Jesus. But you are such an exceptionally pious girl, even though you are only five, that Father Plantin has agreed to give you Holy Communion, and the sisters are willing to open the gates of their cloister to you and only you!"

"Won't you be there, Mimi?" Kitty asked, her eyes widening a little.

"Of course I will," Mimi soothed. "But I'll have to stay and watch from the other side of the grille. They are only opening the cloister for you, my angel!"

Madeleine Langlois was terribly proud of having secured the approval of the Mother Superior of the Sisters of the Five Wounds for her plan. It had taken initiative and daring on her part, but she had the support of Father Plantin, who shared her admiration for the girl. Both saw in Kitty an astonishingly precocious child, blessed with a seriousness and a capacity for awe that seemed to them well beyond her years. Their scheme had taken shape the previous Easter, on the last day of Kitty's stay. Madeleine had found her granddaughter sitting on the front step waiting for her bag to be loaded into the car, elbows propped on her knees and chin in her hand, tears streaming down her smooth little face.

"Are you sad to be leaving us, darling?" she had asked her, wiping her tears with her big white handkerchief.

"Oh Mimi," Kitty had sighed, "I'm so afraid of losing my vocation!"

Madeleine had wasted no time reporting this wondrous utterance that very afternoon to her confessor, who marveled with her at what could only be an extraordinary understanding of the perils she faced upon returning to her Godless parents' faithless household. Together they conceived the plan to bring her back to Ottawa as soon as possible, and to have her make her First Communion before the nefarious influences under which she lived began to corrode her faith and tarnish her soul. The sisters, bless their hearts, had been easy to convince, once apprised by Father Plantin of the child's extreme precocity. Even Jeanne had readily, if unwittingly, cooperated with their grand design.

Now the great moment was at hand. Madeleine's heart rejoiced with God's, for little Catherine had to be the youngest communicant ever to be permitted to approach the altar (and surely the whitest, purest soul ever to receive the Host) in the hallowed confines of this cloister. As she watched her tiny figure enter the chancel and kneel at the foot of the altar, head bowed under the delicate white veil, wearing her crown of flowers like a God-given halo, a fierce joy gripped Madeleine's heart. Tears of reverence rolled down her cheeks. Then, at the moment when Father Plantin, holding the Host between his thumb and index finger, blessed the child, Madeleine felt the prayers of all those present—the sisters in their white habits and black veils behind the partition, the priest, the few lay spectators—go out to her in a great wave that lifted her, onto a new and shining plane. As the child rose to return to her pew, her lovely head bearing its flowery crown with the humility of a saint, Madeleine perceived a radiance emanating from her as though the grace of God himself were descending over the congregation, and tears of ecstasy glistened on her cheeks.

Kitty returned to her grandmother's side and knelt. Her heart galloped with excitement and her closed eyelids fluttered as she tried to concentrate on the prayer she'd been given to recite. The Host in her mouth had all but dissolved. Mimi said not to chew it, because it really was Jesus and it was a great mystery. Her stomach was beginning to rumble from her long fast. She hadn't eaten since last night at dinner. She was hungry now, and she couldn't wait to get back to Mimi and Grandpapa's house to phone her parents and tell them the news.

3

"You just *what?*" Daddy's voice was angry. It gave Kitty a jolt. "Put your grandmother on. Right now!"

Kitty stood there speechless. Tears were beginning to spill out onto her cheeks as she handed the receiver to Mimi, who took it from her with a distressed, uncomprehending look.

"Hello, Michael, you wished ..." she began with her usual assertiveness. "I beg your pardon?... I don't think that's ... Surely you don't ..." Her tone was defensive now, then suddenly indignant: "Well, I never...! Very well, if she must ... I find it most ... Very well. Goodbye."

Mimi had looked more and more flustered and her face had got redder and redder as she spoke. When her son-in-law hung up on her, her pride (and perhaps a kind of instinct that warned her against trying too overtly to divide the child's loyalties) prevented her from visibly registering the insult. She replaced the receiver in its cradle very carefully.

"Why is Daddy angry?" Kitty managed tearfully.

"You must forgive him," Mimi answered in a strangely absent voice, "for he knows not what he has done. Your father thinks you are too young to make your First Communion, darling, but Father Plantin and the sisters knew that you were ready, otherwise they wouldn't have allowed it. Here, dry your poor tears, my angel. Don't let anything spoil this beautiful day. Unfortunately your father has decided that he wants you to go back on the next train. Now you show him how ready you really were. Don't cry, and don't complain. Just forgive him, and ask Jesus to forgive him too."

So Kitty took the next train home. As it pulled into the station her stomach tightened into a painful knot. She wondered who had come to meet her, and what they would say. Secretly she hoped it wouldn't be Daddy, and she breathed a sigh of relief when she saw Mummy on the platform waving to her. She pointed her out to the black porter, who lifted her down the step and held on to her hand until Mummy arrived to claim her. She was smiling happily. Mummy was so beautiful, especially when she smiled like that.

"I missed you!" Mummy said, hugging her over and over. She thanked the porter warmly and gave him a tip. "I was lonely without you!"

"Is Daddy very angry with me?" Kitty asked apprehensively.

"Of course not. He wasn't expecting it, that's all. He's very happy to have you back, you'll see. And so am I. Wait till you see what I've got for you when you get home!"

There was a lovely tea waiting for them, with a platterful of petits fours, which Georgette had made specially. Gabrielle was so happy to see her little girl again, she cried. After tea, Mummy got a kerchief and tied it over Kitty's eyes.

"Don't take it off till I tell you," she said.

Kitty waited, listening carefully for clues, but all she heard was Mummy leaving the room, and then coming back very quietly. Then Gabrielle *ooh*ing and *aah*ing, and Mummy laughing softly nearby.

"You can look now," she said finally.

And there, sitting primly on the chair next to her, was a doll, almost as big as she was. It had thick brown curls and shiny brown eyes, with lids that closed when you laid her down, and red-painted cupid's-bow lips, parted in a smile over pearly teeth. Its chubby dimpled hands and arms reached out asking to be held. It wore a sapphire-blue dress with white collar and cuffs, under a white pinafore.

"Oh, that's just like my dress!" Kitty exclaimed delightedly.

"Exactly the same," Mummy concurred.

"Oh, Mummy, did you make that dress for her?"

"I did. But this is not just any doll, Kitty. Her name is Beatrice. Someone I dearly loved gave her to me when I was your age. Your Great-aunt Florence, who died just before you were born."

Mummy kissed her tenderly. Kitty nestled in her closeness, breathing in the sweetness of her mother's scent, her senses swimming in the warmth and smoothness of her blouse against her cheek. She was too young to reflect on how worried she had been. She had already forgotten the tight knotted feeling on the train and reveled in the safety and comfort of her mother's arms. She always felt uneasy around her father even though he had never scolded her before. In fact if she'd been able to think like a grown-up she would have realized that he hadn't scolded *her* at all. But the fear was there nonetheless. It was there late at night when his voice through the wall would burst in on her sleep, his voice raging at Mummy, even though she could never make out what he was saying. But his anger came through, came through the wall.

"When I grow up I want to stay with you forever," she said suddenly, hugging her mother even more closely.

"When you grow up you'll want to get married, and have a house of your own," Mummy answered, playfully ruffling her blond hair.

"I'm never going to get married!"

"One day some handsome young man will come along and sweep you off your feet, and you won't have any time for your old Mummy then."

"I'll never leave you," Kitty cried out, her eyes filling with tears. "Say I won't have to, say I can live here with you forever!"

The child seemed so genuinely distressed that Jeanne was momentarily taken aback.

"Of course you can," she soothed, stroking her daughter's head, "of course you can stay with me. Forever, if you want to."

4

In reality, though Kitty was too young to realize it, the doll had been given to her as a peace offering, or perhaps a consolation prize. For her mother it also carried a deeper significance since it had been Florence's doll. Its passing from her own into her daughter's hands took on the solemnity of a private rite of passage, but there was more. What had moved Jeanne to part with it was an incident so strange that she had reacted by instinctively resorting to a sacrificial act.

Jeanne had decided to put the week during which Kitty would be away at her mother's to good use by finally tackling the long-deferred task of sifting through the books left her in her aunt's will, many of which were still gathering dust in the very boxes into which they had been hurriedly and unsystematically packed by Florence's executors. Day after day, marooned on the living-room carpet amid the flotsam of her aunt's books, she reflected on her own life. Was it not eerily like those unopened, unread books? With its stillborn hopes indifferently pressed between birth and death, and the meaningless verbiage of matrimony in between? Even the memory of Florence had gradually faded. Sometimes she almost wondered whether she had really existed. She missed her daughter. Her absence grieved her. How deathly futile it all seemed without her here.

But then something happened to stir her dormant memory and briefly breathe old life into her dead heart. A piece of paper slipped out of one of the books, the last shriveled leaf from a long-dead tree. Unbelievably, it was addressed to her, Jeanne, despite its having taken more than five years to find its way into her hands. *Darling*, it read:

I won't be here to see the little one but am praying all goes well with your delivery. No one should ask for anything more than a healthy child, but given my circumstances I feel free to wish you something further: a little girl, that you may know the tender complicity which, though childless, I had the privilege of experiencing thanks to you. It grieves me to leave you, not knowing what future awaits you. Whatever happens my dear know I shall always be beside you in future, for all Eternity,
Florence

The handwriting was distorted, the words slurred by the sickness. The ink was as fresh, the paper as unyellowed as if the note had been written yesterday. She felt its voice calling to her, reaching out over time and distance, the resurrected voice of a young woman in her prime, who knew she was about to meet her Maker. The love it conveyed unsettled and upset her. For a moment she almost managed to repudiate the reality of her surroundings. Then its veil descended once more between her and the memories, and discouragement bore down on her more than ever.

2

Ghosts

1

Montreal, November 1925 MACNEILL RESIGNS FROM BOUNDARY COMMISSION ran the small headline in the newspaper Mick had folded beside him on the passenger's seat. The rain rattled relentlessly against the hood of his car. He shivered slightly in the cold November night. The final act of the Irish tragedy had been reduced to a short news item whose significance few now cared about, and fewer still understood. For such a hard, bloody struggle to meet such a mean end—for the dream of Irish unity to be snuffed out by stealth and petty trickery—was enough to make you give up on the human race.

Mick was anxious to get to the station, knowing that the man whose train he was meeting would at least have an opinion on the subject. He had not seen his cousin in more than five years. The telegram from Halifax came out of the blue. Even though he had only seen him twice in his whole life, Mick was deeply impressed with the young associate of the famous Michael Collins, the hero felled by an assassin in 1922. Four years earlier, when the treaty confirming the victory of the armed struggle against British rule was signed in London, Mick wrote to his cousin, in care of the government of the Irish Free State, to congratulate him and pass on the good wishes of all his Irish brethren in the Montreal section. But his enthusiasm was short-lived. In Ireland, the territorial and political concessions imposed by Britain during the negotiations were quickly denounced, and civil war ensued, bloodier than anything seen during the insurrection.

Mick had no difficulty spotting the big fellow in an Irish frieze coat who had just stepped off the train. He was wearing a tweed cap and carrying one suitcase. Mick shook his hand warmly and the pair exchanged greetings in Irish Gaelic.

"I'd like to stop off at the hotel and change, if that's all right," said Liam O'Neill, in his soft, singing brogue.

"Take all the time you need, Liam, there's no rush. Jeanne isn't expecting us until eight." While Liam hadn't changed physically, Mick couldn't help noticing a terrible weariness emanating from his person.

By the time they arrived at the house, the rain had stopped and the streets glistened mournfully under the glow of the streetlamps.

"Jeanne!" Mick called out as he handed his sodden overcoat to Gabrielle. As soon as his wife appeared, however, coming to greet them at the door of the living room, something tightened inside him. Why did her beauty always take him by surprise? Ever since the episode with the Russian at the beginning of their marriage, anything that made her more attractive in his own eyes made him suddenly wary: he felt defied by her beauty, defeated by it, knowing himself not to be the object of its radiance, but merely an obstacle in its path.

"I want you to meet my cousin, Liam O'Neill," he said stiffly, "from Cork, as my ancestors were. My wife, Jeanne. What can I get you to drink?"

"Just a sherry, if that's all right," answered his guest, shaking Jeanne's hand.

"Come now," Mick insisted a little incredulously, "you can do better than that!"

"Just the ceremonial apéritif, thanks, really."

2

They went into the living room, where the other guests were waiting. Mick proceeded to make the introductions.

"Allow me to introduce Mr. Richard Doyle, senior partner in the firm of Lynch O'Connell Doyle, to which I belong; his wife, Mme Violette Doyle; my father-in-law, the Honorable Charles Langlois, member of Parliament for Bonaventure; his wife, Mme Madeleine Langlois; and last but not least, our very own Mlle Éloïse Prud'homme. We wish you welcome," Mick concluded, thrusting a glass of sherry into his cousin's hands.

"Delighted to meet you, mademoiselle."

"You have before you," Mick went on, "one of the most redoubtable campaigners in existence."

"You are interested in politics, mademoiselle?" his cousin asked politely, in his lyrical accent.

"He's exaggerating," Éloïse protested meekly, her cheeks beginning to color.

"Not at all!" cried Mick, between two swallows of rye. "You should have seen her, just last month, October 29, election day, marshaling the voters in a district of the city where brave men venture only under cover of darkness! That morning, she single-handedly covered the entire voting section around De Bullion Street. Believe me, it's quite a feat. The ladies there, it appears, like to sleep late, and they do not appreciate being roused from their slumber, even less when the culprit is an honest female citizen exhorting them to do their patriotic duty. By golly, what a woman!"

"I didn't just offer them a chauffeured drive to the polling station," Éloïse explained with a glint of mischief in her eye. "I told them, 'Here's our chance'—I meant us women, of course—'to stop the Tories, who sent our boys to slaughter in 1917, from doing the same thing again, this time invoking the defense of the British Empire against the Turks! If we don't do something, girls,' I said, 'you're all going to be out of a job!'"

"You see, cousin, we have our imperialists here, too," added Mick.

At that moment Kitty, following what had by now become a ritual whenever her grandparents visited from Ottawa, entered the room in her dressing gown and slippers, all shiny and fresh-faced from her bath.

"Come, Kit, so I can introduce you to your cousin Liam. He's from Ireland, like our ancestors."

The child shook the visitor's hand.

"Ah, here we have the stork," Mick teased, referring to the wobbly one-legged stance that Kitty had involuntarily struck, the other knee bent, holding her foot behind her. "That's a sure sign she likes you!"

Kitty turned crimson and retreated in confusion into the arms of her grandmother, who shot her son-in-law a disapproving look. Relations between them had been frosty since the incident of the First Communion.

"It's good to see you again, Liam," Mick said, turning to his guest. "The last time we met I couldn't be sure our paths would ever cross again in this life."

"I was luckier than many others ..."

"Here, here, what's all this? A bit gloomy, aren't we, boys?" Éloïse interrupted.

"My dear," sighed Mick, as he did whenever the memory of Gonzague passed like a current between them. "The last time I saw this man was in 1920, at a time when he was living much more dangerously than I was."

"You exaggerate, Mick," the young man muttered uncomfortably. "I carried messages, that's all."

"That's all, you say! At great personal risk to yourself, as you well know. In Dublin streets crawling with Black-and-Tans, secret police, spies, and informers ..."

"The risks I took were negligible compared to the dangers Collins faced every day," answered his guest, becoming animated for the first time since his arrival. "He was the most wanted man in Ireland and yet he was everywhere. Never bothered with a disguise ..."

"But how could he get around without being recognized?" asked Éloïse, who was observing the young Irishman with fascination.

"Well, for one thing, he didn't look the part. He was a big friendly man with a warm, easygoing manner. If he was stopped, he'd answer questions good-naturedly, banterin' and jokin' with 'em, till they let him be on his way. His intelligence system was so sophisticated, he always knew about a raid ahead of time, so he always knew where to sleep on any given night."

"But he died, didn't he?" Éloïse pressed on. "Was he betrayed?"

"Yes."

The Irishman fell silent. He glanced over at Mick.

"He was murdered in '22, during the Civil War," he murmured.

"Michael Collins!" said Mick, raising his glass.

The door to the dining room opened and Gabrielle entered. At twenty-two, she was still girlish, but much more self-assured than when she had first joined the household, which she now ran expertly and efficiently. "Dinner is served," she announced, signaling Kitty to say good night to the grown-ups, who then proceeded to the table.

3

The O'Neills entertained elegantly and often, clients mostly, along with colleagues and cronies of Mick's from the Reform Club. All had their place in the network of supporters and advisers he was gathering around him. Since Jeanne's miscarriage, five years earlier, an unnegoti-ated truce had settled between them. Dr. Stanley had unequivocally decreed, upon her release from hospital, that she was not to attempt to have any more children for the time being. Whether because of the doctor's warning, the fright she had given him, or the guilt he still felt for what had happened, his conjugal ardor had cer-tainly been doused. In return, Jeanne had shown herself more willing to assume the social side of her wifely obligations. Still, if the occasionally intemperate atten-tions of her husband's colleagues were any measure of her skill at serving his ambitions, so too were the envy and suspicion which she sensed just beneath the lac-quered gentility of the women who accompanied them.

The example of the Doyles was typical. Jeanne couldn't help liking Richard, even if after a few drinks he sometimes acted like a boor. He was a big, rather stout man in his forties, with the kind of face that grew more attractive as time rounded out its features and tempered its natural arrogance. His dark, flashing eyes were soft and enveloping when speaking to women, but in the courtroom they could hurl thunderbolts, and strike confusion into the hearts of witnesses even before he began his cross-examination. Despite his graying hair and the heaviness that had set in around his lower jaw, his smile was disarmingly suggestive of the curly-headed, happy baby he must have been. He was profoundly intelligent, a quality Mick revered, powerfully connected, and enormously self-assured. For all these reasons he was the only man who could flirt with Jeanne without arousing her husband's ire, perhaps because the latter took Richard's interest in his wife as a compliment to himself. Violette Doyle on the other hand was a fragile doll who worshiped her husband and was openly hostile to any woman who caught his eye. She detested Jeanne.

4

The first course, a *potage fines herbes* prepared by Georgette from ingredients she grew all winter long on the sill of her kitchen window, was served. The conversation had shifted to Langlois, a man now very much on the decline since his relegation to the back benches by Prime Minister Mackenzie King. Genuinely modest and unvindictive as he was, he had resigned himself to his fate, only once wondering aloud to his son-in-law whether perhaps his loss of influence had anything to do with the affection in which he was held by Lady Laurier, who had an intense dislike of her husband's successor. The time was critical; the Liberal Party was in disarray following its poor showing at the polls, and the Prime Minister was clinging to power by a flimsy constitutional device, which to some was tantamount to usurpation.* Yet still Langlois refused to join the pack of malcontents who were howling for King's head.

"Prime Minister King will surprise us all," the old veteran would reiterate to young doubters like Éloïse, whom her leader, in his four years in power, had impressed as little more than a waffler, a fuddy-duddy, and less pardonably, a bore.

"He's incapable of inspiring anyone," she complained. "If only Talbot Papineau had lived. He was the true heir to Laurier!"

"Oh, stop wringing your hands over Talbot Papineau," Mick interjected, with a hint of irritation. "He's dead, Éloïse, and even you can't bring him back. As for King being a waffler and a procrastinator, that serves him rather well in this instance. It's true the Leader of the Opposition is an eloquent and ferocious opponent, but Arthur Meighen is an imperialist who doesn't understand that this country wants to be a nation. Even worse for him, he's rigid and uncompromising, and he can always be counted on to speak his mind regardless of the political realities of a situation. All King has to do is give him enough rope. He's sure to hang himself, you wait and see."

Later, as dessert was brought in, Mick, reclining rather grandly in his chair at the head of the table, pulled his silver cigarette case out of his jacket pocket.

* The 1925 election yielded 101 Liberal seats (down from 116 at dissolution), 116 Conservative seats (up from 67 at dissolution) and 24 Progressive seats. King chose to hang on to power (although he himself had lost his seat, along with eight of his ministers), over the advice of the Governor General, Lord Byng, and to await the recall of Parliament to try and form a government.

"I take it, Liam," he said, pensively tapping the butt-end of his cigarette against the cigarette case, "you've seen the newspaper today?"

"Yes. MacNeill resigned yesterday," his cousin answered wearily, looking down at his plate and fingering the silver.

"Collins was tricked by Lloyd George." His host grimaced, exhaling smoke through his nostrils in disgust.

"No, Mick!" the Irishman countered tensely. Then, regaining his composure, "Rather, it's not that simple ..."

"Do you think de Valera would have done a better job at the negotiating table?" asked Charles Langlois.

"No," answered the newcomer unequivocally. "De Valera knew, because he was told straight out by Lloyd George in the first days of the Truce,* that neither Parliament nor British public opinion would allow the government to back down on the matter of Partition.** And he knew that if the negotiations succeeded, whoever returned from London with an agreement obtained at such a price would be tainted by the odium of having granted such a concession. That's why, when the time came to negotiate peace with the enemy, de Valera, by far our most experienced and able politician, refused to heed the advice of his ministers, who were urging him to go to London himself, and insisted on namin' Collins negotiator. I can still hear Collins tellin' me that 'twas like the captain of a ship sendin' his crew out to sea while himself remaining to direct operations from dry land. In the end he went, but against his better judgment, and only out of loyalty to de Valera and the need for solidarity at that crucial time."

* between British and IRA forces
** the Partition of Ireland into Northern and Southern Ireland, the former to remain formally a part of the United Kingdom

"You think he suspected what was being done to him?"

"Collins was a realist, a very lucid one. He had gone as far as possible by violent means, and he went as far as he could at the negotiating table. He wasn't had by Lloyd George. On the contrary, he succeeded in obtaining a major concession from the British government. It was up to us to muster the courage and determination to see that it was applied! Collins believed that for the first time in our history we had a shot at creating a society that even those of the other persuasion would have been proud to be part of. Instead," he murmured, with a bitter gleam in his downcast eyes, "we chose to turn on each other, and willfully embrace chaos, civil war ..."

"Obviously," scoffed Mick, "it was to Britain's advantage to prolong the negotiations and hope that all hell would break loose!"

"Be that as it may, when Collins signed the treaty in 1921 he was countin' on the political leadership back home to unite in support of the agreement he had concluded. As President of the Dáil, de Valera took on unprecedented importance, yet he was the first, just three days after the treaty was signed, to denounce it publicly in a letter to the newspapers."

"How Machiavellian," exclaimed Éloïse, her eyes reflecting intense sympathy.

"It wasn't the first time he'd tried to shunt Collins aside. At the height of the Black-and-Tan Terror, he even tried to convince him to leave for the United States. At a time when the enemy was redoubling its efforts to break the back of the movement, when the very survival of all those risking their lives under his command depended on the organization he controlled, and on the reliability of intelligence he alone was in a position to coordinate! He held so many of the strings together in his hands that with him gone, the whole resistance movement would have collapsed into anarchy."

"It makes you wonder," reflected Charles Langlois, "how important a single man can sometimes be to the fate of a nation. One wonders, for example, what would have happened if Lenin had been assassinated during the Russian civil war. Or how things would have turned out in your country if Collins had lived."

"Or here in Canada, if Talbot Papineau had come back from the war," sighed Éloïse.

5

"So, cousin," said Mick as everyone rose from the table. "Are you thinking of settling here, then?"

"No, regretfully, I just stopped to say hello on my way to New York. I've a brother there who's done very well for himself, and who can give me a job."

"You're not leaving Ireland for good, after everything you've been through?" asked Éloïse incredulously.

"So many murders, executions," answered the Irishman in a flat voice, "I couldn't stomach any more ... The Ireland I fought for is dead."

Jeanne shuddered as the others left the room. Her father's reference to Lenin had unsettled her, and now Liam's words reverberated through her memory, summoning forth the shade of another embittered exile, the thought of whom she now avoided the way someone who has nearly drowned avoids the water. Nowadays, if she thought of him at all, it was only with vague resentment at having been so easily left behind.

Just then, she felt two warm hands on her shoulders. She guessed it was Richard Doyle and tried to turn around. They were the only ones left in the dining room. With a powerful squeeze the hands prevented her from moving. He was breathing into the nape of her neck, his lips barely brushing her skin, and chuckling in that low, throaty voice of his. Jeanne tried to summon the energy to act offended, but failed. Coming after the food and wine, there was something sweetly soporific about being held in that way. She fought back the temptation to rest the back of her head on Richard's chest and, watching for Violette through the lace-curtained glass double-doors, disengaged herself. A seraphic smile stretched his plump puffy lips. She caught a whiff of alcohol on his breath. She smiled back and walked away toward the other guests.

"It's late, and my train leaves early in the morning," Liam was saying to Mick when Jeanne joined them.

Her husband eyed her watchfully. The dress she was wearing uncovered most of her graceful shoulders, exposing her lovely neck. He felt his old anger stir within him, as it did whenever he repressed an urge to touch her.

"I can drop you off," offered Éloïse, who in the course of the evening had been transformed from the tomboyish party girl they all knew into a bashful creature who blushed when Liam O'Neill looked in her direction.

6

Later that evening, after everyone had left and Gabrielle and Georgette had retired to their rooms for the night, Kitty was awakened by a fracas on the landing outside her bedroom door. She recognized her father's voice, almost unintelligibly distorted, his words slurred to incoherence as he stumbled noisily up the stairs. Kitty lay frozen with dread in the dark, almost afraid to breathe, not wanting to listen, wanting desperately not to hear the voice crashing against her ears.

"*Go ahead!*" her mother was shouting, the shrill sound jolting through her. "Why don't you! You nearly killed me the last time, why don't you finish the job!"

Kitty had never heard her mother yell in anger. She shrank down under the covers, shrank her snail-self into a tiny shell, limbs curled tightly, hugging her own insignificance, eyes squeezed shut, helplessness dwarfing her, until silence finally returned, and sleep engulfed the nightmare, washed away its imprint, like traces in the sand at high tide.

3

A Seaside Election

In the summer of 1926, the pebble-strewn coves of the
Gaspé coast were awash with more than brine and sea-
weed, and fishermen sometimes earned more from
what they scavenged on the shore than from what they
hauled in from the deep. Nevertheless, their profits
were picayune next to the bonanza that their catch net-
ted party workers of both political hues in their campaign work. For the U.S. Coast Guard, in its continuing
effort to stem the flow of prohibited booze from
Canada, had that year stepped up its surveillance of the
waters along the border, so that would-be smugglers
were regularly dumping their cargo overboard rather
than surrender it to an approaching Coast Guard vessel.
In due time the casks of rum or whisky would float in
on the tide and wash up on the beaches. There they
were quickly collected by the fishermen, whose liveli-
hood did not predispose them to a cultivation of the
profit motive, and who therefore sold off what they
couldn't use at rock-bottom prices. The sharp young
men who ran Charles Langlois's campaign had quickly
moved to corner the supply in their area, where the

incumbent was popular, forcing their Tory *bleu* counterparts to motor far beyond the boundaries of the constituency, where the purchase price of free liquor to oil the wheels of a campaign was considerably steeper, especially for anyone from "outside."

Even though his eager young campaign workers smelled blood, Langlois didn't have to caution them against becoming too complacent. The breathtakingly close contest of the previous year was all too fresh in their memories. Their man had gone down to defeat, only to be saved the next day by a recount—not, however, before the Tories had had a chance to celebrate their "victory" in Cullen's hotel. Frank Cullen was a Conservative. The following night Frank's brother Paul, a Liberal, was serving free champagne to his belatedly triumphant fellow Grits in *his* premises, also known as Cullen's hotel, contiguous to his brother's establishment. This time around Charles Langlois's campaign workers, under Mick O'Neill, weren't taking any chances. They canvassed tirelessly, door-to-door throughout the riding. They packed the front rows at electoral meetings with innocent-looking old ladies, who held their peace sweetly until the hapless Tory candidate rose to speak—whereupon his opening remarks were drowned out by their shrill voices, chanting rhythmically and seemingly indefatigably the words *Con-scrip-tion! Con-scrip-tion!* until pandemonium would erupt in the meeting hall.

2

Éloïse Prud'homme had enthusiastically accepted Charles Langlois's invitation to campaign for him this year. Indeed, the lure of summer in the Gaspé had easily outweighed whatever fascination the hot dusty streets of Montreal's red-light district might previously have held for her. For Jeanne, the presence of Éloïse among her mother's houseguests was a welcome tonic. By selling her house the previous year, Florence's heirs had deprived Jeanne of her yearly retreat and forced her to spend July in the city—which she preferred to having to endure the entire summer in her mother's house. However, this year the coming elections left her no choice: Mick was dividing his time almost equally between Montreal and Carleton each week, and taking the last four weeks before September 14, election day, to devote himself to his father-in-law's campaign. It was Mick who had insisted on bringing in Éloïse, whose talent for recruiting voters more than made up for her being an "outsider."

"Always wait until you're inside the house," she advised Jeanne as they bumped along the backroads in Charles Langlois's venerable Chevrolet. She had just arrived from Montreal that morning, and had insisted on hitting the campaign trail immediately. "The best place to give your little speech is in the front room, the one they use only on Sundays. Make sure you compliment the lady of the house on her lace doilies, or her china if she gives us tea. Ask after her children. Remind her that the federal election is her one chance to vote, that we women can't vote in provincial elections. Then talk about your father and all his great achievements, like the Gaspé railway. Tell her what an honest, honorable man your father is, and how much Sir Wilfrid liked and trusted him. Then talk about the Tories. Not long. You don't want her thinking you take them too seriously. But remind her who imposed conscription, and talk about Tory ties to big business. Remind her who will defend her interests, and who will fight for her old age pension."

"You do the talking, Éloïse," Jeanne demurred. "You're

the pro, you know all these issues backwards. I'm afraid I'm a little out of my depth."

The truth was that "the issues" bored her, and that she had little stake in the outcome of the election other than ensuring that her father, for his sake, was re-elected. Her main motive in accompanying Éloïse on the campaign trail was therapeutic. In her company she found the best available antidote for the poisonous atmosphere of her mother's house.

"Any news from Liam?" Jeanne asked, to change the subject.

"Yes! Oh, Jeanne, he's inviting me to come visit him after the elections. September in New York! I can't wait!"

Jeanne envied Éloïse her infatuation with her husband's cousin. Ever since they'd met a few months before, her friend had been completely transformed. She had lost weight and her face looked slimmer; in fact, she had become much more attractive. Faced with these external manifestations of an affliction with which she was all too familiar, Jeanne had difficulty repressing memories that Éloïse's company painfully revived.

3

Little Kitty, meanwhile, was leading a charmed life in her grandmother's doting care. Together they accompanied the sisters, Mimi's guests, to mass every morning and whiled away the days in their gentle company. Theirs was a hushed, comforting presence, their soothing voices blending with the ever-present murmur of the sea and whisper of the wind. Sometimes, when her father was away, Kitty was allowed to wear the miniature nun's habit that her grandmother's nun friends had made for her, over the objections of her grandfather, who, seeing the child red-faced and perspiring in the midday sun, worried that she might become overheated and faint. Jeanne, watching her daughter flit about on the beach in the distance like a gull feather blown by the wind, and knowing how much Kitty enjoyed the masquerade, refrained from interfering. She feared confusing the child, and dividing her loyalties, by expressing reservations about her unusual pastime. That, she felt, would be more harmful than any hold her grandmother might temporarily have on her.

She had to draw the line, however, the night of the great thunderstorm. Returning alone, drenched to the bone, after going out to an electoral meeting, which in the event was postponed due to the weather, she found a terrified Kitty clinging to her grandmother's skirt as she moved through the house, holding high an oil lamp that cast eerie shadows on the walls and ceiling. She went from window to window, sprinkling holy water and muttering incantations: "God's anger for our sins, child. Beg the Holy Spirit to spare this house!" Jeanne strode in quietly, and not wishing to further frighten Kitty, gathered her daughter into her arms, saying nothing but glaring at her mother reprovingly Later, returning after having calmed the child as best she could and waited until she was asleep, she found her mother standing on the porch in a sort of trance, gazing skyward at the retreating clouds. Sheet lightning periodically lit up the horizon, as thunder rumbled in the distance. She was standing on the edge of the porch, rain beating down on her upturned face, and there was a kind of majesty about the way she stood that conjured up the image of a Montagnais shaman communing with the thunder gods. Jeanne opened her mouth to speak, but found her anger had subsided, soothed perhaps along with Kitty's fear. She went back into the house, unnoticed.

4

Aunt

Miss

1

A thin veil of snow hung in the night, floating like gossamer, or dust from the stars. Not a breath of wind stirred the stillness. The night seemed close and somehow friendly, despite the cold. Jeanne and Mick made their way unhurriedly past the long line of cars parked along Sunnyside Avenue; their footsteps were muted by a film of snow that had settled on the pavement in the preceding hours.

They had already dropped in on one New Year's Eve party and were on their way to another, which was their final destination of the evening. Their host was Trevor Jonas, a young tycoon who had made his money in Great Lakes shipping. Tall, trim, and exquisitely groomed, with blond, boyish looks that promised to last him another thirty years, he was one of Mick's biggest clients. His personality was an unstable combination of effervescent energy and breathtaking arrogance. In 1914, his line of business was declared vital to the nation's security. Thenceforth, he had been too busy building up his empire to volunteer for military service. Later, even conscription had not been a problem. He had had no difficulty in obtaining the necessary exemption, and thus was one member of his generation whose innocence had not been defiled in the Great War. Socially he was third-generation money—North America's version of an aristocrat. As such he didn't need to "wear" his wealth (it was as much a part of him as the blue of his eyes), but as a member of the English elite in a town where the humblest French hod-carrier had roots going back two centuries, he felt it his duty to display it in unequivocal terms. He had built himself a massive limestone mansion near the top of Mount Royal, a veritable palace in the Italian Renaissance style, amid lavishly landscaped grounds that included a tennis court and a swimming pool. The entrance was guarded by two stone lions, now mournfully awaiting summer.

"Mick! Jeanne!" he cried, greeting his guests at the door himself, as was his wont, while the white-gloved butler hovered in the background. "Good to see you! Do come in!"

After being relieved of their coats, the O'Neills were ushered into the cavernous front hall. There, an ancient suit of armor, no doubt acquired by Jonas during his travels, bore silent witness to its long-departed owner's sojourn on this mortal plane. Jeanne always felt a vague unease at this human likeness, so far in time and space from its original purpose, standing vacuously at attention at the foot of Trevor's larger-than-life grand staircase. Her mind lingered on the thought that a human body, anonymous as the unknown soldier, had once sheltered there, and she tried to imagine its face. But these private musings were soon overtaken as the house itself reasserted its claim on her attention. The purpose of its design was clearly to impress, even to awe, as though Trevor could not bear his guests' thoughts to stray from the course on which he sought, architecturally and in every way possible, to lead them.

Three vast reception rooms occupied the ground floor, the largest of which, the ballroom, ran the entire length of the house and looked out onto the gardens at the back. Conspicuously intended to evoke the Galerie des Glaces at Versailles, it had six ceiling-to-floor gilded mirrors along one side, facing and reflecting six French doors on the opposite side, which made the room look twice its actual size. In summer, the doors opened onto the stone terrace. There, visitors sat under a geranium-pink awning amid a profusion of flowering plants in carved stone planters, whose reflection via the mirrors filled the interior of the ballroom with delicate pink light.

"I wanted the room to change with the seasons," Trevor would invariably explain to the gushing superlatives of a first-time guest.

In the dead of winter, the cold snowy landscape outside, or at night the scene of scintillating city lights below, was offset by the warm maroon of the velvet drapes and upholstery, and the brightly burning fire in the two monumental fireplaces at either end of the long room.

An orchestra was playing dance music and the floor was already crowded with couples. In one of the two adjoining rooms a jazz band played to a younger, somewhat wilder set, while the older people clustered around a bar and milled about two long buffet tables laden with fresh oysters, turkey aspics, lobster salads, whole smoked salmon, and for those who could still manage a second course after the weeks of pre- and post-Christmas feasting, trifles, puddings, and cheeses of every description.

As they made their way toward the bar, Mick and Jeanne almost bumped into Richard Doyle on his way out. Gallantly he offered Jeanne the goblet of champagne that he had just obtained for his wife.

"You look positively stunning, my dear," he purred as Mick disappeared to fetch himself a drink and replace that which Richard had given up. "Even more so than usual in that dress."

"This isn't a dress," Jeanne answered him with a throaty laugh, "it's an election ploy! Mick bought it specially for the elections. He insisted I wear it on voting day. He had me stand at the polling station in Carleton, starting at eight in the morning. I spent the whole day shaking voters' hands, while Éloïse reminded them to vote for Daddy!"

"Brilliant!" chortled Richard, taking advantage of the excuse to leer at her from head to toe.

The dress, a swishy Jeanne Lanvin model in ruby-red satin, bared her shoulders and hugged her figure.

"Request permission to kidnap your wife, for two dances at least!" Richard called out to Mick who was wending his way back through the crowd with a drink in each hand.

"Permission granted, Richard. You know I don't dance," Mick replied, keeping a careful eye on his two champagne goblets. "Where's Violette? I'll take her her drink."

2

Richard was a good dancer when he wasn't completely drunk, but his bulk made him difficult to dance with unless pressed against him in a way that was unsettling. At the end of the third number Jeanne excused herself and retreated to the powder room, where two other women were busy touching up their lipstick. Looking into the mirror, she saw her reflection, and in her eyes, the bitterness that assailed her each time she was confronted with the emptiness of her life.

Leaving the powder room she passed into the front hall, which seemed to her as vast and impersonal as the hall of a bank. At its center rose the grand staircase. Jeanne looked up momentarily. At the very top of it a man in a dinner jacket, eyes shaded by the brim of the top hat he wore tilted at a cocky angle on his head, was sitting astride the mahogany banister, appraising the angle of descent. Tipping his hat to the back of his head with a flick of his finger, and thrusting his hands into the pockets of his trousers, he came shooting down, legs outstretched for balance, and landed nimbly on his feet in front of her. He was tall and well-built; and as he adjusted the angle of his top hat, Jeanne was certain she had seen him before.

3

The thought nagged her as she made her way back through the crowd toward the table where Mick and the Doyles had joined dear old Miss Marshall, looking more frail and bird-like than ever in a pearl-gray Patou gown. The dreaded Hutchison, her female bodyguard, was nowhere to be seen.

"Jeanne!" cried Miss Marshall in a thin, reedy voice, extending a tiny claw. "How delightful you look! Sit down, dear girl!"

Jeanne did as she was asked. She was fond of the old lady, although she and Mick saw her only rarely. Her health had been deteriorating for years, as was attested by the wheelchair in which she sat, so that she had long ceased giving dinners in her wonderful house. It must have been a decade at least since anyone had seen her out on the town.

"Where is Hutchison?" Jeanne inquired.

"She's in England," Miss Marshall responded rather excitedly, "for another two weeks. Her father died, poor thing, just before Christmas, and her mother was quite desperate for her to go home and help sort out his affairs. Apparently he left everything in a dreadful muddle. She's an only child, you know, so she couldn't very well refuse to go."

Then raising a blue-veined hand to her mouth, she added, with a glint of mischief in her round, little eyes:

"I could never have come tonight if she'd been here. She would not have allowed it."

"Have you got someone filling in for her, then?"

"Well, yes and no. I do have someone at home performing all the duties she would normally carry out. But that would certainly not include taking me to this party. Heaven forbid!" she giggled, with a breathless little wheeze. "But here I am and my dear, I am having the time of my life."

She pressed one hand to her heart and sighed. Jeanne had never seen her so animated.

"I'm invited to all the parties at this time of year, you know, and it's really rather sweet of all these people to keep me on their guest list year in and year out even though I never turn up. But this year, well. Here I am."

She smiled, now looking less bird-like and rather more like the cat who swallowed the proverbial canary.

"Oh, do tell," Jeanne cajoled, playing along. "How did you manage it?"

"Louis saw the invitation on the mantelpiece among the Christmas cards—Louis, my nephew," she added, "you've met him, I think? And he simply announced, 'You're going,' and that was that. And he is a doctor, so I assume he knows what he's doing. He insisted it would be good for me to get out of the house. He freed himself for the evening and made all the arrangements. My dear, how could I resist?" she beamed.

"Yes, of course," said Jeanne a little distractedly. "I think I've just seen him. On the stairs."

It was all coming back to her now: the cold dawn of the hospital room, the winter whiteness outside, and the tall young doctor, tired at the end of his night shift, the honesty with which he had answered her question, after she'd met with nothing but evasions from the nurse ... Now, all at once, she made the connection between the serious young man in a hospital coat and the nephew in army uniform whom Miss Marshall had once briefly introduced to her at a dinner party at her home.

"Come on, Jeanne, time for another dance," Richard, standing behind her chair, broke into her thoughts.

Mick had gone off to the bar again and Violette was out on the dance floor with Trevor Jonas himself. Jeanne, not wanting to leave Miss Marshall alone, was about to refuse.

"Off you go, my dear," the old lady commanded, before Jeanne could decline. "There is nothing that gives me more pleasure than watching young people enjoying themselves."

4

The orchestra played a waltz but Richard, predictably, was considerably less sober than he had been an hour earlier. His hands were wandering stupidly and Jeanne was on the point of forcibly extricating herself when someone behind her cut in, pushing Richard aside politely but firmly.

"Do you mind? You looked as though you could use some rescuing," said the intruder.

"Thanks! Richard is nice but when he drinks, he's impossible."

"Haven't we met?" he said, with slightly raised eyebrows. He still hadn't introduced himself, but Jeanne knew exactly who he was.

"I ... I know your aunt ..."

"You know Aunt Miss? I really don't see her as often as I should." He laughed softly. She didn't take offense.

"Is that what you call her, 'Aunt Miss'?"

"Actually she's my great-aunt, but I've always called her that. I must have picked it up as a boy from one of her attendants. She's always had to have someone to look after her."

"And they called her 'Miss'?"

"That's right. But tell me, what brings you to this particular den of thieves?"

"New Year's Eve?" Jeanne answered tentatively, obviously puzzled by the unexpected pointedness of his question.

"You like dancing, don't you?" he remarked as the music ended, and without pausing, he said, "Come on," and led her into the next room, where a boisterous Charleston was in progress.

"I really should—" Jeanne began, shouting over the din of the jazz band.

"Don't talk!" he shouted back, holding her firmly by the hand. His admonition needed no explaining, given the concentration required for their feet to keep time with the frantic pace of the music. Jeanne had come a long way since her first dance in 1919 and could Charleston and fox-trot as well as any flapper. The band played one delirious number after another and her new partner, whose lankiness dictated a certain economy of movement, kept right on dancing.

"About time they took a break," he said when the music finally ended. "What's your name, anyway?"

"Jeanne O'Neill," she replied, still catching her breath, and without knowing why, she was immediately sorry she'd said it.

"Come on, then, Jeanne O'Neill," he said, "I'll take you back to your table. I've really got to take Aunt Miss home. It's hours past her bedtime."

She noticed that his dinner jacket was of a rather ancient cut, and a little too big for him. He was visibly not the society type, which, to a woman as deeply bored in "society" as Jeanne, only made him more interesting.

5

"Louis, you dear boy!" Miss Marshall's face lit up when she spotted her nephew coming through the crowd. "He's been dancing with Jeanne, bless him. It shows he has taste, doesn't it, Michael?"

Louis Marshall shook hands with Mick, who was watching him attentively. Then, catching sight of Richard, who had been sitting with his back turned, he said, "Sorry, old chap. I couldn't resist cutting in."

"Don't blame you," Richard muttered vaguely, slightly slack-jawed from drink. With his fleshy mouth and wayward curls, he looked like a pouting baby, and quite endearing despite it all.

"I hate to tear you away, Auntie," her nephew announced regretfully, "but if I don't take you home now, my humble coach will turn into a pumpkin at the first stroke of midnight. Doctor's orders, come on."

Miss Marshall smiled gratefully at her nephew. Positively glowing with pleasure, she said her goodbyes to each person around the table, as he waited, slightly aloof with his hands in his pockets, looking benevolently on in an attitude that signaled her not to tarry too long.

"Good night, all," he said finally, positioning himself behind the frail old woman's wheelchair. "Happy New Year!"

Without realizing it, Jeanne was waiting for him to look at her. The pleasant little jolt she felt when he did made her drop her gaze.

Moments later, or so it seemed, the lights dimmed, the orchestra struck up "Auld Lang Syne," and people in every part of the crowded vastness of the house fell to hugging and kissing each other euphorically and exchanging good wishes. In the elusive instant when the old year fades into the new and the future blurs with ritualistic hope, Jeanne, much as an atheist occasionally glimpses then shrugs off the possibility of life after death, fleetingly beheld a wish, then just as quickly dismissed it. Then Trevor Jonas's New Year's kiss roused her from her reverie. When the music started up again her feet resumed dancing, but her heart felt as wintry and barren as the nightscape outside the great windows, where the lights of the city below glittered coldly under the black sky.

6

It all finally began on a frozen January afternoon, as the pale dusk lingered and imperceptibly faded. The snowy landscape gradually darkened under a sky still suffused with pink. Already there were fewer skaters on the rink than an hour ago, when the sun was still high. In the little hut at the edge of the ice, children huddled round the potbellied woodstove warming their hands, but Kitty was still skating, practicing the figure-eights her mother had taught her. She had just celebrated her eighth birthday and Jeanne, an accomplished figure skater who preferred the larger, better-tended ice surface of the Montreal Coliseum, had taken her to the outdoor rink on the McGill University campus to try out her new skates. Jeanne stopped in front of the snowbank at the far end of the rink from the little hut, with its smoking stove-pipe chimney poking crookedly out of its roof.

"It seems you skate almost as well as you dance," came a voice above and behind her. The earlier cacophony of children's shouts and squeals had largely died down, and Jeanne heard the words quite clearly. But the split second it took her to turn her head left her no time to speculate on who had spoken them. At the top of the snowbank in the gathering gloom, outlined against the mauve sky, she saw the tall figure of Louis Marshall, hands deep in his coat pockets, smiling down at her, and at his feet a big, grinning dog of indeterminate lineage.

"Oh, hello!" Her voice wavered slightly in the cold. He took a few steps down the bank toward her, seeming as he did so to detach himself from the scenery, with the dog bounding next to him, wagging a great *panache* of a tail.

"Do you often come here to skate?" asked Louis, once he was close enough not to have to shout. He was bareheaded despite the cold, and had on a well-worn, loose-fitting tweed coat.

"I live nearby," answered Jeanne, slightly beside the point, just as Kitty skated up beside her.

"Your little sister's not a bad skater herself," he observed with a wry smile, prompting from Jeanne a burst of astonished laughter.

"This is Catherine," she said, tenderly tucking a stray lock of hair under the child's white fur bonnet, "my pride and joy, aren't you, darling? Say hello to Dr. Marshall." Kitty complied, biting her lower lip and smiling shyly.

"Well, young Catherine, this is Winston. Say hello, mutt!" he commanded, but the dog kept right on running exuberant circles around them on the ice, tongue lolling, grinning his best dog grin. "Hopelessly insubordinate. I really don't have enough time for him," he sighed.

"You look cold, young lady," said Jeanne, noticing that Kitty was shivering slightly. "You'd better go and change out of those skates. The hut is nice and warm. We'll go home as soon as you're ready," she added, more to herself perhaps than to Kitty.

"Do you come here to skate?" she asked Louis when Kitty was gone, unintentionally reiterating his opening question, then added quickly, "I don't recall seeing you here."

"And yet, and yet ..." he smiled, teasing her. "You just didn't notice. Seriously, where did you learn to skate like that?"

"I practice three days a week at the Coliseum ..." she volunteered, suddenly worrying that she might appear to be giving out information that would allow him to see her again if he wished, which of course was exactly what she had done.

"You're getting cold yourself," he pointed out, and she realized that she was hunching her shoulders and hugging herself stiffly. "You'd better run along."

"What about you? You're not even wearing a hat!"

"A hothead like me has no use for a hat," he answered wryly, waving her off nevertheless.

His was a self-deprecating kind of humor. Underlying it, like bedrock, she sensed a seriousness that was as integral to him as the amber brown of his eyes. She smiled and waved, then turned away, even though nothing would have felt more natural to her at that moment than to stand and watch him walk away, fading into the scenery in the failing light with his big, shaggy dog. Then she felt Kitty slip her little mittened hand in hers. Her touch was real, as real as the comfort she drew from her childish love. It was the one fact of her life she did not relegate to the level of "circumstance." There were the circumstances under which she was obliged to live, and then there was Kitty ...

7

Despite the chance encounter that sharpened for a time the focus of her existence, placing her in a state of expectation, Jeanne's fate after that brief passage through the rapids resumed its flatly predictable course. Yet every life, no matter how dark, is occasionally illuminated by an event that ascends, flare-like, lighting the horizon with a blaze of hope—the unforeseen, subversive promise of unimagined happiness. Between two people the initial shock of recognition may be confirmed and amplified by a later meeting, but if it has no sequel, it will remain no more than a stillborn moment, leaving only a vague sense of loss, and a periodic ache for what might have been.

However, depending on the force of the attraction and the cruelty of the need, there may come a threshold that must be crossed. In the case of Jeanne O'Neill and Louis Marshall that threshold, although neither of them knew it when they parted company on that snowy January afternoon, was barely more than a glance away. To cross it, Louis need only have looked back, and perhaps he did know it as he stalked off, stiff-backed, eyebrows knitted against the phantom image in his head, as bright as a summer sun on closed eyelids, of her luminous eyes. But he let her go, sensing it was both too early in their acquaintance, and too late in her life's unfolding, to act on the impulse that seeing her had again triggered. As for Jeanne, the thought of Louis eventually erased itself from her mind like the subsiding ripples on the surface of a pond after a stone has been cast into it, yet like a stone he remained embedded, undisturbed, and unretrieved, on the silty bottom of her consciousness.

5

Johnny's in Town

Montreal, Sunday, July 31, 1927 Kitty lay in her bed, staring into the darkness, steadfastly fending off sleep. She was waiting for a sign, out there in the warm night. For weeks now Montreal had been abuzz with anticipation as the arrival of Their Royal Highnesses, the Prince of Wales and his younger brother Prince George, drew near. For the first time the British prime minister was also expected, but the focus of all the excitement was plainly the heir to the throne, whose popularity had not waned since the war, and whose affection for the city was well known. In the dark, Kitty listened to the whispering of the leaves outside her open window, which seemed at times to swell with the murmur of a thousand voices. She was disappointed not to have been allowed to accompany Gabrielle, who along with Georgette had joined the crowd already lining Sherbrooke Street in hopes of glimpsing the Princes on their way to their hotel. Mummy said that Kitty was too young to be out on the streets that late, but that she could go with Gabrielle in the morning to watch the motorcade heading the other way, en route to City Hall.

"Besides," Mummy had argued, "you wouldn't be able to see much in the dark anyway."

Kitty, confident that the city itself would divulge the precise moment at which the Princes finally arrived, was determined to stay awake. At last, just before ten, the first discordant sounds, amorphous and scattered like those from an orchestra tuning up before a performance, wafted up from the direction of the harbor. From the distant bellow of foghorns on the river to the mounting stridency of cars honking from the shore, the sound gradually gathered force as wailing sirens and shrieking whistles joined the chorus. The entire city seemed to explode with the pyrotechnic hissing of rockets and the booming of a twenty-one-gun salute, over the drone and roar of myriad human voices. Then suddenly, as though at the behest of an unseen baton, there was silence. A long silence, which Kitty's imagination strained to fill with the arrival of the majestic S. S. *St. Lawrence*—photographs of the splendid ship as it made its way up the river had been in all the newspapers in the preceding days—approaching the Prince of Wales wharf, which Mummy had taken her to see earlier in the day.

At ten minutes past ten precisely, a great cheer went up in the distance. The sound cleaving the warm evening air electrified her. For a moment she dared to think of dressing and slipping out into the night, to the place not half a block from her house where the motorcade was due to pass. Gradually the sounds rippled closer, through the crowds that thronged the quays and lined the route from the riverfront at the bottom of McGill Street all the way up to Sherbrooke. Soon, as she drifted in and out of sleep, the great river of sound was lapping at the bottom of her street and then rolling along

Sherbrooke like a slow-moving wave, decreasing in volume as its crest moved slowly west. Well before Their Royal Highnesses had reached the Ritz-Carlton Hotel, Kitty Florence O'Neill had fallen fast asleep.

2

In the little township of Mount Royal, in the Montreal district, eager citizens began congregating early. Taking advantage of the perfect summer weather, they drifted in groups toward the CN overpass where, according to the itinerary published in the newspapers, the motors containing Their Royal Highnesses, the Prince of Wales and Prince George, were to drive by on their way to the Golf Club at Laval-sur-le-lac. The bridge over the railway had been colorfully decorated for the occasion, the roadway bedecked with banners and Union Jacks. Young girls fussed over bouquets of flowers, while small children in their Sunday best, sporting miniature flags, were lined up smartly on both sides of the road. Older children staked out positions on the bridge itself, or on the big howitzer squatting mournfully at the center of the intersection.

Three or four times a ripple of excitement traveled through the crowd but quickly ebbed as the motorcade failed to appear. At about two o'clock a clerk came running out of a drugstore with a telephoned message—the itinerary had been changed at the last moment, the drive-by called off—but the crowd was slow to disperse. All over the island of Montreal that day, along the main thoroughfares from Saint-Denis Street to Gouin Boulevard, and on packed front porches in the French-Canadian villages of Cartierville and L'Abord-à-Plouffe along the river, the crowds waited into the afternoon. While church bells pealed in vain all along their expected route, the Royal brothers, traveling at breakneck speed in a closed taxicab, had given everyone the slip, leaving a posse of reporters, photographers, and even Scotland Yard detectives scrambling to catch up. That evening, having spent a more relaxed afternoon on the golf course than would have been the case had they followed the prearranged program, the Princes were in a better frame of mind to acknowledge the acclaim of Westmounters, who left their dinner tables by the hundreds to watch them go by. Returning from a garden party on the mountain, they sat in an open touring car, smiling and raising their straw hats to the women and girls in brightly colored summer dresses who cheered and waved their handkerchiefs along the route.

3

How things change, thought Jeanne, watching impassively as two bejeweled matrons vied for her husband's attention. A few years ago he wouldn't have been caught dead at a garden party in honor of the British monarchy. What a transformation he had undergone from the tense, awkward young man she had known, so ill at ease outside his tight, exclusively male circle of lawyers and politicians. Who would have predicted that the dour, silent man he had become in private would in public be a snake-charmer to the females of the Westmount elite? Struggling to keep the poison in her soul from seeping into her eyes, her smile, her voice, she wondered whether the unhappiness gnawing at her heart was due to more than just the resentment of a captive. Maybe she envied these women, their obvious contentment with their lot, their self-satisfaction. They at least were enjoying themselves. Given the part that they had all been assigned by fate or the accident of birth, moments like these were by all accounts among the finest to be had.

Not far from where they were standing, a clutch of young debutantes, exquisitely turned out in the latest Paris summer fashions, jockeyed discreetly for the best position for a first glimpse of the Prince of Wales—whose car, they were told, had just pulled up outside the Jonas mansion. As they waited they chatted excitedly, exchanging gossipy speculation concerning a certain Madeleine Taschereau (*"A French Canadian, can you believe it!"*) to whom the Prince was rumored to have taken a fancy at the time of his last visit, in 1919. To Jeanne their very silliness was a cruel reminder of a time of life which she had barely known. Now, in the waning months of her twenty-eighth year, she bore the lonely ripening of her own womanhood like a bloom whose core had failed to unfold. Her mood of dispirited isolation prevented her from partaking of the strong stimulant the other guests were indulging in—a heady mélange of snobbish vanity and self-congratulation at having made "the list." With the arrival of Prime Minister Baldwin and his wife a general giddiness had taken hold. The quiet murmur of conversation from the small knots of people scattered about the shady grounds had increased to an expectant buzz, crackling here and there with modulated peals of female laughter as the well-heeled crowd instinctively gravitated toward the central portion of the garden. There stood the small pavilion, topped by the gilded crown and three ostrich feathers of the Prince of Wales's crest, which Trevor Jonas had erected for the Princes' private use. For the honor of flying the royal standard, even the flagpole had been painted in yellow and blue, the Prince's colors.

Then at last the band of the Canadian Grenadier Guards, resplendent in their scarlet tunics against the green of the lawn, struck up "Johnny's in Town," said to be an old favorite of the Prince's. Taking their cue, the royal brothers finally appeared from the end of the garden closest to the house and made their way slowly toward the main pavilion, stopping to shake hands and chat along the way.

"I had the privilege of meeting him last time," a female voice in Jeanne and Mick's group was saying. "He's simply charming. Oh look, he hasn't changed a bit."

"I had no idea his hair was so fair," gushed her neighbor, giving no sign that she was aware of having been upstaged. "Photographs really don't do him justice."

"Trevor has put the entire second floor of the house at the Princes' disposal," added the first woman, pressing her advantage. "One of the rooms has been rearranged so that they can go up for a private drink with someone and even a dance, if they wish. The room has a spacious balcony—you can see it from here, it's the one on the right, overlooking the gardens. It has an absolutely gorgeous view of the river, even better than the one from down here. Trevor's even moved a piano onto the balcony and hired someone to play for them, if required."

Jeanne looked out over the city sprawling on either side of the St. Lawrence below. The view was breathtaking, the weather so clear that the mountains across the American border were visible in the distance. She too had had the privilege of meeting the Prince, but in her case the memory was a painful one, of waiting, of wanting, and of her brutal reward for a blameless evening.

As the Princes and their party were passing, Trevor Jonas spotted the O'Neills. As golden as ever with his blond hair and his summer tan, dressed in white flannels and a nautical navy blazer, he beckoned to them to approach. Placing his hand lightly under his wife's elbow, Mick excused himself from the group and came forward.

"Your Highness, may I present Mr. and Mrs. Michael O'Neill," murmured Trevor, first to the Prince of Wales, then to Prince George.

"Delighted to see you. How good of you to come," replied the Prince of Wales in his slightly nasal drawl. Prince George, who was said to suffer from a bad stutter, simply smiled and shook their hands.

He's changed too, thought Jeanne as the royal brothers and their retinue moved on. Sadness was still etched in his features, but it seemed to have slackened to boredom. The charm was still there, but he no longer put any energy into it. It was as though he too were merely going through the motions, however graciously; as if, however exquisitely polished the exterior he chose to display to the world, the core of him, whatever more there was behind those pale eyes, had somehow died.

4

Ignoring the eddies on the surface of his marriage, Mick O'Neill at thirty-one was nearing, both in age and in experience, an important stage in the life of an aspiring politician. An increasing number of the people who mattered were beginning to consider him ready to emerge from the cocoon of the back rooms into the glare of the public arena. The first tangible signs of this impending apotheosis had come, propitiously enough, in Ottawa on July 1, amid the celebrations for the Diamond Jubilee of Confederation. The Prime Minister, who was known to have personally supervised preparations for the event down to the smallest detail, including the invitation list, had made a point when they met of congratulating Mick on his organizing and fund-raising work in the last two election campaigns. Then Mr. King had gone a step further: "It would be most gratifying to me," he'd added in his rather florid way, "to think that you were beginning to envisage running for us yourself next time ..."

Now, on this sunny Friday in September, Mick O'Neill knew that his ship had finally come in. He had been summoned to a late lunch at the Reform Club by no less a personage than the Honorable Ernest Lapointe, Prime Minister Mackenzie King's all-powerful Quebec lieutenant. The Prime Minister, Mick was told confidentially, was "weeding his garden," slowly but surely retiring the old guard among his MPs, and actively recruiting younger, brighter men to surround him in the coming years. In particular, after the seeming eons King had spent enduring the tongue-lashings of Arthur Meighen (now mercifully seatless), whose scintillating sarcasm he could never hope to equal, he was looking for the kind of candidate who would offer him not only new blood but also a razor-sharp mind, with debating skills to match. Some would have to wait until the general election, but a handful would get their chance now. The Prime Minister was preparing to put a small contingent of well-deserving old warhorses out to pasture in the Senate, perhaps as early as next summer, Lapointe explained. A rash of by-elections would soon follow. One of the ridings under consideration was in Montreal.

"In another year, Michael, you'll be thirty-two. You're already nearing the pinnacle of your profession." Lapointe seemed unaware of Mick's political ambition, proof perhaps that the young man had played his cards well, successfully casting himself as a loyal, dedicated party supporter, whose main ambition lay in private life, where he was doing very well indeed. In fact, he had recently become a full partner of the firm, which, following the death of its founder, now went by the name of O'Connell Doyle O'Neill.

"You're now approaching the peak of your energy and vigor," Lapointe continued, "which puts you in the best possible position from which to leap to the challenge of a new career. The party needs you. The country needs you. The Prime Minister wants you to give the matter the most thoughtful consideration."

"The Prime Minister does me great honor," Mick humbly replied, choosing his words with care, "which I will do my utmost to live up to. Have you any idea of when this riding is likely to become available?"

"It's probably safe to say that the Prime Minister will be acting on it within the year," Lapointe replied. "He wants to give you plenty of time to prepare the ground. Needless to say the seat is extremely safe, but the Leader wants nothing left to chance."

"Please tell the Prime Minister that I deeply appreciate the opportunity," Mick concluded, "and that he can rest assured that he will not be disappointed."

As he stepped onto the sun-drenched street after this momentous interview, Mick looked jubilantly at his watch. Almost four o'clock. A year and two days after Mackenzie King's triumph at the polls. This was an afternoon he would long remember. He drew a deep breath of the sweet, late-summer air, and reached into his jacket pocket for the silver lighter and cigarette case bearing his monogram. Life was good, the gods were kind. The performance for which he had been rehearsing all his adult life—in the courts, at his clubs, in the meeting halls, at the back of shops, and ultimately in the streets—was about to begin. But on that blessedly cloudless day, he would have had to have been a seer to divine that, not ten streets away as the crow flies, his luck had already run out.

6

Girl of
My Dreams

1

At three-thirty on that same September afternoon, Jeanne changed into a black sheath dress with long sleeves of black voile that flattered her slender arms. She put on a stylish new black straw hat with a low, shoulder-width brim, and smiled at Kitty through the mirror.

"What do you think?"

"You're so beautiful," the girl sighed adoringly.

"Let me take a look at you, now," Jeanne said, holding her daughter at arm's length. "Shall I put a bow in your hair? You choose a ribbon."

Kitty selected, from among the special ones her mother kept in a drawer of her dresser, a wide plaid ribbon to match her short navy-and-white tartan skirt. Jeanne tied it into a big, fluffy bow on the side of her head.

"Do you like it?"

"Oh, yes, Mummy. It looks fashionable," Kitty remarked approvingly.

Jeanne smiled at the grown-up adjective.

"Let's go then, miss," she concluded, and after reassuring Gabrielle that they would be back in good time for Kitty's dinner, they were off on their weekly outing. They cut through McGill University and walked in the dappled shade of the big trees lining Sherbrooke Street. They then ambled down Peel Street holding hands, the tall slim woman in the elegant hat and the lanky child in the schoolgirl kilt, chatting animatedly, so that it took the honking of a car horn a few feet away to make Jeanne turn her head toward the street. Someone had just pulled up alongside them, bareheaded and smiling at the wheel of a rather weather-beaten convertible.

"Can I give you two ladies a lift somewhere?" he asked, leaning across the passenger's seat toward them.

Jeanne felt the shock of seeing him again. She turned to Kitty and gave her a look which her daughter was too young to interpret for what it was. It purported to ask her opinion, but in reality it masked the sort of panic a novice diver feels just before springing off the high board.

"Why not?" Jeanne replied at last.

They got into the car, Kitty squeezing in between her mother and the driver.

"Where to?" asked Louis Marshall, looking steadily into the rear-view mirror as he pulled away from the curb.

Suddenly Jeanne felt very silly. Their destination was less than two blocks away. It would seem ludicrous to have accepted a ride to cover a distance which they could just as well have walked.

"We're going tea-dancing," Kitty piped up, unexpectedly coming to her mother's rescue. Jeanne laughed nervously.

"The Mount Royal Hotel," she said, then quickly, self-consciously, added, "It's silly really, it's just around the—"

"Sounds like fun," the doctor cut in, "I could do with a cup of tea right about now. Do you mind if I come along?"

"I'll invite you if you want...!"

Jeanne looked with surprise at her normally shy daughter. Kitty was blushing, but she seemed to like Dr. Marshall instinctively, a fact that Jeanne found reassuring somehow.

"Then it's decided," he declared with a winning smile.

He parked the car and got out. As he came round the front of the vehicle to her side, Jeanne noticed again the slight awkwardness of his long-limbed gait, and the oversized jacket hanging too loosely from his broad shoulders. He opened the passenger door and helped her out. Their hands touched. Jeanne lifted her gaze and his eyes held her. She felt something quicken and well up inside her, like sap rising in a spring heat.

They went inside. In the ballroom they found a table not far from the dance floor, where well-dressed couples were fox-trotting to the strains of Charlie Dornburger's tuxedo-clad orchestra. The waiter, recognizing two of his regular Friday afternoon customers, came over to take their order.

"Well, Miss Catherine," said Louis Marshall when the latter had gone, "how about granting me the first dance?"

The child, too tongue-tied to reply, rose wide-eyed from her chair. Dr. Marshall drew himself up, smoothed back his thick, unruly hair, and cleared his throat. Kitty laughed shyly as he offered her his arm.

Jeanne watched them move stiffly about the dance floor, Kitty biting her lip and looking furtively to right and left while Dr. Marshall talked her through the steps. Time seemed to be rushing by, rolling away like scenery from the window of a train. Soon he would step outside her life again, leaving a memory of no more substance than the dreams that tumbled through her nights, strewing meaningless debris in their wake. But she could no more let him vanish than she could hold on to the passing moment. Tea arrived just as Kitty and the doctor returned.

"Mummy's turn now, right, Catherine?" he declared, looking steadily at Jeanne. Kitty giggled self-consciously as Louis pulled out her chair for her.

"Are you going to be all right here by yourself?" her mother asked her.

Kitty nodded, smiling timidly, her eyes on the plate of cookies in the middle of the table. Jeanne poured her daughter a cup of weak tea with plenty of milk, leaving her to add the sugar herself. "No more than three cubes now, Kitty," she cautioned, as if to resist for a second further the powerful current that was sweeping her away.

They reached the dance floor as the orchestra struck up "What'll I Do?" He turned toward her and wrapped his arm around her waist. "It's good to see you," he said. His voice rasped softly. It was deep and rich. It caressed her. She felt the pressure of his hand easing her against him, the surprise of his body through their summer clothes.

"I can't stay long," he said quietly into her hair as they moved to the slow fox-trot. "They're waiting for me at the clinic. It's only once a week, and people are depending on me."

Jeanne started inwardly. The music was going to end. He was going to leave. Disoriented by the sudden arousal of her senses, she closed her eyes, her mind clinging fiercely to the moment about to end, striving to commit it to memory. The song ended. He pulled back and looked at her searchingly, like someone who is used to weighing consequences. "Can I see you again?" he asked earnestly.

But Jeanne hadn't weighed anything. A thick fog of emotion shrouded her thoughts. She knew only that she had ventured so far out of the shallows that she had lost her footing.

"I'm going to a concert," she blurted almost inaudibly. "At McGill, next week."

"When next week?"

"Tuesday."

"What time?"

"Eight. It's—it's Mozart."

She was having trouble getting the words out, too perturbed by the sudden confluence of dismay and hope to make much sense of what was being said.

"I don't know what time I can make it, but I'll be there. Look for me?"

They made their way back to the table where Kitty was sitting, loudly crunching sugar cubes. She smiled apologetically at her mother's mild remonstrations. Louis helped Jeanne into her chair. He remained standing and gulped down his tea. Then, reaching for the plate of cookies, he helped himself to two. "For the road," he said, popping one in his mouth and the other into his pocket. He gave Jeanne an eloquent look.

"Thanks for the dance," he said, winking at Kitty. Then in a few strides, stopping just long enough to slip the waiter a few bills, he was gone.

2

September 20, 1927 Rain poured down as Jeanne left the house, a drenching, quasi-tropical rain, so aberrantly warm for late September that steam rose from the cobbled pavement, as though summer were being held over for a few more days. She had taken Mick's big black umbrella, but even it was inadequate in such a downpour. The water struck the ground with such force that it rebounded, splashing her legs and the hem of her skirt, but she didn't care. She crossed the street running, less to escape from the weather than in her haste to reach her destination. She wasn't late. If anything she was a little early, but with Kitty doing her homework and Mick away in Quebec City for the week, she saw no point in waiting around the house any longer. In any case, Mick knew she was going to the concert, so there was no danger if he called. The freedom she felt as she ran the few hundred yards to Moyse Hall in the rain was a pleasure she savored with her whole consciousness. Come what might, the heavy boom of reality would fall soon enough. She ran up the stone steps. Pausing for a moment under the high portico like a bird shaking its feathers dry, she closed her umbrella, glancing casually at the faces of the other concert-goers as they hurried up the steps toward her in the pouring rain.

The entrance hall was fairly empty but for a few sodden students standing about, lighting cigarettes, presumably waiting for their companions for the evening to appear. Not wishing to join their number, Jeanne went straight into the auditorium, by now abuzz with a near-capacity crowd. As she made her way unhurriedly to her seat, she scanned the rows of faces as discreetly as she could. She tried reminding herself of what he had said, of his uncertainty about the time, but there was no combating the sinking feeling, the doubt that gripped her.

Applause rippled through the audience as the musicians walked onto the stage, thirteen of them, carrying their shiny wind instruments. Most of them were students from McGill's Faculty of Music, looking improbably elegant in their tails before the damp, weather-bedraggled audience. They sat down, arranged the sheet music on the stands in front of them, and tuned their instruments. Merciful darkness descended and the expectant hush enfolded Jeanne. The program in her hand read:

McGill Music Society
AN EVENING OF MOZART
Tuesday, September 20th, 1927
Performed by students, members, and alumni of the
MCGILL FACULTY OF MUSIC

Florence had been moved to tears by Mozart, but his music had always left Jeanne cold. For all its esthetic and technical perfection, and despite her best efforts, she could not love it as Florence had, a failing she deplored as a defect in herself.

The musicians attacked in perfect unison, and the reflective mood of the opening movement settled on the hall. In her distracted state, Jeanne found that the hushed attentiveness of the audience merely prolonged the suspense, stretching each minute, until the air grew thin and her breathing shallow. She looked down at her program: three more movements after this one. She had already lost interest in the labors of the performers. The primal hope with which she had come into this place was now contaminated with doubt. She loathed the anxiety that came with it, but she could not now retreat back into senselessness. She had returned to the realm of the living, the dominion of pain.

She spent the intermission searching the faces in the lobby, and thought of going home. The second half of the concert dirged on interminably, until at last there came the finality of applause, the lights coming on. As the hall emptied she dithered dejectedly, gathering her purse, her program, her umbrella, pulling on her coat, which was still damp from the rain.

3

As she started down the steps outside she saw a tall figure, waiting on the path. The rain had stopped, but the stone steps still glistened wetly in the warm night. She had to look away to keep from running, to keep the gap closing smoothly between them. He watched her from beneath lowered eyebrows, as though he had been there for a long time.

"I almost missed you," he apologized.

"All's well that ends well," she managed, overcoming the emotion that had her by the throat. It was an understatement but it left her defenseless, feeling naked. An instinctive need for cover made her avoid his eyes. The path, happily, was dark, the air thick with moisture despite the recent rain. The wind blew in gusts that shook the layered canopy of leaves above their heads, spraying them with droplets.

"When are you expected?"

They had begun walking a little uncertainly toward the McTavish Street entrance to the campus.

"I'm not," she murmured without looking up. "Mick is in Quebec City pleading a case ..." She'd said it, mentioned her husband's name, shattered the night with it, but she couldn't account for the shame. Simply agreeing to their meeting was already a betrayal, but it wasn't Mick she cared about exposing. Kitty was still wedged between them, as surely as she had been in the car that day. "He's out of town a lot these days," she added rashly, indefensibly. "He's been asked to run for Parliament in a by-election they're going to call sometime next year."

"For the Tories or the Grits? Not that it makes any difference ..."

"For the Liberals," she answered. "Why do you say that?"

"Bandits, the lot of them," he shrugged, obviously amused by her question. They were nearing the gates and the light from the streetlamps.

"Is that what you meant when you made that remark at Trevor's, about being in a den of thieves?"

"I said that, did I?" He smiled wryly. "Trevor is a nice fellow, but his company is involved in a gigantic price-fixing scam on the Great Lakes. He plays handmaiden to a bunch of American steamship owners and they all make huge profits, a tidy portion of which ends up in the coffers of the Tory Party. But don't get me wrong," he added, turning to face her and intercepting her thought like a fielder catching a wayward ball, "the Grits are no better. They had a royal commission investigate the whole operation, and when the smell got too high they slapped the lid right back on. Now the report's gathering dust somewhere and the Liberal bagmen are counting their cash. Those people live for power. Bah! How was Mozart, anyway?" He took her arm and steered her up the well-lighted street toward Pine Avenue.

"I hate to admit it," Jeanne said, doing her best to keep pace with his long, purposeful strides, "but I've always had trouble liking Mozart."

"Odd what works for different people," he said. "Now what I like is jazz. Ever been to the clubs?"

"The clubs?" Jeanne repeated uncomprehendingly.

"The nightclubs on Saint-Antoine. No? They open around eleven. We could go in my car," he said. "Do you want to?"

Want. It all came down to that, as though at a single stroke all her protective layers had been stripped off and her secret self, writhing like a nymph in its torn cocoon, indecently laid bare.

"But what if someone ..." Blood was rushing to her face in the blessed darkness. They found his car.

"You don't get into those places unless you know someone," he said, dropping his voice reassuringly. "Some of the musicians are friends of mine. You won't run into anyone you know, it's not that kind of crowd."

Jeanne hesitated, her misgivings mired in the depth of her need.

"We don't have to go downtown if you'd rather not," he said sympathetically.

"No, I'd like to," she stammered, horrified at the sea-change of her emotions in the last half-hour, as the wave of anticipation that had carried her all day finally broke on the reef of finite reality.

4

The Owl Club was located over a tavern on Saint-Antoine Street, in a seamy part of town west of the financial district, wedged between the river and the railway lines. It was home to the men who worked on the trains, the Negro porters and their families. In the summer it was infested with bookies, who liked to set up shop close to the money-men for the betting season. Nighttime saw a different population on its streets, of hookers, pimps, and crowds from the Irish working-class neighborhoods along the river, seeking temporary companionship or the superior brand of oblivion available in the jazz clubs and dance halls.

"Hey, Doc!" a tall, smiling black man in a tux called down to them from the top of the stairs leading up to the club. "That's some cute nurse you got on your arm tonight," the man observed with a knowing grin. "I was wondering when you were gonna get somebody to look after you for a change."

Jeanne and Louis exchanged a tentative look, and laughed. The man waved them inside, chuckling and shaking his head.

The atmosphere that met them in the nightclub was warm and thick with smoke and the moisture rising from the tight hive of dancers at the center of the room, some white, but mostly black. Four jazzmen were blowing their horns on the small, cramped stage, their faces glistening with sweat in the bluish light. The floor throbbed with the rhythmic tapping of feet, and the whole teeming place hummed with cathartic energy. Louis checked their sodden coats and Jeanne's umbrella, prompting another warm greeting, this time from the young woman in charge of the cloak-room. Jeanne felt his hand land just wide of the nape of her neck, and glide her along until they had somehow squeezed into the throng. Instantly the churn of bodies all around them pressed them together in a way that would have been unthinkable on a better-lit, less densely packed dance floor. She offered no resistance, buoyed up on the stroking, undulating music, drunk on the mellow grunting whine of the saxophones, eyes closed, her mind buffeted by sensation flooding in, the rough tweed of his jacket, the lean body underneath. "Whispering," the band played. "Girl of My Dreams." It played on and they danced, almost motionless now amid the colliding energy of the crowd, moving in fluid unison like delicately finned fish suspended in the current, adrift on a sensual tide. The song ended. She half-opened her eyes, and started so violently that he felt it and pulled back slightly to look at her.

"Someone's here," she babbled, burying her head against him in panic. The door of the club had just opened to admit a small group of new arrivals, among whom Jeanne had immediately singled out Éloïse, the perennial bachelor girl, who despite her crush on Liam O'Neill had not given up painting the town with "the boys." In one swift movement Louis swung her around to face the opposite side and retreated from the dance floor, pulling her into the semi-darkness of small tables and swaying, clapping patrons on the far side of the room.

"This way," he said, heading for an unmarked door at the back. A big friendly-looking man waved from a nearby table. Louis squeezed his shoulder, shouted a hurried apology as they pushed by.

"Patient of mine," he explained as they neared the door. "He works as a porter on the CPR. Phenomenal guy. His kids are so bright they all learned to read and write before they were three. All gifted musicians too. Just as well for them, because in this town a Negro who doesn't sing, dance, or play an instrument can look forward to nothing but a lifetime of serving whites—in their homes, on the trains, or in the brothels."

In the noisy hall behind them, the band was launching into "Follow the Swallow Back Home." They hurried down the back stairs. The door at the bottom opened onto a side street. Jeanne began shivering almost immediately.

"Who was it?" he asked, wrapping his jacket around her shoulders. Her teeth chattered pathetically.

"A woman I know very well. An old friend of my husband's. They grew up together," she answered in short, quavering bursts, unable to control the tremor in her voice.

"It's my fault. I shouldn't have taken you to such a public place. It wasn't very smart," he said, swinging an arm round her shoulders and drawing her close for warmth.

"It's just bad luck," she said, belatedly aware that the legitimizing context for such intimacy had been snatched away, and casting about in herself for a way to keep the moment from ending. "Your friend at the door," she asked, "is he a patient too?"

"Not exactly. Herb and I go back a long way," he said, walking a little slower now that they were a safe distance from the club, "back to the war."

"You fought in the war?" she interrupted, without meaning to. He seemed much too young to belong to the generation of battle-scarred men who had returned the year Florence had gone missing forever from her life.

"*Fought* is a big word." He shrugged. "I was in med school. I went as a stretcher-bearer in 1917. I saw my fill of bloodshed, but I was one of the lucky ones. I didn't have to do any killing. That's how I met Herb. When I bundled him onto the stretcher I wasn't sure whether he was alive or dead. It was pouring buckets and in the gloom that day he was just another mangled mass of muck and gore. But he pulled through somehow. After that I didn't see him again until I bumped into him in a club just up the street in 1922."

"And you recognized him?" she asked, a little calmer now.

"Not at first," he said, "but he remembered. He had a

long wait in the dugout before he could be moved out through the tunnels to the field hospital behind the lines. We got to talking during the lulls, to keep his mind off the pain. We were both barely twenty. Needless to say there weren't many colored guys like him in the trenches. He was lucky too, I guess, luckier than a lot of others. Right now he's employed as a bouncer, but he makes a little extra in the summer running errands for a bookie. Not much to show for putting your life on the line for your country."

They had reached his car. Jeanne stood rooted to the spot, trembling like a sapling in the autumn wind while he groped in his pockets for the key. It was almost over. In a few minutes she would be home again, alone, empty, and in need.

"They must be in my jacket. No, don't," he said, pulling it back over her shoulders before she could hand it over. He was holding her by the lapels, looking down at her, his face dark save for his eyes reflecting distant light from a streetlamp. Her body longed for touch, to be enveloped, swathed in it. She realized she had been trembling as much from the sudden withdrawal of contact between them as from the shock of seeing a familiar face in the crowd. He let go and unlocked the car door.

"What about the raincoats?" she asked.

"I'll come back for them tomorrow," he said as he went round to his side. He got behind the wheel.

"Do you want me to take you home now?" he asked, staring expressionlessly out at the street ahead.

She hesitated, compelled by emotion so long dormant that it was struggling, like an insect fighting its way out of its chrysalis.

"I really should be getting back," she said, so low that she wondered whether he'd heard her.

He started the car, and an uneasy silence compounded of expectancy, self-consciousness, and vague trepidation settled between them. She caught glimpses of his face emerging from the darkness into the yellow light of passing streetlamps as they climbed Guy, to Côte des Neiges, and on to Pine Avenue. He hadn't turned right at Guy and Sherbrooke, and she made no comment.

"I work in that hospital," he said, to the dark turrets of the Royal Vic hulking up outside the window as they drove by, "fighting another kind of war. One waged by the powerful against the weak—"

"You mean—" she began, but he forged on.

"You might think that disease doesn't discriminate between rich and poor, that death at least is immune to the bribery of privilege, but you'd be wrong. For every Westmount matron who recovers from tuberculosis after treatment at some expensive sanatorium, in Griffintown, in Pointe-Saint-Charles, in the East End, the children go on dying. Because of contagion, because of the cramped quarters in which they're forced to live, the lack of indoor sanitation, the inadequate heating, the filthy air. Because their fathers can't afford to buy them health. Every winter many people have to make a choice between fuel to heat their homes and food to feed their families—except maybe in an election year," he added with a bitter smile, "when they get to barter their vote for a few sacks of coal or groceries. That's why fellows like me get to treat their sickly, underfed children. We help them valiantly fight off bronchitis or pneumonia only to be sent back to the conditions that made them ill in the first place. Meanwhile, I see my colleagues in my own hallowed profession," he said, his tone shifting to audible scorn, "devoting their most productive time to the wealthy few they pamper and fawn

305

over and compete for. To the herd of needy sick they dispense a brand of experimental medicine, masquerading as charity, that lets novice MDs fresh out of med school earn their spurs practicing on the poor in the public wards, working six days and nights a week for no pay, thus affording their teachers, the older doctors with established reputations, the pretense of discharging their so-called social duty."

The car had come to a stop on Lorne Avenue, a side street about two minutes' walk from where she lived. "Do you know what one of my professors said to me when I asked him how much I should charge my patients for my services? *Simply charge a bit more than you think you can get*, he said." He paused, hands on the steering wheel, then turned toward her. "This is where I live." In the semi-light from the streetlamp his eyes stated the question which, if he uttered it, she would have to answer. The street was quiet save for the urgent whispers of the trees rustling in a fitful breeze, the air still swollen with moisture. The starkness of her choices flared in her mind like a catherine wheel spewing sparks into the night. The moment seemed to hang on the rim of timelessness, as a raindrop clings to the edge of a leaf. She got out of the car. The warm, humid night enveloped her. The droplet fell.

5

The apartment was small, with a fireplace in the main room. The furniture looked old but comfortable, the rug Persian but threadbare in places, like the upholstery. The overstuffed cases spilled books onto the floor in neatly ordered piles. There were more books and periodicals stacked on the open rolltop desk, the chesterfield, and any other available piece of furniture.

"Uh-oh," he muttered, spying his dog on the rug in front of the empty fireplace, its head between its paws. "Look at him. See that look he's giving me? Sulking, are we? Come here, mutt," he admonished the animal, whose ears twitched to let its master know it heard him. Otherwise it did not deign to move a muscle in reply. "Jealous." Louis shrugged, motioning her into the kitchen.

"What'll it be, tea? Coffee?" He clapped the kettle onto the stove, then turned and struck a match on the gas burner.

"Coffee keeps me from sleeping," she said, then realized her reply could be construed a number of ways.

"So, which will it be?" He grinned.

"Tea!" she exclaimed, with the flustered giggle of a schoolgirl being teased by a grown man.

"All I've got's Chinese. You mind?"

Jeanne watched him get a bottle of milk from the icebox, which, she noticed, was completely empty. He took two cups and saucers out of a cupboard and rummaged around another, which seemed almost as bare as the icebox. "I trust you don't take sugar," he concluded, setting the cups down on the table.

"No," she said, smiling now.

The kettle began belching steam. He poured boiling water into a small china teapot with a chipped, teastained spout. Then he sat down, facing her across the narrow kitchen table.

"Isn't that the dress you wore to Trevor's last summer?" He leaned back in his chair, stretching out his long legs.

She knew when she put it on that the white silk shift would be only just plain enough, if worn without jewelry, not to make her look frankly overdressed. Her seamstress no doubt designed it to catch the eye of royalty, and eye-catching she knew it to be, which is why she was unable to resist wearing it, however inappropriately, on this unseasonably hot night.

"How do you know what I wore to Trevor's?"

"Couldn't miss you, could I?" he replied, folding his arms over his chest.

"You were there?"

"Only under extreme duress," he conceded, half in jest. "Aunt Miss can't get around at all any more, and the damned thing meant so much to her, I offered to go and be her eyes and ears."

"But why didn't I see you there?" she chided him meekly. "You could have said hello."

"You were surrounded, impregnable. I would have had to fight my way in. It would have caused a scene." The arrogant maleness he exuded was exciting and intimidating. "I've watched you though," he said, in earnest now, "at Trevor's, New Year's Eve, and at that garden party. You go through the motions, but you're not really there, are you?" He was spying directly into her soul. There was no recovering any semblance of composure.

"My mother raised me to be a nun," she said with a hint of bravado, as a compromise between the instinctive need for concealment and the urge to expose herself to his scrutiny. "When I wasn't quite sixteen, she sent me away to become a Carmelite."

Louis's eyebrows went up slightly and his eyes narrowed with curiosity. "Isn't that the religious order whose members aren't allowed to speak to one another?"

"You're not even supposed to make eye contact," she said blankly to the hands in her lap, clasped as though for dear life, "except for two hours every day at meals and during recess."

"I didn't know there was a Carmelite convent here ..."

"The main convent is here. She sent me to the one in Saint-Boniface, Manitoba."

"You were *sixteen?*" he said, grimacing incredulously. "And your mother sent you there? Didn't your father have anything to say about it?"

"You don't know my mother," Jeanne murmured by way of explanation.

"How did you manage to get out?"

"I became gravely ill ... because of the privations ... I now realize I only married Mick to get away from her," she added, conceding an oblique answer to his initial observation about her not really "being there." "What about you, have you never wanted to be married?"

"Aunt Miss had a go at me when I came back from the war," he said, pouring tea at arm's length into their two cups. "She was very partial to debs, having been one herself."

He had large, beautiful hands, with wide palms and long, tapered fingers, like the hands of God in a reproduction her father had of *The Last Judgment* by Michelangelo.

"What happened?" she asked, her smile masking a vague apprehension, as though she sensed that his answer had the power to inflict grievous wounds.

"You remember there was a rash of balls after the war. There were so many marriageable young women for so few eligible men, especially that year. Demobilization was painfully slow in the beginning. I was lucky—again—to be on one of the first transports home. But that was small comfort at the time, because no matter how eager a girl was to understand, I was numb, worn out, like so many others ..." She wondered whether he was speaking of someone in particular, someone he'd met, and talked to, the way they were talking now. It was a thought with a sharp point to it, and it gave her a fierce little stab. He spoke matter-of-factly, without taking his eyes off hers. He was in fact telling two stories, one in the past tense, the other, pressing and immediate, in the wordless here and now.

In the next room, the dog rose stiffly to its feet, stretching its front legs and yawning hugely, and trotted into the kitchen.

"Okay, okay, pooch," Louis humored the animal, as it stood wagging its tail and whining hopefully. "Hey, mind your manners," he said to curtail its insistent sniffing. "Dog's a hermit," he muttered, massaging its head and ears with obvious affection, "just like his master."

6

"I really should be going," Jeanne heard herself whisper.

"Oh. All right," he said, getting up and running his hand through his hair as though he'd forgotten something important. "You. Stay," he commanded the dog.

He followed her into the next room, hands in his pockets, the spell apparently broken. They reached the door of the apartment.

"I'll pick up your things tomorrow. How do you want me to get them to you?" he said, leaning one shoulder against the doorjamb. Then, almost neutrally, from what seemed to her like a great height, he said, "Don't go."

She hesitated. Alarm, sweet and sharp, rippled through her. His hand alighted on her, just the fingertips on her skin, steadying her, then tugging her slowly toward him. His back was propped against the door as he pulled her against him, his arms enveloping her. The drumbeat of blood in her head—his? hers? She felt the coarse-grained skin of his throat, the rough smoothness of his jaw, then his mouth, seeking, transfixing her with softness, prying her open, delicately, like a succulent fruit slaking a pilgrim's thirst.

"How old are you, anyway?" he whispered, so softly it made her shudder. "You kiss like a kid."

His hands barely alighting on her waist, she felt only the warmth of them through the silk of her dress as they glided upward. Her heart was jumping at her rib cage like a fish in an angler's net. He led her by the hand to the door of the room where he slept. Her dress had silk buttons all the way down to the small of her back. In the darkness he freed them one by one, his fingers moving over her naked skin like wind in grass, bending each glistening blade. He was laying her down in grass so sweet she could taste it, in her nostrils, on her tongue. Her body was yearning toward him, swelling like the sea, naked in his hands, sweeping softly, swiftly, down the long beach of her belly to the dark bloom, delicately parting petals, baring a quivering pistil, playing it with his fingertips, drawing from that virgin flesh a melody so sharp, above the pounding of her blood, that it pinned her like a butterfly, palpitating on the point of ecstasy, until her body quaked and quaked—

"What did you do?" she whispered.

"Warm enough?" he said, pulling the eiderdown up around her nakedness and holding her close. They were lying face to face with only his clothes between their skins.

"Don't you want to—" she began. Bashfulness kept her from finishing.

"Next time," he said, with a smile that suggested he already knew more about her than she'd ever told him. Outside the trees still whispered fitfully in the breeze. "You mustn't fall asleep ..."

"What time is it?"

He reached for the lamp. It was twenty past one. She nestled for a few minutes more in his arms, then resigned herself. She got up, pulled on her dress, and sat down with her back to him on the edge of the bed, where he lay with his hands folded behind his head.

"Pinch me," he said, instead of doing up the proffered buttons of her dress.

She turned her head questioningly.

"Pinch me," he repeated. "Know how many times I've had this dream?"

"You mean ..."

"Whenever I see you, it's like fire, like hot embers," he said, lifting a strand of hair away from her cheek. His face was flushed and his eyes shone with something like fever. "I knew right away, at Trevor's, the first time I saw you," he said, rising on one elbow and nuzzling her.

She resisted the urge to tell him it hadn't been the first time, that he'd seen her before, twice. She savored her secret knowledge of him, as if she had it from someone else, someone he didn't know.

"Come on, I'll take you home."

Later she lay in her bed, cradling the newly blessed vessel of her body, for once dreading the oblivion that sleep brought. Outside the open window, the night had cooled, its fever finally broken.

7

Manitoba

When she awakened the next morning from an unusually dreamless sleep, she was immediately back in the
relentless, unforgiving present. Her life was a trap whose
jaws had once again snapped shut.

"Monsieur called last night," Gabrielle said, setting
down the breakfast tray with the pained expression of
someone offering a difficult condolence. It was hard to
tell from her wise young face how much she knew, but
her sympathetic intention was discreetly obvious.
"Monsieur will call again, today or tonight."

"What time was it when he called?" Jeanne asked,
more sharply than she would have wished.

"About eleven, Madame. He sounded a little ..."

"Was he angry?"

"I don't think so, Madame. I think he was spending
the evening with friends and called on the spur of the
moment. He sounded in good spirits, Madame ..."

Mick made sure he was sober when he called that

night. He was coming home a day early, he said, leaving Jeanne to mourn the hours she'd wasted waiting for his call instead of meeting Louis to retrieve her raincoat and Mick's umbrella. The following day she had found both on the back seat of her car, and the wretchedness that had overcome her at the thought of him standing under her windows as she slept had never fully left her. Time had her in bonds endlessly gnawed by need. Need was the kiln in which her will was slowly churning, where she unendingly languished, content on good days to trace and retrace the imprint of Louis on her memory, as though priming her senses with words and images that could somehow bring back each moment in the flesh. On bad days she was exiled from her feeling self, save for the hollow sensation, like hunger, in the pit of her stomach, and the tension in her body that refused to abate even in sleep.

For weeks she was plagued by a desperate malaise, a sense of drowning. She fell prey to dreams that exhumed cruel memories of a Lenten fast, of the woeful passion with which, day after day, she had once devoured her one daily meal of thin broth and brittle bread, with furtive glances at the brown-robed figures aligned on both sides of the rough-hewn refectory table. She wondered at the staunchness that enabled them to survive on sheer abstinence and the love of God. Now she pined all through the shallow nights and fathomless days for the comfort of his arms around her, containing her, defining her. She moved in a kind of Hades, where even Kitty seemed at times no more substantial than a shade, except that those around her were very much alive, while it was she who had departed from their midst.

Even though prudence demanded that he not call her, every ring of the telephone, its sharp shrieks reverberating through the house, made her start out of her skin. Each night when Mick ensconced himself in the living room with his sherry and his paper, she watched grimly for any sign that his suspicions might somehow be aroused, all the while waiting at his whim for the opening she craved. Eternity trickled on for a full three weeks before he finally announced for the end of October, less than ten days away, the long-anticipated northern hunting trip he made each year with a group of clients and friends.

2

She waited that evening until Mick had left the house for a meeting of the riding association that was courting him. She took a little longer than usual tucking Kitty into bed, then procrastinated further until she was sure the little one was asleep. She circled the telephone, eyeing it warily like some black instrument of Fate. Finally she made the call, and then the ringing at the other end jangled her nerves beyond bearing. Five times. Six times ... Carefully she placed the receiver back in its cradle. There was no answer, nor would there be, because he wasn't there.

Brutally her own telephone screamed through the house and her whole body started to quake. She picked it up on the third ring.

"Hello?" she said. There was a long pause.

"Jeanne?"

"Yes," she answered, her senses straining blindly, like antennae, toward the sound.

"Did you call me?" The voice was like a probe, sounding depths where only her own voice was normally heard.

"Louis!"

"The phone was ringing when I got in the door. I didn't get there in time—"

His words spilled in, their rich, rough tones cascading through her, committing themselves to her memory.

"How did you know?"

"I didn't. Just a crazy hunch."

"You sound tired ..."

"I've been spending all my time at the hospital. I'm not sleeping much these days," he said, "so I might as well be up working. You?"

"I called to tell you—" She hesitated. Her heart was pounding almost painfully in her chest. "I've got five days. The twenty-fifth to the thirtieth. It's short notice, I know—"

"I'll think of something. Are you all right?"

"Better now," she said, twisting the black cord round her fingers till it hurt. She closed her eyes, tethered to his voice. Their conversation had dwindled almost to a whisper. They would have dispensed with speaking altogether, if only they had been face to face.

3

The road led north through small villages, each huddled around a church whose tin roof and slim spire glittered in the morning sun. October this year had been warmer than usual, delaying by a fortnight the sudden blaze of color that was now sweeping through the countryside, soon to leave only scorched fields and shorn, blackened trees in its wake. The sharp autumn sunlight gilded the edges of the brittle bushes and grasses shivering raptly in the ungentle breeze, and the trees whose majesty would soon be stripped from them. The light set the very air to shimmering, like a mirage on the cusp of memory. The physical proximity of Louis after the long weeks alone, the riot of colors outside, even the hurtling motion of the car filled her with an unbridled sensual keenness, the foretaste of a joy that might be the last. Tomorrow was a precipice over which the present thundered like a torrent.

"Where are you taking me?" he repeated.

"On a pilgrimage," she said, remembering.

Gradually, as they topped a small rise just past a little village, the Laurentian foothills came into view, crouching low, a distant barrier across the horizon.

"My aunt used to have a hunting lodge in the mountains. She was going to take me there after I had Kitty. It was the year of the flu epidemic. She got sick and died the day the armistice was signed. She'd lost her husband in the war and had no children of her own, so she left me the hunting lodge in her will. I've never had the heart to go there, until now ..."

She felt him squeeze her hand, threading his fingers through her own. She realized that she was speaking of those dark times as though she were reading about them in the newspaper. She was shedding her past as quickly as the car was speeding toward the mountains.

"More wasted lives ... Take my own Aunt Miss, poor devil. They say she used to be a fiend for parties. Quite a dancer in her prime, according to my father. Even had a beau, once. The marriage was called off after she contracted tuberculosis. By some miracle she managed to recover from the disease itself, but not before it attacked her joints and her spine. She was never able to walk again. Her body just wasted away. Even her doctors don't know how she's managed to last as long as she has."

"Are your parents still alive?"

"My mother died when I was ten."

"It must have been ..."

"It was. It's not easy, at that age. You remember everything, and you go for years needing something no one else can provide."

"And your father?"

"He raised me almost single-handedly after Mum died. He was a transatlantic, like me. Born in England, but with his roots here. His own father, Aunt Miss's only surviving brother, didn't get on with their old man, the one who built that beautiful old house on Drummond Street where she still lives. Instead of going into my great-grandfather's import business over here, he went back to England, married my grandmother, and made his own fortune in the South African diamond rush. He sent my father to public school, and from there Dad went on to Cambridge and a career in the Colonial Office. He was posted here, in Ottawa, as an attaché to the governor general. He met my mother and married. I was born here. Later Dad was called back to London and we followed. When Mum died he asked to be posted back here, and after about six months he pulled me out of my boarding school in England and brought me over to be with him."

"You mean you were raised partly in Ottawa?"

"Yes, I was. Too bad we didn't meet earlier ..."

All at once she measured the time she had wasted not knowing him.

"Is your father still alive?"

"No. When the war broke out he went back to England. He left me here, largely in the care of Aunt Miss, I suppose because he knew I couldn't be with him anyway, and he didn't think it useful to uproot me again, even though my grandfather was still alive and could have looked after me. Maybe he just felt I'd be safer. But here I stayed ..."

Their tightly twined hands looked like the delta of two converging rivers flowing out to an unknown sea. Jeanne now marveled at the capriciousness of fate, which might have decreed that they should never meet.

"For a while I got letters from him regularly," he went on. "Then there was a long period without news of any kind. Eventually I got a letter from His Majesty's government. By then I'd started medical school at McGill, and my response to the situation was to enlist on the spot. As it turned out it was probably the best thing I could have done. As a battle-field orderly I had plenty of outlets for my grief."

At that moment the dog, who had been asleep in the back, sat up and, plonking its head on its master's shoulder, poked its nose out the window.

"Hannibal! Down, boy!" Louis complained.

"Hannibal! I thought his name was Winston."

"Oh, that's just his nickname, isn't it, pooch?"

The road had been rising so gently that the change in the scenery took them by surprise. Suddenly the mountains were all around them. They were low and rounded, barely higher than hills but massive and ancient. Spruce forests covered them like dark shag on giant slumbering beasts, with enough maples and birches woven in to produce a rolling tapestry of breathtaking color. From time to time a sheer gray cliff loomed, with strangely contorted pine or tamarack growing vertically out of the rock face, clinging for dear life with talon-like roots dug right into the stone.

"Sure you know where you're going?"

"I have my map," she laughed, flourishing the yellowed paper Florence had left. "I've written to the blacksmith. They used to board their horses there. I understand there's just a trail into the woods. It's quite inaccessible by car, but I don't know if there are any horses there now that we can use. We'll just have to see. Even if we can't get to the cabin, I'll still be glad we tried."

"We'll find a way. We can always go on foot, if necessary. We couldn't have picked a better day."

4

The village they were looking for was nestled in one of the small valleys transected by the railway line, surrounded by the mountains on all sides. At its hub a slender steeple, glinting in the autumn sun, thrust its silver needle up at the sky. The tiny village itself straggled along its two perpendicular streets, which led out of it and beyond to distant hamlets hidden in the bosom of the mountains. The blacksmith's forge was next to a stable on the Rue de la Gare, between the train station and the church. It was a simple wooden structure, similar to a barn, with a great sliding door high and wide enough for a plow horse to get through. It was open, and from the dark bowels of the building came a rhythmic clanging of metal on metal.

At first Jeanne saw only the red glow of the forge and sprays of sparks raining onto the earthen floor. As her eyes adapted to the lack of sunlight, she made out the sooty black-aproned figure of the blacksmith, stooped over the anvil. His dirty face shone with sweat, and his huge hands, and bare, bulging forearms, gripping the hammer and tongs, were black from the work. His expression was set in a wary scowl, his instinctive hedge against flying specks of hot metal. Looking up, he set aside the horseshoe he'd been pounding.

"Yes, Madame," he said, mopping his face with the roll of his sleeve.

"M. Loiseau? My name is Jeanne O'Neill. I hope you received my letter?"

"Yes," he said, his eyes registering recognition now,

"my wife did, sure. She's over at the store. Better talk to her. She looks after all that sort of thing."

"The store? Is that the building next door?"

"The other side of the stable there," he said, like a man who doesn't have all day. "She'll tell you anything you want to know."

The blacksmith's wife was a prim, pleasant woman in her forties, whose engaging manner showed that she was used to dealing with queries from passing strangers.

"Is there something I can help you with?" she asked, smiling behind the long counter with its colorful jars of hard candy.

"The store" was in fact the only business in the village, a general dry-goods store displaying on its shelves all manner of merchandise, from rope and nails to clothes, boots, soap, horse ointment, and friar's balsam. Jeanne introduced herself again.

"Mme O'Neill," the woman exclaimed. "I remember your uncle and aunt well. Such nice people." Her face was smooth and pink, with no trace of wrinkles save for the few lines etched by decades of looking on the bright side of life. "M. Talbot used to come up all the time with his nephew."

"His nephew?" said Jeanne with some surprise. Florence had never mentioned her husband's nephew.

"Oh, Madame," the woman gushed, "you never saw such a good-looking boy. Monsieur used to joke about how the nephew was almost as old as the uncle. They used to come by for the horses, always laughing and joking like a couple of schoolboys. They never shot more than a few partridges or pheasants. Never bigger game— I think Mme Talbot disapproved."

"That sounds like her," Jeanne said wistfully.

"After M. Talbot's death, she came up here once or

twice a year, always on her own. She was a great lady, your aunt. She always brought presents for the children. They were all small in those days. Such a shame."

Jeanne agreed distractedly. She could feel the warmth of Louis behind her, even though they were not touching.

"Will you be wanting the horses? There's no road, you know, for the motor," said the blacksmith's wife, admiring the car outside the glass storefront.

"How far is it from the road?" Louis asked, in his slightly accented French.

"More than five miles, Mr. O'Neill," said the blacksmith's wife. Jeanne thanked heaven for her Irish-sounding married name. "And it's uphill through the bush. You wouldn't want to walk it."

"Is there a track?"

"It's overgrown by now, but it's well marked in red paint, every few trees, all the way up. You shouldn't have any trouble following it. I sent my boy up to open the place and air it out, soon as I got your letter."

"That's very good of you. You must tell me what I owe you for that."

"Oh, it's my pleasure. Mme Talbot left something to cover the upkeep of the horses, and as it stands, we had the use of them all that time until they died. So naturally you're welcome to use ours. It's too bad because the other ones knew their way up, but you won't have any trouble finding it after I explain to you where it is."

By noon, the horses were saddled and the provisions which Jeanne and Louis had assembled in a shop in Cartierville had been transferred to saddlebags provided by the blacksmith's wife. They set off in the balmy air, past the church in all its autumn glory, up the little dirt road that led north out of the village, with the dog trotting purposefully alongside.

"I trust you realize I've never been on one of these before," Louis announced when Jeanne began to pick up the pace. "If I fall off, you're on your own."

"There's nothing to it!" she laughed, only half believing him. "Just hang on tight with your knees." She nudged her horse into a slow canter.

"I'll get you for this!" he yelled. He was behind her, but by the sound of it, closing fast. Suddenly she was laughing uncontrollably, caught up in a vortex of conflicting rhythms, the lunging of the horse's great shoulders, the drumroll of hooves so close behind, her racing heartbeat, her syncopated breathing. He was gaining on her all right. Out of the corner of her eye she could see the head of his horse thrusting in and out of her field of vision.

"Guess you didn't bet on her giving me the faster horse, eh?" he shouted, streaking past her with a loud, gleeful whoop. Jeanne tried to keep pace but by now, giggling helplessly, was barely clinging to her horse, and had to concede.

"Never ridden a horse, my eye!" she managed between hiccups when she had almost caught up with him. He had slowed right down to a walk and was busily poring over Florence's hand-drawn map. The back of his yellow shirt billowed slightly and his sleeves rippled in the breeze, outlining the muscles of his arms. He didn't look up but smiled the faintest of smiles.

They had come to the end of the valley, to a point where the road veered off and began to climb, where boulder-strewn meadows gave way to brushwood along the forest edge.

"There," Jeanne said, spotting a tree bearing the telltale dab of red paint they had been told to look for.

"This is where Larry here starts earning his grub. Go on, boy, show the way!"

"Larry? But I thought...!"

He pointed into the woods, urging the dog on. Following its lead, they left the road and penetrated under the high vault of the trees. The foliage overhead was a pale, translucent yellow, to which the sun's glow imparted a diffuse radiance, endlessly modulated by the breeze. Below the canopy the air was cool and still, the silence deep, resonant as the inside of a cathedral magically alive. Suddenly, directly ahead, a deer leapt across the disheveled path, its darkly bulging eye askance, its presence strangely godlike in its otherness, like a totem or a portent. In two bounds that barely stirred the underbrush it was gone. Neither Jeanne nor Louis spoke. The dog, having gamboled off sometime before, reappeared up ahead, meandering back from its reconnaissance through the tall ferns and pliant saplings that had taken over the trail. The ground was beginning to slope more steeply now as they made their way up, following the base of the lichen- and moss-covered rock face that rose abruptly above them, baring the mountain's ancient core. From deep fissures sprouted scrawny maple saplings whose frail, blood-red crowns shivered with every breath of wind. The muffled sound of their horses' hooves sinking into the moist carpet of leaves and earth was the only counterpoint to the echoing sighs of the breeze and the intermittent creaking of trees swaying against blue sky. As they climbed higher and the valley, still visible through gaps in the wood, fell away, the physical act of scaling this fragment of eternity only magnified the sense of transience that smote her heart, and the certainty that nothing after today could ever be the same again.

5

"What is it?" she asked in a tone that wavered uneasily between squeamishness and curiosity.

"Not quite direct from the rainforests of Brazil," he said over his shoulder with self-deprecating humor, his back tactfully turned, hunched forward for the few seconds it took him, "made exclusively from the milky sap of the ancient sacred tree, according to a closely guarded secret formula, ladies and gentlemen, God's own answer to the Malthusian dilemma ... vulcanized rubber!" He was sitting on the edge of the narrow bunk, framed in brightness from the window. Jeanne watched the subtle rippling in the muscles of his back. "You may well laugh!" he protested, turning to her. His head was wreathed in sunlight filtered through leaves the color of marigolds, translucent as stained glass. He lay down beside her. She gasped softly as their skins touched. His was flushed and hot, its smell foreign, deliciously male, tasting of sweet salt. The heat of him singed her like a hapless moth swirling in the vortex above an open fire. She was naked in cold sunshine and he was rubbing his cheek against her belly, her thighs, bestowing unimagined tenderness upon her with his tongue, kindling a tiny flame that flickered and grew and spread, churning itself to a chanting incoherent prayer as it swept through her, easing into wet slippery oneness, widening, rushing, tumbling her like a pebble in crashing surf...

"You see, it's so easy," he said, gasping and laughing, "you just hang on tight with your knees ..." His face glowed, his eyes shone, he beamed like a boy sprawled in grass after a run. He raised himself on one elbow and grinned, then launched into a series of high, panting cries that made Jeanne blush violently.

"How did you know?"

"What?"

"About ..."

"About this?" he whispered, his fingers alighting softly

on the acutely tender site of his discovery. "I had a good teacher."

"Who?"

The small, plaintive word had escaped on her breath, spilled from her through the narrowest possible aperture of her lips.

"A woman," he said, laughing, sweeping her hair off her shoulder in a lazy caress. "A friend of my father's. I'm sure he put her up to it before going off to the war."

"Did you love her?"

"In a manner of speaking."

"Then how did *she* know...?" but the words caught on the cruel image forming in her mind, of Louis in the arms of—

"Look at me," he said. "Haven't you ever—? Don't look so horrified," he laughed. "Why do you think we're made like this, with such an aptitude for pleasure? Our whole bodies are exquisitely tuned for it. Where other animals have reproductive organs, we have an almost limitless capacity for ecstasy and wonder. You think it's an accident? Here," he coaxed, taking her hand. "Touch," he said, guiding her gently until she touched him, touched the oddly anonymous, homely appendage that was raising its smooth, featureless head in some blind affirmation of life. Transparent shadows played across his face, ever-shifting shadows of the leaves outside, shivering in the afternoon breeze. He pulled her back into his arms. "Every day I thank heaven I'm alive and able to feel," he said.

"Because of the war?"

"That, and because I've always felt this way. As a kid I used to fall asleep praying that I wouldn't die during the night. I've always had this feeling of having been spared, rescued from nothingness. Sometimes it almost seems like a mad game of musical chairs—you know, the game where if you're caught standing when the music stops, that's it, you're out. To be alive, you see, is to know the music can stop at any moment ..."

6

The sun was already waning in the sky when they finally ventured out of the cabin in search of kindling for the stove. The air had turned colder.

"Look at it all," he said as they paced the russet woods, "we haven't been cast out of Paradise, it's all around us."

He stopped and, leaning his back against a tree, pulled her backwards into his arms. Below them in the valley the little dirt road snaked its way toward the tiny village, its roofs reddened by the setting sun, while all around them the amber and scarlet mountains alternately blazed and smoldered in the lengthening shadows.

"*Manitou-ba.*"

"Hmm?" he murmured, hugging her closer.

"It means *the land where God speaks.* Coming here, it's easy to understand why some people believe ..."

"It's no use approaching it with logic or reason," he said, his voice drifting on the dusky air like a thought on the rim of sleep. "We're not equipped to do that. When you consider the true scale of things, it's like asking an ant to fathom a human being. It's beyond our mental capacity. As for God, what an irritant for our poor primitive brains ..."

He wanted her again. She could feel it through the autumn thickness of their clothes. They watched the shadows deepen in the valley as the light seeped away to the west, and the sky in the east darkened imperceptibly from mauve to violet. In the shed behind the main log house, the horses whickered softly. Every sound lingered on the twilight air. Time itself was so ripe, so full, it seemed to have slowed, as a great river in its final approach to the sea.

Through the long, soothing night their whispers mingled with the sighs and occasional groaning of the logs in the stove, while the wind gusted and flailed at the trees outside. In the morning the woods were bare. A thick rusty carpet had settled on the forest floor.

8

One Life

1

December 1927 Thick, heavy snow swirled slowly down out of the darkness on a sluggish wind. The big, wet flakes that landed on the windshield melted almost immediately. Inside the car it was cold, the damp, dull cold that penetrates through layers of clothing. Jeanne could see her husband's breath as he groped in his coat pocket for his cigarettes. He cocked his lighter and the small blue flame leapt upward, illuminating a classic smoker's scowl as he huddled over it, eyebrows knit, eyes half-closed, hand cupped against the cold. The brief trudge from the front door to the car had turned her feet to wet ice. The tension between her shoulder blades intensified.

"I'm going to leave you, Mick," she heard herself say.

Her voice had a dull, disembodied ring. She saw his hand freeze, then almost imperceptibly tighten its grip on the slender, silver lighter. He turned his head slowly.

"What did you say?" He spoke in a taut whisper. His eyes glinted in the shadows.

"You heard me," she murmured. Her throat went into a kind of spasm. She tried hard to swallow. The sudden constriction had caught her at the end of an exhalation, her lungs empty.

"You've certainly picked your moment, haven't you?" Mick said harshly. He couldn't have spoken a truer word. They were on their way to the biggest Liberal fund-raiser of the year, a pre-Christmas social event in its own right, one at which Mick, whom everyone knew to be the Prime Minister's choice to stand for the party in the soon-to-be-called federal by-election, intended to shine. "It'll have to wait," he concluded tersely. "We'll talk later."

At that a hot, angry geyser of feelings erupted inside Jeanne, her lungs instantly expanding again. "I'm serious, Mick," she said, with such rancor she felt as though she'd roared it, even though she hadn't raised her voice. "I want a divorce."

"A divorce," he repeated, incredulously. "Have you gone mad? Why should I divorce you? On what grounds?"

Timing had been her only available weapon, and her calculation seemed to be paying off. For the moment, as she had anticipated, he was more exasperated at the inconvenience of her outburst than anything else. Tonight of all nights, he could not afford to let anything distract him from his chosen course.

"Adultery," Jeanne answered, as calmly as she could, fixing her gaze on the windshield where melting snowflakes had begun to coalesce into floe-like clusters, inching their way down the sloping glass.

Mick lowered his head and gripped the steering wheel with both hands.

"Who?"

"Louis Marshall."

"The son of a bitch," he said, his bitterness dignified with a tinge of irony.

"What you think of him is irrelevant."

He looked up sharply. "You obviously don't know much about him," he said with a strange, unpleasant smile.

"What is that supposed to mean?"

"Don't you know? This is no ordinary doctor you've gotten yourself mixed up with. Hasn't he told you?" He was taunting her now, rubbing her face in something, but what? "I'm surprised he didn't have the decency to warn you. He's an abortionist. I guess to a good Catholic girl like you that makes him a murderer, doesn't it?"

"You're lying!"

She felt her stomach heave, as though to retch up so much hatred.

"Ask him yourself."

"You disgust me," she cried.

"I'm telling you the truth. It wouldn't do me much good to make it up!" he shouted back.

"Prove it! If it's true, then why hasn't he been thrown in jail by now?"

"Connections. I understand a number of people who matter owe him some favors of a rather unsavory kind ..."

"I don't believe you."

"As you wish," he said, dropping his voice deliberately, willfully reining himself in, "but ask yourself this: are you prepared to have your father's name dragged through the mud? As for divorce, you know his long-standing opposition to it, it's in Hansard for all to see. You know a divorce can only be obtained through petitioning Parliament. Are you prepared to put your father, a sitting member whose views are well known, through such a public humiliation? Because I'll tell you right now, I'm not, nor will I ever be. Do you know what a scandal like that would do to your father, even assuming the facts concerning your friend's occupation never came out, which I can't guarantee?"

"Listen, Mick, you don't give a damn what it would do to my father. All you really care about is what it will do to you!"

"I'm amazed you've even stopped to consider that."

"You're right, it's the least of my concerns!"

"Then think of your daughter, goddamn you!"

"I plan to send for her as soon as I can," she retorted, much more tentatively than she would have wished.

"Over my dead body." He said it softly, through clenched teeth, each syllable one slow turn of the knife.

Before she knew what she was doing Jeanne had leapt out of the car and was running up University Street in the opposite direction to that in which Mick's car was facing. Over her own loud gasping as she ran she heard the car engine snarl briefly, then, tires skidding in the slush, it pulled away. He made no attempt to bring the car around after her. Still she kept running uphill, clumsily, like a child on unsteady legs. As her breath got shorter her lungs began to burn, her legs heavier with each dwindling step. Then as she rounded the corner of Prince Arthur the ground gave way and she was stumbling downhill, trying to adjust her stride, but her legs were numb, unresponsive. Finally she was walking, but her breath still raced ahead of her heartbeat. For now, she had managed to outdistance her anger, temporarily exhausted her anguish. Curiously, at that moment all that remained was relief. The relief of having freed herself from the lies and the months and years of dissembling, the relief of having unburdened herself of her fear.

2

There was no wind now. The snow was falling in big, cottony flakes that seemed to absorb all sound, throwing a quilt of silence over the city streets. As her breathing got steadier, the crushing weight of Mick's accusation bore down on her, disfiguring Louis in her memory, skewing, warping her emotions. She had been forcibly inoculated with something deadly. Perhaps there was still time to get help, if a remedy existed.

She entered his apartment building and for the first time felt like an intruder there. The sudden silence of the place was clamorous, a rebuke. She pressed the light switch at the bottom of the stairs. By the time she'd reached the second-story landing the urge to turn and flee trilled through her like a current. Paralysis, more than anything, and a stubborn, lovesick need kept her rooted to the spot. The light, which was equipped with a timing device, turned itself off, leaving the hallway in darkness save for the light reflected up the stairwell from the lobby two floors below. She knocked on the door of the apartment and, drawing no response, had to fight twice as hard against the undertow that sucked ever more powerfully at her hopes. Still she could not bring herself to leave. She let herself sink to the floor and propped her back up against his door.

Gradually she realized how cold she was. Her fashionable evening coat was damp through with melted snow, her elegantly buttoned black boots had soaked up the slush so that her feet ached with almost the same kind of pain as the tightness in her throat, a desperate, intractable, burning hurt. After a time she heard the front door open then clang shut downstairs, and belatedly wondered how she might look to a passing tenant, sitting on the floor in the dark at Dr. Marshall's door in her soggy clothes. Footsteps came up the stairwell, slow, tired steps. She wondered why the landing light hadn't come on. The heavy tread started up the second flight toward her. He was coming up the stairs, head bowed, shoulders uncharacteristically stooped, a sprinkling of snowflakes in his thick brown hair. Jeanne struggled to her feet. Her heart froze as he looked up into the darkness of the hallway, his face registering neither surprise nor curiosity.

"Who's there?" he asked, his voice guarded but kindly.

He reached for the switch, and the light came on. It was his face, his eyes. The distortions wrought by shock and doubt dissipated like a bad dream. The tenderness leaping from his face at that moment was real. He was real.

"God, Jeanne, you look as though you've seen a ghost. What's happened?" he said, putting down his leather bag.

She registered his hand on her shoulder, the smell of damp tweed from his coat. With his free hand he felt around his coat pocket for his keys. He pushed the door open.

"What is it? What is the matter?"

He was kind. Gentle. Patient. Everything he did matched, to perfection, everything she knew about him. Her head was spinning now. He sat her down in the armchair by the fireplace, not thinking to take her coat, or remove his own for that matter. The dog emerged from the bedroom, wagging its tail in welcome.

"I told Mick," she said, choking out the words. There was no avoiding his eyes. He was crouched in front of her, his face inches from her own.

"Yes," he said, urging her on. "And...?"

"I told him—" She struggled against the gag Mick had stuffed into her mouth, a gag of fear, that the ground was shifting beneath her, threatening to gape open at any moment. "That I was going to leave him ... that I wanted a divorce—"

"What did he do? Did he hurt you?"

"He asked me who it was, so I told—told him." Her voice was quaking too now. "He got angry. He said—"

"Jeanne, what did he say? Tell me." his voice coaxed softly. She opened her eyes.

"I can't! I can't say it!... I told him I didn't believe him, I said he was lying—"

"Jeanne," he said slowly, patiently, "what did he say?"

"He said I obviously didn't know much about you, about what you do, he said you were a ..."

"A what?" he said calmly. "He said I was a what?"

"An abortionist," she mumbled, slurring the word.

Louis's face had always been like an open book. He didn't seem to have a devious bone in his body. His eyes had never been so clear, his gaze more direct. His expression hardened slightly, into bittersweet resignation.

"And you've come to hear me out," he asked gently, but, to Jeanne's despair, almost impersonally. She nodded in agreement, too unsure of her own voice to speak up. "Bless you for that," he said, squeezing her hand.

It was a gesture of consolation, the kind doctors resort to when they can no longer offer hope. Or of farewell. He stood up and, digging his hands into the pockets of his overcoat, turned to face the empty fireplace, at first exposing only his profile to her scrutiny. She was able to look more calmly at him now that he was not looking directly at her, and it was just as well. He came straight to the point.

"He told you the truth, but what he said was a lie, and here's why." He took a deep breath and turned to face her, head high, eyes candid. "During the war I saw my share of blood, spilled guts, and shattered bodies. Men still breathing with most of their faces blown off. Men with holes in their bodies big enough to put your fist through. Appalling wounds, filled with mud and shrapnel. We carried those torn bodies along miles of stinking trenches barely wide enough for the stretcher, over a moving floor of corpses buried inches beneath our feet. And every time the trench got too narrow and we were forced out on top, into the enemy's line of fire, I swore if I ever got out alive I'd make it up to those who didn't, I'd make my life count for something."

He turned and looked into the dead fire, peering distantly as though flames still danced amid the charred remains of logs in the grate. "After it ended I went back to med school. I worked at the Vic, first as an intern, then as a resident. I saw a lot more death. Mostly children—gastroenteritis, pneumonia, meningitis, congenital syphilis. A lot of tuberculosis. A lot of poverty. As an intern I often worked the emergency department at night, and after almost two years on the battlefield I thought I'd seen it all. In emergency, at night, you see all kinds of things you normally don't see during the day.

"What struck me most was the women, all ages, married, unmarried, some of them barely out of girlhood, women I could do absolutely nothing for, except watch them bleed to death. Because they couldn't afford the kind of doctor who for a handsome fee would gladly have relieved them of their pregnancies without also robbing them of their lives. They were dying because their lives weren't worth saving, literally. Of course, the two or three doctors who provide the service were, are, shunned by their colleagues, who nonetheless refer their well-to-do clients to them whenever the need arises. Eventually I set up a free clinic in Griffintown one day a week. I saw a lot of sick babies, a lot more tuberculosis, venereal disease. A lot of what I did was simply convincing people to go to the hospital, or to use prophylactics to protect themselves from unwanted pregnancies and venereal disease. Then one night, one of the young mothers whose baby I'd been treating came and asked for me at the emergency."

He spoke clearly, evenly. He seemed neither contrite nor defiant, like someone who stood on the rock-hard ground of belief.

"She was distraught and obviously frightened. She pleaded with me to come with her, but she wouldn't tell me where or why. She was on foot, claiming to have been driven to the hospital by a friend, so we took my car to a rooming house in a dark side street. She led me up three flights to a dingy room to which she had the key. There was a bed in one corner and an old woman kneeling there, crying over a rosary in her clenched hands. In the bed lay a young girl, not fifteen, pale as death, covered in blankets. There was a pile of bloody sheets on the floor next to the bed. I pulled the blankets back as gently as I could. Someone had bunched another sheet between the girl's legs to try and stanch the bleeding. In my head I saw the kid I picked up one day on the battlefield, who had been hit by shrapnel in the groin. Everything she was lying on, the mattress, everything was saturated with her blood. I took the girl's pulse, knowing there was nothing I could do for her. I don't remember what I said but I spoke to her as softly as I could. Five minutes later she was gone. Bled to death. 'Who did this?' That's all I could say to the other two women, I was so angry. And even through their grief and their tears, their eyes froze with fear. I felt ashamed, for the hypocrites in my own profession—those who treat the few doctors who perform abortions like pariahs, while willingly referring to them the wives and daughters of their well-heeled clientele; those doctors themselves for restricting their compassion to patients who can pay for it; and those like myself, who felt the same outrage again and again every time reality spattered itself all over their pious, sympathetic inaction. Not long afterward, a young woman came to see me, apparently referred by my visitor of that night. She was pregnant and had just been informed by her boyfriend that marriage was out of the question. She spoke in terror of her father, under whose roof she still lived, and made it clear that if I refused her, she was prepared to risk the same fate as her friend's little sister rather than face the consequences once her condition began to show. I felt *duty-bound* to help her, do you understand?" he said quietly, but as he turned to face her, his eyes glittered with bitterness.

"And having helped her, how could I as a matter of conscience turn away someone else in similar straits? The Church and the law say it's a crime, but I say outlawing it is murder. All any one of us gets is one shot at life. One life, that's all. Why should a woman be condemned to die for a mistake the man can simply walk away from? Turning her away when you know the possible consequences is morally no different from refusing to treat anyone else whose life is threatened."

"Why didn't you tell me?"

Jeanne spoke but made no sound as when, boarding the slow barge of sleep for the nightly expedition up the tributaries of her subconscious, she saw Louis's lifeless body rolling in the current, or by the cruel alchemy of dreams, deaf and mute with shame, she spied him writhing in the coil of some opulent female.

"Must I tell you about the woman whose baby died of meningitis this morning while in my care? Or the one with malnourished children whose husband is too debilitated by unemployment and drink to feed his family? Do I mar what time we have with the sadness and hopelessness of daily existence? Do I force you into a moral dilemma over a decision I have had to make, out of rage and pity for people so much worse off than you or I, but for whom I feel responsible nonetheless?"

"But you could be arrested."

"There's not much danger of that," he said wearily. "The police know, just as they know about the others. They see the same bloody mess." Then he seemed to come out of his bitter trance.

"Look," he said, helping her to her feet. "I'm sorry. I didn't mince my words. It isn't pretty and it isn't fair, especially not to you, any of it. I can't change the things I believe in, any more than I have any right to expect you to embrace them for my sake. You need to make up your own mind about this. But," he said with an earnestness that put him far beyond her reach, "now isn't the time. Come, let me take you home."

Her tears were flowing freely now. When she stood up the floor seemed to tilt upward slightly, then down, like a raft.

"Hold me," she said, almost inaudibly. "I couldn't bear to be away from you ..."

The sobs came, and she couldn't stop for a long time, as though to purge herself of the poison attacking her heart.

Outside it was still snowing, albeit less heavily.

Judging from the feathery coating on Louis's car, they couldn't have been talking for very long. He drove her right to her door, as though he no longer cared who knew. She walked up the steps, fumbled in her handbag for her key, opened the front door, removed her boots, hung up her coat as she did every day, but it was no good. This was no longer her house. She tiptoed upstairs, not wishing for company of any kind. The pain was getting worse and there was only one way to make it stop. She let herself into Kitty's room and sat gingerly down on the edge of the bed. Kitty was sleeping on her side, her hair spread loosely over the pillow. She took her small hand in her own. The little one's face was barely discernible in the darkness. The desperate tenderness she felt toward Kitty only heightened her distress. Here was the half of her that was to be immolated, that the other might live, that other who could no more survive without the one she had just left than a plant can survive without light, or an animal without nourishment. *Over my dead body.* A cold hand gripped her heart as the full force of Mick's words finally struck. This was the vital, redemptive part of her own self, to be left in escrow after she tore free. Free. How could she ever be free when her very soul was racked by famine, of the kind that drove mothers to devour their young?

3

Albina Provost had been a tall, handsome woman, before her disease shrank her big frame and ravaged her flesh. By degrees, but with stunning speed, she had lost the use of her body until even her voice was taken from her. Death's dreadful talons were slowly tightening around her throat as the muscles there became inert. She was in constant danger of choking and yet her expression, now banished from the wasted slackness of her face into the flickering recesses of her eyes, still managed to convey warmth and recognition when Dr. Marshall came to see her. For several weeks since her distraught family had brought her back to the hospital to die, Louis had turned up at her bedside every day at the end of his watch, even though she was no longer officially in his care, her case having long ago been taken over for teaching purposes by a specialist in the neurology department.

"What do you say I take you away from all this, Mme Provost?" He could lift her like a child now, despite her size. He put her down gently in the wheelchair, wedging pillows here and there to prop her upright in the seat and keep her head from falling forward on her chest. Then he took her into the corridor, past the Christmas tree donated and decorated by the Ladies' Auxiliary, down a narrow hallway to a small room once used by interns to bunk down for a few hours between shifts, and now designated as storage. Its main attraction was an ornate antique of an upright piano, incongruously elegant amongst the panoply of janitorial implements and drums of disinfectant. Having positioned the wheelchair so as to be able to catch the sick woman's eye as he played, Louis settled himself on the slightly too-high stool and, unable to tuck his long legs under the keyboard, half sitting, half standing, played for her a medley of old army songs and vaudeville tunes. From time to time he would look up and almost sense the effort it must have taken her to keep her eyes trained on him as she did, and he would feel a strengthening bond with the dying woman, knowing that the two sons she had lost in the war would have been about his age, and that she herself was not much older than his own mother would have been, had she lived.

There was a knock on the door.

"Sorry to interrupt ..." The nurse's voice in the doorway was discreet.

"Not now!" Louis grumbled without looking up or slowing the pace of his fingers on the keys.

"I'm afraid you're wanted in Outpatients," the nurse countered sympathetically.

"I'm not due in Outpatients today," he muttered.

"The person insists you have an appointment," the nurse explained.

Louis took the time to return Mme Provost to her bed. By the time he'd jogged down to the Outpatients' waiting room at the other end of the hospital, Michael O'Neill had been waiting for twenty minutes. The two men did not shake hands.

"I'd like a word with you in private," Mick said matter-of-factly. He appeared self-possessed, sharp, a lawyer speaking on behalf of a client.

"We should be able to find an empty office somewhere," Louis answered him warily.

The sight of the man induced in him an unpleasant combination of hostility, apprehension and reluctant pity. Leading the way, he became aware that the fellow couldn't quite keep up, and to his own annoyance, he found himself shortening his stride.

"I've come to ask you," Mick began tensely after Louis had shut the office door behind them, "to stop seeing my wife."

"That's something I can't do," Louis answered evenly, looking the other man steadily in the eye.

"You must realize," Mick continued, barely containing his spite, "that there is more at stake here than what people will say. Jeanne and I have a child together. We are a family. Quite aside from what it will do to her or to me as individuals, there is the matter of a little girl's life being thrown into turmoil. You haven't the right to inflict mental anguish on a child by your actions. My daughter needs her mother."

Louis was visibly uneasy now—not, as Mick might have surmised, out of any personal sense of guilt, but rather because the natural advantage that his size conferred on him disturbed, at some profound level, his congenital sense of fair play. Nonetheless he replied, with his customary directness: "What Jeanne decides is entirely up to her. What happens to her daughter, however, is clearly in your hands, since you refuse to grant her custody."

"She has chosen to abandon the conjugal home," Mick reminded him abruptly, his face beginning to color. "The law is clear on that, especially in view of her avowed intention to leave the country."

"What choice does she have?" Louis demanded, his voice dropping to a low rumble in an effort to contain his mounting hostility. "A woman who leaves her husband is a renegade, virtually a criminal. She'd be shunned like a leper if she stayed here, and so would her daughter."

"Precisely. She doesn't have a choice," Mick replied, his ice-blue eyes narrowing implacably. "*Quod erat demonstrandum*. It's a ridiculous fantasy of hers to think she ever had."

"Look. Jeanne isn't happy in her marriage. That won't change. Even if you could force her to stay, that still wouldn't change."

"She may imagine herself to be happy with you for the moment," Mick countered, going on the offensive. "But Jeanne is nothing but a pious little convent girl at heart. She won't be able to sustain for long the rejection of the society that molded and shaped her. You're talking to someone who has known her since she was seventeen years old! I'm asking you one more time to do the decent, honorable thing and end your relationship with her before it's too late."

"Too late?"

"I have here a signed affidavit," Mick said with a note of disdain, and reaching into his jacket pocket he took out a document, which he opened, "by two prostitutes residing on De Bullion Street, to the effect that on the fifteenth of March, 1926, you procured an illegal abortion to a Miss Elodie Vallières at—"

"I dare you to use that," Louis interrupted him with deadly calm. "In any case, it changes nothing. Now if you'll excuse me, I have patients to see."

4

Kitty's mother was lying on the living-room couch in the failing light of mid-afternoon. One side of her face was white, in the light from the window, the other deep in shadow. She spoke softly, her voice a satin whisper, her fingers cool as silk on Kitty's forehead. In the gray daylight her pale eyes glistened, even though her cheeks, when Kitty kissed her, were dry. Oh, how she kissed her, again and again. To Kitty it seemed she had never loved her mother more than at this moment, never wanted more fervently than now for her to be happy. She had been so unhappy for so long. Just three days ago, on Christmas Eve, she and Daddy had been here, in this very room, dressing the Christmas tree whose ornaments now winked over there in the gloom. Daddy was climbing the stepladder, with the angel in his hand. He was shouting in that way he sometimes did, something about "a bloody Englishman, from England! Christ! And if that wasn't enough, a damned Communist. Bloody hell!" Kitty had never heard so many swear words strung so close together in the same sentence. She would have marveled at it if she hadn't been so sad. In any case, what he said made no sense to her, so she preferred to stare intently into the fire, feeling its delicious heat on her face, and in her clothes against her skin, until the voices behind her blurred and faded into meaninglessness.

"Daddy and I have not been happy for a long time. It isn't Daddy's fault," her mother was saying, and her voice came over her like the warm sea breeze ruffling the curtain at nap time, in her grandmother's summer house. "When that happens, sometimes it's best not to go on living together. And so Daddy and I are going to get unmarried."

"What will you do?" Kitty asked.

"Do you remember Dr. Marshall? He took us tea-dancing last summer."

Kitty nodded. "Are you going to marry him now?"

"I hope to, very soon. I love you," Kitty's mother whispered, taking her into her arms. "Do you understand?"

Kitty, holding on tightly to her mother, nodded again. Her mother's love was like the accolade bestowed by King Arthur upon his knights of the Round Table, a magical blessing, for which the knights gave undying fealty, forever. "Where will you go?" she asked simply.

"Right now I don't know where we're going to live," her mother said, still speaking in a low voice, almost a whisper, as though she couldn't bear to say some things out loud, "but we'll be going to England for a while. They say it's a beautiful country."

"Can I come with you?"

"Not right away, but soon," her mother said, holding her very close now, the way she always did when Kitty hurt herself and needed consoling in some way. "I'll send for you as soon as we're settled, I promise."

5

The night air swirled with snow. In the sky above, churning mists had drawn a black veil across the face of the moon. It was bitterly cold. As they made their way against the wind toward Windsor Station, Jeanne held Kitty's mittened hand more tightly in her own. They went everywhere together these last days, they clung to one another physically, seeking tangible reassurance that the bond between them could not be severed, that it would survive. They arrived on the platform just in time to watch the big black engine chug into the station and come to a stop with a mighty screech of metal upon metal. Still hissing steam like some mythical beast in the arctic cold, the train they had come to meet began disgorging its passengers into a flurry of redcaps vying for their luggage. Finally, Charles Langlois stepped onto the platform, and immediately towered over the rest of the crowd.

"Grandpapa!" Kitty called out excitedly. "Grandpapa!"

Charles Langlois bent down and let the child throw her arms around his neck. Only when he straightened himself did he finally meet his daughter's gaze. He seemed careworn, almost frail now despite his great size. His cheeks were hollow, his eyes sunken. He seemed to have aged dramatically in the few months since Jeanne had last seen him. "Jeanne," he said finally, as though everything he had ever felt or believed in somehow hinged on that one word.

"Daddy," Jeanne said, a wave of tenderness overtaking her annoyance, "why did you come?"

"I came to try one last time to persuade you to stay," he said, eyeing his granddaughter with concern. "Are you sure it was a good idea to bring the little one?"

"Kitty knows," Jeanne answered categorically, instinctively drawing the child closer. "She understands. There is no reason to make her feel as though things are going on behind her back. They are not. I have nothing to hide from her."

"Well, you know best," her father said resignedly. "But do you realize how much she will be made to suffer from the scandal that is sure to follow?"

They stepped outside into the angry night, the unforgiving cold.

"Daddy, I've explained to you already. The situation had become unlivable, for Kitty just as much as for anyone else," she replied, trying to keep the exasperation out of her voice.

"Jeanne, for the love of God," he cried, "think of your husband, think of your family! Think what this will do to us all!"

"Daddy," she relented slightly before her father's distress, "our lives were hell. It's the only way that any of us has a chance of being happy!"

"You think that right now," he countered, in a tone as close to bitterness as Jeanne had ever heard from that fundamentally gentle and decent man, "it makes sense to you in the heat of the moment, but what if you regret it six months from now? A year from now? It will be too late to undo what you will by then have done. Think about it. Think hard! There is still time to change your mind!"

"Daddy, no matter what may or may not happen to me in the future, I could never remain in a marriage that brought everyone concerned so much unhappiness."

"I fear for you, Jeanne, I fear for you, for Kitty, for Mick, and I fear for your poor mother. I don't see how she will ever get over the heartbreak. So much grief in store for us all, Jeanne."

"Please, Daddy," Jeanne said, as softly as she could, "try to forgive me. You're the only one I can ask that of. Try to understand."

She looked up into his face, a merciless wind roughing up his white hair. But if forgiveness was already implicit in her father's soft voice and in his eyes, rheumy with the cold, his stooped, crestfallen demeanor told her that he didn't, that he could never, understand.

6

Jeanne started down the stairs of the house that had been her home. Downstairs on the front hall carpet her small suitcase seemed to float, like flotsam from a wreck at sea. She was taking nothing, not the books or Florence's portrait or the Victrola or her piano. Having against her will to abandon her child, she instinctively sought atonement in renouncing her few prized possessions, moved by some need for expiation, perhaps hoping to temper by sacrifice a guilt whose exactions she could not yet imagine.

"I'm leaving them with you for safekeeping," she had told Kitty evenly, denying her grief free rein in this most sensitive of farewells. Kitty gazed up at her with eyes unclouded by doubt. There was a reasonableness in this child, put in the service of boundless, unconditional devotion, that filled Jeanne with remorse and denied her the balm of forgiveness, since in the eyes of her daughter she could do no wrong. Kitty put her arms around her mother's waist. From her silence Jeanne could tell that she too was holding herself in check. It was time to go.

Jeanne stepped gingerly down the stairs as though fearing a fall, with Kitty noiselessly following close behind. Gabrielle and Georgette were waiting at the foot of the stairs. Gabrielle's face was red and puffy from crying. The stolid Georgette's features were quite inscrutable. Jeanne kept her goodbyes to both women to a minimum, having already made arrangements with Gabrielle regarding correspondence between herself and Kitty.

The front door opened, letting in a sharp gust of early spring. Mick picked up the suitcase without a word and went back out to the car. Ten years almost to the day. As she slid first one arm, then the other into the coat that Gabrielle held out for her, a sickly fear momentarily subverted her resolve. Then Kitty slipped her hand in hers. They went out to the waiting car in the crisp evening air. The wrenching contradictions of the last four months were almost at an end. But first, like a rite of passage, the final journey in the compressed space, the oppressive silence of the car. On the one hand, the physically distressing proximity of Mick, fueling an almost reckless need for speed—he was driving even more circumspectly than usual, prolonging the torture, perhaps deliberately. On the other, the equally fraught reluctance to expedite the parting—Kitty's hand in hers, the years since her birth, vanished, in the winking of an eye. Flesh of her flesh, soon to be excised from her and brandished like a trophy by this man ...

They passed Saint George's Church. Jeanne's mind groped at the memory, however somber, of the funeral that had so delayed their departure. At least dear, gallant Miss Marshall had had the decency to pass away peacefully in her bed before she could be told. Louis, fearing a rumor might reach her first, had gone to make the unavoidable disclosure, but she'd died during the night; her body had just been found. She didn't deserve and so apparently had been spared the sorrow that his revelations undoubtedly would have brought her. Still, having named him the executor of her will, she had unwittingly, posthumously, stretched the painful business between herself and Mick beyond anyone's endurance. Moreover, having bequeathed the bulk of her estate to the McGill University Medical School, she had ensured that Louis would feel honor-bound to handle matters himself, directly with the university. Jeanne shuddered a little at the thought of Miss Marshall's poor little cadaver, like the shriveled corpse of a bird, tiny claws delicately folded, awaiting the spring thaw in the charnel house at the foot of Mount Royal. Jeanne and Mick had attended the funeral ceremony together at the back of the church. Only Louis had accompanied her remains to their temporary resting place.

The car came to a stop. Mick got out, opened the trunk, handed her suitcase to a porter. He moved stiffly, eyes front, scowling slightly. When they reached the platform Jeanne turned toward him and, failing to draw his attention, placed a hand lightly on his arm.

"I'm asking you again, for Kitty's sake, to allow me to part with you on friendly terms."

He made no answer.

"I'll write you from New York," Jeanne continued, more tentatively still. "The boat leaves in a week. I'll write again as soon as I get there."

Their eyes did not meet. He kept his fixed on a point at some distance along the track. Jeanne bent down and kissed Kitty's cool, smooth cheeks slowly, fervently. Something began to swirl inside her. She was emptying faster than water down a drain. When she turned to board, she was sucked down, down ...

When she came to, she was being helped to her feet by the porter. Kitty's voice reverberated in her head,